continued . . .

Berkley Prime Crime titles by Laura Childs

Tea Shop Mysteries

DEATH BY DARJEELING
GUNPOWDER GREEN
SHADES OF EARL GREY
THE ENGLISH BREAKFAST
MURDER
THE JASMINE MOON
MURDER
CHAMOMILE MOURNING

BLOOD ORANGE BREWING
DRAGONWELL DEAD
THE SILVER NEEDLE
MURDER
OOLONG DEAD
THE TEABERRY STRANGLER
SCONES & BONES
AGONY OF THE LEAVES

Scrapbooking Mysteries

KEEPSAKE CRIMES
PHOTO FINISHED
BOUND FOR MURDER
MOTIF FOR MURDER
FRILL KILL

DEATH SWATCH
TRAGIC MAGIC
FIBER & BRIMSTONE
SKELETON LETTERS
POSTCARDS FROM THE DEAD

Cackleberry Club Mysteries

EGGS IN PURGATORY
EGGS BENEDICT ARNOLD
BEDEVILED EGGS
STAKE & EGGS

Anthology

DEATH BY DESIGN

Stake & Eggs

BERKLEY PRIME CRIME, NEW YORK

THE BERKLEY PUBLISHING GROUP
Published by the Penguin Group
Penguin Group (USA) Inc.
375 Hudson Street, New York, New York 10014, USA

Penguin Group (Canada), 90 Eglinton Avenue East, Suite 700, Toronto, Ontario M4P 2Y3, Canada (a division of Pearson Penguin Canada Inc.) • Penguin Books Ltd., 80 Strand, London WC2R 0RL, England • Penguin Group Ireland, 25 St. Stephen's Green, Dublin 2, Ireland (a division of Penguin Books Ltd.) • Penguin Group (Australia), 250 Camberwell Road, Camberwell, Victoria 3124, Australia (a division of Pearson Australia Group Pty. Ltd.) • Penguin Books India Pvt. Ltd., 11 Community Centre, Panchsheel Park, New Delhi—110 017, India • Penguin Group (NZ), 67 Apollo Drive, Rosedale, Auckland 0632, New Zealand (a division of Pearson New Zealand Ltd.) • Penguin Books (South Africa) (Pty.) Ltd., 24 Sturdee Avenue, Rosebank, Johannesburg 2196, South Africa

Penguin Books Ltd., Registered Offices: 80 Strand, London WC2R 0RL, England

This is a work of fiction. Names, characters, places, and incidents either are the product of the author's imagination or are used fictitiously, and any resemblance to actual persons, living or dead, business establishments, events, or locales is entirely coincidental. The publisher does not have any control over and does not assume any responsibility for author or third-party websites or their content.

PUBLISHER'S NOTE: The recipes contained in this book are to be followed exactly as written. The publisher is not responsible for your specific health or allergy needs that may require medical supervision. The publisher is not responsible for any adverse reactions to the recipes contained in this book.

ISBN: 978-1-62090-901-0

BERKLEY® PRIME CRIME
Berkley Prime Crime Books are published by The Berkley Publishing Group, a division of Penguin Group (USA) Inc., 375 Hudson Street, New York, New York 10014.
BERKLEY® PRIME CRIME and the PRIME CRIME logo are trademarks of Penguin Group (USA) Inc.

PRINTED IN THE UNITED STATES OF AMERICA

ALWAYS LEARNING   **PEARSON**

For my husband, Dr. Bob,
who was scheduled to retire, but taught
an additional six years so I could have my shot
at mystery writing.

Acknowledgments

Heartfelt thanks to Sam, Maureen, Tom, Niti, Jennie, Dan, Dawn, and all the designers, illustrators, writers, and sales folk at Berkley Prime Crime. You all do so much! And a special thank-you to all the booksellers, reviewers, librarians, bloggers, and wonderful readers who have helped put *Eggs Benedict Arnold* and *Bedeviled Eggs*, the previous books in this series, on the *New York Times* bestsellers list. Who would have ever thought a couple of funky little cozies about three middle-aged women would land *there*?

CHAPTER 1

ICE pellets blasted the windows of the Cackleberry Club. Ticking and clicking like angry molecules, they crystallized on impact as the afternoon's eerie whiteout morphed into a late afternoon snowstorm that rolled like a freight train out of Canada, flash-freezing the entire Midwest like a package of Mrs. Paul's Fish Sticks.

Inside the little café it remained cozy and warm. Afternoon tea on this Monday in mid-January had just concluded, the scant number of customers rushing off to grocery stores to stock up on milk, eggs, bread, beer, and lottery tickets in preparation for the coming storm.

Suzanne Dietz, the entrepreneurial owner, part-time waitress, and major domo of the Cackleberry Club, paced the pegged wooden floor, worried that Old Man Winter had pretty much canceled her meeting. Clutching a hand-knit cashmere shawl around her shoulders, she pushed a hank of silvered blond and bobbed hair from her face. Even though Suzanne favored slim-fitting jeans with white shirts tied at the waist, she possessed a cool elegance and a quiet confidence. When her husband, Walter, had passed away some ten months earlier, she'd taken stock of her situation, rolled the dice, and, without too much fanfare or too many sleepless nights, opened the Cackleberry Club. Now her heart-warming little café was the go-to joint for Kindred locals as well as travelers who cruised Highway 65 and were drawn in for breakfast, pies, or afternoon tea.

"The mercury is hovering at zero," observed Toni, one

of Suzanne's two enthusiastic partners, "while our Suzanne hovers at the window." Toni was string-bean skinny, favored cowgirl outfits, and piled her frizzled reddish blond hair atop her head like a wanton show pony. Even though Toni dressed like a hottie patottie twenty-two-year-old, she was no spring chicken. Toni was slaloming toward the high side of forty, just like her cohorts.

"You sure Ben's even coming?" asked Petra. She was the third member of the troika, a big-boned Scandinavian who wore old-fashioned aprons over jeans and loose-fitting blouses, and shucked her size ten feet into comfy bright green Crocs. Her kindly face and bright brown eyes were perpetually welcoming as well as reassuring.

"He said he'd be here," Suzanne replied. "Ben and I were supposed to nail down plans for Sunday's Winter Blaze." Ben was Ben Busacker, the new president of Kindred State Bank. Although Suzanne found him relatively easy to deal with, most of the residents in Kindred didn't see it quite that way. Busacker was the company man for Mills City Banks, a large holding company that had recently swept in and taken over what had been their local bank. Busacker and Mills City Banks were said to be tougher than a Brazil nut, and had quickly earned a reputation for squeezing customers on payments, seizing properties, and being seriously parsimonious when it came to granting loans to small businesses.

The tell-tale, high-pitched whine of a snowmobile sounded from behind the Cackleberry Club.

"That must be Ben now," Suzanne told Petra. "When he called earlier he said he was driving out on his new Ski-Doo. Going to test it out."

"Funny to think of a banker riding a snowmobile," said Toni, a smile spreading across her attractive face. "Think he wears a three-piece suit and gold watch underneath his parka?"

They were gathered in the café, a homespun place with wooden tables, a marble soda fountain counter salvaged from an old drugstore, and shelves populated with colorful ceramic chickens and roosters. All manner of eggs were whipped up for breakfast here, hence the Cackleberry Club moniker. But they also served tasty, creative lunches and elegant afternoon teas. As elegant as one could get in a re-habbed Spur station, that is.

"I think Busacker's trying hard to fit in," said Petra, who always strove to find the good in people. "People in Kindred haven't exactly welcomed him with open arms."

"His wife, Claudia, is awfully stuck-up," said Toni. "She carries one of those fancy purses with *G*s all over it." She thought for a minute. "Or maybe it's intertwined *C*s." She shrugged. "Whatever. Claudia walks around with her nose stuck in the air, and if you say something to her she acts like she smelled a cow pie or something."

"You think anybody who doesn't wear a cowboy shirt is stuck-up," said Petra.

"No ma'am," said Toni. "Ben and Claudia have acted uppity since the day they hit town. And now they're trying to worm their way into civic clubs and things." Toni grabbed a snickerdoodle cookie from a plate on the counter, popped it into her mouth, and chewed vigorously. "I just hope they don't try to join our romance book club."

"I don't think they're the bodice-buster type," Suzanne smiled, as the shrill of a second snowmobile filled the air.

Petra was suddenly annoyed, her eyes rolling skyward in disapproval. "I absolutely *detest* the sound of those infernal machines. They're constantly rip-roaring across the countryside and popping up out of ditches when you least expect them. Scaring the crud out of you." Wiping her hands on her blue plaid apron, she added, "Really stupid if you ask me. And dangerous."

"Aw," said Toni, "snowmobiles are fun." She grabbed a striped scarf off a straight-back chair and wrapped it around her neck until she looked like a burrito. "Don't tell me you never went 'biling."

Petra gazed at Toni with a mixture of amusement and

horror on her broad face. "Never have and don't care to start now."

"Where's your sense of adventure, lady?" joked Toni.

"At home in my sock drawer," said Petra.

"What we need to do," Toni told her, "is bust you out of your rut. I'm gonna organize a moonlight trail ride, get a bunch of friends, and . . ."

Vrrrrmmm! Crash! Whack!

Teacups suddenly rattled in the cupboard, and the noise instantly grabbed everyone's attention.

"What the hale holy heck was that?" Petra yelped.

"Sounds like somebody plowed their car right into the back of our café," said Toni. "Maybe skidded on the ice?" She dashed through the swinging door into the kitchen and peered anxiously out the back window. "Huh, I don't *see* anything." She pressed her nose against the cold glass. "Then again, it's darn near a total whiteout."

"That didn't sound like a car," said Suzanne, who'd followed her in. "Not nearly heavy enough." *More like a snowmobile?* she wondered. Had Ben been hot-dogging through her back woods and overshot the parking lot? Lots of amateur riders underestimated the horsepower on those machines.

"Something sure went smackeroo," said Toni.

"I better go out and take a look," said Suzanne. "Make sure Ben's all right." She grabbed her parka off a wooden peg and struggled into it. Then she pulled on boots and wooly mittens, too.

"Aren't you the intrepid one," said Petra, as she joined them. "You look like Admiral Byrd setting out to conquer the North Pole."

"Or maybe Big Bird," Toni giggled.

"Wish me luck either way," said Suzanne, pulling open the back door.

"Ehh!" cried Petra, shrinking back as wind and snow pellets whooshed in. "Cold!"

But Suzanne had already slipped out the back door,

where snow swirled in mini cyclonic arcs, prickling her face like so many tiny frozen needles.

Doggone, she thought, pausing on the back steps. This was awful weather. Were they even gonna make it home tonight? Or would they have to camp out in the Knitting Nest?

Then Suzanne cast her eyes toward the back of her property. Even though she couldn't make out all that much through the curtain of falling snow, the high-pitched snowmobile whine had grown louder. Definitely an engine revving wildly. Grasping the handrail, Suzanne clambered down two snowy steps, then stumped across the parking lot where her Ford Taurus was pretty much just a hump under more humps of drifted snow.

No other cars. Has to be a snowmobile. Has to be Ben's.

She narrowed her eyes against the biting snow and was able to make out a yellow beacon of light some twenty yards back.

Yup, a stalled snowmobile, was Suzanne's initial thought. Then she quickly changed her mind, deciding it had to be a crashed snowmobile. Of course, that's exactly what she'd heard. A snowmobile plowing headfirst into her rickety little back shed, where she kept a serpentine coil of rubber hose, an old-fashioned push lawn mower, and a bag of defunct, half-sprouted grass seed. Although now that winter was here, it was probably in suspended animation.

She toddled toward the back woods, feeling like the Michelin Man in her poufy down coat, her footsteps immediately puddling with snow as she made her way.

If the snowmobile crashed, then where is its owner? she wondered. *Hurt? Dazed? And what about the second snowmobile we thought we heard? What happened to that machine, or that driver?*

Suzanne quickened her pace. She hated the thought that Ben, or anybody for that matter, might be lying on the ground hurt or badly injured. Especially in this raging storm.

The buzzing grew louder and even more annoying. Like an angry hornet batting against a screen door. Perhaps Petra was right. Maybe snowmobiles were infernal contraptions. Suzanne grabbed a snow-laden spruce bow and pushed it aside, setting off a mini avalanche. And yes, indeed, there was a snowmobile, canted on its side, the red nose of the thing practically run up the side of her shed. A headlight shone brightly, like a single yellow eye, while the engine continued to roar full throttle.

But where's the rider? Where's Ben?

She decided Ben must have pitched off in the crash. Which meant he was either hurt or deeply embarrassed.

Or drunk? That possibility raced through Suzanne's brain for an instant. But, no; if she recalled correctly, Ben wasn't much of a drinker. He wasn't part of the good-old-boy scene that congregated Friday and Saturday nights in Schmitt's Bar in downtown Kindred to hoist a brewski or help themselves to a snort or two of Jameson. Or three or four.

"Got to find him," Suzanne said out loud. She walked another few steps into the woods. "Ben!" she called, trying to make herself heard. "Are you out here?"

But even if Ben was lying in a snowdrift with his arm broken, she wasn't going to hear him call out. Not with that machine wailing away like a crazed banshee.

Suzanne doubled back to the snowmobile. *How do you turn this stupid thing off?* she wondered, hovering over it. *Where's the throttle or button or starter gewgaw or whatever it's got?*

She fiddled around, hit a black rubber switch, and, just like that, the noise died. From more than 175 nasty decibels to a silence so still she swore she could suddenly hear the wind whispering through the pines.

Straightening up, Suzanne was suddenly aware of how fast the storm had rolled in, how violent the blizzard had become.

I need to find Ben, then batten down the hatches. And

pray the roads aren't drifted over. And that the plows are out.

Suzanne walked out ten feet to where a cornfield lay buried under ten inches of snow and stretched like an undulating white canvas for almost eighty acres. Her cornfield, really. Leased to a rail-thin farmer named Reed Ducovny, who grew tall stalks of Jubilee and Golden Cross Bantam that commanded premium prices. In growing season, that was. The *other* season here in the Midwest.

Gazing out across the field, silent and white and swirling, Suzanne couldn't spot any sort of trail.

Wait a minute. A trail. All I have to do is follow the snowmobile trail.

The notion struck her as being incredibly simplistic.

Then why hadn't she thought of it sooner? The answer came easily. Because that nasty machine had been buzzing like a killer gnat inside her brain.

Back at the machine, Suzanne peered at the rounded depression in the snow. The snowmobile had come from the west, obviously wending its way through the small woods that stood at the back of the Cackleberry Club. She stepped onto the trail, sinking down to the tops of her boots. Then, ducking around a stand of birch, she plunged down the trail, wending her way past buckthorn, poplars, and cedars. Fifteen feet, twenty feet, dodging trees, until she suddenly caught sight of a dark shape lying motionless in the snow.

Dear lord.

That had to be Ben, slumped in the snow. Not moving, not even twitching.

Her first thought was that he must have hit his head to be lying so still. After all, the snow was so deep, it would have been merely cushiony if he'd just dumped over sideways.

Hurrying toward the lump, she called out, "Ben, are you okay?"

But she knew he wasn't. He needed an ambulance, a doctor, a nurse, anything. Pronto.

Suzanne faltered, almost falling forward, as the toe of

her boot stubbed against something. She caught herself, took another half step, then reached down and put her hands firmly on Ben's shoulders. She decided the best course of action would be to roll him onto his back. That was the safest position for a back or neck injury. Then she'd dash back, grab a blanket, and get an ambulance out here.

"Okay now," she said, keeping her voice calm and even, just in case he could hear her. "I'm going to ease you over . . ." Suzanne knelt down in the snow, slipped her arms around the shoulders of his shiny blue-and-yellow snowmobile suit, and gave a gentle push.

Ben rolled over fairly easily. Except for one weird thing. Only his torso and legs seemed to roll.

Huh?

Suzanne scrabbled backward in the snow as new flakes continued to rush down from the sky. She was staring. Gaping. Trying to figure out what was wrong with this picture. And suddenly realized there was just a mangled bloody stump where Ben's head should have been.

"Uhhh!" she cried out, frantically backpedaling away from him.

"He's . . . he's . . ." she babbled. "Is that what I stumbled . . . ?" But her mind refused to go there. Her reluctant, darting eyes took in Ben's limp body, while her mind chose to retreat to a safer place for now. Suzanne clambered to her feet so rapidly her knees popped, then she leaned against a birch tree and vomited softly. Thought about Ben. Headless. Vomited again.

It was only when, limp and sick, she sank to her knees, hot tears streaming down her face and quickly turning cold on her skin, that Suzanne saw Ben's head lying in the snow. His eyes were squeezed shut, a red knit stocking cap still covering his dark hair.

Like Lot's wife, struck by the angels of deliverance and turned to stone, Suzanne froze and stared straight ahead. And that's when she caught the faint glint of wire stretched tautly between two wooden stakes.

CHAPTER 2

THEY called Sheriff Roy Doogie, all of them jabbering into the phone at the same time, shouting for help and probably scaring the poop out of the dispatch operator at the Law Enforcement Center.

"We've got eight calls ahead of you," the dispatcher told Suzanne. The dispatcher was a woman named Molly Grabowski, who was also the county's go-to foster mom when it came to providing emergency shelter for kids in need. "Plus there's a jackknifed semi trailer out on Highway Eighteen," Molly continued, "as well as a stuck school bus and a smoldering tire fire behind Cragun's Auto."

"We've got a dead guy here," Suzanne blurted out. "My dead guy trumps your jackknife and everything else."

There was a sharp intake of breath. "Seriously?" said Molly.

"Ben Busacker pitched off his snowmobile," Suzanne explained. "Behind the Cackleberry Club."

"And lost his head," Toni muttered, her voice constricted, her eyes wide with fright.

"What was that?" Molly asked. "I didn't quite . . ."

"Never mind," said Suzanne. "Just send Sheriff Doogie over here as fast as you possibly can." She hung up the phone and gazed into the stunned faces of Toni and Petra. Before they could say anything more, she sat down hard in a chair and touched a hand to her stomach. She still couldn't wrap her mind around what she'd seen out there in the blizzard.

"Honey, are you okay?" asked Petra. Concern lit her face as she bent down toward Suzanne.

"No," said Suzanne. "Not really."

"It must have been an awful sight," said Petra. "I can't imagine. Can I get you some tea or anything? Water?"

"No, thanks," said Suzanne.

Petra straightened up and exchanged glances with Tony. They both knew that Suzanne tended to take on too much. And took it all to heart. On the other hand, they also knew what a tough cookie their friend was.

"Now what?" asked Petra.

"Well," said Suzanne slowly, "we can't exactly pack up and go home."

"I don't know if this is appropriate right now," said Toni, "given the . . ." She crooked her head toward the back door. "You know, what happened out there and all. But we've got corn chowder and blueberry muffins left over," she added slowly. "Maybe we could warm everything up and wait for Doogie in the Knitting Nest?"

"Cozy in," suggested Petra.

Suzanne cocked an eye at them. After what she'd just seen, cozy didn't quite cut it.

Petra looked suddenly sheepish. "I mean . . . as cozy as we can get with a dead guy lying out back?"

Toni peered nervously out the window. "A dead guy who's probably turning into a popsicle even as we speak."

"Let's do that," said Suzanne, making a decision. "Let's stay calm and hunker down in the Knitting Nest." The Knitting Nest was a small shop adjacent to the Cackleberry Club café, right next to their Book Nook. The Knitting Nest was best because it boasted comfy rump-sprung chairs and a space heater. It was also cheery, with hundreds of skeins of gorgeous yarn tucked into virtually every corner, plus Petra's shawls, wraps, and sweaters displayed on the walls.

"I'll heat the soup," Petra offered, grabbing a sauce pan from her overhead rack.

"Thank you," said Suzanne. She suddenly thought of her

dogs, Baxter and Scruff, who'd need tending to. She'd have to make a quick call to her neighbor, Mrs. Wendorf, and ask her to feed her pups and let them out into the backyard.

Toni remained glued to the kitchen window, eyes darting nervously. "You don't suppose . . ."

"Don't say it," said Suzanne. She knew how Toni's mind worked.

"Don't say what?" asked Petra.

"Coyotes," Toni said in a stage whisper.

"There," said Suzanne, throwing up her hands, "she said it."

"What if they come sneaking around?" asked Toni. "The little pests have been all over the place this winter."

"They won't," Suzanne promised. *They better not.*

But Toni had a one-track mind and a fascination with the macabre. "I heard this awful story about an old lady who died all by herself at home. And her . . ."

"Not the cat story!" Petra shrieked.

"Yes!" said Toni. "The cat! And it . . ."

"Never happened," Suzanne interrupted. "That tale's an urban myth. Just like the choking Doberman story." But deep inside, she couldn't help but give a little shudder.

THEY were halfway through their fairly somber meal of chowder and muffins when they heard the *clump clump clump* of heavy boots on the front porch.

"Doogie," said Toni, starting to rise in her chair.

"Took his own sweet time," said Petra.

Suzanne glanced at her watch, a silver-and-gold Timex that Walter had given her for their ninth anniversary. Unfortunately, poor Walter had never made it to their tenth anniversary.

"Suzanne?" Doogie was stumping around in the café now, kicking clods of snow from his boots, generally making a slushy mess.

The three women came flying out to greet him.

"Thank goodness, you're here," said Suzanne. Sheriff Roy Doogie's face and ears were red as pickled beets. He wore his modified Smoky Bear hat and an oversized dark green snorkel parka over his khaki sheriff's uniform. He was a big man, broad across the shoulders, beamy in the hips. But right now, his hooded gray eyes darted back and forth. Sheriff Doogie was on full alert.

"Where is he?" asked Doogie.

Toni hooked a thumb. "Out back."

"And you're sure it's Ben?" asked Doogie.

"Ninety-nine percent sure," said Suzanne.

"And you're sure he's dead."

"If he's not dead, it would be a miracle," said Suzanne.

"Okay," said Doogie. He blew breath onto his hands to warm them, then said, "I'll go have a look."

"Come through the kitchen," said Suzanne, gesturing. "It's easier going."

"You want us to come out, too?" asked Toni. She'd gotten over her initial shock and was suddenly all jacked up about viewing the body.

"You stay put," said Doogie. "This is not a paramilitary operation." He cocked a rheumy eye at Suzanne. "You, too."

"What am I?" said Petra. "Chopped liver?" They had all three followed Doogie into the kitchen. But Doogie threw them a warning glance, then slipped out the back door.

"He didn't warn you, because you're the non-snoopy one," Suzanne told Petra. "The one least likely to get involved."

Petra frowned. "When a murder happens at the Cackleberry Club, we're *all* involved."

"Good point," said Suzanne. She nibbled at her lower lip. And realized that this was really very bad timing. Kindred's big Fire & Ice Festival was due to kick off in two days' time. This nasty little incident could definitely put a crimp in things. And she'd already spent time, money, and beaucoup energy on a couple of events the Cackleberry

Club was slated to host, like Thursday's Crystal Tea and Sunday's Winter Blaze.

Still, a man had *died* out there. That certainly trumped a lot of other concerns. Suzanne suddenly wondered about Ben's wife, Claudia. How was she likely to handle this dreadful news? Even snooty people had feelings, Suzanne thought, hard as that could be to believe sometimes.

Doogie stomped in from the cold some five minutes later. "Yup, he's dead as a doornail," he declared, clapping his hands together.

"You saw the wire?" Suzanne asked.

"Yup, I did. Even in that snow-washed world. Amazing what the eye can sort out when it needs to." Breaking out of his parka, Doogie lifted his big head and gave a suspicious sniff, as if he might be sourcing a leftover sticky bun or cinnamon donut.

Petra, who was leaning against the big industrial stove, arms folded across her ample chest, said, "So that's your expert opinion?"

"It is," said Doogie, pulling off his suede mitts, ubiquitously known as choppers. "Since I don't know of any transplant operation that could remedy his type of situation."

"That bad, huh?" said Toni.

Doogie nodded.

"Maybe I should go out and take a look," said Toni.

"Don't!" Suzanne, Petra, and Doogie all cried together.

"It looks to me like there might be other snowmobile tracks out there," said Doogie, "but it's awful hard to tell for sure. The snow's coming down hard and the wind is ripping like crazy, so everything's drifted." He pulled out his cell phone and stared at Suzanne. "You guys got any leftover sweet rolls or donuts? I ain't had dinner yet and it's gonna be a long night."

"Out in the café," said Suzanne.

Doogie nodded as he punched in numbers. "Got a couple of calls to make. You ladies give me a little privacy, then I'll be out in a jiffy."

* * *

DOOGIE sat at the counter munching a donut while the three women clustered around him.

"You called for an ambulance?" Suzanne asked.

Doogie brushed a spray of colored sprinkles from the front of his shirt. "And the coroner. No big hurry, though." He drained his coffee cup noisily, then said, "Got any more? Hot?"

Petra grabbed a pot from the burner. "It's mostly dregs."

"Works for me," said Doogie.

"I can make fresh," said Petra. "We might be here awhile."

"You want another donut, too?" Suzanne asked.

"Bring it on," said Doogie.

Suzanne placed a glazed jelly donut on a clean plate and slid it across the counter to Doogie. He reached out with a chubby finger and towed it toward him. "Thanks," he said. He took a bite, swallowed, seemed to be ruminating about something, and then said, "You say Busacker was coming out here for a meeting?"

Suzanne nodded. "To talk about the Fire and Ice finale. We're hosting the big party this year."

"Did you see or hear anybody out back?" Doogie asked. He pulled a pencil and small spiral notebook out of his shirt pocket.

"Maybe," Suzanne said slowly. "Maybe there might have been two snowmobiles."

"She's right," said Petra. "We heard one buzzing around a few minutes before the other one crashed."

"So you heard two different machines?" asked Doogie. He was taking notes now.

"I guess so," said Suzanne. "No, I'm pretty sure we did." She thought about the implication of that, then asked, "Does that mean somebody else was sneaking around out back, stretching that wire?"

"The killer was scoping us out?" said Petra. She looked deeply unsettled.

"Whoever stretched that wire had to know Ben was coming here," said Doogie. "For your meeting."

"Who would know that?" asked Toni.

Suzanne thought for a minute. "Everybody. It was written up in the *Bugle*."

Doogie stopped jotting notes and looked up. "Huh?"

"Courtesy of Gene Gandle," said Suzanne, "our intrepid local reporter. When it comes to meetings and civic activities, he writes down every little nit and nat and sticks it in the newspaper." Gene Gandle wore several hats at the *Bugle*. He covered hard news, crop reports, high school basketball, hog prices, and sold advertising space. Not necessarily in that order.

"Conscientious son of a gun, ain't he?" said Doogie.

"I think Gene's still hoping to win a Pulitzer," said Suzanne.

"That's gonna be a cold day in—" Toni began.

"Kindred," finished Petra.

"The thing is," said Suzanne, "Ben was coming along a trail that lots of folks use. They come hot-dogging along Highway Sixty-Five on the shoulder. Then, when the ditch starts to get too steep, they cut behind the Journey's End Church and zip through my woods."

"So everybody knows about the path . . . the trail," said Doogie. He scratched his nose with the eraser end of his pencil.

"Most snowmobilers do, anyway," said Suzanne. "Especially if they're coming here."

"Can't you just question all the people who own snowmobiles?" asked Toni. "Seems like that would be a likely place to start."

Doogie let loose a sharp bark. "Hah! That would be half the people in Logan County."

Petra sighed. "All those people making a racket. It's practically criminal."

*   *   *

FIFTEEN minutes later, there was a new racket at the front door. And, seconds later, Dr. Sam Hazelet came rushing in. Surprise bloomed on Suzanne's face as she jumped up from her stool at the counter. "What are *you* doing here?" Sam was tall, early forties, good looking, with tousled brown hair and blue eyes. Of course he looked adorable with a navy North Face parka pulled over his blue medical coat.

"Doogie called me," said Sam, glancing around.

Suzanne was delighted to see him, of course. It was all she could do to resist rushing up to him and planting a great big smackeroo on his lips. Fact was, she'd been keeping company with the good doctor for the past couple of months and was feeling more and more romantically inclined. But she still wasn't comprehending why Doogie had called him.

"Did you forget?" Sam asked her. He spread his arms wide. And, as if it were the most natural thing in the word, Suzanne stepped into his embrace. "It's my turn to play duly appointed county coroner."

Suzanne pulled back suddenly and made a face. "Oh."

"Exactly my reaction," Sam said, his mouth twitching up at the corners. "But hey." He gave her a chaste peck on the top of the head, then gazed around the room and became all business. "I understand there's been a snowmobile fatality?"

"That's right," said Doogie. "Ben Busacker."

Sam did a kind of double take. "The new bank president?"

Doogie gestured with his thumb. "Out back. Happened maybe fifty minutes ago."

"Suzanne found him," said Toni.

A look of professional concern crossed Sam's face. "You're sure he wasn't still breathing?"

"Trust me," said Suzanne. "He wasn't."

CHAPTER 3

TUESDAY was Confetti Fried Eggs day at the Cackleberry Club. Fresh eggs sizzled in enormous cast-iron frying pans, French toast crisped on the grill, and the mingled aromas of Kona coffee, spicy sausage, and fresh-squeezed orange juice filled the small kitchen where Petra reigned supreme.

Mornings at the café were always about eggs, of course. Scrambled eggs, eggs balderdash, eggs in a basket, eggs mornay, fried eggs, and Scotch eggs. Eggs were the specialty at the Cackleberry Club, and they did it amazingly well. Which also meant they drew a tremendous number of customers each morning, including folks who snarfed their breakfast down fast, then enjoyed lingering over their coffee. It was especially so this morning.

"We're getting hammered," said Suzanne, as she pushed through the swinging door into the kitchen.

"Because the storm rolled past," said Petra, as she cracked eggs, one-handed, into a large speckled bowl. "And the roads are clear."

"The snowplows must have been working all night," said Toni. She was dealing out white plates like a deck of cards, setting up for Petra's cheesy scrambled eggs that were shot through with bits of sizzled onion, red pepper, green pepper, and diced zucchini.

"And the one thing that's on everyone's lips," said Suzanne, giving a nod toward the café, "is the shocker here yesterday."

"A terrible accident," said Petra.

"That was no accident," snapped Suzanne. "That was murder!"

Petra half turned, a look of unhappiness on her broad face. "Are you sure about that, honey?"

"There was a wire," said Suzanne. "Someone deliberately placed it there. And remember, Ben's head was—"

"Okay, okay," said Petra, busily checking her order slips. "I get the picture."

"Trust me," said Suzanne, "you don't want that picture engraved on your brain." She'd had a fitful night, filled with restless, haunting dreams about being chased through a hostile, wintery landscape and stumbling over strange body parts.

"My big question," said Toni, "is will the Fire and Ice Festival go on?"

"It has to," said Petra. "What else is there to do in January when there's six feet of snow covering everything?"

"For starters, there's a funeral to plan," said Suzanne, thinking of Ben Busacker. "And a bereaved wife who might need a little comfort and sympathy." The three women pondered that sober reality for a moment. Suzanne continued, "Between the murder, digging out from the blizzard, and anything else connected to this . . . the festivities could get derailed. Or at least postponed."

"Oh, don't say that," said Toni. "I've got my heart set on finding the treasure medallion and winning the grand prize."

"There's a prize?" said Petra.

"Three thousand smackeroos," said Toni.

"Seriously?" said Petra. "Last year the winner got a fifty-dollar gift certificate for Schmitt's Bar and a sack of high-oil-content sunflower seeds from Chalmers' Feed Store."

"Well, thank goodness it's been seriously upgraded this year," said Toni. "And when I get my hands on that pot of cash, I'm gonna buy myself a pair of baby blue cowboy boots to match my eyes."

"Even if they're custom-made," said Petra, "you'll still have a pile of money left over."

"That's what I figure," said Toni as she placed garnishes of sliced strawberries on each of the plates. "So what I'm gonna do is hire a big-shot attorney and finally get my divorce from Junior."

"Really?" said Petra.

"Finally?" said Suzanne.

Toni had married Junior Garrett a couple of years ago. After a super-quickie courtship, the two love birds had flitted off to Las Vegas and gotten married at the Elvis Wedding Chapel. Unfortunately, theirs was a union that had been fueled by too much Jack Daniel's, groping over the gearshift of a Ford F-150, and lacy red lingerie. Just weeks after their till-death-do-us-part vows, it had all begun to unravel. Of course, the real pièce de résistance for Toni had been the moment she'd discovered Junior's penchant for bar waitresses who favored cheap angora sweaters and hot pink extensions in their hair.

Petra looked concerned. "I hate to say this, honey, because I love you, but your marriage was snakebit from the very beginning, from the moment the plane touched down on the tarmac on your return trip from Vegas. You should've just bitten the bullet and marched directly to the courthouse for an annulment."

"I realize that now," said Toni, a tad wistfully. "Our marriage careened from one natural disaster to another. In fact, once Junior and I moved in together, he was basically roadkill." Toni wrinkled her nose. "He just laid around in his underwear until he started to smell."

"Ugh," said Suzanne, feeling sympathy for Toni. "That's another image we don't need engraved on our brains. So on that happy note . . ."

"I'll plate these orders so Toni can run them out," said Petra.

* * *

"WHAT's that fantastic aroma emanating from your oven?" asked Suzanne.

Petra ginned. "That's my lemon cornbread."

"Something new and fabulous you're trying?"

"Something new, anyway," said Petra. "But remember the words of Yoda, my fave Jedi Knight: 'Do or do not. There is no try.'"

"Seems kind of weird to quote the teachings of a Star Wars character," said Suzanne.

"Well, I am quite religious, too," said Petra, who was a pillar as well as a volunteer at the Methodist church.

"Your church is having a booth at the ice-fishing contest this year?" asked Suzanne.

"That's the plan," said Petra. "We're going to sell chili and mini tacos."

"I hope you're not going to use the chili as filling for the tacos."

"That was proposed by others," said Petra, "and vetoed by me. Honestly, I'm a chili purist. It's a meal all its own, way too good to just cram inside a taco shell. It's got dignity. It needs space. I mean . . . all those aromatic spices need to *breathe*."

Suzanne smiled and shook her head. "Whatever filling gets stuffed inside those tacos, we're all going to be crazy busy this week. You've got Stitch and Bitch on Wednesday night, then the Crystal Tea and fashion show here on Thursday . . ."

"And Sunday we host the Winter Blaze party," said Petra. "That's gonna be a biggie. We really need to do some planning!"

"Plus there are umpteen other events that are supposed to go on all over town," said Suzanne, "like the parade, the community play, the ice-carving contest, the fishing contest, and dog sled races. I wonder what Baxter and Scruff will think of those?" she added, referring to the dog sled races. "Maybe I'll bring the little demons to the sled races and see if they want to give it a go."

"I sure hope last night's murder doesn't derail all this good old-fashioned fun we've got planned," said Petra.

"Hey, guys," called Toni, as she leaned in through the pass-through. "Doogie's here."

"Maybe we'll get an update directly from the horse's mouth," said Suzanne.

"Or the horse's something else," Petra murmured as Suzanne slid out the door.

SHERIFF Doogie was hunkered at the marble counter, twirling a spoon in a cup of coffee that Toni had just poured for him. Deputy Eddie Driscoll, a young, lanky newcomer to the force, accompanied him. Standing a few feet behind Doogie, like some kind of armed guard, Eddie was on alert, seemingly waiting for orders.

"Morning, Sheriff," said Suzanne. She was aware that pretty much every face in the Cackleberry Club was now turned toward them. Conversation was muted, too; the better to eavesdrop.

Doogie nodded at Suzanne, then said, "Driscoll, you head out back and snap those pictures like we talked about."

"Yes sir," said Driscoll, eager to be put to work, no doubt dreaming about single-handedly cracking his first big case.

"Got some sticky rolls here," Suzanne said to Doogie.

"Don't mind if I do," he said, swiveling on his stool to watch her.

Suzanne grabbed a caramel roll strewn with pecans from the glass pie saver, put it on a plate, then added three pats of butter. Doogie was a big butter eater. No concerns about cholesterol for him, though truth be told he probably *should* have been concerned.

"Got anything cooking?" Suzanne asked, as she slid the plate in front of him.

Doogie dropped his voice to a conspiratorial low. "Not much yet. I'm hearing mostly idle speculation and innuendo." He slapped a whole pat of butter on his sweet roll and took a bite. "Turns out Ben Busacker wasn't exactly Mr. Popularity around Kindred."

"That's what I heard," said Suzanne.

"What have you heard?"

"Nothing concrete," said Suzanne. "Just a lot of rumblings about him foreclosing on properties and calling in loans and things."

Toni stopped by to throw in her two cents' worth. "Busacker did away with free checking accounts, too. Now you gotta keep at least fifty bucks in your account at all times or you get smacked with a six-dollar fee every time you go under." She looked exasperated. "Who can do that? I mean, keep fifty bucks in your account twenty-four/seven? Especially when you gotta pay bills! At Busacker's rates, I'll have to take out a loan just to maintain my bank account."

"Nobody's going to murder a banker over a checking account," said Suzanne.

"No," said Doogie, "it had to be something bigger."

"You find a motive," said Suzanne, "you find the killer."

Doogie aimed an index finger at her. "That'd be the general plan. And the first place I'm gonna start looking is at the bank. Try to find out which customers were unhappy or involved in some sort of dispute."

"So you think Busacker's murder was bank-related and not some personal vendetta?" asked Suzanne.

"I do," said Doogie.

"Well, people reelected you, Sheriff, because they believe in you," she said. "Because they trust your judgment."

Toni leaned in to them. "Have you heard anything about the Fire and Ice Festival? I mean, they're not going to cancel it, are they? I'm really counting on finding that treasure medallion."

"Turn on the radio," said Doogie, motioning with a big paw. "Last I heard, Mayor Mobley was gonna do a live broadcast this morning. Give a little law-and-order pep talk to the citizenry, then let everybody know if Fire and Ice is still on."

Petra's voice floated out from the kitchen. "Of course he is. The man loves to hear himself talk. I'm surprised he doesn't lobby for his own radio talk show." She snorted. "*Mobley in the Morning* or some crappy, self-serving title like that."

Suzanne reached up to the shelf where flocks of yellow, black, and orange ceramic chickens were clustered, and turned on the radio, an old brown plastic Emerson clock radio that looked like it had been around since the fifties.

There was a burst of static, then Paula Patterson's voice came through. She was the genial host of the morning *Friends and Neighbors* show on WLGN.

"What's she sayin'? What's she sayin'?" asked Toni.

Doogie put a finger to his mouth. "Sssh."

Suddenly, Mayor Mobley's voice brayed out over the radio. "There's been some talk, Paula, that the town fathers of Kindred were going to cancel our Fire and Ice Festival. But that's just not the case. Fire and Ice will go on as planned, and it will be bigger and better than ever. That much I can guarantee!"

As Toni broke into a wide smile and gave a thumbs-up, they heard Paula say, "Mayor Mobley, what can you tell us about the manhunt that's currently underway?"

Suzanne glanced at Doogie and lifted her brows. "That would be you," she whispered.

"Will the perpetrator be caught?" asked Paula. "Are the people of Kindred in any danger?"

"Absolutely not," said Mobley. "In fact, they couldn't be safer. Our law enforcement people are following up on several leads right now."

"Are you?" Suzanne asked in a low voice.

Doogie lifted a shoulder. "Deputy Driscoll is snappin' pictures."

Mayor Mobley continued in a boastful tone. "I can say, with complete and utter confidence, that the perpetrator is definitely a person from outside our community and that we expect an arrest in a matter of days."

"Those are some big promises he's making live on air," said Suzanne, shaking her head.

"And I'm the one who has to make good on them," said Doogie. He looked suddenly unhappy.

Then Paula Patterson was talking to her radio audience in her familiar, chatty voice. "So there you have it, folks. Fire and Ice will kick off tomorrow as planned. And we'll be announcing the very first treasure hunt clue right here . . . first thing tomorrow morning. So be sure to tune in!"

"Hot dog!" blurted Toni. "I can almost feel those sweet dollar bills spilling through my fingers."

Suzanne reached up and snapped off the radio. "You know what they say . . ."

"I know," said Toni, "don't count your chickens before they're hatched." She grinned. "But, hey, this is the Cackleberry Club. So that counts for something!" Her grin faded as the front door flew open and a large, solid-looking man walked in and planted himself in the middle of the café. "Who's *that?*"

Suzanne and Doogie swiveled their heads to look.

The man, who had a beefy red face and the jowls of a Saint Bernard, gave the room a cursory gaze. Then his eyes seemed to settle on Doogie. He strode forcefully across the room, peeling off his overcoat as he went. Dressed in a three-piece city suit, the man was a distinct contrast to the good old boys (and gals) who hunkered at tables in the Cackleberry Club, enjoying their breakfasts and morning coffee.

"I was told I'd find you here," the man said to Doogie without preamble.

Doogie didn't bat an eye. "Then I guess you found me."

CHAPTER 4

THE man gave a cursory smile and stuck out a hand, which was smooth and manicured. A gold watch gleamed from his wrist. "Ed Rapson. I'm regional manager for Mills City Banks."

"Nice to meet you," said Doogie, shaking hands. He looked the stranger up and down with hooded eyes, then leaned back on his stool and said, "Sorry about your man getting killed."

"That's what I want to talk to you about," said Rapson. He glanced at Suzanne, a cool, appraising look that clearly conveyed *This is a private matter. Please go away.*

She did. Suzanne had an impression of steely, super-confident efficiency as she sidled down to the end of the counter, where she busied herself with the coffeemaker, dumping in a fresh scoop of French roast and humming tunelessly to herself. But, of course, she could still hear the conversation just fine.

Ed Rapson launched into a little song and dance about the importance of justice being served and of the killer being quickly apprehended. Doogie, the consummate professional, kept a neutral look on his face and assured Rapson that he was running a tight, professional investigation.

When Rapson asked to be kept in the loop, Doogie did a bit of verbal tap dancing, but basically remained noncommittal. Then Rapson nattered on some more about resolving this incident quickly before any more customers got spooked. And how critical it was to keep his bank running smoothly, as he was sure the sheriff understood, without any glitches to gum up the works. It was your basic yadda-yadda-yadda conversation during which Doogie's eyes seemed to glaze over slightly. The whole thing ended with the two men shaking hands. Then the front door opened again and Hamilton Wick, also know as Ham, stuck his head in. Ham was a pale, mousy fellow in his late forties, who'd been the long-time vice president and loan officer at the bank.

"You almost done here?" asked Ham. He shrugged and looked apologetic. "It's getting cold out there." He tugged at the collar of his light brown parka.

"Yeah, yeah," said Rapson. He struggled back into his overcoat and retreated out the door with Wick. Watching them go, Suzanne realized Rapson had never even asked her for a cup of coffee. But neither had she offered him one. Or anything else.

Suzanne drifted back to Doogie. "Is Rapson heading back to the home office?" She was pretty sure the home office was somewhere over in Sioux Falls, some hundred and fifty miles away.

"Says he's gonna stick around," said Doogie.

"Is that going to be a problem?"

"Depends how much trouble he manages to stir up while he's here," said Doogie.

"You don't look very happy," observed Suzanne.

"Ah," said Doogie, "Rapson's one of those guys who says he wants to have a conversation with you, but what he really does is talk at you and deliver a few thinly veiled threats."

"Threats about what?" asked Suzanne. "Closing the bank? Taking his business elsewhere?"

"That and how he's had reassurances from Mayor Mobley about how quickly law enforcement will resolve this case."

"That's not good," said Suzanne. Mayor Mobley, bless his wretched little black heart, was said to have his sticky little fingers in quite a few deals around town. Particularly when it involved new businesses or real estate developers who wanted to gallop in and throw up an ugly cinder block building or a row of tract homes devoid of color or character.

"The other thing," said Doogie, "is that Rapson pretty much enjoyed talking down to me. He treated me like I had tufts of straw sticking out of my collar and shirtsleeves. As far as I can tell, though, he and I put our pants on the same way."

"Sheriff! Sheriff!" Deputy Driscoll suddenly appeared before them, his eyes wide and his face bright pink, displaying a lethal combination of cold and excitement. He'd popped through the kitchen and obviously had major news.

"What's up?" asked Doogie.

"You need to come outside and take a look at something this minute!" urged Driscoll.

Doogie eased off his stool. "See you later."

"Keep us posted, okay?" said Suzanne.

But Doogie was already grabbing his parka and striding out the back door.

SUZANNE turned her attention back to the café, making the rounds of her customers with a pot of fresh-perked coffee in one hand and a pot of freshly brewed Darjeeling tea in the other. She slipped between tables with a smile and a cheerful good-morning, all the while wondering what Driscoll had been so hot and bothered about.

When her curiosity finally got the best of her, Suzanne went into the kitchen and pushed her nose against the window, trying to see out into the frozen landscape. But Petra had more pressing business at hand.

"Suzanne, would you please deliver this three-cheese omelet to table twelve?" Petra asked. "Oh, and this rasher of bacon goes to table five." She glanced around. "Where the heck is Toni? She's supposed to be on top of these orders."

"She's working the cash register right now," said Suzanne. She glanced over her shoulder. "What do you imagine Deputy Driscoll was so fired up about?"

"No idea," said Petra. "But the fact that he was so worked up scares me to death."

"Doogie's on this," said Suzanne. "And I'm positive we're not in any real danger." But she said it with more confidence than she actually felt. A life had been lost out here behind the Cackleberry Club, and in the most gruesome manner. Who was responsible? And why had it happened? Did someone actually hate Ben Busacker enough to want him dead? Were there any other intended targets? And who in creation would ever think of using a stretched wire to kill someone? She shuddered slightly.

Petra, rattling pans, said, "It still feels like we're in danger."

Toni popped back in the kitchen. "Feels like what?"

"In danger," Petra said again. "It creeps me out to think that somebody set such a nasty trap back in our woods. And that they would go to all that trouble in the middle of a major snowstorm. And that, ultimately, their trap snared poor Ben Busacker!"

Toni glanced at Suzanne. "Can't say I've ever heard a banker referred to as poor. Especially not this one."

"You know what I mean, honey," said Petra, shaking her head. "This whole thing's got me on edge."

"Time for a group hug?" said Toni.

"Couldn't hurt," said Suzanne.

The three friends embraced, grabbing comfort, strength, and support from one another. Then Petra reached for the Red Wing crock that sat on the shelf. It held a bunch of affirmations the women had stuck in there over time. "A little inspiration couldn't hurt, either," said Petra. She extended the crock to Toni. "You go first."

Toni drew a piece of paper from the crock. She unfolded it and read, " 'Winter, spring, summer, or fall, all you've got to do is call. I'll be there, yes I will.' "

"James Taylor! How perfect," said Suzanne.

"Actually, Carole King *wrote* that song," put in Toni. "She's the genius behind those words and music. Remember *Tapestry*? Oh lord, I loved that album. But Taylor's really the one who made the song a big hit."

"I love that song no matter who wrote it or sang it," said Suzanne. "Okay, your turn," she said to Petra.

Petra fished around and drew out a yellow Post-it note. "It says, 'I pay my bills with love, and I know abundance flows freely through me.'"

"Good one," said Toni.

"Now you," said Petra, shoving the crock toward Suzanne.

Suzanne drew a crumpled piece of paper and read it out loud. "This one says, 'The wise person listens to everyone. But the wiser person takes her own advice.'" She hesitated. "Hmm."

MUCH to Suzanne's consternation, Doogie never came back into the café. She figured he'd either found a tantalizing clue outside and had dashed off to follow up on it, or he'd come up with a big fat zero and was too sheepish to stomp back in and admit it.

Actually, Suzanne thought, *scratch that*. Sheriff Doogie wasn't sheepish about *anything*.

Either way, it was time to gear up for lunch.

Petra had planned a dazzling luncheon menu, the ideas swirling around in her head for the past couple of hours just like the mass of snowflakes that had piled up outside. Suzanne could smell the aroma of bacon frying in the kitchen as she went to scrawl the day's specials on the chalkboard.

Petra's soup of the day was aptly called Veggie Supreme. It was a hearty vegetable broth crammed with bits of celery, carrots, zucchini, broccoli, and yellow squash, plus a decadent dash of cream just in case the whole thing sounded a little too healthy and righteous for its own good.

The soup was one of Suzanne's favorites, and on a cold winter's day like today there was no way it could miss. She wrote it on the board in yellow chalk and drew a cartoon bowl of soup.

"Okay, how about the salad?" Suzanne called to Petra.

"I'm doing my Egg Salad Eggstravaganza," Petra said. She meant her tasty showstopper of an egg salad, seasoned with delicious pieces of pimento-stuffed olives and bacon, as well as a healthy dab of Dijon mustard.

Suzanne jotted that down in pink chalk, then added the rest of the day's lunch servings as Petra rattled them off: Grilled Cheese Louise. Carrot quiche. Blueberry Pie with Whipped Cream to Die For.

Just as a group of early lunch customers filed in, Suzanne stepped away from the chalkboard so everyone could see it.

As Suzanne dusted her hands on her red checkered apron and took a deep breath, Gene Gandle, the *Bugle*'s persistent and insanely intrepid reporter, came charging into the café. Slat-thin, head bobbing atop his stalk-like neck, Gene Gandle looked skinny even in an over-stuffed olive drab parka. Shaking himself like a wet dog, Gandle stomped snow from his boots and peeled off his gloves.

"Will wonders never cease," said Suzanne, in a low voice to the others. "Look what the Chinook winds just blew in."

Toni swung her gaze to the front door. "Of course, the news guy is here. The Cackleberry Club is the place to be. Everybody knows that. We're Grand Central Terminal right now. Who wouldn't want to be here on a day like today?"

"I just wish fewer murderers wanted to be here," murmured Suzanne.

"Hi there," said Gandle. He was perky and faux friendly as he hunched onto a seat at the counter in front of Suzanne.

"Hi, Gene. What can I get for you?" Suzanne asked. Gene took his job as a reporter as seriously as Woodward and Bernstein. He bordered on pesky, veering into obnoxious. "Maybe a cup of coffee to start?"

"Sounds good," said Gandle.

"And we've got some great veggie soup today," she told him. "A real favorite and good for you, too." She knew Gandle liked to eat healthy. "Care to try a bowl?"

"Sure," said Gandle, "why not?"

As he settled himself at the counter, Suzanne delivered his coffee, then ladled out a steaming bowl of soup. There was a distinct buzz in the café now, as a few customers glanced over from their tables. Word had obviously spread fast about Ben Busacker's death, and people were naturally curious. Maybe they thought Suzanne would share some inside information with Gandle. Or maybe they figured Gandle would dig up some new dirt.

Suzanne could only imagine the questions her customers must be asking one another. She tried to stay focused as she placed a cinnamon muffin on a plate and delivered that to Gandle, too.

It soon became clear, however, that Gandle wasn't there for coffee, soup, or anything remotely culinary. He took a quick, perfunctory swallow of coffee, then pulled out a notebook, a pen, and a small digital recorder, arranging them all on the counter. With a deft move, he switched on the recording device. "Mind if I ask a few questions?"

Suzanne could see the glow of the tiny red light, indicating the machine was grinding away in record mode. "Sure," she said, working hard to remain neutral. "Go right ahead. Ask away." She managed a smile. "You oughta dig into that soup, though, while it's still hot."

Gandle obeyed her, taking a quick sip and then wiping his mouth. "That's mighty tasty," he said, taking a few more hurried spoonfuls.

Suzanne began to relax. Maybe this was going to be easier than she thought.

Gandle nibbled at his muffin and then, still chewing, looked at her and said, "So?"

"So?" said Suzanne in return.

"Yesterday. Talk to me about what happened."

"The storm? It came barreling in before we knew what hit us. Pretty much a complete whiteout. We barely got out. The plows hadn't come through yet, and we . . ."

"Cut the crap, Suzanne. I know a man died out there last night," said Gandle directly. "Ben Busacker, the bank president. Some sort of snowmobile accident during the storm. What do you know about it?"

"So awful," said Suzanne, shaking her head. "Such a shame."

"Of course it is," said Gandle. "What happened?"

"That's what we're all wondering," said Suzanne, careful as ever.

Gandle frowned. "Tell me something I don't know, Suzanne. I'm working on a story here. A *major* story. And rumor has it you were the one who found Busacker's body."

Suzanne hesitated. "Who told you that?"

Gandle arranged his face in a mirthless grin. He knew he'd struck a nerve. But he didn't answer her directly.

"Sheriff Doogie's working the case," put in Suzanne, "so he's the one you should be talking to."

"Already did," said Gandle. "What I'm after are a few fresh details." He gave a look that was halfway between a smile and a sneer, then took another sip of soup. "It's the little details that make a story, Suzanne. And the reason people read the *Bugle*."

"Really? I thought they read it because it's the only newspaper in town."

"I'm just trying to do my job, Suzanne."

"Really, Gene . . ." She hated that he was trying to mousetrap her.

Gene leaned forward and lowered his voice. "Did you see Busacker's body?"

"Yes, I did, and I fervently wish I hadn't," said Suzanne.

"I heard he'd been . . . decapitated?"

Suzanne sighed. "You heard right."

Gene's eyes took on a predatory glow. "What did it look like?"

"Shame on you, Gene."

"If I worked for the *New York Times*, you'd be bending my ear about this," said Gandle, pouting. "Or if I was a reporter for CNN."

"Look," said Suzanne, "the investigation is underway and I'm sure Doogie and his team will have it figured out in a matter of days." She swallowed hard. "And we'll all be relieved once it's over."

"One more question," said Gandle.

Suzanne puckered her mouth in exasperation.

"Do you think it was an accident, or murder?" asked Gandle. His eyes carried a nasty gleam, and Suzanne was pretty sure he knew darn well that a wire had been stretched deliberately. Pointing to . . . calculated murder.

Suzanne chose to deflect his question. "That's the burning question of the day, isn't it? And now, if you'll excuse me, I have lunch orders to deliver!"

SPEEDING from table to table, Suzanne did her best to quiet whatever rumors snaked their way to her as people paused between bites of food. For the most part, she was successful.

Until Charlie Steiner walked in. Steiner was a taciturn farmer who lived a hardscrabble life running a small dairy farm. His mood was generally dour, and he rarely had a kind word for anyone. Still, Suzanne grabbed a menu and greeted him with a big smile. "Table for one?"

Steiner gave a surly nod and clumped after her. Once he sat down, he planted his elbows on the table, creaked back in his chair, and declared, "Don't need no menu, just bring me a grilled cheese and coffee."

"Right away," said Suzanne. She hustled off, hoping Steiner's dismal mood didn't spread to her other customers.

And like a self-fulfilling prophecy, Suzanne's fears came true. Because when she circled back some ten minutes later,

Steiner was munching on his grilled cheese, lecturing to everyone at the surrounding tables.

"That Busacker was one mean son of a gun," said Steiner. "Tough and hard-hearted. I missed a couple payments on my farm, and Busacker started legal action to take it away from me!" His face was a thundercloud. "Can you believe that? A hard-working, tax-paying veteran like me!"

"Charlie," said Suzanne, sidling over to him, "take it easy, okay?"

Steiner seemed not to even notice Suzanne. "But justice has been duly meted out. Ben Busacker is *dead.*"

"Charlie, please," said Suzanne, a little more firmness in her voice. "Dial it back."

Steiner tilted his head back, raised both arms, and turned his palms outward, as if receiving a blessing. "The man spit poison and greed, and now he's received his comeuppance from the Almighty!"

A man at a neighboring table, a volunteer fireman named Mike, said, "Charlie, you sound like you're happy that Ben Busacker is dead."

A slow, wolfine grin crept across Steiner's craggy face. "I'm not *un*happy, I can tell you that."

Back in the kitchen, Suzanne quickly related to Toni and Petra what she'd overheard.

Petra sucked in her breath. "Steiner's actually celebrating the fact that Busacker's dead? Good lord. What's his heart made of? Stone?"

"It's his pebble brain that worries me," said Toni. "I mean, don't you think Steiner sounds entirely too happy about this whole Busacker thing?"

Petra was the first one to make the frightening leap. "You don't think Steiner could have *engineered* something, do you?" she asked. They all looked at each other.

"I don't know what to think," said Toni.

"He did seem awfully angry at being foreclosed on," said Suzanne, thoughtfully. "I suppose he could have . . ."

Petra gave a shudder. "Please don't tell me the killer is

sitting out there eating one of our grilled-cheese sandwiches."

"We don't know that for sure," said Suzanne. "We just
made a crazy assumption."

"Still," said Toni, "we should probably tell Doogie about
this guy's rant. After all, what do we really know about
Charlie Steiner anyway? Is he a decent guy or is he an angry jerk?"

"Angry jerk," said Petra.

"Jerk doesn't necessarily translate to killer," said Suzanne. At the same time, she knew that Doogie had a right
to know about this. It might be secondhand information, but
it was still information. And Gene Gandle, who was still
sitting at the counter jotting notes, had surely heard everything Charlie Steiner had blurted out. So Gandle was probably planning to stuff a heavy dose of that vitriol into
whatever sausage of a story he was cooking up for Thursday's edition of the *Bugle*. In which case . . . the whole
town would know.

"I love it when you do those crisscross strips on top," said
Toni. Petra was putting the finishing touches on a couple of
apple pies. "They let all the hot, cinnamony apple goo bubble up through the top."

"That would be the general idea," said Petra. She stuck
her hand into a calico oven mitt, opened the door, pulled out
a pan of muffins, and slipped in her pies.

As sweet baking aromas filled the Cackleberry Club,
Suzanne suddenly thought to herself, *Walter, how I wish
you were here.* His memory suddenly flooded back to her,
sharp as cut glass. Where was Walter when she needed
him? Where was he at any time of day or night, for that
matter? Hopefully in a better place, encircled in the arms of
the Lord.

Sometimes it didn't make sense to her that Walter had
been dead for almost a year, a victim of pancreatic cancer.

Or that Donny, Petra's husband, was lying in a nursing home suffering from Alzheimer's. Yet she knew they had to carry on, that they both *were* carrying on.

Living was a special gift. Unfortunately, it often took a tragedy to make one fully realize that.

Giving a quick glance around the café, Suzanne noted that everything seemed under control. Gandle had finally left, Steiner had departed, a handful of customers were finishing up. Excellent.

Crossing the floor, Suzanne slipped into the adjacent Book Nook. It was a cozy place where sagging wooden shelves were packed floor-to-ceiling with books. Where a threadbare Oriental carpet covered the floor, and two cushy overstuffed velvet chairs served as the perfect place to plop down and sit a spell.

UPS had delivered three cartons of books this morning, and Suzanne eagerly ripped them open. It was fun to unearth new treasures, to shelve them in the various sections they'd designated, such as as Mystery, Romance, Fiction, Culinary, History, and Children's. Surrounded by books, Suzanne always experienced a great sense of calm. The books helped her to feel centered, to grab a tiny bit of Zen.

She reached into the box, pulled out a book titled *Tea & Tidbits*. She smiled, turned the book over to read the back cover, then was suddenly aware of hurried, heavy footsteps heading toward her.

Suzanne glanced up just as Reed Ducovny, her neighbor from across the way, came roaring in. A shade past sixty and tough as an old boot, Ducovny stomped into the Book Nook. His normally placid face was scrunched into an unhappy grimace, and his mouth worked soundlessly.

"Reed," said Suzanne, suddenly concerned. "What's wrong?"

Ducovny reached up and pulled a purple stocking cap off his head, revealing a tousle of gray hair. "Sheriff Doogie!" he exclaimed breathlessly. "Sheriff Doogie says I'm a suspect!"

CHAPTER 5

SUZANNE was shocked beyond belief. And not just by the raw outrage that poured out of Reed Ducovny, a man who cared more about corn and soybeans than nearly anything else in his life. No, what really shocked her was the fact that a steady stream of people with incredibly urgent problems kept finding their way to the peaceful, cozy Cackleberry Club.

Was it just her imagination, or had the Cackleberry Club become the eye of the storm in less time than it took to say "homemade rhubarb pie topped with French vanilla ice cream"?

And Suzanne felt that she herself was at the center of the vortex—either being dumbstruck by a grisly killing, or dishing out food and advice, or dealing with the chaos and craziness that swirled around her.

A quick recount, thought Suzanne: First Ben Busacker was killed. Then Doogie dove in and started munching his way through the investigation. Then Mr. Fancy Pants Banker with the Gold Watch showed up, followed by Gene Gandle, slavering for juicy details to stick in his newspaper exposé, and then Charlie Steiner, who'd vented like the second eruption of Mount St. Helens.

Wow, Suzanne thought. *No wonder my head is spinning like a top.*

She half wished she could rewind the hands of time and start the week over again. *Could we just kick it off with a garden-variety winter snowstorm and end with tasty tea and scones? Wouldn't that be loverly? And while we're at it, let's toss in a couple of plump muffins, a delicious cup of Kona coffee, and some friends, good books, beautiful yarns, and other nice-and-easy things that tend not to upset any apple carts. Or lop off any heads.*

As Suzanne studied the man standing in front of her, exasperation and intensity dripping from his face, she suddenly realized how very personally Ducovny was taking all of this.

"Why would Sheriff Doogie think you're a suspect?" she finally asked. "Why you? That doesn't make any sense." She shook her head. "There has to be a mistake."

Ducovny shook his head. "Sheriff says the wire that killed Ben Busacker was the same kind of wire that's in my fences! And now that he knows this, he says he can't ignore it. He says it puts me under suspicion. That it's . . . what did he call it? Damning evidence."

But Suzanne, who owned the land and only leased it to Ducovny, was already thinking, *Actually, that would mean it's the same kind of wire from* my *fences.*

Ducovny paced back and forth, practically in hysterics now. "Suzanne," he pleaded, "you've got to help me!"

"Me?" said Suzanne. *Why do I have to help him? If the wire's really from my fence, I might have to help* me!

"You've got a big in with Doogie," said Ducovny. "He likes you. He trusts you. You've known each other for a long time."

"I don't really have an in with him," Suzanne said slowly, mulling over everything Ducovny had just lobbed her way. Why would wire samples suddenly put Ducovny under suspicion, she wondered. Weren't there miles of wire out there that just happened to be the same make and model, so to speak? Everyone around the county could have the same kind of wire, for all she knew. This part of the state was filled with great stretches of farms, fields, and pastures that were wired off and divided by ownership rights, land surveys, and whatnot. And all of that wire had to come from somewhere, and it probably all came from the same factory. Exactly what had Doogie and his deputy discovered when it came to this particular wire?

Suzanne realized she needed some inside information, courtesy of Sheriff Doogie. And quick.

Yes, Doogie was a friend of sorts. But Suzanne also figured the real reason he hung around the Cackleberry Club was because she never charged him for all the platefuls of food he snarfed down on a regular basis. Did the man ever pay for anything? No. Did she ask him to pay? No. And neither did any other local café.

Talk about a job with excellent benefits. No wonder some folks kept running for office. And not just in Kindred, Suzanne thought, but across the entire country!

Still, it was comforting to have Doogie's bulky, familiar presence around the Cackleberry Club, just in case some crazy tweaker or 7-Eleven rip-off artist got it in his fool head to try to grab fistfuls of money from their cash register. After all, a Saturday night special worked just as well on a busy Monday morning.

"I came to you, Suzanne," Ducovny continued, "because you're smart. Last fall, you figured out who killed that guy Peebler. And I know you worked on a couple of other crimes before that, too. Seems to me you've been investigating murders ever since you opened this place."

"I got lucky with the Peebler case," said Suzanne.

"No," said Ducovny, "you got good." He strode a few paces, whirled around, and knocked a couple of books off the shelf. *Blue's Clues* went tumbling. So did two new thrillers by David Baldacci and John Sandford that Suzanne had just unpacked a few minutes ago.

"Calm down," said Suzanne, bending to pick up the books. "This is just a case of simple misunderstanding. I'm sure we can get everything straightened out."

"Oh yeah? Tell that to the other fellow who was with

Doogie. The guy who kept egging him on and wanted me arrested right on the spot! Before I even had a chance to defend myself!"

Suzanne frowned. "You're talking about Doogie's deputy? Um . . . Driscoll?"

"No, I am not," said Ducovny. "This was some pretty-boy bank manager. Some out-of-towner who seemed proud of the fact that he didn't hail from Kindred, by the way."

"Oh crap," said Suzanne. "Was it a guy by the name of Rapson?"

Ducovny bobbed his head. "That's it. You know him?"

"I ran into him briefly," said Suzanne. "Rapson stopped here this morning to buttonhole Doogie and spread a little cheer. He's apparently the regional manager for Mills City Banks. Sent here to bat cleanup."

Ducovny grabbed a copy of John Grisham's newest thriller from the shelf and squeezed it between his work-worn hands. "I don't like him."

"Join the club," responded Suzanne. "Neither do I."

There. She'd said it out loud. She'd admitted it in the light of day, and to someone other than Toni or Petra. And guess what? She wasn't a terrible person for it, either.

"Then you'll help me?" asked Ducovny. "You'll set Doogie straight?"

"I'll try," said Suzanne, wondering exactly what she was promising.

AMAZING aromas wafted throughout the kitchen and swirled out into the café as Suzanne, Toni, and Petra turned their full attention to prepping for afternoon coffee and tea. This was their most elegant time of day, their civilized respite from the rest of the Cackleberry Club craziness. And even in the middle of winter, the day after a major snowstorm, they knew they'd get pretty near a full house.

Suzanne was proud that she'd managed to subtly introduce afternoon tea to their customers. Of course, they'd pretty much had to point a loaded gun at the heads of the men to get them to order tea. But, much to her delight, the women of Kindred and the surrounding environs had embraced tea service like shoppers at a 70 percent-off clearance sale. The café often filled with women eager to ditch their winter sweatshirts and jeans for vintage wool skirts, fancy sweaters topped with lace, and warm, frilly scarves. These newly converted tea lovers mingled with friends, sipped Darjeeling and oolong tea from bone china teacups, nibbled on dainty finger sandwiches and other goodies, and caught up on the latest news in the romance-book world.

With tea service, life was good.

AFTER whisking together flour, sugar, salt, eggs, melted butter, and more, Petra popped her famous oat-and-almond scones into the oven. Meanwhile, Suzanne and Toni buzzed about the café clearing away the detritus from lunch and trading ketchup bottles for silver creamers and crystal bowls filled with sugar cubes.

Suzanne glanced around and realized how grateful she was to have daily rituals like this to keep her grounded and remind her of what really mattered in life. It also helped her keep thoughts of Ben Busacker's grisly death at bay.

I like thinking about tasty finger sandwiches and pretty lace tablecloths, she thought. *I enjoy brewing healthy green tea and malty Assam tea, and serving it in dainty cups and saucers. And these two crazy BFFs in my life, Toni and Petra . . . Okay, I know it sounds squishy and a little bit lovefesty, but I don't know what I'd do without them!*

Suzanne smiled to herself as she sidled into the kitchen. "I can't stand it much longer," she said to Petra. "How soon are those scones going to be ready? The smell is making me ravenous!"

"Didn't you eat?" asked Toni, who'd cribbed a triangle sandwich and was munching on it.

"Be careful," Petra warned Suzanne. "You're starting to sound like Sheriff Doogie."

"Just as long as I don't end up looking like Doogie," said Suzanne. She watched over Petra's shoulder as she opened the oven door to reveal giant scones that were turning a gorgeous golden brown.

"Two more minutes," Petra declared. She turned and stared at Suzanne. "Are you going to let us in on the conversation you just had with Reed Ducovny or keep us in the dark and guessing?"

"Let you in?" said Suzanne. "I figured you must have heard it. I figured *everybody* heard it."

Toni narrowed her eyes. "So Doogie sees Ducovny as a suspect?"

"Apparently so," said Suzanne, "since he paid Ducovny a visit."

"That's just plain silly," said Petra. "Everybody knows Ducovny wouldn't hurt a fly."

"Tell me about it," said Suzanne. "He won't even use weed killer on his crops. He's organic all the way."

"Little green caterpillars and all," agreed Petra. "We need more conscientious people like him."

"You have to talk to Doogie," Toni urged, popping a final bite of sandwich into her mouth. "Set him straight."

"I'll try," said Suzanne.

"So much going on in Kindred right now," mused Petra. "Although, some of it's actually positive." She had a little twinkle in her eye. "Like Lester Drummond getting fired." Lester Drummond had been the warden at a nearby for-profit prison. Hardly anyone in Kindred had wanted the place built, but Mayor Mobley had found a way to ram it through, arguing that the prison would lead to new jobs and bring increased revenue to local businesses.

Some of that was certainly true, but a cement bunker surrounded by razor wire didn't exactly enhance the beauty of an historic town filled with cute cottages, Victorian homes, and a picturesque downtown of yellow-brick buildings. And all of it surrounded by towering bluffs on one side and the meandering Catawba Creek on the other.

"I'm glad Drummond was finally fired," said Toni. "Especially after that dog-fighting scandal." She shook her head. "Just awful."

"Janell down at Kuyper's Hardware told me Drummond's furious about losing his job," said Petra.

Drummond was a big man, almost pro-wrestler size, who, with his tattoos and shaved head, looked like one of the prisoners he'd reigned over. And now that he'd been drop-kicked through the prison gates, Drummond was probably in an awful frame of mind.

Which made for a fairly lethal package, Suzanne decided.

"And now there's a new warden," Petra continued as she stirred chocolate sauce at the stove. "Some guy name Fiedler."

"Is he cute?" asked Toni. "Is he single?"

"Even if he is," Petra said, in an arch tone, "you're not."

"Don't sweat the details," said Toni, with a flick of her head. "Because I will be soon."

She'd barely spoken the words when the front door of the café swung open with a loud bang.

"Customers?" said Toni.

Suzanne poked her head out the door just as Claudia Busacker, Ben Busacker's widow, stepped briskly into the café. Claudia paused, looking unsure of her surroundings.

"Oh!" said Suzanne, startled. She glanced at Toni and Petra and said in a stage whisper, "Claudia Busacker."

"Here?" whispered Toni. "Why?"

Petra rolled her eyes. "You know why. Suzanne," she hissed, "you go out and greet her!"

Suzanne touched a hand to her chest. "Me? Why me?"

"Because you're our fearless leader," said Toni.

Suzanne steeled herself, drew a deep breath, and went out to greet Claudia. In her heart, she knew it was the right thing—the kind thing—to do.

"Claudia? Mrs. Busacker?" she said as she crossed the café. "Hello." She stretched out a hand. "I'm Suzanne Dietz. We've . . . I . . . well, I'm just so very sorry . . ." She didn't know Claudia all that well, but she'd certainly seen the woman around town.

"Suzanne . . . yes," said Claudia, giving a faint smile. As always, Claudia was beautifully groomed and well put together. She was trim and elegant in her black mink coat with every hair on her honey blond head perfectly highlighted and blow-combed. But even with high color in her cheeks from the winter cold, Claudia looked drained. And upon closer inspection, Suzanne noted dark circles under her eyes and tension lines intersecting her forehead.

Claudia didn't waste time with pleasantries. "I want to see where it happened," she said to Suzanne in a clipped, no-nonsense tone.

Suzanne's heart went out to Claudia. She clasped her hands in front of herself and said, "Oh, honey, you really don't."

"Yes, I do," said Claudia. She set her jaw so hard that Suzanne was afraid she'd crack a filling.

"There's really nothing to see," Suzanne said, trying to sound practical. In fact, that was pretty much the honest truth. Ben Busacker's body was no longer lying out back, nor was his smashed snowmobile there. Sheriff Doogie, Sam Hazelet, and Deputy Driscoll had seen to that almost immediately. Everything had been hauled away for preservation as well as investigation.

Toni suddenly crept in beside them. "There's crime-scene tape," she piped up helpfully, looking directly at Claudia. "And the stakes are still there. So, you could see that."

Claudia made a pathetic little mewling sound. She put a gloved hand to her mouth and looked like she was about to collapse.

"Too much information," Suzanne whispered to Toni.

Claudia waved a hand. "No, I want to see it . . . I really do."

"You really don't have to," said Suzanne.

But Claudia was adamant. "I want to see where my husband drew his final breath," she said firmly. "I'll never forgive myself if I don't do this." She gazed at Suzanne and then at Toni. "I need closure."

"Got it," said Toni.

Suzanne gave a helpless shrug. A here-goes-nothing shrug. Then she motioned with her hand. "Come this way."

Claudia followed Suzanne into the kitchen, waited a few minutes while Suzanne slipped into her boots and parka, then followed her out the back door.

The winter sun was lasering down, forcing the two women to shield their eyes from the strong glare that danced off icy snowdrifts and crystallized trees.

"So bright," murmured Claudia.

You should have seen it yesterday, thought Suzanne. *Big difference. Night and day. Ha-ha*, she thought as that notion capered madly in her brain.

Together, they slogged across the drifted parking lot and disappeared into the woods. The snow was knee-high, so it was tough going, and branches slapped at their faces. Every once in a while, Claudia would utter a surprised little "Ooh."

Finally, they arrived at a small clearing where the snow was tromped down and yellow crime-scene tape fluttered desolately in the wind.

Claudia stared in stoic silence while Suzanne looked on in sympathy. The new widow took in the yellow tape and then the wooden posts, probably imaging the wire that had been stretched between them. Then, just as Suzanne figured would happen, Claudia's lower lip began to quiver and her eyes welled with tears.

Suzanne leaned over and touched Claudia's arm, rubbing it gently, offering whatever solace she could as they both breathed in the brittle, cold air. "I'm so sorry," she repeated.

"I wasn't thrilled about moving to Kindred," Claudia said, in a kind of hoarse croak. "But it was a huge opportunity for Ben." She dug in her purse for a Kleenex and dabbed at her eyes. "A wife's role is to support her husband, isn't it?"

Suzanne wanted to say, *Not necessarily*, but didn't. Claudia didn't need a women's-lib pep talk right now.

"Anyway," Claudia continued, "I left my old home and my friends and moved here." She heaved a sigh that was almost a shudder. "Now what am I going to do?"

Suzanne put her arms around Claudia and pulled her close. "For one thing, you're going to stay here for now," said Suzanne. "And I promise that your new friends will rally around you. In fact, I'll make sure of it."

"Thank you," Claudia said in a whisper. "You're very kind." A few more tears spilled down her cheeks, and then Claudia's body began to shake with sobs.

Suzanne's gaze traveled from Claudia to the crime scene, then back to the stricken widow. All she could think was: *What a brave woman.*

AT three-thirty, just as they were clearing away the last vestiges of their tea service, Sheriff Doogie dropped by. He swung his bulk onto a creaky stool and slumped over the counter. "Coffee. Black," he said.

"We're going to try something new today," Suzanne told him.

"Huh?" Doogie was already eyeing her with suspicion.

"I'm going to pour you a lovely cup of tea."

Doogie blinked in disbelief. "My pinky finger won't fit through those dinky little teacup handles," he complained.

Suzanne grabbed a sturdy ceramic mug and splashed in a helping of Assam tea. "No problem."

Doogie sniffed his mug of tea as if she were a wicked witch offering him a lethal dose of strychnine. "What kind is this? Like Lipton's?"

"It's Assam, and it's fresh brewed from tea leaves grown in India. Go ahead, try it. It's good for you," Suzanne told him, as Toni cut a slice of apple pie for Doogie.

"Smells funny," said Doogie.

"Malty," said Suzanne. "That's a good thing. Tea should broaden your horizon as well as your taste buds."

"Doogie's horizon is already plenty broad," Toni chortled as she set his pie in front of him.

"Hey, smart mouth," said Doogie. "Watch it!" He took a sip of tea, considered it for a few moments, then said, "Not bad."

"I'll make a convert out of you yet," said Suzanne.

"The Methodist preacher's been saying that to me for years," said Doogie.

"Well, this might be a somewhat easier task," said Suzanne. She hesitated, then said, "I want to talk to you about Reed Ducovny."

Doogie nodded. "I suspected you did."

Suzanne spread her hands wide and said, "Why. On. Earth?"

"Evidence," said Doogie.

"A little piece of wire?" Suzanne snorted. "That's not evidence, that's a coincidence."

"No," said Doogie, "the wire was cut directly from his fence. We even found the place where it had been cut. It's a *fresh* cut."

"Even so," said Suzanne, "if it was cut from his fence, anybody could have done it. You can't come down hard on Ducovny just because he's convenient. Because the fence was convenient."

Doogie held up an index finger. "Don't lecture me, Suzanne."

"I have to," said Suzanne, realizing she might be pushing it a little, but not caring. "Because Ducovny had no *motive*. He's a guy who cares about corn, not about offing some full-of-himself banker. The two men didn't even *know* each other, for gosh sakes, except to maybe exchange a polite nod on the street."

"I gotta look at all the angles, Suzanne."

"I understand that," said Suzanne. "But Ducovny? Jeez."

"It's what I got," said Doogie.

"Please don't let Ed Rapson drive you in the wrong direction," Suzanne cautioned. "He wants Busacker's murder wrapped up in a nice, neat package so he can go back to the home office and deliver it as a trophy."

"I get it, Suzanne," said Doogie. Now there was a definite edge to his voice.

"I'm not finished," said Suzanne firmly. "That darned Charlie Steiner was in here for lunch, running his yap about what a non-tragedy Ben Busacker's death was. Apparently, Busacker was about to foreclose on his farm?"

Doogie nodded. "Got the whole story, blow by blow, from Gene Gandle."

"I figured as much," said Suzanne. "So you're going to talk to him?"

"To Steiner? Yes," said Doogie. "He's next on my list."

"Okay, then," said Suzanne.

"That make you happy?" asked Doogie, with a frown.

"For now, yes," she said.

"I'm gonna blow this pop stand, okay?" called Petra. She was standing at the front door, her camel hair coat pulled around her, a white knit cap stuck like a poufy marshmallow atop her head.

"Have a great night!" called Toni. She was poking a broom underneath one table, trying to hook an errant French fry.

"Give Donny a hug for me," called Suzanne. Donny was Petra's husband, who lived in the Center City Nursing Home.

"I will," said Petra. A cold breeze swooped in, and then she was gone.

"Got any special plans for tonight?" Toni asked Suzanne.

Suzanne smiled. "Sam's dropping by for dinner."

"Ooh, the good doctor is coming a-courting. Lucky you."

"Lucky me only if I figure out a suitable menu. I was thinking veal chops, then I decided steak would . . ." Her words broke off as another cold gust suddenly swept through the café. "Petra?" she said, glancing up. "Did you forget . . . ?"

But it wasn't Petra who stood in the doorway. Suzanne was suddenly staring into the dark, sparkling eyes of Carmen Copeland.

"Hello, ladies," Carmen purred. She was wrapped in a floor-length sable coat that was so lush it fairly crackled. A caramel-colored cashmere muffler was coiled around her neck.

"Carmen!" said Suzanne, going over to greet her. "I had no idea you'd be stopping by." Carmen Copeland was a local author who'd made it big as a romance writer. She had something like twenty-two novels to her credit with multiple trips to the *New York Times* bestsellers list. Even though Carmen's success and fame were prodigious, they'd done nothing to soften her personality. Carmen remained aloof, abrasive, and difficult.

"I wanted to make sure we were all on the same page for the fashion show this Thursday," said Carmen. A year ago, Carmen had opened the Alchemy clothing boutique, and her clothes were going to be featured at the Crystal Tea.

"The same page," said Toni, pointing her broom at Carmen. "Ha-ha, very good."

Carmen's eyes hardened. "This is no joke, ladies. In fact, after what happened here yesterday, I seriously considered moving the event."

"What?" yelped Suzanne. "But we're already sold out!

Our plans are all in place. We've ordered flowers and food and . . . everything!"

Carmen sighed. "So you have."

"Which means we can hardly afford a last-minute change," finished Suzanne, somewhat breathlessly.

Carmen gazed down at her leopard-spotted boots. "No, I suppose not."

"So, the show must go on," said Toni, trying for humor, failing miserably.

"Realize, please," said Carmen, "that I don't want my boutique to be associated with anything as tawdry as murder."

"We don't like it any more than you do," said Suzanne, "but it's pretty much blown over by now."

"It has?" said Toni.

"Sure," said Suzanne. "Fact is, we had a full house for breakfast, lunch, and teatime, so I can't imagine anyone will stay away come Thursday."

"I'm going to hold you to that," said Carmen haughtily. She gazed about, then slipped out the door, as quietly as she'd come in.

"Ding-dong the witch is dead," quipped Toni.

"Not quite," said Suzanne. "We still have to deal with her on Thursday."

"I just wish she wasn't so snooty," said Toni. "It's not like Carmen is an ambassador for the United Nations or something. I mean, she writes books, for cripes sake. Bodice-busting romances."

"Romances that sell like crazy," said Suzanne.

Toni's shoulders slumped. "I guess."

The two women stared at each other.

"Doggone it," said Suzanne. "Now I know how Doogie felt earlier today when Ed Rapson confronted him from his high horse."

Toni wrinkled her nose. "Whadya mean?"

"With her fur coat and sparkly rings, Carmen makes me

feel like I'm some backwoods granny, sucking on a corncob pipe and wearing hand-me-down gingham."

"Just because Carmen's got money and prestige doesn't mean she's particularly well-liked," said Toni. "She's a rottweiler who's hound-dogged after every man in the county. And *still* she remains single."

Suzanne smiled a faint smile. "There is that."

CHAPTER 6

TONIGHT was a night Suzanne was secretly excited about. In fact, she'd been looking forward to it ever since she and Sam had marked it (in ink, of course!) on their calendars a couple of days ago. But with the press of business at the Cackleberry Club, the Fire and Ice Festival about to begin, and the crazy swirl of activity surrounding Ben Busacker's death, she'd had to batten down the hatches on excitement. She'd had to focus on the storm that was directly in front of her nose.

Life was like that sometimes, she thought. She hadn't had more than a minute to think about this special night. But even though her plans had been on the back burner, she was simmering tonight. Because Sam was coming over to her house, and she was going to cook.

"Are you sure you're up to it?" he had asked on the phone earlier this afternoon. Before she could answer, he added, "Especially after the Busacker incident? Really, Suzanne, I don't want to put you to any trouble."

Suzanne smiled as he spoke to her. She couldn't help it. What was it about this man that sent a shiver through her bones?

She had an image of Sam on the other end of the line as they spoke. Tall, check. Handsome. Oh yeah. Tousle of brown hair with a slightly unruly forelock spilling onto his forehead. Bit of a crooked smile. A kind, inquisitive face. And those strong but slender hands . . .

Where'd this guy come from, anyway? How had he

landed in her life? She wondered what forces in the universe had put them on a collision course and then brought
them together.

In so many ways, Sam Hazelet was just what the doctor
ordered. Except, of course, he *was* the doctor.

"I'm fine," she'd said into the phone. Sounding calm,
even as her heart was beating a little faster. "Not to worry.
You know that cooking's my thing."

"And a fine thing it is."

"So, come on over," she said. "Around sixish."

"What can I bring?" asked Sam. "How about a bottle of
wine?"

"Perfect."

"Red or white?"

"Up to you, but we're having steak."

"Mmn," said Sam. "Red, then."

SUZANNE bustled around her kitchen, an apron tied at her
waist and the nape of her neck still slightly wet from the
shower she'd taken just minutes before. She cubed a few
slices of brioche, tossed them into a bowl with four beaten
eggs, then added butter, raisins, milk, sugar, and cinnamon.
That went into the oven.

Now what?

Suzanne opened the refrigerator and grabbed her steaks.
She unwrapped them, knowing it was always better to let
meat come to room temperature before cooking it.

When she glanced around, she saw two dogs sitting
there, eyes lasered on the steaks.

Baxter was sitting there with limpid eyes and a softly
graying muzzle. He was Mr. Cool Dude Dog, pretending
not to care but salivating over the idea of grilled steak.

Scruff was just plain anxious, his tail thumping constantly, no pretense of being laid back or blasé. Then again,
Scruff was a rescue dog, a poor pathetic pup she'd found
wandering on a lonely highway one night. Now, almost

three months later, he was starting to relax and getting used to being in a warm, loving home. Suzanne had been dropping subtle hints to Sam that he should adopt Scruff, but he hadn't taken her up on it yet.

Hands on hips, Suzanne gazed at the dogs. "What? You guys are hoping for scraps already? I haven't even started dinner."

The dogs continued to stare at her. Casting polite but pathetic glances at the food.

"Okay, but kibbles only," said Suzanne. She grabbed two aluminum dog dishes, filled them with a scoop of kibbles each, and placed the dishes on the kitchen floor. Two muzzles dug in eagerly, sending little avalanches of kibbles over the side.

SUZANNE had stopped at the market on her way home and picked up a few more of her favorite ingredients for dinner. Besides the New York strip steaks, she'd gotten a bunch of asparagus, a French baguette, and an enormous heirloom tomato that wasn't in season but had hopefully been flown in from some warm and wonderful South American country where it *was* in season.

Now she bustled about what she thought of as her dream kitchen with its Wolf gas range, Sub-Zero refrigerator, granite countertops, and fabulous collection of copper pots and pans. She thanked her lucky stars for the umpteenth time that she'd been able to renovate this kitchen exactly to her taste and standards. When you put great care into something, she decided, it became yours in the truest sense.

Chopping off the woody portion of the stems, Suzanne popped her asparagus into simmering water for a quick blanch before she tossed it on the Jenn-Air grill. Then she seasoned the steaks with fresh cracked pepper, whipped up a pan of her special béarnaise sauce, and sliced the baguette and slathered it with garlic and butter. Tonight she wasn't counting calories.

With the grill heating, the asparagus simmering, and the béarnaise sauce bubbling like a mini volcano, Suzanne set out ivory-colored linen placemats on her butcher-block table. She added silverware and two Reidel wine goblets. As a finishing touch, she placed two silver candlesticks with tall white tapers in the center of the table, then lit the candles.

Suzanne gazed at the table. A cozy, inviting place setting for two. It looked so perfect, it brought a lump to her throat.

Just as she placed the steaks on the grill, she heard Sam's footsteps outside the front door. There was a loud *da-ding* and then the dogs were whirling and swirling their way to the door.

"Right on time," she said, pulling open the door.

"Smells great in here," Sam said as he clumped in, kicked off his boots, and gave her a quick kiss. "Looks great, too," he said, smiling at her.

"Compliments will get you everywhere," laughed Suzanne as she took his parka and hung it in the hall closet. She glanced out the narrow front hall window that was etched with ice crystals. "Still so cold out?"

"Brutal," said Sam. "But even with icy intersections, people are tearing around like mad."

"Good for business," said Suzanne.

"Ski season's always my prime time," laughed Sam as they linked arms and strolled into the kitchen, the dogs following at their heels. "All those broken bones."

Sam produced a bottle of cabernet sauvignon and set it on the kitchen counter.

"What kind?" said Suzanne.

"Ah, something I read about in *Wine Spectator,*" said Sam. "They gave it ninety-six points. Then again, they're generous and tend to give everything ninety-six points."

Suzanne handed Sam a corkscrew, and he opened the wine with a *pop* and a flourish, as she tossed her asparagus onto the grill next to the sizzling steaks. Five minutes later, with the steaks looking caramelized and smelling great, Suzanne plated everything and carried it to the table.

"Wow," said Sam, as she hit the rheostat and dimmed the lights. "Very impressive. Fine dining à la Chateau Suzanne."

"Did I ever tell you my secret dream?"

"You mean running your own fine-dining restaurant? Yes, you did. And I think you should follow that dream. Of course, I'd insist on a small piano bar where I could tickle the ivories when the mood struck me."

"You really play the piano?"

"Are you kidding?" Sam made a Groucho Marx expression with his eyebrows. "I can play show tunes with the best of them."

They dug into their food and wine then, relishing the end-of-day peacefulness and the chance to be together. Both had demanding work schedules and were responsible for other people, so it was a blessing to sit down and share a few hours.

"This is so civilized," said Sam. "I could get used to it."

Suzanne grinned. "I'm already used to it."

Reaching across the table, Sam grasped her hand and gave it a knowing squeeze.

They chatted comfortably then, but it wasn't long before their talk turned to the news du jour in Kindred: Ben Busacker's untimely death. Suzanne told Sam all about Ed Rapson showing up that morning. And about Charlie Steiner's rant against Busacker, as well as Reed Ducovny suddenly becoming Doogie's prime suspect.

"Ducovny?" said Sam. "Your Ducovny? The guy who won't kill a beetle?"

"Exactly," said Suzanne. "That's what I told Doogie. He's, like, mouse potatoes."

"What's that?"

"I don't know, I just made it up. I guess I meant small potatoes. Nothing there. That Doogie is way off base."

"Except for the wire," said Sam.

"Anybody could have cut that wire," said Suzanne. "It was just . . . I don't know, there for the cutting."

"And Ducovny really asked you to intercede?" said Sam. He paused, a fork in one hand, a knife in the other. "Please tell me you're not going to."

"No, of course not," said Suzanne. Feeling a little guilty that she hadn't told him the whole truth, she took a quick gulp of wine, then said, "Oh, and then Claudia Busacker showed up to take the grand tour and see exactly where her husband spent his last few moments on earth."

"Bad day at Black Rock."

"You have no idea," said Suzanne. "Poor Claudia, I felt terrible for her. Can you imagine what she put herself through by going back into those woods? To visit the very spot where her husband was killed? Of course, I also thought she was incredibly strong-willed to be able to do that."

"I've seen a lot of that over the years," said Sam. "People who just need to have a sense of certainty and gain a sense of closure and peace."

"Even though the circumstances of their loved one's death might be considered horrific?" asked Suzanne.

"Yes," Sam replied. "The bereaved often have the need to physically view the place where their loved one died. They need to burn the particular details into their memory. Otherwise, they end up regretting it for years after, wishing they'd gone back for a look. So for Claudia's mental health, it was probably better in the long run that she saw the place where her husband was killed."

"She didn't seem better off," said Suzanne. "In fact, she seemed more upset."

"That's because she's still processing it," said Sam.

"But the circumstances . . ." Suzanne hesitated. "It keeps gnawing at me. I mean, how exactly does someone get decapitated by a stretched wire?"

Sam looked at her with some concern. "You want the clinical details?"

Suzanne nodded. "Maybe I do."

"I'd say Busacker's death was brutally clean and effi-cient," said Sam, switching to a more professional, medical tone of voice. "It would appear the wire caught him directly on the neck, under his chin, where he was most vulnerable. Couple that with his high rate of speed on the snowmobile, and it was a recipe for disaster."

"He was decapitated," said Suzanne. "So that's the *cause* of death?"

"After being deprived of circulating oxygenated blood, his brain died within minutes," said Sam.

Suzanne winced. "Did he feel any pain?"

"Most likely not," said Sam. "I think the whole episode happened too quickly for him to experience pain or for his brain to register any reaction. Kind of like . . . the old French guillotine."

"Wow."

They were both quiet for a moment, almost as if they'd mutually agreed to observe a moment of silence for Busacker. The only things moving in the room were the candles flicker-ing in front of them, slowly dripping rivulets of white wax.

"I'm nearly positive I heard a second snowmobile," said Suzanne. "Just minutes before Busacker was killed."

"You think someone else was out there?"

"I do, but I can't prove it. The snow was pelting down like crazy, pretty much obliterating any other tracks." Su-zanne sighed. "So . . . I don't know. Maybe Busacker was being chased? Maybe that's why his sled was running so fast when he died?"

"Could have happened," said Sam. "Now it's up to Sher-iff Doogie to sort everything out. I imagine he stopped by today?"

"A couple of times," said Suzanne. "First thing this morning, then again mid-afternoon."

"And?" prompted Sam.

"Doogie's certainly made the case top priority. He's ask-ing questions and digging around."

"He's a good man," said Sam.

"But there aren't a lot of clear-cut clues," said Suzanne, "so it could take time. Of course, Mayor Mobley thinks the whole thing should have been wrapped up in about two hours."

"I can't believe that buffoon got reelected," said Sam.

"Rumor has it he stuffed the ballot box," said Suzanne. She reflected for a moment, thinking back to last night again. "How often do you see a grisly accident like that?"

"Exactly like that one?" said Sam. "Never have before. But I have encountered some unbelievable things in my medical career. Gruesome injuries and deaths that really have no place, if you don't mind my saying, at this wonderful dinner table of yours."

"But how do you have the stomach for the really tough stuff?" she asked. "How do you handle it? Because I don't think I could."

"I think you could," said Sam. "For example, you'd probably do well in a morgue, where medical students put in their time studying gross anatomy."

"I don't know about that," said Suzanne.

"If you have the stomach for understanding a beheading, then you have the stomach for, let's say, looking inside a human kneecap, or studying the gnarled bones of a ninety-eight-year-old woman's hand, or stitching up a terrible gash on the side of someone's jaw."

Suzanne grimaced. "I think even the kneecap is pushing it for me."

Sam smiled. "Oh, I think Suzanne Dietz is one tough lady."

"Maybe she is," said Suzanne. "But she's also wise enough to know when it's time to let this conversation go."

Sam leaned back from the table and stretched. "Time for me to help with the dishes?"

"Time for dessert," said Suzanne. "I was going to serve bread pudding with an optional scoop of French vanilla ice cream."

"Wow. You really know how to pile on the calories, lady. I'm going to have to do double crunches and pull-ups at the gym tomorrow."

They ended up watching a thriller on HBO and sipping cheggnog, Suzanne's blend of eggnog and chai tea. Curled up together on Suzanne's cushy couch in the living room.

My home feels complete, Suzanne thought to herself a little later, as they lay cuddled together. It feels warm and comfortable to have a man back in my life again. Her mind flew briefly to thoughts of Walter. What they had together, what they shared. Then she brought herself back to the here and now, where she really belonged.

Try to live in the present, she reminded herself. *After all, that's one of the affirmations Toni, Petra, and I have in our little collection.*

When the ten o'clock news was over, after the weatherman had warned of more sub-zero temperatures rumbling down from Canada, Sam stretched, stood up, and padded to the window in his stocking feet. "Awfully cold out there," he said.

Suzanne walked up behind him and circled her arms around his waist. "Maybe too cold."

"Mmn, you might be right."

"Nice and warm upstairs," she said.

He turned around and pulled her close. "That's the best offer I've had since . . ."

"Last week?" She grinned. He'd been over for dinner last week, too. They definitely, officially, were becoming an item. And as they climbed the stairs, hand in hand, Suzanne thought to herself, *Correction: we* are *an item.*

Two hours later, a cool muzzle tickled her arm. Baxter asking to go out. Slowly, carefully, without waking Sam, Suzanne slipped out from beneath the poufy down comforter. In the chill air of her dark bedroom, she dressed hurriedly, pulling on fleece pants and a long-sleeve shirt. Downstairs she added boots, a parka, and a knit cap.

Then they were out the door and crunching down the sidewalk, Baxter and Scruff straining at their leashes. The snow had frosted all the trees up and down her block, and the nearby homes looked gingerbread perfect. Very snug and picturesque with puffs of smoke curling up from the chimneys.

If I were an artist, Suzanne thought, I would paint this scene. I'd even try to capture the scatter of stars, strewn like a game of glittery jacks, high in the inky black sky.

But as Suzanne led the dogs back to her house, she couldn't help wonder: In this picture-perfect little town, who really had murder in their heart?

CHAPTER 7

SUZANNE arrived at the Cackleberry Club bright and early Wednesday morning, energized after her night with Sam and ready to jump in and serve the morning's breakfast crowd.

Petra was already presiding over her stove, rattling pans while pancetta sizzled and popped in one of her cast-iron skillets. Batter for red-velvet chocolate-chip pancakes sat at the ready.

"Morning, sweetie," Suzanne said, greeting her. "What'd you conjure up for breakfast today?"

"Hey," said Petra, turning with a smile on her face. "I've got something new to rock your world."

"Lay it on me."

Petra flipped the pancetta onto paper towels to drain. "Poached eggs stuffed inside popovers."

"Yikes," said Suzanne. "What do you call something like that?"

"Nest Eggs," grinned Petra.

"Isn't that cute?" asked Toni, as she pushed her way into the kitchen, looking like a rodeo star in her hot pink cowboy shirt and tight blue jeans. "Isn't our Petra a creative genius?"

"As well as a kitchen genius," agreed Suzanne. She was forever thankful that Petra's broad Scandinavian face was the one she saw every morning at the stove wearing her oversize apron and funky clogs and taking infinite care with everything she prepped and cooked.

"So," said Toni, popping a couple of purple grapes in her mouth, "how was your dinner last night?" She paused, chewing. "Yep, I've got my trusty shovel out, digging for girlfriend dirt."

Suzanne was suddenly busy with a stack of plates. "Oh, it was fine. Just fine."

"Anything special you want to tell us about?" pressed Toni. "Because enquiring minds won't be satisfied with a noncommittal 'fine.' Enquiring minds want to hear a few juicy details." She reached up and popped the top button on her shirt, revealing a smidgeon of lacey pink bra.

When Suzanne shook her head and smiled, Toni blurted out, "Come on, Suzanne, spill it. Throw us a bone. Or do Petra and I have to browbeat it out of you? You know darn well we're not easily vanquished."

"Unless there's a bottle of Jack Daniel's involved," said Suzanne.

"Oooh," said Toni, balling her fists, frustrated.

"Face it," Petra said to Toni, "a good-looking guy like that? Suzanne probably had a magical night. Fireworks and pinwheels."

"Did you?" asked Toni.

"All you need to know," said Suzanne, "is that Sam and I had a terrific dinner together. Steak, wine, and all the fixings."

"Couldn't you just elaborate on the fixings?" Toni pleaded. "Like the kissing and the hugging and the—"

"I'm happy for you, Suzanne," cut in Petra, as she pulled a pan of enormous popovers from the oven and placed it on the counter. "It's a thrill to see you really enjoying life again."

"I didn't enjoy life before?" asked Suzanne.

Toni and Petra exchanged glances.

"After Walter died," said Petra gently, "it was difficult. You were always so quiet and serious."

"But for good reason," said Toni.

"And because I was honchoing the grand opening of this place!" said Suzanne.

"Yes," said Petra, "but you were grieving, too. Probably still are."

"Can you still grieve for someone and fall in love again?" Toni wondered.

"Sure you can," said Petra. "But it takes a special person to . . . I don't know what you'd call it . . . compartmentalize those experiences." She smiled at Suzanne. "One who has her head on straight."

"Speaking of heads . . ." said Toni.

"Oooh, don't you dare bring that up!" said Petra. Now she looked deeply perturbed. "I don't want to hear about Ben Busacker anymore. I just want that whole nasty episode to be done with!" She put her hands on her broad hips. "Do you ladies realize how busy we are?" Then, without letting them answer, she continued. "Fire and Ice kicks off today, I've got Stitch and Bitch tonight, and tomorrow is our Crystal Tea. And if that isn't enough to worry about, we'll probably have Sheriff Doogie schlumping around here looking for clues." She threw up her hands. "Lord love a duck!"

SUZANNE kicked it into high gear then, brewing pots of Sumatran roast coffee and English breakfast tea, and making last-minute adjustments to table settings before her early morning customers came tumbling in. And, all the while, she was thinking about the bottom line. The Cackleberry Club was a business, after all. And Suzanne was well aware that making a profit was a far cry from just making a living. What she liked to think of as her diversification—the café, Book Nook, and Knitting Nest—had proved to be a lethal business combination. And for some strange reason, when one wasn't contributing its fair share to the bottom line, the other two seemed to kick in and do amazingly well. Go figure.

Ruminating about finances led Suzanne back to thoughts of that beefy-faced regional bank manager, Ed Rapson,

who'd stormed his way in here yesterday. And the pressure
he was undoubtedly exerting on Sheriff Doogie to solve the
Busacker case practically overnight.

Rapson bothered her. And not just because he'd tried to
sic Doogie onto poor Reed Ducovny. No, Rapson carried an
air of fat-cat slicko about him. He was aggressive and edgy
and seemed to have something personal on the line.

What was Rapson so worked up about? Suzanne wondered. Somehow it seemed to go way beyond simply losing
a valued employee. Suzanne turned that notion over in her
mind as she stacked fat jelly donuts in the glass pie saver.
And suddenly made a scary leap in thought: Could Rapson
have been involved in Busacker's death? Had Busacker discovered some problem at the bank? Or had Busacker been
a problem? And had Rapson neatly eliminated that problem? Could have happened.

Of course, there was no way to know at this point. She'd
have to wait and see what developed.

Minutes later, customers began trickling in for breakfast.
They pulled off caps, hats, and mittens, stomped snow from
their boots, all the while murmuring how warm and cheery
it was inside the Cackleberry Club. Suzanne guided them to
tables and got them settled in as the smell of Petra's tantalizing bacon and sausages drifted out from the kitchen.

Soon, every table was filled and breakfast service was in
full swing. Toni joined Suzanne in the café, taking orders,
delivering fresh-squeezed orange juice, coffee, and tea,
then dashing back into the kitchen to grab platters of food
hot off the grill.

Petra's Nest Eggs were an instant hit. And a low, comfortable murmur filled the café as customers enjoyed their
breakfast entrees, as well as seconds and thirds of morning
coffee.

Suzanne was pouring out a mug of hot cocoa made with
Belgian dark chocolate when Petra called to her through the
pass-through.

"Suzanne," said Petra, making a little whirring motion

with her hands, "turn on the radio. It's time for the first treasure-hunt clue to be broadcast!"

"Holy *ka-ching!*" cried Toni, hustling over to the counter. She wiped her hands on her apron and dug out a pen and order pad. "I've got to catch this baby. I'm ready to go on the hunt!"

Suzanne reached up and snapped on the radio. A quick announcement on winter wheat and hog prices crackled out over the air, then Paula Patterson's cheery voice came on: "Good morning, Kindred, and thanks for joining us!"

A hush swept through the café, as customers perked up their ears and listened in. Obviously, Toni wasn't the only one chomping at the bit to hear the first clue.

"As all of you probably know," continued Paula, "our much-awaited Fire and Ice Festival kicks off today, and we're ready and raring to share the first of five clues with you." She paused. "Does everybody have paper and pencil handy? Because you don't want to miss any part of this!"

"I'm ready, I'm ready," said Toni, staring intently at the radio and nervously tapping her foot.

"This year," Paula went on, "a grand prize of three *thousand* dollars goes to the person who discovers the treasure medallion. And every morning, starting today and continuing for the next four days, we'll announce a new clue. That's right, folks, five clues in all, until Fire and Ice culminates on Sunday night with a grand bonfire and cookout at Kindred's own Cackleberry Club."

Suzanne, Petra, and Toni looked at each other and smiled. Always good to get a nice on-air plug! Especially when you didn't have to pay for it!

"Without further ado," said Paula, "here's our first clue."

Everyone seemed to hold their breaths as Paula read the clue:

Join the hunt, and try your hand
At winning this very special three grand.

Look high and low and where it's frozen,
Find the medallion first, and you'll be chosen!

Toni dutifully wrote it all down, then stared blankly at the radio. "Wait, that's it? That's the clue?"

"Start your detective work . . . now!" urged Paula, then the radio station segued to a piece of lively music.

"It's awfully vague," said Petra as she stood at the stove, gently dropping eggs into hot water.

"It's beyond vague," said Toni. "It's useless." She glanced down at her notes. "The clue says look where it's frozen? The whole town is frozen! There's five feet of snow everywhere, and where there isn't snow, there's ice! Everything's practically *freeze*-dried."

"With a grand prize of three grand," said Suzanne, "you can't expect this treasure hunt to be easy. There's not going to be any sort of 'X marks the spot.' They're going to make you scramble for it."

"I guess," said Toni, scratching her head. "Jeez, maybe we should call a psychic hotline. 1-800-READ-MY-MIND."

"The clue does say high and low," said Suzanne, "so that's something to consider. Maybe the medallion is tangled up in the branches of a tree?"

"Sure, but there's about a billion trees in town," said Toni. "And most of them are covered with snow."

Petra leaned forward and called through the pass-through, "Don't you worry, Toni, you'll noodle it around in that clever little head of yours and come up with something. Besides, there are four more clues to come."

"Maybe," said Toni. Her enthusiasm had waned enormously.

"I can't believe Carmen put up the prize money," said Suzanne. She turned to the coffeemaker, dumped in a scoop of fresh coffee, and flipped the switch.

"I bet she did it for the publicity," grumped Toni.

"Carmen does love a mention in the *Bugle* or a chat on

the radio," said Suzanne. "She's no fool. It helps drive book sales. Every mention or appearance just ups her notoriety."

"I'm sure Carmen will probably be yakking up the prize money at the Crystal Tea tomorrow," said Toni.

"Toni?" called Petra. "Focus please, your orders are up."

Suzanne did her café ballet then, whirling and twirling and pouring refills, clearing tables, setting out fresh cups and silverware and napkins for the steady stream of customers that continued to ease their way in. And just as she hustled back to the counter to whip together a ham and Swiss cheese sandwich for a take-out order, Lester Drummond, the ex-prison warden wandered in and took a seat at the counter.

"Hello, Suzanne," Drummond said, with a gruff voice and a quick nod. He was a big man with a shaved head, craggy face, and a forehead full of worry lines. Suzanne always thought Drummond had the kind of hard face and hard muscles that came from serving hard time. Except, of course, Drummond had *run* the prison. But now that he was out of a job, Drummond spent most of his days pumping iron at the Hard Body Gym on the edge of town.

"Mr. Drummond," said Suzanne. She whipped a paper napkin down in front of him and laid down a clean fork, knife, and spoon. "Coffee to start?" Even though she disliked him, Suzanne resolved to treat him with the same courtesy she'd give any other customer.

"Lester," said Drummond, "call me Lester. And, yeah, coffee sounds good."

"Lester," said Suzanne, pouring out a steady stream of coffee into his cup.

He smiled at her, all piercing eyes and Chiclet-sized teeth. "Looking good, Suzanne."

"Thank you." Her smile was brittle at best. "Lester."

"No, I mean it," said Drummond, dumping at least a quarter cup of sugar into his coffee. "You're a fine-looking woman. You remind me of some of the women back east, the ones who graduated from those fancy colleges."

But Suzanne was all business. "We've got Nest Eggs

today, which is a poached egg tucked inside a fresh-baked popover, scrambled eggs with pancetta, red velvet pancakes, and . . . let's see . . . I'm pretty sure there are a couple orders of pork sausage left."

"Scrambled eggs," said Drummond. "Whole wheat toast."

Suzanne made a note. "Got it."

"You going to the play Friday night?" he asked. The Community Players, a local troupe, were putting on a stage presentation of *Titanic*.

"Maybe," said Suzanne. *Unless Sam and I get together again.*

"I've got one of the lead roles," Drummond boasted. "I play the captain."

"Who goes down with his ship," said Suzanne. "Perfect casting, I'd say."

He peered at her. "You think?"

Suzanne regarded him with a steely gaze. Should she bring up the little bit of unfinished business that hung between them? Why not? "Might I remind you, Lester, I still have a poor, innocent little dog in my care. One that barely managed to escape that stable of fighting dogs you had squirreled away out in the countryside."

A muscle in Drummond's jaw twitched. "There was never any proof those dogs were mine."

"Not yet," said Suzanne.

Now Drummond shook a finger at her and grinned. "You better be nice to me, Suzanne. I just might be the next bank president around here."

"What?" Suzanne was shocked. In fact, this was the most ridiculous thing she'd heard since Bob Connors claimed to have found a two-headed snake wriggling through his pasture!

But Drummond was suddenly full of swill and swagger. "That's right. I've already met with Ed Rapson and put in my application for the job." His chest puffed slightly. "And I think I have a darned good shot at it."

Suzanne said carefully, "Is that really the right type of job for you? I mean, don't you have to understand how the Federal Reserve operates . . . How bonds and interest rates work? Things of that nature?" She was about to add *And know how to get along with people*, but decided not to push it.

"Look, Suzanne," said Drummond, forcefully, "I ran a prison for three years. It's exactly the same as being CEO of a major corporation. You govern from the top down, hire the right people, and focus on the big picture. Plus, I have organizational skills and an excellent head for finance. As for the minor details, I can learn those as I need to."

"I suppose," said Suzanne slowly. "After all, there's nothing like on-the-job training. Particularly when it's for a bank position where people's lives are at stake—and maybe their entire futures, too."

"YOU want to have a good laugh?" asked Suzanne as she pushed her way into the kitchen.

"Lay it on me," said Petra, who was standing at the counter, whipping a big bowl of frosting by hand.

"What's up?" asked Toni. She balanced a gray plastic tub full of dirty dishes she was about to stack in the dishwasher.

Suzanne grinned. "Lester Drummond applied for the job of bank president."

"What!" said Petra.

"Shut the front door!" whooped Toni. "Are you serious?"

"Drummond certainly is," said Suzanne.

"That's plum crazy," said Petra. Then she stopped to consider Suzanne's words. "Do you think he's got a chance?"

"Maybe," said Suzanne. She thought about Ed Rapson, the regional manager, and decided Drummond might be just the kind of man Rapson would like. Tough-minded and hard-driving. The kind of guy who wouldn't buckle under to a farmer's pleas for credit or a small mom-and-pop business asking for a loan.

"Oh man," said Petra. "If he gets the job, I'm going to have to move my checking account."

"Ditto," said Toni. "In a heartbeat."

"How," wondered Petra, "could a guy with a bad reputation and an even worse temper get considered for a job as bank president?"

"What would you do after being a prison warden?" Toni asked.

"Interesting question," said Suzanne. "Maybe . . . go work for Martha Stewart?"

"Good one," said Toni, aiming a finger at her.

"This is just another indication of the instability in our country these days," reflected Petra. "Things that were rock solid and reliable aren't necessarily so anymore. The banks. Our car companies. Even the stock market."

"Don't forget the government!" said Toni.

"Federal, state, or local?" asked Suzanne.

"The whole shootin' match!" cried Toni.

"But Drummond as bank president," said Petra, sounding mournful. "That's just way too much to wrap my mind around. I mean, he was *fired* from the prison because of those fighting dogs!"

"Unfortunately, the charges never stuck," said Suzanne.

"How did he slither his way out of that anyway?" asked Toni.

"The dog kennel wasn't on his land, so there was some technicality," said Suzanne. "The county prosecutor didn't have an ironclad case. I guess that pricey, big-city lawyer Drummond hired did exactly what he was paid to do."

"I know one thing," said Petra. "Anybody who mistreats poor defenseless animals is not someone I want near my money." The others nodded as she added, "If he hurt those poor dogs, who knows what he'd do to all of us?"

* * *

FEELING the need for a small bit of calm, Suzanne wandered into the Knitting Nest. She instantly felt at ease in this room, with its overstuffed chairs, finished sweaters and shawls adorning the walls, and crazy-quilt collection of gorgeous yarns and fibers tucked into every nook and cranny of the room. Petra had stocked the Knitting Nest with skeins of mohair yarn, alpaca, and even a few skeins of cashmere.

Some new shipments of knitting needles had arrived, too, including fresh sets of bamboo single- and double-point knitting needles. They were sure to knock the socks off knitting aficionados, Suzanne decided, as she ran her fingers across a smooth wooden set. The bamboo needles were much lighter than the aluminum kind, and were even said to improve with age.

Soft footfalls behind her caused Suzanne to spin about. "Oh!" she said, putting a hand to her chest. "Hello."

Elise Steiner, the wife of Charlie Steiner, stared at her, a cautious look on her face.

"Sorry to startle you," said Elise, "but I saw you walk in here and I . . . well, I wanted to talk. Um . . . privately."

Elise Steiner was a sweet, if slightly wan-looking woman with an almost ivory complexion and the kind of white blond hair you only see with true Scandinavians. Elise was a devout Lutheran who volunteered at the library and was also a member of Petra's Stitch and Bitch group. Although Elise always pointedly referred to it as her stitching group.

Suzanne couldn't help it: Charlie Steiner's angry outburst in the café yesterday came instantly to mind. And she wondered if Elise would dare mention it. Or did Elise even *know* about it?

She knew.

After a few false starts, Elise asked, "Did my husband say anything to you that was, er, slightly out of the ordinary?"

Suzanne decided to play dumb. "Why do you ask?"

Elise's pale skin turned bright pink. "I received a phone

call from Gene Gandle at the *Bugle*. He told me Charlie was talking up a storm about Ben Busacker's death during breakfast yesterday. I'm embarrassed to ask, Suzanne, but do you know exactly what Charlie said?"

Suzanne recalled that Charlie had pointedly talked about missed mortgage payments, which would put anybody on edge. But to spare Elise some embarrassment, she said, "I think he was unhappy about his financial situation at the bank."

Elise ducked her head and said, "So you know about that?"

"Well . . . yes."

"We're way behind on our loan payments," said Elise, looking grim.

"Have you tried dealing directly with the bank?" said Suzanne. "Asking for more time? A grace period, perhaps?"

Elise nodded. "It didn't work. They're putting our farm into foreclosure."

"That's awful." Suzanne felt a surge of anger for all the hard-working folks who were going through this kind of financial nightmare right now. It just wasn't right.

Elise looked down at her feet and mumbled, "I'm terrified about Charlie. He's been talking crazy for a couple of weeks now. Muttering threats and cooking up imaginary scenarios. You know, ways to get back at the bank."

"But Charlie wouldn't actually *do* anything, would he?" said Suzanne. "He wouldn't . . . retaliate?"

Elise shifted from one foot to the other, obviously upset and nervous. "Uh, I just don't know."

"Dear lord," said Suzanne, "have you mentioned any of this to Sheriff Doogie?"

Elise's face twisted in pain. "No! If I did, the sheriff might come out and arrest Charlie!"

"Well, I know that Gene Gandle definitely overheard Charlie," said Suzanne. "So, chances are, Gene's already mentioned Charlie's rants to Doogie." In fact, she knew he had.

"Oh dear," said Elise.

"I wish I could help, but . . ."

"You *can* help," said Elise. "The investigation into Ben Busacker's death is centered right here at the Cackleberry Club. Maybe you could kind of, you know, keep your eyes and ears open. See what suspects Sheriff Doogie comes up with. And then . . . let me know."

"I'd feel funny doing that," said Suzanne.

Elise took a step forward and gripped her arm. "Please!"

Suzanne gazed into the desperate face of Elise Steiner. "Okay," she said. "I can't promise anything, but I'll see what I can do."

"Bless you," said Elise. Her voice was practically a sob.

Still, Suzanne was conflicted. *Her husband might be about to lose his farm to a greedy bank,* she thought. *But I shouldn't have promised to spy for her. Oh man, but I did.* And then, directly on the heels of that thought was: *What if I find out that Charlie Steiner really did engineer Ben Busacker's death? Then what? Would that put me in danger?*

CHAPTER 8

IT seemed like an eternity before Elise Steiner finally released her vise-like grip on Suzanne's arm. But she did. And even though she gave another whispered, "Thank you," worry still draped the woman's face like a shroud, and her narrow shoulders sagged.

Suzanne watched as the wounded Elise retreated from the Knitting Nest and trudged out into the icy landscape. Then she gave a sigh of relief.

She needed to play major catch-up with Doogie concerning the investigation. It had been less than twenty-four hours since she'd last talked to him, and now she was wondering exactly what sort of progress he'd made. Had Doogie learned anything more about the wire? Had he pinpointed any disgruntled bank customers who might be suspects? Was he getting anywhere at all?

Doogie, where are you on this thing? she thought to herself. *Talk to me. Call me. Text me. Send an SOS. Something.*

Gazing around the Knitting Nest, trying to organize her thoughts, Suzanne couldn't shake the notion that Charlie Steiner might possibly be connected to that awful night. Her mind kept stumbling over one thought: could an angry farmer have been *that* angry that he actually stretched a deadly thin wire in a snowstorm, in the middle of winter in order to lop off someone's head?

The notion chilled her. It would mean Steiner had slipped from normalcy into seriously psychotic behavior.

Was that what had happened?

Suzanne had no idea. All she had was a bushel basket full of conjecture. And now she was trying to placate a nervous, desperate wife who was worried about her husband's culpability.

Jeez.

Suzanne picked up a stray strand of soft, white fiber and wound it around her finger. Then she shook her head to try to clear her thoughts. How on earth, she wondered, did professional psychologists and psychiatrists hack it? Chewing over the hidden motives and misexpressed emotions of highly imperfect people, all with their troubles and confusions, definitely had to be challenging. In fact, it could drive a person crazy!

Stepping out into the café, Suzanne noted that Toni was standing at the counter, ringing up the last of their morning customers. Which meant . . . holy guacamole! It was almost time for lunch. And time to put herself on fast forward.

It wasn't until she had peeled a mess of carrots for Petra's carrot-apple cole slaw that Suzanne mentioned her conversation with Elise Steiner.

"Are you going to help her?" Petra asked.

"I kind of promised I would," said Suzanne, "but now I'm nervous about the whole thing."

"That's because you're playing both ends," said Petra. "Trying to get information from Doogie while conveying any concern he might have about Charlie to Elise."

"Yes," said Suzanne. "That's about the size of it. So how do I get out of my predicament?"

"You don't," sang Petra. "A promise is a promise."

"You're no help," said Suzanne.

"You just need to find out how Doogie's investigation is going," suggested Petra. "If he's moved in another direction, then the whole Charlie Steiner thing is a moot point."

"You think?"

"No," said Petra, "I don't." She dipped a wooden spoon into a simmering vat of soup and tasted it. Cocked her head, then added a pinch more salt.

"Chalkboard time," said Toni, as she careened into the kitchen with her last tub of dirty dishes. "Better get the lunch specials up on the board before the thundering horde makes a return appearance."

Suzanne grabbed a stick of yellow chalk and gazed at Petra. "So what's it gonna be?"

"Our soup du jour," said Petra, "is tomato and egg drop soup served with a chunk of toasted Italian bread. That's pretty much a meal in itself."

"Got it," said Suzanne. "What else?"

"Seize-the-Day Caesar Salad," said Petra, "topped with sliced chicken. And Toasted Tuna Melties with carrot cole slaw, and gingerbread cake to round out the menu."

Suzanne got busy with the chalkboard then, writing everything down and adding prices. When she got to the gingerbread cake, she scrawled $2.99 next to it, then erased the price with her hand and changed it to $3.99. She decided a few extra bucks would help fluff the bottom line.

Ten minutes later customers began showing up.

"It's a slam dunk day," Suzanne said to Toni, as they stood behind the counter grabbing more coffee cups and silverware.

"You got that right," said Toni, wiggling her hips.

"You're in a feisty mood. And what, pray tell, is with that peek of pink bra you've been sporting all morning?"

"Helps generate tips," said Toni.

"Ah," said Suzanne. "And is it working?"

"Oh yeah, baby," grinned Toni. "It's working. *I'm* working."

"Just . . . take it easy, okay? This is the Cackleberry Club, not the Victoria's Secret runway show."

"That's okay," said Toni, giving a slow wink. "'Cause I'm no angel!"

AT quarter to one, just when Suzanne thought lunch was winding down, just when she thought she could take a break, Ed Rapson pushed his way into the Cackleberry Club trailed by the pale, mousy Hamilton Wick. Both men were dressed in conservative black suits and white shirts. The only color in their outfits was the narrow, red-striped rep ties they wore.

"Gentlemen," said Suzanne brightly, as she showed them to a sunny table. "Nice to see you both. Even though circumstances at the bank aren't the best, I hope you've brought your appetites."

Rapson and Wick settled in at their table.

"Nice to see you, Suzanne," said Ham Wick. He was a pleasant man, who always spoke kindly to her.

"I was so sorry about Ben Busacker," she told Wick. "Especially since it all . . ." She made a gesture that ended up as a shrug.

"Happened here," said Wick, nodding. "And I'm equally sorry for you, Suzanne. I know it couldn't have been easy for you."

Suzanne saw what looked like true sorrow in Wick's eyes, and said, "I understand Busacker's funeral is going to take place tomorrow?"

"That's right," said Ed Rapson, jumping in. "The body's been released, so there's no reason to delay."

"Are you coming?" Wick asked.

"Certainly," said Suzanne. Her heart went out to Ham Wick, who she knew had been passed over for bank president in favor of Ben Busacker. Would probably be passed over again, if Lester Drummond had his way.

"I'll have the soup," said Rapson, who obviously wasn't in the mood for small talk.

"Tuna melt," said Wick, smiling at Suzanne.

But as Suzanne jotted down their orders, Ham Wick surprised her.

"Suzanne," said Wick, "perhaps you might consider giving Mr. Rapson here your vote of confidence."

Suzanne looked up and blinked. "Excuse me?"

"You know," said Wick, "vouch for me. You being a local business owner and all."

"Vouch for what?" asked Suzanne.

"He's lobbying for the bank president's job," Rapson barked out. He also seemed amused.

"Is that so?" said Suzanne. She didn't know what else to say. Hamilton Wick had never struck her as a go-getter. In fact, he'd probably be the least-effective bank president she could think of.

"Anyway," said Wick, almost stumbling over his words now, "your vote of confidence would go a long way."

"Would it really?" Suzanne asked Rapson.

A smarmy smile crawled across Rapson's beefy face. "Sure. Why not?" he said.

"I think," said Suzanne, tapping her pen against her order book, "that a kinder, gentler banking environment would be a breath of fresh air in Kindred. And if Hamilton Wick can make that happen, then so much the better."

"Thank you," said Wick, beaming.

"Hrmmp," said Rapson.

"GUESS what?" Suzanne said to Petra in the kitchen. "Now Ham Wick wants to be bank president."

"Good lord," said Petra. "The man is afraid of his own shadow."

"I need two more tuna melts," said Toni, pushing her way into the kitchen.

"Hold your horses," said Petra. "We've just had a hot news flash." She gave a wicked grin. "As opposed to a garden variety hot flash."

Toni glanced from Suzanne to Petra. "What are you crazy ladies talking about?"

"Hamilton Wick is lobbying for the bank president's job," explained Suzanne.

"Our Ham Wick?" said Toni. "The guy who's the spitting image of Mister Rogers? The guy who drives, like, two miles an hour even when there's bare pavement? *That* guy?"

Suzanne nodded. "Yup."

"He'd be terrible," said Toni. "He's walking milque-toast."

"But maybe a better choice than Lester Drummond?" said Petra.

"Those are my choices?" said Toni. "Heck, I'd rather do my banking online."

"Don't do it!" cried Petra. "You'll end up losing your money to some crazy offshore bank in the Caymans or some Nigerian scam artist. Besides, honey, you're not that computer savvy to begin with."

"I could learn," said Toni. "I could buy myself one of those iPods."

"iPads," said Suzanne.

"Whatever," said Toni.

"HERE you go," said Suzanne, dropping off the orders for Rapson and Wick. "And don't forget, we've got ginger-bread cake for dessert."

But Wick was suddenly looking downhearted, as if Rapson had been chewing him out. Or putting him down.

"Don't you think, Ms. Dietz," said Rapson, "that our bank requires a candidate who projects an air of absolute confidence?"

Hamilton Wick's face turned strawberry pink.

Suzanne cleared her throat. Even though she didn't think Wick was the right candidate, she hated to see the man pil-loried. "The bank president's job requires the most qualified candidate you can find," she said, addressing Rapson. "From a public-relations standpoint alone, it's a vital position in Kindred."

"What's Kindred got to do with it?" said Rapson sharply.

"Beg your pardon?" said Suzanne.

"Mills City Banks is going to choose the best person for the job according to our corporate criteria," snapped Rapson. "Not Kindred's needs." His brows beetled together. "This is hardly a popularity contest."

"I'm not suggesting that," Suzanne replied firmly. "All I'm saying is that the townspeople view the person who holds that particular post as a civic and business leader. Someone who understands the ins and outs of banking, as well as the economic needs of the people who live here. Your choice of bank president would hopefully take that into account."

"That's a lot for a one-horse town like Kindred to ask," said Rapson, snickering. "A one-horse town with a one-horse sheriff, I might add. Your man Doogie acts like he just walked off the set of *The Andy Griffith Show*." Rapson let loose a belly laugh while Wick ducked his head and turned an even more embarrassed shade of red.

"Excuse me," said Suzanne, her eyes blazing. "You're referring to *this* town? The one where your bank is located? Because if you don't feel our residents are *worthy* of your financial services, I'm sure we could make alternate arrangements with the bank in Jessup."

Rapson's eyes narrowed into piggy little slits, and his mouth opened and closed like a catfish that had been snagged and was drawing its last breath. "You've got a smart mouth on you, lady," he snarled.

"Maybe," said Suzanne, "that's because I'm a smart lady!"

But as she stepped away from the table to tend to her other customers, Rapson muttered after her, "You haven't heard the last from me—or my bank. No matter what kind of town you think you live in."

CHAPTER 9

CHILLS trickled down Suzanne's spine as Rapson's words drifted after her.

Taking a deep breath, she willed herself not to turn around or show any fear. *Hold it together, girl,* she told herself. *It's like dealing with an aggressive dog. Never react, never show fear. You're the one in charge.*

But inside she was spitting mad.

Who did Rapson think he was, anyway? God's gift to the financial world? The bank czar? And he was going to have the sole vote when it came to choosing Kindred's next bank president? Rapson's arrogance and rudeness were practically beyond belief.

Once she was safely behind the counter, Suzanne looked around the café at her happy, good-natured customers—all but two of them, anyway—and tried to shake it off.

Enough. She wasn't about to let Ed Rapson get under her skin. On the other hand, her instincts told her to keep a sharp eye on him, just in case. There was something about the man, besides his arrogance and foolish words, that made her more than a little jumpy.

"What's wrong, kiddo?" Toni had edged up beside her.

"Rapson," Suzanne said, under her breath. "Acting the fool again."

Toni glanced over at Rapson and said, with all seriousness, "I don't think he was acting. I think he really is."

Which caused them both to dissolve in giggles.

"Maybe we should give him the Cackleberry Club Egghead Award," said Toni.

"We have that?" asked Suzanne, playing along.

"Sure," said Toni. "Big gold statue that kind of looks like a bowling trophy, only with an egg. Or we could give it to Lester Drummond, whatever tickles your fancy." She lowered her voice. "I saw Drummond flirting with you earlier." She poked an index finger toward her mouth and said, "Gag."

"You got that right," said Suzanne. Then she sobered slightly. "But the weird thing is, both those guys are sort of mixed up in this murder case."

"A lot of people are."

"Unfortunately, there don't seem to be any solid suspects," said Suzanne.

"Doogie's got nuthin'?" asked Toni.

"I don't know what's going on with him," Suzanne said as she reached to grab the phone. "But I'm gonna give him a call and find out."

"Atta girl," said Toni. "See what's shakin'."

Suzanne dialed Doogie's number from memory, waited a beat, and then said, "Oh crud, voice mail."

"Leave him a message anyway," Toni urged.

Suzanne nodded, then said into the phone, "I know you're hard at work doing your job and all, Sheriff, but it's important I know where you are with a couple of things. If you could drop by the Cackleberry Club, today yet, that would be great. Oh . . . and there's cake. We've got cake."

"Gingerbread cake," said Toni, leaning in to the receiver.

"Okay, thanks," said Suzanne, and hung up.

"Think he'll show up?" asked Toni.

Suzanne shrugged. "Dunno. Hope so. Cake's always a major incentive." She reached for a sleek black tin. "I think I'll shake things up today and brew jasmine tea."

"Yum," said Toni. "And Petra's got lemon scones baking in the oven."

Suzanne tilted her head toward Rapson and Wick. "As soon as those two hunyucks leave, we'll set up for tea. White tablecloths, sugar cubes, lemon slices, the whole nine yards."

"Maybe I'll go help things along with Tweedledum and Tweedledee over there," said Toni. "Deliver their tab and start clearing dishes."

"Do that," said Suzanne. She danced around the counter and cut across the café, over to the sputtering cooler that sat against the wall. Its shelves were stocked with jars of fat dill pickles, canned jellies and jams, and wonderful gouda and Swiss cheeses. These were all items that local producers brought in to the Cackleberry Club to sell. It was pretty much a win-win situation for all concerned. Suzanne took a small percentage of retail sales, and the growers and producers got the lion's share. But as Suzanne's eyes scanned the shelves, she noticed they had nary a loaf of homemade bread. She made a mental note to call Shar Sandstrom, one of their top bakers of banana and cranberry bread, and ask her to pretty please bring some more loaves in.

Then, because Petra's Stitch & Bitch was happening tonight, Suzanne popped into the Knitting Nest to check on things. She'd tried to do that before, but the appearance of Elise Steiner had pretty much derailed her efforts.

Just as Suzanne finished stacking a pyramid of colorful yarns, she heard a rumble in the parking lot out front.

Doogie? Already? Hope so.

Suzanne walked out into the café and glanced around. Rapson and Wick were finally gone, the tables were draped in white linen, and tiny white candles flickered in glass candle holders. Perfection.

But what on earth was that awful racket outside?

Suzanne pushed back a drapery sheer and looked out the window.

"What's going on?" called Toni. She was polishing a silver spoon on her apron.

Suzanne gazed through frosted whirls and swirls, and said, "I think it's Junior."

"No way!" Toni's voice rose in a squawk, and she flew across the café. "What's that lamebrain doing here? He's supposed to be at work. If he got fired again, I'll . . ." She cocked an arm and made a threatening fist.

"Maybe he's come to see you," said Suzanne.

"You think?" Toni suddenly looked pleased.

"Wait a minute," said Suzanne, catching her dramatic shift in mood. "I thought you were hot to get a divorce."

"I am," said Toni. "Except that . . . wait a minute, is he . . . ? I think he's driving a different car. Yup, that's one of his clunkers. Hmm. Looks like he finally got that old Chevy running." Junior, who'd studied car repair after reform school, was a magnet for junked cars. If a car didn't run, had a bad transmission, or was propped up on blocks, Junior fell in love with it, no matter how useless or defective it might be. Go figure.

They watched through the window as Toni's juvenile-delinquent husband climbed from his car. Dressed in his typical black leather jacket and saggy jeans, Junior took his own sweet time, as if he didn't have a care in the world.

"What's he up to?" muttered Toni.

Instead of heading for the warmth of the Cackleberry Club, Junior strolled around the car, as if conducting an official vehicle inspection. Finally, he glanced over at the window, saw them watching, and gave a wave.

"Oh, for Pete's sake," Toni said under her breath.

"What's he doing?" asked Suzanne.

"Something about his car."

"I think he wants us to come out there," said Suzanne.

Junior motioned to them again. He was a bandy rooster with a dark complexion, and his dark hair was swirled and slicked into a pompadour that would have made James Dean proud.

"What?" Toni mouthed at the window.

"I gotta show you guys something," came Junior's faint voice.

Suzanne opened the door and leaned out. "What's going on? Car trouble?"

"Come on out," said Junior. "I got a kind of demonstration."

"Outside? In the cold?" said Suzanne.

Junior extended both arms and gave an exaggerated nod.

"Humor him," said Toni as they shrugged into their coats and trooped outside.

"What's up?" asked Suzanne, her breath pluming in front of her.

That was the precise opening Junior was waiting for. He suddenly walked to the hood of his burgundy Chevy Impala and pulled it open with a flourish of his grimy hands.

"This is it," he announced. "My newest invention."

Toni frowned. "What are you talking about?"

Junior grinned and pointed.

Suzanne and Toni gazed down at Junior's oil-crusted engine. To the left of his corroded battery, a battered bread pan had been wired to the top of the manifold.

"What is it?" Suzanne asked.

"A car cooker," said Junior. He rubbed his hand back and forth, caressing the Chevy's front bumper like it was a stripper's thigh. "Can you believe it? I'm this close to busting with excitement. I couldn't wait to drive over here and show you all. This is the latest and greatest. Gonna make me a million bucks."

Petra suddenly tromped out onto the front porch. "What's going on?" she asked. "Car trouble?"

"Car cooker," said Junior. "My new invention."

"It looks like you wired on a bread pan," Petra observed.

"That's just one of several specialized attachments," said Junior. "This one's been carefully engineered for cooking meatloaf."

"Engineered? Meatloaf?" said Suzanne, incredulously.

She seemed to be having trouble grasping the concept of actually cooking food inside a car's engine.

Toni blew out a breath in exasperation. "Next to the gerbil farm, this is the stupidest scheme you've come up with yet."

"No, it ain't," Junior replied patiently. "Mark my words, this is the next big thing in engine-block cooking. It's true automotive cuisine!" He gazed at them like they were a troop of third graders who needed a remedial explanation. "All right, lemme explain. Let's say you're headed out on a long trip. So first you mix up your meatloaf at home, and then you set it going in the cooker. Then, when you're driving along and your hunger pangs start to kick in, well, you just stop by the side of the road and have yourself a nice tasty dinner."

They all stared at him.

"Think about it," Junior boasted. "It sure beats going into some greasy spoon diner in some godforsaken place and paying six ninety-five for a blue plate special that probably came out of a can."

"Makes sense to me," said Petra.

Suzanne gazed at Petra. "You are officially scaring me."

Petra shrugged. "They don't teach this in culinary school, but at least it's home cooking."

"No," said Suzanne, "it's car cooking. Big difference. Think about it, do you really want your meatloaf seasoned with a splash of WD-40?"

"Mmn," said Petra, wrinkling her nose. "Perhaps not."

"So Junior," said Suzanne. "Supposing this really does work, exactly how long does meatloaf have to cook in that thing?"

Totally in his element now, Junior flashed a self-satisfied smile and said, "Four hundred degrees for one hundred and twenty miles."

"STUPID," said Toni. She picked up a ceramic mug and banged it against the counter. "Stupid, stupid, stupid."

"His invention wasn't *that* bad," said Suzanne. Now that they were back in the warmth of the Cackleberry Club, she could afford to be charitable.

"Wasn't it?" said Toni. She shook her head. "He told me he'd find a use for that old Chevy, and he did. Can't hardly drive the thing 'cause the rear end shimmies so bad."

"Maybe Junior could add some kind of cocktail-shaker attachment," Petra said, with a wicked grin.

"In this weather?" said Suzanne. "Only if you're making frozen daiquiris."

Petra gazed at Toni. "I think you're still in love with Junior." When Toni blushed, she said, "Yeah, you are. I can see it in your face. He reels you in like a fish. You can't help yourself around that greasy little bumpkin. You're just stuck, girl."

"Am not," said Toni, but she smiled and ducked her head.

"Love is blind," said Suzanne.

"Yeah, well, if love is blind," said Toni, "why is lingerie so popular?"

"Is it?" said Petra.

Toni nodded vigorously. "Oh yeah. Junior's forever buying me these frilly little teddies. I can barely figure out how to get them on, never mind take them off. I have no idea where he gets them or *when* he gets them. Lord knows, the man doesn't have time to file his income taxes or replace his bald tires. But these teddies, he can make time for. For all I know he's a Victoria's Secret junkie!"

"Excuse me," said Petra, "but if we're talking about underwear—and I think the conversation just veered that way—I plan to stick with my granny panties, thank you very much. There's nothing to hook, button, buckle, or untangle. That's how underwear should be. Simple and uncomplicated."

Toni burst out laughing. "Petra, I never knew you had such strong feelings about this subject. Where have you been hiding this philosophy of yours? This is a whole new side of you!"

All three of them were laughing now, giggling like a bunch of schoolgirls. It felt good to let loose and kick back a little.

"But here's the thing about a man who gives you lingerie," said Toni, after a minute. "If he's not sophisticated enough to order it off the Internet in a brown, unmarked package, it means he's endured the embarrassment of going into a lingerie department to actually shop for you. Which indicates that he's *serious* about you."

"A sort of baptism by fire," mused Suzanne. "I can see that."

A *clump clump* sounded at the back door.

Petra glanced back. "Joey." Joey Ewald was their sixteen-year-old slacker busboy and dishwasher.

"Hey, Joey," said Toni as he strode in dressed, as usual, like a Detroit rapper in a black puffer coat, low-slung jeans, and clanking chain jewelry.

Joey glanced around the café and gave a little wave. "Hey, guys."

"You're just in time," said Suzanne. "Any minute now we're going to be invaded by hordes of customers who want tea, coffee, and afternoon dessert."

"Uh, okay," said Joey, unplugging one of his ubiquitous earbuds and fiddling with his iPod. Then he peered at them shyly. "Are you guys okay? I mean, I heard about what happened out back the other night . . ."

"We're just fine," Suzanne said hastily.

"That's right," chimed in Petra. "Sheriff Doogie is taking care of things."

"Really?" said Joey. He seemed jittery.

"Hey, big guy," said Toni, "you ready for action?" Joey was a favorite of hers, and she kidded him unmercifully about his tattoos, piercings, and chain jewelry.

"Ready," said Joey. But his answer was flat as a pancake, and his usual enthusiasm just wasn't there.

"Then come on with me," said Toni, grabbing him by the arm. "Let's get started, my friend."

Suzanne smiled as she watched them head off, but her smile faded quickly. For some reason, Joey didn't seem quite like himself. Was he nervous about Busacker's murder, or something else? Sure, Joey had his sullen moments, like a lot of teenagers who were at that awkward age between boy and young man. But he hadn't quite made eye contact with her, and Joey always—

"Doogie," Petra rasped suddenly, glancing out the window. "Doogie's here."

All thoughts of Joey flew from Suzanne's brain.

Petra wiped her hands against her apron, looking anxious. "Listen, if you're going to talk to Doogie about the murder, and I know you are, can you do it in the Book Nook? After all, we've got customers coming."

"No problem," said Suzanne, even though the last couple of days had definitely been fraught with problems. She made a dash for the front door, and just as Doogie stepped in, Petra's prediction came true. Three more cars, all bearing customers, pulled up outside.

"WHATCHA got?" asked Doogie, once he'd settled into one of the chairs in the Book Nook.

"You tell me," said Suzanne. "What's new and improved on your end? Specifically in the Busacker case?"

Doogie rubbed the back of his hand against his stubbly chin. "It's pretty much been nonstop since I saw you last. We've been conducting more tests on that wire, and I've been following up on a couple of new leads."

Suzanne waggled her fingers. "Concerning . . . ?"

"Unhappy bank customers," said Doogie.

"Are there unhappy bank customers?"

Doogie frowned. "I just said there were."

"Anyone I know?"

"I can't really divulge that information."

"Sure you can," said Suzanne. "You've told me everything else."

But Doogie remained stubborn. "Not really. Besides, you're too involved as it is, Suzanne."

"I'm involved because the murder happened *here!*"

Doogie held his hands out flat, in a placating gesture. "I understand that, Suzanne. But I can't spill the beans on everything. I'm the duly elected sheriff. As such, I have to—"

"Yeah, yeah, spare me the reelection speech. Seeing as how you've already been reelected."

"I'm just saying," said Doogie.

Suzanne thought for a minute. "Would you like a piece of cake?"

"Cake?" A light sparked in Doogie's eyes. "Sure." He held up a big paw. "No strings attached though, right?"

"No strings attached," said Suzanne. She went out to the café, cut a double slice of gingerbread cake, placed it on a dinner plate, and got a fork and napkin. Then she carried it all back in and handed it to Doogie.

"This is mighty nice of you," said Doogie, digging in. "I didn't get much lunch."

"Mmm," said Suzanne. Leaning over slightly, she picked up a copy of *The Wind in the Willows* and held it loosely in her hand. "You'll never guess who stopped in here today."

Doogie chewed thoughtfully. "Oh?"

"Elise Steiner," said Suzanne.

Doogie stopped chewing. "What the Sam Hill did she want?"

"She wanted me to keep her in the loop concerning the investigation."

Doogie's eyes bugged out. "She what?"

Suzanne almost smiled at Doogie's startled response. "Elise Steiner seems to think her husband is your prime suspect. As you can imagine, she's scared that you're going to drag him off to jail and beat him senseless with a rubber hose."

"He ain't my prime suspect," said Doogie.

"Really," said Suzanne. "Then who is?"

Doogie shifted his khaki bulk in the chair. "Are you kidding me, Suzanne?"

"No, I'm not."

Doogie looked suddenly nervous. "Heck, Suzanne, we got so many suspects right now, they're piling up like cordwood!"

CHAPTER 10

BY seven o'clock that night, Petra's weekly Stitch and Bitch meeting was in full swing. The knitters, quilters, and crocheters, twelve strong tonight, were hunkered down in the cozy confines of the Knitting Nest.

With its array of fine yarns, knitting needles, embroidery threads, and stacks of jelly rolls and quilt squares, this was a home away from home for the devoted group, which had been gathering here week after week, rain or shine, summer or winter.

But tonight, instead of sitting around the room in over-stuffed chairs, with needles clacking and gentle voices murmuring, the atmosphere was one of excitement.

A shipment of luxe Berroco Nanuk yarn, one of the most popular yarns to hit the needle-arts scene in ages, had just arrived. Sixty-seven percent wool and thirty-three percent nylon, this yarn lived up to its marketing and promotion hype and truly "begged to be touched."

Petra, wearing blue jeans and a loose-fitting cowl-neck sweater and her short, no-nonsense hair pulled back with clips, was totally in her element. She dug into the newly arrived box of yarn and passed the super-soft skeins around to her group as if each mound of yarn were a precious newborn puppy.

"Okay, you fiber freaks," said Petra. "What do you think?"

"It feels like a cloud," said Toby Baines.

"Almost as soft as alpaca," said Letitia Sprague, who

actually raised sheep and alpacas on her farm outside of town.

"Just like a whisper or a gentle caress," said Petra. "And can you believe these scrumptious colors?"

There was narwhal, a delicious light milk-chocolate brown; caribou, an attractive mix of tan and brown; sila, a soft shade of brushed gray that appeared to lighten or darken, depending on the light; and polaris, a richly hued light lavender.

"And my favorite," said Petra, holding up a skein in rich, vibrant red. "Claus. I'm going to use this to knit an afghan for Donny. To help brighten his room." Petra's husband, Donny, currently resided at the Center City Nursing Home in the memory-care section. Unfortunately, his Alzheimer's had progressed to the point where he didn't seem to recognize Petra anymore. But that cruel twist of fate had never put a dent or a divot in Petra's devotion. She would sit with Donny for hours on end, reading poems by Walt Whitman, bringing him brownies and snickerdoodles, making sure he had enough warm blankets and fresh glasses of water. They'd watch TV together, mostly game shows or talent shows, and Petra would reach over and hold his hand.

Did any of this make a difference to Donny's overall health? Petra thought so. She thought it made him calmer and happier. And if Donny didn't realize that it was his devoted wife who sat there right next to him—well, yes, that fact was hard to deal with. But Petra had prayed hard and had finally arrived at a certain peace.

"Petra," said Dede Meyer, not looking up from the shawl she was knitting, "what's going on with the murder investigation?"

The atmosphere in the room was suddenly electric. Needles paused, eyes darted, shoulders tensed.

"Sheriff Doogie is doing his best," said Petra with a slightly clenched jaw. "He's pretty much been in and out of here all day."

"But are there any suspects?" asked Dede. At this, all the women seemed to lean in closer, the better to hear.

"I'm not . . ." began Petra, looking flustered and suddenly ready to cry. Then she glanced up and saw Suzanne in the doorway. "Suzanne!" she exclaimed, hugely relieved at her friend's sudden appearance.

"Just checking on things," said Suzanne.

"Good for you," said Petra, locking eyes with her.

But Dede was not to be put off or dissuaded. "We were just asking Petra about the Busacker murder," she said. "We're all kind of wondering . . ."

"We're all wondering about that, too," said Suzanne, cutting in smoothly. "And I guess we just have to hope that our law-enforcement officials are on their toes and doing their jobs."

"Are they?" asked Letitia. She was knitting something that, to Suzanne, looked to all the world like a big bug cocoon.

"They seem to be," said Suzanne. "But, please ladies, enough about cold-blooded crimes. I just wanted to pop in and give a big hello, then get back to the task of preparing tea and some tasty snacks for you."

The prospect of tea and snacks seemed to dispel any more questions about Busacker's murder, and the group breathed a collective sigh.

"Are you going to join us tonight?" asked Toby.

"Sure wish I could," said Suzanne, "but the closest I've ever come to knitting is wrapping one of Petra's shawls around me on a chilly night. You guys are the ones with talent."

"We could teach you," piped up one of the women. She smiled from behind a pile of multicolored yarn that was attached to the sweater she was working on. Her fingers and needles flew so fast that Suzanne could barely see them.

"I'm sure you're all the best teachers in the world," said Suzanne. "No doubt about that. And knitting is still on my bucket list. One of these days I'll learn."

That produced a flurry of *I'll teach you*s and *There's no time like the present*s as Suzanne backed out of the room.

Whew, she thought. Close call. Especially when it came to dishing about Busacker's murder. But of course they'd want to talk about that. Everybody in town was gossiping about poor Ben Busacker losing his head. The whole ball of wax would probably be splashed across the front page of tomorrow's *Bugle*.

Sighing, Suzanne hustled into the kitchen to prepare the evening's snack for the group.

She put a kettle of water on the stove, then opened the industrial cooler and pulled out a selection of cheeses. A creamy goat cheese, a stout cheddar, and an always-reliable Swiss. She sliced the cheeses on a cutting board and arranged them on a bright blue ceramic platter. Toni had painted it at one of those paint-your-own-dish places over in Jessup. She'd started out painting bluebirds, then halfway through had pooped out and switched to fish. So kind of a reverse-evolutionary-cycle design.

Suzanne added rows of sliced green apples and put piles of almonds, cashews, and pecans in all four corners. Two crusty French baguettes were also sliced and went into wicker baskets.

When the tea kettle whistled softly, she made two pots of tea, a honey vanilla variety and a strong black Keemun. As the delicious aromas mingled and drifted through the kitchen, Suzanne breathed deeply, feeling herself relax. Teapot aromatherapy, she decided. You could always count on the soothing effects of tea.

Suzanne grabbed a dozen small blue-and-white Chinese teacups without handles, as well as paper napkins, milk, sugar, and utensils, and set everything on a silver serving tray. In two trips, she'd carried everything to the Knitting Nest.

She was met with a bevy of *ooh*s and *aah*s and *thank you*s from all the women.

"This is so kind of you," said Toby, reaching for a chunk of baguette and a cube of Swiss cheese.

"My pleasure," said Suzanne. "Enjoy."

The women nodded happily as they dug into their snacks.

Suzanne's next stop was the Book Nook. Flipping on the lights, she walked to the shelf where she kept her needlecraft books. She grabbed a stack of books on knitting, crocheting, quilting, as well as three general crafting books, and carried them to the counter. Then she grabbed a pink-and-peach afghan that Petra had knit, spread it carefully on the small round table at the front of the shop, and arranged the books on top of it, piling them up, then standing a couple of books upright. A few skeins of yarn and a stack of quilt squares completed her arrangement. Oh, and she couldn't forget. She dashed into her office and grabbed a new book on cross-stitching that had just arrived and added it to her display.

Suzanne knew that, sooner or later, the knitters and stitchers would get up to stretch their legs. And when they did, they'd wander into the Book Nook to snoop around and see what was new. It never failed. Suzanne typically sold five to ten books this way. All in all, a nice little add-on that helped boost the Cackleberry Club's profitability.

THREE hours later, the Stitch and Bitch was over. Platters were bare, with nary a crumble of bread left over. Half-finished knitting projects were stuffed into tote bags. And all of the ladies had departed, with Petra waving her good-byes, too, then darting out the front door directly on the heels of her knitters.

Suzanne, weary from her long day, was still hunched at her desk, working her way through a stack of paperwork. Luckily, there hadn't been any nasty surprises. No past-due invoices, no cut-off notices from vendors, no phony-baloney bills that had mistakenly been paid. Fact was, the Cackleberry Club was chugging along fairly well, even in the midst of this "Great Recession," something the economists said had ended a couple of years ago. Thanks to the good folks of Kindred and everyone else who ambled down Highway 65, they'd managed to eke out a small profit when many other small businesses weren't even able to cover their operating expenses.

Just as Suzanne was contemplating her good luck, she heard a faint jingle at the back door of the Cackleberry Club.

She sat up, suddenly alert.

What was that? Someone tippy-tapping *at the door? Trying to get in?*

Even from where she sat in her office, she felt a cool breeze waft across her ankles.

She set down her pen and listened carefully.

Someone *was* in. Could it be Petra who was pussyfooting around so quietly? No, it couldn't be. Petra, the perpetual hard charger, had never moved quietly a day in her life.

Okay, then, maybe one of the knitters had forgotten something. A skein of yarn they'd purchased? A knitting bag? A wallet?

Suzanne listened harder.

Now—nothing. No sounds at all.

How odd.

But somebody had opened the door, hadn't they? Or was she just jumpy and spooked because of the Ben Busacker incident?

Suzanne suddenly couldn't stand the tension. The place was way too quiet now and feeling strangely eerie. No way could she sit here and try to work—she had to investigate!

Quietly, like a mouse trying to steal its way into a larder, she slid her chair back and stood up.

The tiny hairs on the back of her neck prickled, and she felt a serious twitch of nerves.

Ben Busacker had been murdered out in the woods just two days ago. That hard fact scared Suzanne, worried her enormously. Had the cold-blooded killer come back for a return engagement?

Should I dial 911? Try to get Doogie over here? Or Sam?

A footstep sounded.

Oh man. No time to call for help now! Someone is definitely in my kitchen!

Heart beating wildly inside her chest, Suzanne moved across the darkened café slowly and stealthily, like a jungle cat stalking its prey.

Pausing at the swinging door, knowing someone was on the other side, Suzanne glanced about frantically, searching for a weapon.

The butcher knives were all lined up nice and neat in the kitchen. So what could she use to defend herself? Or launch an all-out assault if need be?

Slowly, quietly, Suzanne reached an arm overhead and grabbed a yellow ceramic chicken from a shelf crowded with chickens. This was it, she decided. She'd have to make her stand with a paint-and-plaster chicken statue! And clobber whoever came walking through that door.

The door creaked on its hinges and suddenly swung open!

Suzanne lunged forward, ready to bring the chicken crashing down upon the intruder's skull. And checked herself midstrike.

A boy stood in the doorway. A teenager dressed all in black. Black jacket, black pants, black boots. Like a youthful ninja. He had short, jet-black hair, pale skin, and worried eyes that glowed with tones of yellow in the faint light that spilled over from the Book Nook.

"What. The. Heck!" Suzanne blurted out. Her fear was suddenly mingled with anger. Who was this dumb kid who'd just broken into her place and scared her half to death?

She dropped her eyes and glanced at his hands, almost as an afterthought. Thank goodness he wasn't carrying a weapon! At least nothing she could see. So, what did this kid want? What on earth was he *doing* here?

Suzanne's left hand reached out and frantically batted the light switch. Warm yellow light flooded the café and thankfully calmed her racing heart just a bit.

The kid stared at the chicken still clutched in Suzanne's hands. "Oh jeez, you were gonna smack me with that?" he cried out. "You coulda killed me!"

"You got that right!" said Suzanne. She used her stern voice, the one she'd used when she used to teach at Kindred Middle School. The one that could usually intimidate youthful offenders.

She motioned toward a nearby table, brandishing the chicken as one might a gun. "Sit down. You've got some serious explaining to do."

The kid shuffled over to a chair and sat down, never taking his eyes off her.

"Who are you?" she demanded. First things first.

"Umm . . . Colby," he said, sputtering, stumbling over his words.

"Colby?" said Suzanne, drilling him. "Colby what?"

His eyes shifted across and around the room, then back to her. His hands fidgeted and twisted together like a pretzel, and his feet were positioned awkwardly, as if he'd been caught midstep. Which, of course, he had been.

"How'd you get in here?" asked Suzanne.

Colby gave an offhand shrug.

"Look, buster," said Suzanne, "we can do this the hard way or the easy way."

"What's the hard way?" asked Colby, sounding petulant.

"I call the sheriff."

An uptick of one side of his mouth. "You wouldn't do that."

Suzanne took a step toward the wall phone. "Watch me."

Colby's bravado seemed to falter. "And the easy way?"

"You tell me the honest truth, and I don't wring your scrawny neck."

Colby thought for a long minute. Then he said, "I got a key."

Suzanne was stunned. "You got in with a key? No way. I don't believe you." There were only four keys to the Cackleberry Club, and she knew exactly who had each of them.

Colby dug a grubby hand into his voluminous jacket pocket and pulled out a key. With just a hint of a smile, he dangled a small brass key in front of her eyes.

Suzanne reached out and snatched the key from his hand. "Where'd you get this?" she demanded. She glanced at it, saw the key was attached to a familiar looking fob. "Oh crap. You got this from Joey." Her voice was like ice now. "Did Joey give this to you?" Under her breath she muttered, "That little weasel."

Colby seemed to hunch up as if he was chilled to the bone. "We met a couple of days ago, yeah. We're kind of like friends now."

"Excuse me," said Suzanne, "but *why* did Joey give you this key? To the best of my knowledge, I don't believe you had a job interview scheduled for nine o'clock this evening."

Colby's dark eyes burned into her. "I was hungry."

Suzanne was taken aback. "So why sneak in here? Why not just go home?"

Colby turned his head, as if to deflect her question.

Suzanne suddenly understood. It hit her like a thunderclap. "Because you don't have a home," she said in a soft voice. "You're a runaway, aren't you?"

The kid didn't answer. He just sat still as a statue. The only thing that gave him away were his eyes. They were wild, slightly haunted eyes that gave him the look of a caged animal, restless and scared. Or a wild animal caught in a leg trap.

Suzanne decided to try another angle. "Where's your family?"

"Don't have one," Colby replied with a toss of his head.

Suzanne sucked in a small breath. This revelation—if

true—pretty much floored her. "There has to someone we could call," she pressed. "Your mom or dad? Brother or sister?"

"No way," said Colby.

Suzanne tried again. "A friend?"

Colby pursed his lips.

"Where have you run away from?" she asked.

"None of your business," Colby said sharply.

"You're a tough guy, aren't you?"

"You better believe it."

More than anything, Suzanne wanted to keep this conversation rolling, the better to draw out information. So she softened her voice and said, "You say you met Joey a couple of days ago. Does that mean you've been staying at his house?"

Colby shook his head.

"Then where have you been sleeping? You do sleep, don't you?"

Colby looked suddenly uneasy. After a pause, he said, "I been spending nights in that big barn across the way." He saw the look of surprise on her face, and added, "But it's okay. There are two horses there to keep me company."

"My horses," said Suzanne, smiling a little. "Well, actually a horse and a mule. Mocha and Grommet."

"They're yours?" Now Colby seemed surprised.

Suzanne wasn't about to tell him she owned that particular property, and she sure wasn't going to let this kid crawl back there and sack out in the hayloft again. An overnight in the Cackleberry Club wasn't an option, either.

"Listen," said Suzanne, "it's getting late, and we need to find you a place to sleep."

"I'll be okay," said Colby.

"Doubtful," said Suzanne.

"I said I'll *be* okay."

"Look, kid," said Suzanne, "I hate to do this, but you're probably gonna have to spend the night at the Law Enforcement Center here in town."

"You're gonna turn me in to the cops? Send me to jail?" Colby's eyes blazed with outrage. "You said you wouldn't do that if I played straight with you!"

"Take it easy," said Suzanne. "I'm not having you arrested. I just want you to have a safe, warm place to spend the night. Tomorrow, you can sit down and talk to the social services people. They can help you sort things out."

"Why can't I sleep here?" asked Colby. "I won't hurt anything."

Suzanne's heart softened. "I'm sure you wouldn't. But it's just not going to happen." She stood up. "I'm going to call my friend, who's the sheriff, then I'll drive you over there."

Colby flashed a sullen glance and crossed his arms. He seemed both angry and despondent.

"Tell you what," said Suzanne. "How about I make you a nice turkey sandwich first? And warm up a piece of apple pie. Then we'll drive you over there. Deal?"

Colby sighed deeply. "I guess."

SUZANNE pulled off her coat and tossed it on the hall table, too tired to even hang it up. Her scarf, hat, and mittens were added to the pile. Dropping Colby at the Law Enforcement Center hadn't exactly been a piece of cake. The kid was angry and mistrustful of authority, and Doogie's normal blustering hadn't been much help. But the whole thing was over and done with and, hopefully, no longer her problem. She had high hopes that Molly Grabowski, the dispatcher, or Sandy Preston, a grandmotherly woman who worked in social services, would be able to connect with Colby and somehow coax him back to his family.

Baxter stood at the edge of the living room wagging his tail, looking sleepy but happy to see her home.

"Sorry I'm so late, sweetie. Tough night."

Baxter padded over to Suzanne and stuck his muzzle in her hand, welcoming her with hot doggy breath and a wet tongue.

"I love you, too, Bax," she said, as the phone rang. "Oh man, I hope this is just a later-than-usual telemarketer." She sighed. "And not bad news."

"Is he with you?" asked Doogie, the moment she picked up.

Suzanne was momentarily confused. "Is who with me?" Was Doogie talking about Sam? Her heart lurched. Had there been some kind of accident?

"The kid," said Doogie. "Colby. Is he with you?"

"No," said Suzanne, frowning. "He's with you."

The line went silent.

"Doogie, what?" said Suzanne. "What happened?"

"Aw, I feel like a colossal doofus," said the sheriff. "That kid gave us the slip."

"What?"

"The thing is," said Doogie, sounding sheepish, "we turned our backs for like two seconds, and suddenly he was gone. Just like that. Blew out the door like some kind of junior Houdini."

"Rats," said Suzanne. She wondered if Colby had made his way back to the barn. Or if he was trudging across the frozen soybean field right about now, hoping to burrow under the straw and stay warm.

She shook her head to dispel that thought. *Don't think of him being out in the cold*, she admonished herself. It was his choice. Then her heart softened, and she thought, *How can I not worry? He's just a kid.*

"I'm sorry, Suzanne," said Doogie. "At least our intentions were good."

"But it pretty much shoots the whole plan," said Suzanne. "I was hoping somebody over there might be able to gain his trust and worm a little information out of him. Send him back home to his parents."

"We'll find him," said Doogie. "I'll put the word out to all my deputies first thing tomorrow."

"I guess," said Suzanne, knowing it was the best they could hope for. What was that old saying? You can't close the barn door after the horse is out? She drew breath, and said, "Listen, after we talked this afternoon, I was wondering if anything new turned up? Any clues on the Busacker case?"

"I'm bringing Ducovny in for questioning tomorrow," said Doogie.

"Why on earth?" Suzanne sputtered. "You can't do that. The man's innocent!"

"Yeah, I guess," said Doogie. "You've got me pretty convinced of that. Unfortunately, a whole bunch of people think otherwise."

"You've got to keep digging," said Suzanne. "Ducovny's not your man!"

"It's tough when Mayor Mobley and the fancy bank man, Ed Rapson, think otherwise," said Doogie. "They think he's guilty as sin."

"And after tomorrow," said Suzanne, "when Gene Gandle's story comes out in the *Bugle*, the whole town will probably think Charlie Steiner is guilty, too!"

"They probably will," sighed Doogie.

"What a mess," said Suzanne.

CHAPTER 11

SUZANNE stood in front of the mirror in her bedroom penciling a little more definition into her brows. It was Thursday, 7:30 A.M., and the morning of Ben Busacker's funeral.

She'd smudged on a little taupe eye shadow to her normally au naturel face, then wiped it off with a Kleenex. Too raccoony. Too . . . Kardashian. So, what else? Maybe just a dab of pale peach lipstick. After all, she was going to a funeral, not Hoobly's Roadhouse.

Blinking at herself in the mirror and catching a glimpse of her somber expression, Suzanne thought, *This is the real deal, isn't it? Yup. Funeral time.*

Funerals left no wiggle room. Suzanne had been to enough services over the years to comprehend this hard-and-fast truth. When that gunmetal gray casket came rolling down the center aisle, there was no avoiding or denying the reality of the situation. It was a visceral, gut-wrenching confirmation that a friend or loved one was dead and gone. Forever.

Except in this case, Busacker the banker wasn't exactly viewed as a "loved one" by the folks in Kindred. Coldly efficient banking practices didn't exactly win friends and influence people. Especially when it meant jacking banking fees sky high, or ripping people's homes out from under them.

As Suzanne kept an eye on the clock—she had to leave in about ten minutes—her unhappy thoughts strayed to

Claudia, Ben's wife. The poor woman, how was she faring? Was Claudia getting any rest, any respite from her nightmare? Suzanne decided she'd try to say a few comforting words to Claudia after the service. It seemed only fitting.

As Suzanne tried to tame some flyaway strands of blond hair, hair that definitely warranted a touch up at Root 66, she wondered if anyone ever found peace after their beloved had been mowed down in cold blood. And by a killer who still hadn't been identified or apprehended! To know that the killer was still lingering in their midst, and might even attend the funeral today, was beyond creepy.

That's when it hit her: After today, she'd have something in common with Claudia Busacker. After today, they'd both have buried their husbands.

On that unhappy note, Suzanne snapped off the bedroom light and headed downstairs. She had to feed the dogs, shoo them out into the backyard, and try to gulp down a piece of toast. Then she'd head over to Hope Church. She figured she'd run into Doogie there and that he had probably rounded up the elusive Colby by now. She also held out hope that Doogie had been blessed with some sort of brainstorm concerning Busacker's killer. Because the trail of the killer was getting as cold as a Minnesota lake in the dead of winter. Time was passing, and people were getting impatient. *Namely me,* she thought.

As she drove over to the church, a hazy sun shone down but did nothing to dispel the chill or mantle of ice that covered the small town of Kindred. On Main Street, the shoulder-to-shoulder yellow brick buildings seemed to hunch together as smoke plumed from their chimneys and furnaces worked overtime. The trees in Founder's Park were frosted with ice, and as she pumped her brakes at an intersection and began a slow, sickening skid, Suzanne realized the roads were just as slick!

Luckily, her tires were good steel-belted radials, and in a matter of minutes, she'd navigated her way to Hope Church.

Pushing open one of the double oak doors, Suzanne stepped inside one of the oldest houses of worship in Logan County. Thin January sunlight streamed through tall stained glass windows filling the church with warmth and a kaleidoscope of colorful dancing beams. Massive hand-carved wooden arches spanned the width of the white plaster ceiling, giving a sense of majesty.

An usher, wearing a dark suit that smelled faintly of mothballs, handed a memorial program to Suzanne. She opened it quickly and scanned it, almost wondering if there'd be an advertisement inside for Mills City Banks. Thank goodness, there wasn't.

Spotting Sheriff Doogie in the middle of the church, Suzanne tiptoed down a side aisle to join him in his pew. The church was sparse on mourners but abundant with flowers. Elegant sprays of blue hydrangeas, delphiniums, and white roses were banked on either side of the altar. Clearly, the Mills City Banks people had opened the corporate checkbook and gone all out for Busacker's big send-off.

"Good morning," she said as she slipped in next to Doogie.

Doogie swiveled his big head. "Morning," he said. His sparse hair was freshly combed, and his khaki uniform looked pressed and spiffier than usual. And did she detect a hint of Drakkar Noir aftershave? Could be.

Suzanne scooted closer to Doogie and whispered, "Did you find the boy? Colby?"

He blinked. "Not yet."

"Well, I hope you at least pried some information out of him last night."

"Not much chance," said Doogie. "Kid slipped into his boogie shoes and was gone."

"Then have you talked to Joey Ewald? My busboy? He might be able to shed some light on Colby's whereabouts. They're supposedly friends."

Doogie sighed heavily. "I'll get to it when I get to it."

She looked at him. "We're talking about an underage boy—"

Doogie beetled his brows. "Look, Suzanne, I only got so many deputies and so many hours in the day."

"—an underage boy who wiggled out of your grasp," she added. "At the Law Enforcement Center, for crying out loud."

"Job number one right now is to catch Busacker's killer," said Doogie without emotion. "Not chase down some random kid."

"Not random—a runaway," said Suzanne.

"You don't know that for sure," said Doogie. "He might live next town over, in Jessup. Just here to visit friends or hang out."

"He *told* me he was a runaway," said Suzanne, as a burst of organ notes erupted from the choir loft above them. "He said he'd been sacking out in my barn." Any more words were drowned out by Agnes Bennet, the longtime organist, who was now pumping away like the Phantom of the Opera. The notes of "Amazing Grace" filled the church with a rich, sumptuous sound, underlining the gravity of the situation.

Suzanne dug in her handbag and pulled out her cell phone. She scrolled through her contacts list, found Joey's phone number, and wrote it down on the back of an old grocery list.

"Here," she said briskly, handing the paper to Doogie. "Call Joey. And if he stonewalls, I want to know. I'm positive he wants to keep his job at the Cackleberry Club, so I can always lean on him."

"If you ask me," said Doogie, "that kid Colby was probably hanging around selling drugs."

"He didn't look like any kind of dope dealer to me," said Suzanne, "just a scared runaway kid."

"Hmph." Doogie gave an offhand shrug.

"You always think the worst of people," she said.

"That's because I deal with the worst people," snipped Doogie.

Which pretty much rubbed Suzanne the wrong way.

"And another thing," she whispered. "I want you to lay off Ducovny." She had an urge to shake her finger under Doogie's nose, but managed to contain herself, since they were in church. "The man had absolutely no motive to kill Ben Busacker. You know it, and I know it."

Doogie shifted on the hard bench and crossed his meaty arms. "Oh yes, he did."

"What are you talking about?" Suzanne was about ready to spit a mouthful of tacks.

"I did some more checking this morning," said Doogie, not bothering to look at her. "And found out Ducovny was turned down for a bank loan." He paused. "By none other than Ben Busacker."

An icicle of fear jabbed at Suzanne's heart. "A loan for what?" she stammered.

Now Doogie turned his flat gray eyes on her. "Apparently, he wanted to make an offer on your farm."

"To buy it?" Her question came out in a high-pitched squeak. She quickly ducked her head, hoping no one was listening.

"Yup. That's what I'm saying."

Suzanne stared straight ahead at the altar, where dozens of votive candles flickered wildly. And wondered: Did Ducovny really have an axe to grind? Had he set up some sort of strange trap for Busacker? Maybe not to kill him, but to grab his attention? So he could make a final plea for a loan?

She knew it could have happened that way, but fervently hoped it hadn't.

"I still think Ducovny's innocent," Suzanne muttered as a dramatic change in organ music signaled the start of the funeral service.

One by one and two by two, the mourners stood up and turned their attention toward the back of the church. And the sad procession began.

STAKE & EGGS ·

Reverend Strait, with his fine head of silver gray hair and decorous black suit, led the way. Directly behind him, a shiny gunmetal gray coffin, topped with a spray of white roses and Asiatic lilies, clacked along on a squeaky-wheeled casket carriage, escorted by six pallbearers.

Suzanne strained to see who these plain-faced, black-suited men were, and decided they were either Mills City Banks employees who'd been strong-armed by Ed Rapson, or characters direct from central casting. Or both.

Then Claudia Busacker's pale face came into view. Dressed in a black skirt suit and a demure white silk blouse, Claudia, the distraught widow, clung to the arm of George Draper, owner of Driesden and Draper Funeral Home. Claudia's hair was meticulously done, and her makeup was flawless beneath her short black veil. But she seemed incredibly frail and vulnerable as she took baby steps down the center aisle, pausing every few seconds. At one point she leaned heavily against George Draper. Draper, who was tall, gangly, and slightly stooped, was amazingly solicitous, gazing at Claudia as though she were a Dresden figurine.

Is she even going to make it? Suzanne wondered. Draper seemed to be half supporting her, half escorting her. But Claudia eventually made it to the front of the church, where she dramatically pressed her lips to the casket, then took her seat.

Reverend Strait blessed the casket and said the opening prayers as everyone bowed their heads. After the prayers came the eulogies, of course. And first up was Ed Rapson. For someone usually so slick and glib, Rapson seemed stiff and uncomfortable during his speech.

"He was loved by all," Rapson reeled off without emotion. "He was a friend to everyone. A model employee. We shall miss his hard work and steady collegiality."

Suzanne wrinkled her nose. His words, dashed off like so many empty platitudes, sounded like something out of a handbook on what *not* to say at a funeral.

When it was his turn to speak, Reverend Strait, by contrast, was engaging and heartfelt. In warm, friendly tones, he spoke of Busacker's devotion to his wife and Claudia's devotion to him, despite several career moves that took them across multiple states. He looked kindly at Claudia, and said, "This was a decent man." He spoke of how Busacker had struggled to put down roots yet again, in middle age, and how he had served the residents of Kindred as best he could.

Listening to the melodic hymns that followed, Suzanne glanced at the program again, then twisted slightly in her seat. And was surprised to see quite a few more people sitting in the back of the church.

Interestingly enough, Suzanne spotted Charlie Steiner and his wife, Elise.

Lester Drummond was also among the assembled, staring straight ahead, an impassive look on his craggy face.

Could one of those men have wanted Busacker dead? Suzanne wondered. Steiner was losing his farm and had aimed his anger like a rapier at the bank.

Drummond, for his part, badly needed a job after losing his prison-warden gig. Could he have lusted for Busacker's job and fat salary so much that he would have killed for it?

Suzanne tried to focus on the service, but her mind kept drifting. Back to the murder, to the motive. Who else could have wanted to get rid of Ben Busacker?

Her eyes flashed on Ed Rapson, and her reptile brain, the primitive brain, did a slow *Hmm?*

What if Rapson really was the killer? The thought had occurred to her before, but she hadn't given it serious consideration.

But what if things at the bank had somehow reached crisis stage? What if Busacker had alienated too many people, or the books weren't balancing, or there was something very, very wrong? And whatever that terrible something had been, what if Rapson had been catapulted over the edge?

Suzanne drew in a sharp breath, causing Doogie to give her a curious sideways glance.

It could have happened that way, she thought. But had it? *How can I find out? How can I know more about circumstances at the bank?*

For one thing, she decided, she would talk to Hamilton Wick. Maybe try to draw him out with a little friendly conversation. Probe and pry a little, but in a concerned way, so he wouldn't think she was meddling. Be the business ally he'd been looking for.

Minutes later, the casket came rolling back down the aisle. Claudia still looked ready to collapse, while the black-suited pallbearers still looked staid and inscrutable.

After firing a final warning shot at Doogie to stop hassling Ducovny, Suzanne hustled out the door to find Claudia.

And found her hunched outside, next to the long black hearse. She watched her husband's casket being loaded, while George Draper practically stood guard by her side.

"I'm so sorry, Claudia," said Suzanne. She leaned forward and gave her a hug.

"Thank you, dear. Thank you for coming," said Claudia, in a thin, brittle voice. Her eyes were glazed, and she seemed to be operating on autopilot.

"Kind of you," said George Draper, offering his perfunctory funeral director's smile.

Suzanne could sense that this day, this whole experience, had taken a terrible toll on Claudia. She was as frail as a dove with a broken wing.

"I wish there was something I could do," said Suzanne.

"You've been very kind," said Claudia. She offered a weak smile, then said, "I'm so sorry to miss your Crystal Tea this afternoon. I was planning to attend, but now . . ." She made a vague gesture with her gloved hands.

"If you feel better in a few hours," said Suzanne, "you really should come anyway. You'd be among friends, people who care about you."

"That's so kind of you," said Claudia.

Suzanne grasped her hands, then released them. "Really," she said, moving away, "you'd be amazingly welcome."

As Suzanne scurried toward her car, Mayor Mobley emerged from a throng of mourners to accost her.

"Suzanne," said the rotund mayor, holding up a finger. "A word?"

Mayor Mobley, who'd managed to squeak by in the last election, was pond scum as far as Suzanne was concerned. He was greasy, sleazy, and an all-around untrustworthy guy. He'd honchoed the building of the for-profit prison, promising it would bring jobs to the town. Now that razor wire monstrosity sat on Kindred's outskirts, looking dreary and foreboding.

"What?" Suzanne said sharply. She didn't care for the pompous Mobley, with his bad comb-over. To her he represented small-town bureaucracy at its worst.

The mayor scuttled up to her, dressed in dark plaid slacks and a long-sleeve Izod shirt underneath his too-tight putty brown parka. Beads of perspiration dotted his pink scalp even in the freezing cold.

"I imagine Sheriff Doogie's been out at your restaurant investigating?" Mobley belted out to her.

"He's probably been all over town," Suzanne said, diplomatically. She didn't like Mobley, and she knew he knew it.

Mobley rocked back on his heels. "Fact is, I don't understand for a minute why this case isn't wrapped up yet."

"Maybe because it's more complicated than you think?"

Mobley's mean little eyes flashed up and down her. "When was the last time he was out at your place?"

Suzanne set her jaw firmly. "Why don't you ask Sheriff Doogie?"

"I'm just lookin' out for the town, Suzanne," said Mobley. "For our citizenry."

"Understood," said Suzanne. "But Sheriff Doogie was recently reelected to office. Which sends a pretty strong message that the people of Kindred are behind him one hundred percent. They believe in Doogie and have faith that he'll solve Ben Busacker's murder."

"Is that so?" said Mobley.

"And I have faith in Doogie, too," said Suzanne, as she backed away from Mobley.

Mobley sucked air through his front teeth and let loose a harsh laugh. "I'm glad somebody does."

CHAPTER 12

A blast of warm, toasty air hit Suzanne as she stepped through the back door of the Cackleberry Club and into the kitchen.

"Are we ever glad to see you," trilled Toni. "We're busy, busy, busy."

Petra cocked a sympathetic eye at her, and asked, "How was the funeral?"

"Sad," said Suzanne. "And not all that well attended."

"Probably because Busacker wasn't all that well liked," said Toni.

"Still," said Petra, as she flipped sizzling strips of bacon and stirred a bubbling pan of cheese sauce, "you always hope your final send-off won't be a mammoth disappointment."

"At least the flowers were lovely," said Suzanne. "And Reverend Strait's words were quite uplifting."

"Still sounds like a bummer," said Toni. "Hey, did I ever tell you guys about my uncle Otto's funeral? About when they did a twenty-one-gun salute and released a flock of white doves?"

"That sounds almost presidential," said Petra, hefting her frying pan off the stove.

"Not really," said Toni. "Problem was, they released the doves just before the rifle salute."

Petra hesitated, her spatula midair. "Oh no."

Toni shook her head. "Poor little birds, never had a chance."

Suzanne grabbed an apron and tied it around her waist, anxious to move the subject away from funerals. "How can I help? Looks like you have some orders to deliver."

"Give me one minute," said Petra, as she continued plating. She dished out French toast, sausage and eggs, and their Thursday special, Eggs Mornay. "Okay." She grabbed a dozen order slips from her overhead rack and matched them up against the plates. "Now you ladies can hustle these breakfasts out to our customers."

Suzanne and Toni were busy then, delivering breakfasts, pouring refills of coffee, and ringing up to-go orders at the cash register.

"We're hoppin' and boppin' like a sweet sixteen party," said Toni as she brushed past Suzanne.

"Does it make you feel young again?" grinned Suzanne.

"Cookie, I *always* feel young."

Back in the kitchen, Petra was pink-faced and hustling. "Suzanne," she said, "can you grate a couple cups of cheese while I whip up another pan of Eggs Mornay?"

"I'm on it," said Suzanne. She grabbed the grater and a big block of cheddar and started whittling away. Petra, meanwhile, rough-chopped a bunch of fresh parsley, even as she grabbed a wooden spoon and stirred madly at the stove. Then she plopped her eggs into a shallow baking dish, sprinkled on a mound of bread crumbs, ladled on her cheese sauce, and popped the whole thing into the oven.

Peering through the pass-through, the comforting clink of coffee cups and silverware—plus murmured conversation, punctuated by occasional bursts of laughter—reassured Suzanne that all was well in the café.

And once the third and final pan of Eggs Mornay had emerged from the oven, all golden brown and bubbling, and the last group of breakfast customers had been served, the women were able to take a welcome break.

"Did you forget to listen for your treasure-hunt clue on the radio?" Suzanne asked Toni.

Toni grabbed her copy of the *Bugle* and thumped two

fingers against it. "Don't need to. The clue's posted in here today." She raised her penciled brows and pursed her lips. "Along with Gene Gandle's big scoop of the century."

"How bad is it?" asked Suzanne, thinking it was unfortunate that a story about Busacker's murder had to come out the same day as his funeral.

"Yellow journalism," said Toni.

"More like purple prose," Petra snorted.

"Whatever the color," said Suzanne, "are you telling me it's a hatchet job?" She'd almost let herself forget that Gene Gandle had taken copious notes during Charlie Steiner's rant. "What does Gene's headline say?"

"You ain't gonna like it," said Toni.

"Read it to me anyway," said Suzanne. "I'll try to get a grip."

"*Huh-umh.*" Toni cleared her throat. "It says, 'Banker Found Dead; Mystery Still Unsolved!'"

"That's not so bad," said Suzanne. Fact was, it was all true.

"Unfortunately," said Toni, "the story takes a nosedive from there. In fact, the words 'decapitated' and 'Cackleberry Club' both appear in the opening sentence."

"Maybe you better read the whole thing to me," said Suzanne, alarmed now.

"'Kindred officials,'" began Toni, "'have launched an urgent investigation into the death of local banker Ben Busacker, whose decapitated body was found during Monday's snowstorm behind the Cackleberry Club café on Route 65.'"

"Holy Coupe de Ville," said Suzanne. "What do you think that's going to do to business?"

"It gets worse," said Toni. "'A suspicious and tautly stretched wire was also found nearby. Authorities believe there's a possibility that the wire had been deliberately strung to harm Busacker, the president of Kindred State Bank.'" Toni stopped reading and looked up. "Heard enough?"

"Yes," said Petra.

"No," said Suzanne.

Toni passed the paper to Suzanne. "Here, kiddo. Maybe you should read it for yourself."

Suzanne scanned the story. It wasn't good, but it wasn't terrible, either. Gandle mentioned how Busacker was new in town, that he left behind his wife, Claudia, and then went on to suggest that Busacker hadn't been all that well liked because of his "take-no-prisoners approach to local banking."

Again, that was all true, she told herself.

But it was the next paragraph that made Suzanne gasp. "Oh no!"

"I thought that part might stand you on your ear," Toni muttered.

Gandle's story went on to detail that "Ms. Suzanne Dietz, owner of the Cackleberry Club, was the first to discover the body in the snow." And that she'd told the *Bugle* she "fervently wished she hadn't seen it."

"I wish Gene hadn't mentioned me," said Suzanne.

"Keep reading," said Toni.

"Oh my lord," said Suzanne.

"What?" said Petra.

"Gandle's gone so far as to name suspects," said Suzanne. "Listen to this: 'The office of Sheriff Roy Doogie says it questioned several individuals who may have possible knowledge concerning the unfortunate incident. Recently, suspicion has fallen on two Logan County farmers, Reed Ducovny and Charlie Steiner.'"

"Holy hairballs," said Petra. "Can he say that?"

"He just did," said Suzanne.

"I mean," said Petra, "is it even *legal* to mention names like that?"

"What do you think's gonna happen?" asked Toni in a rush of words. "You think Doogie's gonna arrest Gene Gandle for overeager journalism and throw him in the clink? Or slap him on the wrist?" She shook her head. "Never happen."

"No," said Suzanne. "Doogie will just seethe silently and hope the story blows over."

"While he continues to plod along," said Toni.

"Doogie's doing the best he can," said Suzanne. She glanced at the newspaper again. "But this entire story makes me queasy."

"Do a quick affirmation," said Petra. "Tell yourself, 'After each deep, cleansing breath, I will release all negative thoughts and sadness.' Then, with each follow-up breath, think, 'I accept positive thoughts and happiness.'"

Suzanne closed her eyes and inhaled a lungful of air. Then she blew it out in a long stream. "Better," she said after a moment.

Petra leaned over and gave her friend a quick hug. "You'll be okay. We'll all be okay."

"You're probably right," said Suzanne, "even if you do sound like a self-help paperback." She brushed back strands of silver blond hair, and said to Toni, "Let's get back to something lighter. What about the treasure clue?"

Toni snatched up the *Bugle* and flipped to an inside page. She scanned a few columns, running a bright red manicured finger along. "Here it is!"

She read it aloud to Suzanne and Petra:

Focus now and you can do it
Try to pause and look right through it.
Take care to gaze into the ice
The extra cash would sure be nice.

Toni looked up. "Gaze into the ice? What on earth does that mean? There's ice all over this blasted town. I could be searching for months! Right up until the spring thaw!"

"At least this clue's a little more specific than the first one," said Suzanne.

"No, it's not. I still have no idea where to start," Toni sputtered.

"You were so excited about the treasure hunt," said Petra, "and now you've turned all mopey."

"Duh . . . yeah," said Toni. "Because the clues are gibberish." She nibbled at her lower lip with her front teeth. "Maybe . . . you guys could kind of throw in with me?"

"What do you mean?" asked Suzanne.

"You sound like an old prospector asking for a grub stake," chuckled Petra.

"I kind of am," said Toni. She scratched her head vigorously. "I think I need serious help."

"Here's the thing," said Suzanne. "With clues this vague, nobody else is going have an aha moment, either."

"You make a good point," said Toni.

"So let's wait until we have three clues under our belt," said Suzanne. "Then we'll put our collective heads together and go on a treasure hunt."

"That's the spirit!" said Toni. "All for one and one for all!"

"Like the three Mouseketeers," said Petra.

Suzanne and Toni looked at her sharply.

"You said Mouseketeers," said Toni.

"Did not," said Petra, fussing at her stove.

"Did, too," said Toni. She was bending over, laughing, practically in stitches now.

"I think you did," said Suzanne, giggling. She waved her hands in the air. "Wait a minute, wait a minute, I almost forgot to tell you guys."

"What?" said Petra, happy to change the subject.

"We had a night visitor," said Suzanne.

"When?" asked Toni. "Oh . . . you mean last night?"

"Yes, last night," said Suzanne. "An intruder of sorts."

"What?" said Toni and Petra in unison.

Suzanne told them all about Colby. How he'd come skulking in, looking for food. Aided, of course, by Joey's key.

"He nearly scared me right out of my skin," said Suzanne.

"I can imagine," said Petra. "After . . ." Her eyes rolled toward the back window. "You know."

"We sure do," said Toni. She turned to Suzanne. "So, then what happened?"

"After I beat him senseless with a club," said Suzanne, "I drove Colby over to the Law Enforcement Center." She paused. "Where the little ragamuffin promptly gave them the slip."

"No way!" cried Toni.

"Way," said Suzanne. "In fact, it was under Doogie's eagle-eyed watch that he got away."

"Your tax dollars at work," said Toni, dusting her hands together.

"So what happens now?" asked Petra. "Are they going to try and track him down?"

"Doogie said he put the word out to all his deputies," said Suzanne, "to be on the watch for Colby. But who knows? They're busy chasing down leads on the Busacker murder."

"More like chasing their tails," said Toni.

"But what about the kid?" asked Petra. "What's going to happen to him?"

"No idea," said Suzanne. "But just in case he comes skulking back here, keep an eye out. Colby admitted to me that he'd been bunking in the barn across the way, so there's a possibility he could show up again." She paused. "Yeah, I have a feeling Colby might be back." *And let's just hope, that if he does, he's not dealing drugs like Doogie suggested.*

SUZANNE was stacking sugar donuts in the pie saver, piling them up like a mini load of sugar-coated inner tubes, when Junior came stomping in. He was dressed in his pegged jeans, motorcycle boots, and studded leather jacket. No gloves or hat.

"Will you look at that," Toni remarked. "The man can't stay away from me. I must be totally irresistible."

Junior was stomping his feet and blowing warm air on

his red, chapped hands. "Cold out there!" he exclaimed, when he saw Suzanne and Toni looking at him.

"Big surprise," said Toni. "It's January."

"Why is it so hard to get a kind word around here?" asked Junior. "All I want's a little lunch."

"How come you're not using your handy, dandy car cooker?" asked Suzanne.

"I am," said Junior. "I'm making goulash, but my noodles ain't cooked yet. I got another sixty miles to go."

"Maybe we better fix you a sandwich," said Toni. "Just in case."

"Or soup," said Suzanne. Then to Toni, under her breath, "Whichever's faster. We don't want Junior lingering here too long."

"Good point," was Toni's quick reply. Her cowboy boots sounded like castanets as she hustled across the café floor to seat Junior. "I'll make you a sandwich," she told him, "but you gotta hurry up and eat. Get your sorry butt out of here before our real customers show up."

"I'd appreciate it if you'd really piled on the meat and cheese," said Junior, easing himself down at a table. "I need all the calories I can get."

Suzanne knew she'd regret it, but had to ask. "Why is that, Junior?"

Junior flashed a cheesy grin. "I'm training for a marathon."

Toni hooked her thumbs in her belt and cast a skeptical eye at him. "Seriously?"

Junior gave a self-satisfied chuckle, happy that he'd sufficiently mousetrapped them. "I'm fixing to watch me a *Baywatch* marathon. Netflix just delivered!"

"THAT man seriously rattles my molars," said Toni, as Suzanne printed their abridged luncheon menu on the blackboard with pink and orange chalk. She'd just written "crab chowder" and was starting on the sandwich du jour.

"In a good way?" asked Suzanne. She wasn't quite sure what Toni meant. Sam sometimes rattled her world, but certainly not her teeth.

"Let me put it this way," said Toni. "Junior keeps me on my toes."

"You're a ballerina in cowboy boots," said Suzanne. She printed "ham salad on rye."

"But Junior did promise to take me treasure hunting," said Toni. "Not that I don't want to go with you guys, too," she added hastily.

"Excuse me," said Petra, leaning out the kitchen door. "Does this mean you've reconciled with Kindred's very own aging juvenile delinquent?"

Toni sighed. "Junior's not without his charms."

"Honey," said Petra, an edge to her voice, "I've heard that tune before."

"One day you want to divorce him, the next day you're having second thoughts," said Suzanne. "Please don't start up with him again until you give this relationship some very serious consideration. Remember, it wasn't so long ago that you were crying buckets because Junior was mooning over that floozy waitress at the VFW."

"Tiffany," spat out Petra. "The one with the big . . ."

"Bouffant hair," said Suzanne.

Toni dropped her head. "I know. I remember."

"The point being," Suzanne continued, "Junior, aka the Rat, walked out on you."

"You know what you do when a man walks out on you?" said Petra.

"Shut the door?" said Suzanne. "Make sure you're on one side and he's on the other?"

"Yes!" said Petra. "And then you lock it!"

"Aw, you guys," said Toni.

"I'm serious," said Suzanne, as the wall phone shrilled. "You gotta be careful about letting Junior worm his way back into your life again." She picked up the phone. "Cackleberry Club." She listened for a few moments, then said,

"Are you sure? It's our . . . yes, okay, I understand." She shook her head and hung up the phone.

"What?" said Petra.

"That was Joey," said Suzanne. "He can't come in to-day."

Petra threw up her arms. "Terrific! Lunch starts in five minutes, then we've got the Crystal Tea! Now what?"

"Now we work our butts off," said Toni. She glanced at her watch, a battered Timex that perpetually ran five minutes slow. "We've got, like, two hours before all the models and boutique people and hair and makeup people come trooping in. And three hours before our guests arrive."

Suzanne went back to her chalkboard, finished printing out "chicken hot pot," then paused. Looking around, making sure she wouldn't be overheard, she murmured, "And I just pray that Busacker's killer isn't among our guests."

CHAPTER 13

THE abbreviated menu saved them. With only four choices, customers ordered fast and seemed to eat even faster. Which was just fine with Suzanne. She was even thinking they could hustle everybody out by one o'clock. Which was exactly when Ed Rapson and Lester Drummond showed up for lunch.

Gritting her teeth, Suzanne greeted them pleasantly, as if she didn't have a care in the world, and asked if they'd like coffee to start. But before she could fetch their hot drinks or ask them what they'd like for lunch, Lester Drummond flashed a big smile, showing off his mouthful of scary-big white teeth.

"You'll be pleased to know," said Drummond, "that I'm getting closer to a new job every minute."

Suzanne was startled by his bluntness. "Beg your pardon?" she said, trying to keep her voice even-keeled.

"I was just telling Ed here that I'm eager to get to work," said Drummond. "As the new president of Kindred State Bank."

"Is that right?" asked Suzanne. She scanned Ed Rapson's face for some kind of sign—agreement, surprise, bewilderment, something. Instead, she saw a face as impassive and immobile as a sheet of steel.

"I'm the kind of guy who hits the ground running," Drummond droned on. "No ramp-up time for me. No sir." His eyes drilled into Rapson. "You'd see results with me my very first week on the job."

Rapson continued to stare straight ahead. Now he looked more like an Easter Island statue.

"That's because I'm a fast learner," Drummond went on. "Fastest on the planet. I don't waste time, and I don't tolerate people who do." He flashed a smile at Rapson. "My hiring could be the best thing ever for your bank. Not to mention the people of Kindred."

This wasn't just a sales pitch, Suzanne thought, this was a full-fledged bells-and-whistles PR campaign! Since when had Lester Drummond, former prison warden and thug, become so outright and unabashedly promotional?

Since he's been desperate for a job, Suzanne realized. Drummond probably had a pile of bills sitting on his kitchen counter and not enough scratch in his checking account to cover them!

Suzanne didn't make a single comment. In fact, she was still trying to get over her shock at seeing the two men sitting together at the same table. The muscle man Drummond and Mr. Slick Banker Rapson. Definitely an odd couple!

After taking the men's orders—crab chowder for Rapson, an egg sammy for Drummond—Suzanne beat a hasty retreat to the kitchen.

"How many customers left?" asked Petra.

"Um . . . about six," said Suzanne.

"So these are the last lunch orders?"

"I fervently hope so."

In between delivering lunches, ringing up tabs at the cash register, and doing general troubleshooting, Suzanne managed to glance over at Drummond and Rapson every so often. The two men seemed to be involved in earnest conversation as they slurped, munched, and drank coffee. Drummond kept poking his finger at Rapson, punctuating the air. And now Rapson seemed to be nodding in agreement.

Toni caught their dynamic, too, and leaned over to Suzanne. "Please tell me Drummond's not going to get the bank job," she whispered.

"Hope not," said Suzanne. She continued to monitor them out of the corner of her eye. And couldn't help thinking: Were they talking about what had happened to Ben Busacker? Maybe each a little suspicious of the other? Were they giving each other a good sniff?

Which made her mind immediately jump to Sheriff Doogie and his investigation. Had he hauled Ducovny in for questioning? Had he talked to Charlie Steiner again? Or had Doogie moved on to another unsuspecting suspect?

Before she could make another stop at their table, Suzanne saw Drummond stand up, throw a few dollars down, then shake hands with Rapson. As Drummond quickly exited the café, Rapson seemed to be lingering, savoring his last sips of coffee while he checked messages on his BlackBerry.

Suzanne sidled over to his table. "Could I interest you in some apple pie for dessert?"

"No, thanks," said Rapson, giving an offhand wave. "Sounds tempting, but . . ." He stared intently at his BlackBerry screen as if it contained all the mysteries of the universe.

Suzanne took a deep breath. "Ed. Mr. Rapson. I have to ask you. You're not *seriously* considering appointing Lester Drummond as bank president, are you?"

Rapson eyed her carefully. "I might be. Problem?"

"What about Ham Wick?" she asked. "Is he in the running, too?" Suzanne knew that Wick would be weak and ineffectual, but he would still be better than Lester Drummond. Anybody would be.

"Here's the thing," Rapson said sharply. "I want to see how badly both men want this job."

"You mean like a contest?" said Suzanne, trying to keep calm but realizing she wasn't succeeding. "You want them to duke it out like some kind of cage-fighting match on cable TV?"

Rapson looked strangely pleased. "Something like that." He nodded, liking her analogy. "Both men have demonstrated an avid interest in the position, so now I want to see how much fire they have in their bellies. Figure out who's toughest and has the thickest skin."

"This isn't the Wild West you know!" said Suzanne, exasperated. "Besides, you know Drummond's the tougher of the two."

Rapson grinned. "You think so?"

"You don't have any other candidates?" Suzanne asked. She thought back to all those black-suited, bland-faced men from the funeral this morning. How about one of them? Wouldn't one of them be infinitely better? Even if he turned out to be a stuffed shirt?

Rapson shrugged. "I'm going to let this little rivalry play out a while longer."

Great, thought Suzanne. *Next thing you know our new bank president will be strapping on a pair of six guns and firing away. And who knows who the target will be?*

TONI had a dozen teapots lined up on the counter when the front door creaked open and a chill wind blew in. Suzanne glanced over, ready to tell their latecomer that they were closed. And, instead, saw someone who brightened her mood instantly.

Sam Hazelet stood in the doorway, sending his devastating smile her way.

Thrilled, Suzanne rushed over to greet him. "You got away from the clinic for lunch!" she cried. "You never get away!"

"I felt something calling to me," said Sam, planting a kiss on her cheek as he enfolded her in a warm embrace. "Something in the air."

As she leaned closer to him, Suzanne smelled his aftershave. Citrus with a hint of amber. And maybe a hint of Betadine?

"You were no doubt drawn by our soup," said Suzanne. "Our crab chowder has a way of wafting its magical aroma clear across town." She stepped back and looked up at him.

Brown hair hanging over his forehead, flashing blue eyes, hint of dimples, healthy glow on his face. *How does this guy always look so good?* she wondered. *Even straight from work. It sure is a mystery. But a good kind of mystery!*

Sam slipped onto a seat at the counter as Suzanne bustled about, grabbing a steaming bowl of soup for him and prodding Petra to construct one of her famous hot roast beef sandwiches au jus.

"Too much, too much," Sam protested, when she put it all in front of him.

"No," said Suzanne, smiling, "it's just right."

So of course she had to tell him about her little tête-à-tête with Ed Rapson. And how Rapson had been lunching with Lester Drummond.

"Do you think Rapson will give the bank job to Drummond?" Suzanne wondered.

Sam chewed thoughtfully. "Sounds like it would be a terrible mistake to do that."

"I can't imagine how this thing is going to play out," said Suzanne. "Plus, we still have a murderer on the loose!"

Sam gazed at her. "We?"

"Um . . . I meant Sheriff Doogie."

WHEN Sam's soup bowl was almost empty, Suzanne said, "How much time do you have?"

He glanced at his watch. "About two minutes. I gotta get over to the hospital. I think there's an appendectomy waiting for me."

But Suzanne grabbed his hand and guided him into the Book Nook.

"I sure love this little shop," said Sam. He cast an interested glance at the History section, but Suzanne pulled him into the Romance section. And there, surrounded by book covers that depicted pirates, Victorians, and couples of English nobility locked in passionate, bodice-busting embraces, Sam leaned in and kissed Suzanne.

So wonderful, she thought. *So unexpected in the middle of a crazy hectic day. I could get used to this. For good.*

"See you tonight?" said Sam.

"For the parade." Suzanne smiled. "Absolutely."

"WHAT were you two lovebirds up to?" asked Toni once Sam had left.

"Nothing," said Suzanne. "Just . . . hanging out with the books."

"Didn't sound like nothing," said Toni. "Sounded more like . . . steamy romance."

Suzanne chuckled. "You think?"

"Oh yeah," said Toni, as she shook out a white linen tablecloth. "Which is always a good thing." She settled the tablecloth onto a battered wooden table, and said, "Presto, change-o. Instant tea salon."

"Now all we need are the candles and flowers and cream and sugar."

"And the food," said Toni. "I love it when Petra makes tea sandwiches. They're just so . . . petite!"

"Let's see how she's doing," said Suzanne, putting a hand on the kitchen door. "See if she needs me to slice off crusts or something."

But when she walked into the kitchen, she was once again startled by the sight of an unexpected visitor.

"Colby!" Suzanne cried.

Colby, the juvenile getaway artist, was sitting cross-legged on a chair. Contentedly munching one of Petra's double-decker roast beef sandwiches and swigging sips from a can of Coke, he looked like he didn't have a care in the world.

"You little rat!" said Suzanne, putting a hand to her heart. "I was so *worried* about you!"

Colby stopped chewing for a moment and raised one upturned palm in a nonchalant, I-got-no-problem gesture.

"I had visions of you sleeping on the floor of some cold

garage," Suzanne scolded. "And don't you dare try to look innocent!" Then she whirled on Petra. "And *you*. Why didn't you tell me he was here? And why on earth are you feeding him like he's some prodigal son who's just returned to the fold! Why are you treating him like . . . like . . ."

"Like some big-shot poobah!" filled in Toni. She'd come in to see what all the fuss was about.

Petra looked suddenly sheepish. "I . . . well, he was hungry. And he just slipped in here, quiet as a mouse, and quite politely, I might add, while you were hanging out with Sam in book world over there. And, besides, I just had to feed him . . ."

Suzanne tapped her toe.

"Like I already said," said Petra, "he was hungry!"

"Starving," said Colby, through a mouthful of food.

"Kid," said Suzanne, focusing her energy back on Colby and realizing she was much more relieved than she was letting on, "you not only owe me an explanation, you owe me an apology."

"Suzanne," said Petra, ever the champion of stray dogs, homeless army veterans, and even turtles that had wandered away from their ponds, "we *have* to help him out."

"Oh really," said Suzanne. "From the way he's chowing down, it's a good thing he hasn't eaten us out of house and home."

"Hey," said Colby, swallowing hard, "I'll pay you back. I mean it, I really will."

Now Suzanne was amused. "Sure you will. Even though you're homeless and—I'm taking a wild guess here—unemployed."

"I'll tell you what," said Colby. "I'll *sing* for my supper."

"What are you talking about?" said Suzanne. She gazed at Toni, who was still watching the whole exchange with mostly stunned silence. "Do you know what he's talking about?"

Toni shook her head. "Nope. But it's interesting to say the least."

Colby stood up, as if to add emphasis to his words. "I mean I'll help out around here." He swept his arms wide. "You got stuff that needs doing, right? So, slap an apron on me and put me to work. I'll sweep floors, take out the trash, do whatever you guys need."

Suzanne considered this with some amazement. Was this really the same kid who'd slipped out of Doogie's grasp last night? That kid was surly and combative, while this kid was offering to help. And actually seemed sincere. She was comfortable enough now to let her guard down a bit.

"We *could* use some help with the tea this afternoon," said Petra, in a hopeful, slightly wheedling tone.

"There you go," said Colby, sensing an in. "You're having a fancy tea party. Which means you're probably gonna need a busboy or maybe even a waiter."

"We do need help," put in Toni.

Suzanne considered Colby's offer. Should she risk it, or would he duck out again? That remained to be seen. "Okay," she said, finally. "But only because we're going to be ferociously busy this afternoon."

"I'll work my fingers to the bone," Colby promised. "Believe me, you won't regret it."

Suzanne held up a finger. "I better *not* regret it. And, kid . . ."

Three pairs of eyes stared at her.

"I still have a few questions that need answering," said Suzanne. And to herself she thought, *I really do have to call Doogie.*

CHAPTER 14

WHILE Petra worked in the kitchen, Suzanne, Toni, and Colby got to work on the decor. And in a few minutes' time instantly upgraded the casual café with winter white linen tablecloths, sparkling crystal stemware, pink-and-cream-colored Spode plates, cups, and saucers, and tea light candles in glass candleholders shaped like snowflakes.

"You want slipcovers on the backs of these chairs?" Toni asked.

"Absolutely," said Suzanne. "The white ones, the ones we use for bridal showers."

While Toni and Colby tied slipcovers over the wooden chairs, transforming them into elegant seating, Suzanne frosted the windows with snow spray, adding yet another touch of crystal-perfect winter wonderland.

"I love that stuff," said Toni. "Except once I sprayed it in my hair, for a kind of snow-maiden effect?" She wrinkled her nose. "Stuff wouldn't come out for weeks!"

"What else?" asked Suzanne, gazing at the tables. They were almost perfect, except for . . . "Ah, the flowers!"

"I'll get 'em," offered Colby.

"In the cooler," said Suzanne. Buds & Blooms had delivered the flowers just this morning. And stashing them in the walk-in cooler on top of the butter and cheese had seemed, to Suzanne, the smart thing to do. She just hoped they hadn't gotten smooshed.

Colby was back a few minutes later. "These are great!"

he exclaimed, hauling two heavy green plastic pots stuffed full of blooms. "What are they exactly?"

Suzanne touched a hand to the white blooms. "Roses and lilies," she told him. She glanced over to where Toni was down on her hands and knees pulling a half dozen crystal vases from a small wooden cupboard.

Which was when the door flew open and Carmen Copeland strolled in.

"Well, isn't this a sight to behold?" she snickered.

Embarrassed, Toni whirled around. "Huh?"

Looking as exotic as ever with her long, dark hair swept off her neck in an artful updo, Carmen had her fur coat thrown casually over the shoulders of her bright red silk dress. A black handbag dangled from her slim wrist, her feet and legs were sheathed in black patent-leather high-heeled boots. Carmen gazed about the newly decorated café with an imperious air, not saying anything terrible, but not saying anything particularly nice, either.

Finally, she announced to no one in particular, "We're here to set up. I assume we may commandeer your crafting room?" This time she deigned to direct her glance at Suzanne.

"The Knitting Nest, yes," said Suzanne, vowing to remain calm. "Let's get you and your models settled in and comfortable. We've been looking forward to your fashion show for weeks! We're sold out, you know."

"I would expect nothing less," said Carmen, spinning on her heels. Behind Carmen strolled a gaggle of tall, leggy, and impossibly smooth-faced models, six in all. They clustered after her, like chicks around a mother hen, wardrobe bags slung over their shoulders and duffel bags filled with makeup, high heels, undies, and clip-on wiglets. Bringing up the rear was the blond and blue-eyed Missy Langston, manager of Carmen's Alchemy Boutique. In her early thirties and, Suzanne thought, easily one of the sweetest people in Kindred, Missy was struggling under another half dozen wardrobe bags, all crammed to the point of bursting.

"Let me help you with those," Suzanne offered quickly. Missy willingly surrendered three bags from her narrow shoulders. "Thank you," she breathed. "I feel like a pack animal."

Suzanne knew that Carmen treated Missy exactly like that, but she held her tongue. This wasn't the right time to give her a pep talk about finding a new job. Instead, she steered the group to the Knitting Nest and helped them stow their things. Just as she was offering water, tea, and whatever else they needed, Gregg from Root 66 rolled in to do hair and makeup. He was tall, blond, and ethereal, one of two gay fellows who owned Kindred's premier hair salon. Gregg had signed on a month ago to help out as stylist.

"Suzanne, sweetie," said Gregg, hugging her and administering elaborate air kisses. "Don't you think it's high time we did something about those roots?" His gaze had focused on her hair.

"You don't like my two-tone look?" Suzanne asked. Really, were her roots *that* bad?

"Mmm," said Gregg, "just a bit skunky for my taste. But who am I to judge? Only your hairdresser, stylist, and all-around confidante!"

"You guys need any help?" asked Toni, pushing her way into the increasingly crowded Knitting Nest. Then she looked around, noticed the elegant clothing and gorgeous models, and said, "Wow." In her Western shirt and jeans, she was a stark contrast to the sophisticated clothing from Miu Miu, James Perse, and Stella McCartney.

"Fun, no?" said Gregg.

"Fun, yes," said Toni. She reached tentative fingers out to touch a midnight blue mohair jacket that looked as light and delicious as spun sugar.

"Please don't touch the merchandise," Carmen snapped.

Toni pulled her hand back. "Sorry." She backed up, a little nervous now, and turned to Gregg. "Could you, *would* you, take a look at my eyebrows? I've got these two squiggly little caterpillars, and I really need an expert's advice."

"Let me take a look," said Gregg, sweeping her bangs out of the way.

"I don't know whether to fluff, buff, or pluck," said Toni.

"*Excuse* me," said Carmen with attitude. "This really isn't the time to start freeloading."

All the models' heads swiveled in Toni's direction, their red, pouty-perfect lips open a little at the sudden tension in the room.

"Take a chill pill," said Toni. "I'm just asking for a quickie opinion, not a complete spa day."

"That's right," said Suzanne, jumping in to defend Toni. "She's allowed. We're all friends here, right?"

"Please," said Carmen, her voice coming out in a hiss. "Today is *not* the day."

That did it for Toni. She threw up her hands and murmured to Gregg, "Never mind." But as Toni stomped out of the Knitting Nest, her back to everyone but Suzanne, she rolled her eyes and stuck out her tongue.

Suzanne had to work hard to stifle her laughter.

PETRA'S elegant four-layer cake sat on the marble counter in the café. Like an artist putting finishing touches on a canvas, Petra applied decorative swirls of white icing to the top and sides of the cake. Then, using hot strands of glossy white sugar, Petra fashioned three spectacular snowflakes for toppers.

"How do you like my winter whiteout?" she said proudly. "All made of sugar."

"Sweet," said Suzanne.

Colby clumped over to them. "Is this okay, ma'am?" He held up a crystal vase filled with flowers for Suzanne to see. "If it is, I'll do the rest just like it."

"It's perfect," said Suzanne. She was impressed at how well Colby was doing. Joey Ewald, their regular busboy, required constant prodding and positive reinforcement— kind of like training a new puppy—but Colby seemed to be able to take charge on his own. "When you're finished with the centerpieces, let's put an apron on you and you can help serve."

"You trust me that much?" asked Colby, his eyebrows raised.

"You've done very well so far," said Suzanne. Then she lowered her voice and touched his arm. "Colby, I need to ask you something." She paused. There was no way to soft-pedal this. "I heard a rumor that you might be dealing drugs on the side. Is that true?"

"No way!" blurted Colby. Then: "Who'd you hear that from?"

"It doesn't matter," said Suzanne.

Colby's dark eyes flashed. "It does to me."

"Really," said Suzanne. "If I hurt your feelings, I apologize."

The boy stared at her. "Well, I guess," he finally grunted.

SUZANNE had just lit the white candles and stepped back to admire their handiwork when the slam of a car door sounded outside. Then, like a friendly, happy tide, friends and neighbors came spilling in from the cold. And within moments, the Cackleberry Club was jammed with tea party guests alive with conversation, laughter, and excitement. Coats were hung on a borrowed coatrack, women circled the tables excitedly looking for place cards with their names on them, and everyone *ooh*ed and *aah*ed over the gorgeous transformation of the Cackleberry Club.

"It looks like a proper British tea shop in the Cotswolds!" exclaimed Lolly Herron, one of their tea regulars. She was a fan of old BBC movies and always dressed in classic Miss Marple style. That meant tweed skirt, sensible shoes, and small brooch pinned at the neck of her ruffled blouse.

"Doesn't it?" said Mrs. Minerva Bishop. She was an old dear who loved taking tea. "And they're even serving four courses today."

"That's right," said Suzanne, stepping in. "Lemon scones, cheddar ricotta quiche, an assortment of tea sandwiches, and Petra's almond cake for dessert."

"Sweets and savories," said Lolly with delight. "Just like you read about in those fancy tea magazines."

Within minutes, everyone took their seats, and Suzanne and Toni were moving about the tea room pouring cups of Darjeeling and Lapsang souchong tea.

"All but one chair filled," whispered Toni. "We're a hit!"

But Toni had spoken too soon. Suddenly, Carmen rushed out from the Knitting Nest and wrested open the front door. "Claudia!" she exclaimed. "You came!"

Claudia Busacker, wrapped in her black mink coat, stepped shyly across the threshold. Her blond hair was smoothed back, and she wore fresh lipstick, but the worry lines etched in her forehead and the purple smudges under her eyes didn't escape Suzanne's notice.

She probably just came from her husband's gravesite, Suzanne told herself, *which has to be really tough. And no matter what lush fur Claudia has draped over her shoulders, she still looks like she's carrying the weight of the world.*

Every woman in the place paused to stare at Claudia, some even stopped in midsip. But as Carmen and Claudia clutched each other's bejeweled hands in friendship, the women began to smile. And conversation started up again on a very positive note.

"How brave," said one woman.

"I'm so glad she came today," murmured another.

As Carmen escorted Claudia to the one empty seat, everyone around them nodded and smiled. Where many of the women in the room had once given Claudia the cold shoulder around town, today they were warm and welcoming. They obviously felt badly that she'd lost her husband, and they quickly moved their bags and wraps aside to make a special place for Claudia in their little group.

Seeing their kindness warmed Suzanne's heart. Of

course they'd be cordial and inclusive to Claudia. She was a wounded bird who desperately needed help. And the women of Kindred always rallied, always set aside their petty differences and closed ranks when they saw a need. When Walter had died, Suzanne had been showered with loaves of banana bread, gallons of soup, jars of homemade jam, and plates of home-cooked food. One woman had even left an enormous basket of chocolate-chip cookies on her doorstep. Their tenderheartedness had been the only good thing in her life for many days, Suzanne reflected. Just thinking about it still brought tears to her eyes.

Their sound system cranked out the pleasant strains of a piano concerto as Suzanne, Toni, and Colby ferried out three-tiered stands of tea sandwiches and presented them to each table with a flourish. There was even a flurry of applause when Suzanne pointed out the chicken almond sandwiches gracing the top tier, ham and apricot pinwheels on the middle tier, and wedges of roast beef, mortadella, and flatbread on the bottom tier.

Pleased that their guests were so appreciative, Suzanne and Toni popped into the Knitting Nest to see if Carmen was ready to kick off her fashion show.

"The scones are mere crumbs, and the women have started on their quiche and tea sandwiches," said Suzanne, in a jovial mood. "So anytime you want to begin your show would be just perfect."

Carmen glanced at two of her models who were busily gabbing away. "Juliet, Coco!" she said. "If you could control your blathering for just a moment. And do lose the chewing gum!" She looked around the room, coolly appraising each of her carefully coiffed and outfitted models, then said, "We're ready now." She pressed a CD into Suzanne's hands. "Will you kindly cue up my track?"

"Of course," said Suzanne.

"Which outfit are you gonna start with?" asked Toni. She'd trailed Suzanne in, fascinated by the transformation of the models. The girls, who'd looked tall, gangly, and about eighteen years old just an hour ago, now looked like sophisticated Parisian women. Their eyes were smoky and rimmed with kohl, their lips were dramatically red, their hair was angled into modern do's, and they wore tiny size-two suits, skirts, and designer jackets.

Carmen never bothered to glance at Toni. "We'll kick off the show with the Cavalli tunic. The dolphin blue."

Toni scrunched up her face. "You mean like Flipper?"

Suzanne gave Toni's arm a sharp tug. Better to get her out while the gettin' was good. "Let's go out and do a quick introduction," she suggested.

Toni jangled a tiny bell, and its high-pitched ring caused conversation to cease and curious faces to turn toward them. Then Suzanne stepped to the center of the room to kick things off. "Welcome, ladies, to our Crystal Tea," she said, smiling. "I hope you're all enjoying the luncheon. We'll continue to circulate with fresh pots of tea—jasmine and peach paradise for this go-round—but if you'd prefer something else, please just ask." She paused. "As you know, our own reigning mistress of romance novels, Carmen Copeland, is with us today. And she's brought with her some of the finest pieces from her Alchemy Boutique." There was light applause, and then Suzanne said, "Carmen, why don't you come out here and show us exactly what you found on the runways of Paris!"

More applause sounded, and Carmen strolled out, looking cool and relaxed, like some kind of languid jungle cat.

"Ladies," Carmen began theatrically, "I know that most of you aren't used to this kind of high fashion. But I beg of you, please keep an open mind." She spread her arms apart in a dramatic gesture. "Fashion is what separates the soulless from the sophisticates. What feeds the senses and soothes the eye. And today, I am going to rock your world!" She turned to Suzanne and nodded, and Suzanne pushed a button on the CD player.

Katy Perry's hit song "Firework" rang out as Carmen snapped her fingers and the first model strutted out, swinging her hips to the beat.

"Coco is turned out in a Cavalli cashmere tunic with matching leggings," said Carmen in a slightly breathless voice. "Soft, supple, and ever so elegant."

"Baby, you're a firework" went the music as Coco coolly circled the room.

"Our second model is wearing a purple Yoji Katoshi power suit," said Carmen. "As you can see, dramatic shoulders are back. Which gives a lovely structured look, and is oh so slimming for the hips."

"Come on show 'em what you're worth . . ."

"Now this jacket and skirt," said Carmen, with all sincerity, "is truly investment dressing."

Standing against the wall, watching the show, Toni whispered to Suzanne, "When a store charges too much for an outfit, they always tell you it's investment dressing."

"Sophia, our next model," said Carmen, "is wearing a gorgeous silk jersey leopard-print dress. As you can see, it boasts a plunging neckline and body-hugging fabric that shows off every feminine curve and leaves nothing to the imagination!"

This time Toni whispered, "Leopard print? Is she serious?"

"Sshh," said Suzanne, trying to keep a straight face.

"It's just so . . . so . . ." Toni began.

"Don't say it," whispered Suzanne. "If you can't say anything nice . . ."

"Tacky!" spat out Toni, in spite of herself.

CHAPTER 15

As the fashion show continued, Suzanne circled the tables discreetly, making sure her guests had plenty of tea, lemon slices, and bowls of Devonshire cream. Colby, much to his credit, carefully cleared dishes after each course. He had a light touch and a swift hand at the tables and seemed to be doing a fairly credible job.

"You've done this before," said Suzanne as he brushed past her, carrying a tub of dirty dishes. "You've had some experience in the restaurant business, am I right?"

"I worked as a waiter at a place in Minneapolis," answered Colby.

"Is that where you're from?"

"Nah." He shook his head. "That place is too square."

"Then where?" she asked

His eyes shifted a bit and a light seemed to go off. "Nowhere special," he said. "Just . . . around."

While Carmen continued to narrate and the models managed their amazingly quick costume changes, Suzanne slipped into the kitchen and phoned Doogie.

"Guess what?" she said energetically, once she had him on the line.

"You solved the murder," put in Doogie. "My work here is done."

"No!" said Suzanne.

"Then what?"

"The kid showed up," said Suzanne. "Colby."

"What?"

"He returned to the scene of the crime, so to speak."

"That little demon," fumed Doogie. "Did he say *why* he gave us the slip last night? When all we were trying to do was give him a warm bed and a square meal?"

"He didn't offer an explanation," said Suzanne. "Just showed up here hungry. I still have no earthly idea where he spent the night."

"And you say he's still there at your place?" asked Doogie.

"Working for me," said Suzanne. "And busing dishes like a pro. Why do you ask? Are you gonna come here and get him?"

There was a long silence. Then Doogie said, "No, I wasn't planning to. I was hoping maybe *you* could bring him over to the Law Enforcement Center."

"We tried that once," said Suzanne. "Didn't work out too well, as I recall."

"He's dealing drugs," said Doogie in an ominous tone.

"He swears he's not," said Suzanne, "but if it makes you feel any better, I'll ask him again."

"He'll just deny it."

"Then I *won't* ask him," said Suzanne. "What do you want, Doogie? You can't have it both ways! And you can't always think the worst of people. You can't go through life being a total pessimist!"

"Ah . . . jeez," said Doogie, breathing hard into the phone, "the last thing I need is a lecture." Then: "Is that music I hear?"

"We've got a fashion show going on," said Suzanne.

"Fashion show!" snorted Doogie. "Who's got time for that?"

"Obviously not you," said Suzanne. "You sound funny. Gruffer than usual. Are you okay?"

"No, I'm not okay. I feel like I've been kicked and trampled by a pack of mules."

"Tell me," said Suzanne, "did you question Reed Ducovny again?"

"That I did."

"And?"

"None of your business, Suzanne."

"You've got nothing, right? Because he's innocent."

"I ain't no judge and jury," said Doogie. "As the duly elected sheriff, all I do is catch 'em."

"Did you talk to Charlie Steiner again?"

There was more heavy breathing on the line, and then Doogie said, "I gotta go." And just like that, the line went dead.

Holy halibut, thought Suzanne. *What's this guy's problem now?*

"Is Doogie being ornery again?" asked Petra. She was standing at the butcher block table, slicing pieces of cake and carefully transferring them to the bone china dessert plates that Suzanne had found at a tag sale a couple of years ago. They were decorated with pink-and-white floral designs and marked with a fancy blue *M* on the back, which made Suzanne suspect they were Mavaleix Limoges from France.

"He's just Doogie being Doogie," said Suzanne.

"Which means his sparkling personality is shining through," said Petra.

"I wish," said Suzanne.

Petra licked frosting from her finger and cocked her head, listening. "Sounds like Carmen's show out there is starting to wind down."

"Which means it's time for you and Toni to serve your cake and for me to hustle into the Book Nook," said Suzanne. In her marketing zeal, she'd set up several nice displays of fashion books, along with a few fashion magazines and tins of tea. Maybe their guests would find their way into the Book Nook and be enticed into making a small purchase.

It would seem Carmen had the exact same idea.

"I think I should sign a few of my books," she said, buttonholing Suzanne the minute she emerged from the kitchen.

"Sounds like a fabulous idea," said Suzanne. She hadn't put any of Carmen's books on display but knew she could snatch a row off the shelf and make a nice arrangement on the counter. Then Carmen could sit behind the counter on a stool and sign books to her heart's content. Until doomsday if she wanted.

"The fashion show went extremely well, don't you think?" asked Carmen, as they threaded their way to the Book Nook.

"A huge hit," said Suzanne. "As was the tea service."

Carmen stopped suddenly and gazed meaningfully into Suzanne's eyes. "We're a lot alike, you and I."

"You think so?" *No, we're not.*

"We're both smart women," said Carmen. "And we're both hard-charging entrepreneurs."

"I suppose we do what we can to get by," said Suzanne, trying to sidestep whatever point Carmen was trying to drive home.

"No," said Carmen, "you're a tiger, just like I am." She lowered her voice and added, "Not like most of these other women."

"You mean the ones here today?" said Suzanne. "Our friends and neighbors?" She watched as Toni and Petra served cake to all the dear women who had believed in the Cackleberry Club and supported them from the get-go. The same women who also volunteered time and energy at the hospital, knitted socks for soldiers, and taught kids with disabilities how to read. Suzanne was suddenly steamed. "You're talking about the women who *ooh*ed and *coo*ed over your clothes?"

"But most of them won't set foot inside Alchemy," said Carmen. "It takes a special woman with contemporary taste and more than a few discretionary dollars to do that."

"But you said Alchemy was doing well," said Suzanne. It always surprised her that Carmen managed to sell designer duds in such a small town.

"Yes, thanks in part to Claudia," said Carmen as she slipped behind the counter and pulled out her black Montblanc pen. "Lately, she's almost single-handedly kept me in business."

"How lucky for you," said Suzanne, wondering just how long Claudia Busacker was going to stick around Kindred now that her poor husband was dead.

AN hour later, with dozens of books and tins of tea sold and wrapped in peach-colored tissue paper, with models scrubbing off their exotic makeup and turning back into pumpkins, Suzanne walked their last guest to the door. She waved brightly, closed the door firmly, and sagged against it. Then, on impulse, she cranked the latch and locked it tight.

There. Done and done. If somebody wants back in, it's not going to happen. Because I'm pooped and my feet are literally killing me.

"Petra! Toni!" Suzanne limped into the kitchen. "How are you guys doing?"

One look and Suzanne knew they hadn't fared that well, either. Petra was sprawled on a folding chair massaging her neck, while Toni was scrunched on a wooden bench with her back propped against the wall.

"How does it *look* like we're doing?" said Toni. "We're wiped."

"We are," said Petra, "but it's nothing that can't be remedied by a serious hit of sugar." She hauled herself up, cut a generous serving of cake, and proceeded to attack it with a fork.

Suzanne kicked off her loafers just as Colby pushed by her carrying a load of dirty dishes. "I think I wore the wrong shoes," she said. "Or I need gel insoles or something."

"You need an Oriental foot massage," said Petra. "I saw a diagram in a magazine once. If you hit the right pressure points, the pain just goes away. Poof!"

"No, no, no," said Toni. "She should be wearing cowboy boots. Cowboy boots all have some kind of lethal metal arch inside. You can be on your feet all day long, even get tromped on by a horse, and nothing will faze you."

"I've been tromped on by a horse," said Suzanne. "My own horse. And it fazed the heck out of me."

Toni shrugged. "Go figure."

Petra scraped up a bit of frosting as she glanced around the kitchen. "The thing to do now," she said, "is sell the place." Petra was a bit of a neat freak, so a messy kitchen, especially one that had just cranked out breakfast, lunch, and then a large and complicated tea party, catapulted her into a nervous frenzy. She tended to wring her hands and walk in circles.

"Who'd want to buy it?" said Toni.

"Maybe we could sell it to Carmen," Suzanne joked. "She certainly fancies herself a big-time entrepreneur."

Toni looked glum. "You think I'd work for *her*? No way, José!"

"Is there some problem I'm not aware of?" said Petra, glancing up.

"Just the usual chicken-poop stuff," said Suzanne. "Carmen wasn't exactly charitable to Toni."

"Carmen loves to snip and snipe and put me down," said Toni. "She enjoys looking down that surgically enhanced nose of hers."

"Oh, Toni," said Petra, "I don't think she means it. Carmen pretty much treats everybody with the same amount of disdain!"

"She may be an equal-opportunity snob," said Toni, "but face it: Carmen still thinks she's better than we are." She tugged at her blouse. "Maybe if I had different clothes?"

"Clothes don't mean a thing," said Petra. "Look at me. I wear T-shirts and crop pants and bright green Crocs. I look like the love child of Mario Batali and the Jolly Green Giant. And nobody's putting me down."

"That's 'cause you're so sweet," said Toni. "And everyone loves you." She nodded to herself. "Yup, I should probably stop dressing like a character out of *Annie Get Your Gun.* I probably need more sophisticated clothes."

"I bet you wouldn't like 'em even if you had 'em," said Petra. "I bet you wouldn't feel comfortable."

"I could at least *try*," said Toni.

Suzanne thought for a minute. "You know, Missy left a garment bag full of clothes in the office."

Toni sat bolt upright, like a prairie dog that had just received an electric shock. "She did? Really? You think I could try 'em on?"

"I don't see why not," said Suzanne, "as long as you're verrrry careful."

Toni dashed from the kitchen.

"Whoa, girl," said Petra, "don't let that swinging door hit you in the . . ."

"Head," said Suzanne, as Colby trudged through again.

Petra rested a hand on Colby's shoulder. "Honey, if you could bring in the crystal water glasses, I could get started with the hand washing."

"Sure thing," said Colby.

"You know," said Petra, hoisting herself up again, "I'd better help you. That glassware is awfully fragile."

Alone in the kitchen now, Suzanne wolfed down a leftover triangle spread with chicken salad and sliced herself a small piece of cake.

A sharp knock at the back door startled her.

What?

She glanced up, feeling edgy and nervous. Her first thought was: *Who's hanging around my back door? Please tell me it's not one of Carmen's models who's forgotten a tube of mascara. And I sincerely hope it's not the same wacko who strung the wire a couple of nights ago!*

But it was Reed Ducovny's familiar face that peeped in through a frosted sliver of window.

"Oh, hey," she said, pulling open the door and feeling instantly relieved. "Reed, come on in."

"Afternoon, Suzanne," said Ducovny. He shuffled in but

remained resolutely by the door, not wanting to track snow all over her kitchen floor.

"I guess you're here because of Doogie, huh?" Of course, he was.

"Ayuh," said Ducovny. "The sheriff is pretty much driving me batty with all his darned questions and innuendos." He shrugged out of his brown parka and pulled a stocking cap off his head, revealing a crazy tangle of gray hair. He looked, Suzanne thought, like some of those pictures she'd seen of Albert Einstein in his later years.

"I told Doogie you were innocent," said Suzanne, "and asked him to ease off. But he's obviously not listening to me."

"No, he's listening to that banker guy, Ed Rapson. And, I guess, Mayor Mobley, too."

"Mobley wants every problem to be wrapped up nice and neat," said Suzanne. "Without regard to what's right or wrong."

"Life doesn't work that way," said Ducovny. "You know that."

"Reed," said Suzanne, "I want to ask you something . . ."

He stared at her, twisting his hat in his hands.

"You went to Ben Busacker looking for a loan," said Suzanne. "But then you were turned down."

Ducovny cast his eyes downward. "It was a bitter pill to swallow," he said in a kind of half croak, "when they told me my credit wasn't so hot. You see, I wanted to make an offer on your farm."

"I understand that," said Suzanne, "and I'm truly flattered. But I still have to ask . . ."

Ducovny shifted from one foot to the other as the snow on his pac boots melted and formed two little puddles.

"You didn't do anything, did you?" said Suzanne.

Ducovny's eyes suddenly lasered into her. "What do you mean?"

"You didn't do anything, um, strange or unusual to get Busacker's attention, did you?"

"Of course not!" The ferocity of his reply unnerved Suzanne. She took a step back just as the kitchen door swung open and Petra peered in.

"Everything okay in here?" Petra asked. She saw Ducovny, smiled sweetly at him, and said, "Hello, Reed."

Ducovny bobbed his head. "Howdy, ma'am."

Petra clapped a hand to her ample chest. "You, too! Another ma'aming. Do I look that old?"

Ducovny shook his head and smiled a bit. "No, ma'am."

"Ooh, he did it again," said Petra. Glasses rattled behind her, and Petra held the door open so Colby could gingerly ease his way in with his tub full of glassware.

"Set 'em right here, hon," Petra said, pointing toward their industrial sink. She blinked, looked around at the mess that hadn't budged, and said to Colby, "Maybe you should take the garbage out, too, before we end up with a real stink-fest."

Suzanne and Ducovny continued to stare at each other as Colby fussed with the garbage, pulling one bag out of a red plastic bin, trying to force it into another bag.

"One bag's enough," Petra told him. "It's not like it's nuclear waste or anything."

"Anyway," said Ducovny, eyeing Suzanne as he pulled his parka back on, "anything you can do with the sheriff would be welcome." He tugged at his zipper. "Help get me off the hook."

"I understand," said Suzanne. It was impossible to talk frankly with Ducovny while Petra and Colby continued to struggle with the garbage. "We'll talk later," she told Ducovny, as he backed out the door.

"Pull the string tight," said Petra, grabbing one of the bulging bags. "Now haul it outside and toss it in the Dumpster."

But instead of finishing his task, Colby suddenly looked panicked. He glanced at the back door, as if he'd seen something strange, or his mind had drifted somewhere else.

Suzanne picked up on it. "What's wrong, Colby?"

He grabbed his jacket off a peg and shrugged into it. "Time to get moving," he said as he hastily slung the trash bag over one shoulder.

"I don't understand," said Suzanne. Colby was suddenly acting suspicious. As if *he* were wanted for murder.

"Colby?" said Petra. She saw his sudden unease, too.

"What's bothering you?" asked Suzanne, taking a risk—but needing to ask.

"Nothing," said Colby. The boy had totally shut down; he would not even meet her eyes now.

"Did something just happen?" asked Suzanne.

"No," said Colby.

Suzanne cocked her head. "Something you just remembered?"

"Maybe," he said.

Suzanne had a sudden thought. "Colby, did you see something out here the other night?"

He twitched like a Mexican jumping bean. "Um . . . I don't think so."

Suzanne pressed him. "Were you out back the other night when the man on the snowmobile was killed?"

"Um . . ." Colby hesitated. He met her gaze, looked away, then looked back at her. He seemed shaky and uncertain, just this side of fearful. "Maybe," he choked out.

Suzanne could barely breathe. *How much more can I push this kid without losing him?*

"Colby, did you see who killed the man?" Suzanne asked.

"No," he said in a small voice.

"Are you sure?"

"Yup," he said, but his hand was pulling at the doorknob.

"Colby," said Suzanne, "did you see who stretched the wire?"

But there was no answer. Just a whoosh of cold air, and then Colby was gone before she could even react.

CHAPTER 16

RECOVERING quickly, Suzanne struggled into her coat and dashed out the back door after Colby. The sun was just beginning to set and was spilling the last of its golden beams across the snow-covered ground while the sky overhead turned an eggplant purple.

"Colby!" Suzanne called out. "Colby, come back!"

Peering at shadows and whorls of snow that shape-shifted in the wind, Suzanne looked every which way, pausing whenever she saw the slightest movement. But instead of spotting a boy fleeing through the snow, all she saw was a black plastic garbage bag dumped in a snowbank.

Where'd he go? Suzanne wondered. Was this kid some kind of world-class speed demon?

She walked back into her woods toward the shed and looked across the expanse of snow-covered field to her farm, the farm Ducovny had wanted to buy. She saw nothing but a lone crow dive-bombing down, hoping to unearth some leftover corn cobs. But definitely no Colby.

As Suzanne rubbed her arms to warm them, she now felt sure that Colby knew something about the night Ben Busacker had been killed. Maybe not everything, not the whole picture, but he might be able to nudge one of the puzzle pieces into place, get her closer to a solution. The problem was how to find Colby. And, if and when she found him, how to gain back his trust?

* * *

"So, where'd he go?" asked Petra when Suzanne stepped inside. She was up to her elbows in sudsy water working on the glassware, her sponge making little squeaks and blurps.

"No idea," said Suzanne. "But he's sure as heck gone. Just . . . disappeared."

"Who's disappeared?" asked Toni. She suddenly reappeared dressed in a pair of tailored black slacks and the midnight blue mohair jacket she'd admired earlier.

"Colby," said Suzanne. "The kid just hightailed it out the door again."

"Kids will do that," Toni said matter-of-factly. She made a quick pirouette. "So, what do you guys think? Do I look like I just stepped off a runway or what?"

"You look great," said Suzanne. She was a little distracted, her thoughts still focused on Colby.

"You look quite sophisticated," said Petra, "but I still prefer you in your old clothes."

Toni was startled. "Huh? Why is that?"

"Because this isn't the real you," said Petra. "It's some lady who goes out for lunch and snarfs down a twenty-dollar salad and a little too much chardonnay."

Toni looked thoughtful. "That's what I look like?"

Petra nodded. "Those new clothes kind of take over. They . . . I don't know how to say it, exactly . . . they kind of obliterate your personality."

"What she means," said Suzanne, "is that the clothes are front and center instead of you."

"Maybe," said Toni. "But I'm still gonna wear 'em tonight to the parade. See what kind of reaction I get."

"If you do," said Petra, looking skeptical, "you better not let Carmen see you."

"She's right," said Suzanne. "If she sees you in that jacket, she'll have your hide!"

A brisk winter wind whipped down Kindred's Main Street, ruffling flags and kicking up rooster sprays of snow. But that didn't stop a soul from turning out for the ever-popular Fire and Ice Parade. Residents both young and old were bundled up in burly parkas with fur-trimmed hoods, puffy down jackets, and thermal-lined wool coats in red-and-black buffalo plaid.

Some folks had brought along folding chairs and had cantilevered them into snowbanks. Other hardy folks sat atop sleeping bags, while some huddled against the turn-of-the-century brick buildings with their cozy little thresholds and decorative overhangs. Adults cupped hands around warm Thermoses filled with coffee and even stronger spirits while kids sipped warm cider and munched sugar cookies with red and white sprinkles, a surprise freebie from the mayor's office.

Easing her car into the first snow-free space she could find, Suzanne made her way though the jostling crowds to a spot on Main Street, directly in front of Root 66. Sam had promised to meet her there at 7:15 P.M. sharp, in plenty of time to catch the start of the parade.

"One more patient," he'd texted her earlier. "Then I'll dash over from the clinic. C u soon."

"Sounds good," she'd texted back. "Can't wait."

Just five minutes later, she spotted Sam in his navy North Face parka making his way down the street, dodging and weaving through the bundled-up crowds.

He smiled broadly as their eyes locked.

This man is so handsome, Suzanne thought for the umpteenth time. *Especially when he smiles.*

"There you are!" Suzanne exclaimed as he approached.

They fell into a comfortable embrace, no longer worrying what others might think of their blossoming relationship.

"Quite a crowd out tonight," said Sam. "I was nervous I wouldn't be able to find you."

"I wasn't," said Suzanne.

Hand in hand they wandered down the street enjoying the sight of so many people. The Kindred Department of

Public Works had strung tiny decorative red and white lights on all the frozen, snow-laden trees along Main Street. And now the lights sparkled against the inky black sky, lending a festive, majestic touch.

"How'd your tea go today?" asked Sam.

"Great," said Suzanne. "A packed house with a great time had by all." She stopped abruptly.

"Except for . . . ?" said Sam, picking up on her change of mood.

"Oh, that kid Colby turned up again," said Suzanne. "Remember the one I told you about?"

"The runaway."

"That's the one. Right after lunch, just after you left, I wandered into the kitchen and there was Petra, stuffing Colby's face full of goodies."

"So why is that a problem?" asked Sam.

"It's a problem because he took off again. Right after Reed Ducovny walked in."

"You think Ducovny scared him off or something?" asked Sam.

Suzanne stopped in her tracks. "I'm not sure. Something went down, that's for sure. I got a funny vibe that Colby might have even seen whoever strung the wire, but really, I just don't know." She shook her head. "What can I say? He's a hinky kid."

"Which means he'll probably turn up again," said Sam. He sidestepped closer, bumping hips with her. "Don't worry about it. Just put a little pile of cheese and bologna on the back step, and he'll probably come sniffing around again."

Suzanne slugged Sam on the shoulder. "He's a kid," she said, "not a stray cat."

"Just get Doogie out there searching for him."

"Easier said than done," said Suzanne.

They walked along enjoying the people, the lights, the festive mood. And just as they scored a prime viewing spot for the parade, they noticed Toni and Junior emerging from Schmitt's Bar.

As usual, Junior had on his saggy blue jeans, but at least tonight, instead of a white T-shirt, he wore a black bomber jacket against the cold.

"Hey!" Junior crowed when he caught a glimpse of Suzanne and Sam. "Lookie who's here!" He grabbed Toni's arm and steered her through the crowd. "Did you guys just get here? We was in Schmitt's having a couple a' belts." He made a drinking motion with one hand and giggled wildly.

Junior's silly grin gave away the fact that he'd been drinking, but Toni said, "It's still nice and peaceful in there. No fights, nobody slamming a folding chair on top of somebody's head."

"Good thing," said Sam, trying to be friendly. Then he noticed Toni's midnight blue mohair jacket and said, "Nice duds."

"Thank you," said Toni, standing a little straighter.

"We're celebrating," Junior announced, wobbling on the run-down heels of his motorcycle boots.

"Junior got some good news today," said Toni, patting the collar of her jacket.

"What's that?" asked Suzanne. *His probation is finally up?*

"I placed a very important call today," said Junior, "and had a conversation with the marketing manager at a major consumer-products company."

Suzanne did a slow, reptilian blink. "And why would you do that?"

"To see if we could put together some sort of deal," said Junior. "You know, for my car cooker."

"What kind of company did you contact?" asked Suzanne. *An auto salvage yard?*

"A Crock-Pot manufacturer!" said Toni. She grinned and said, "I know, I know, I said Junior's car cooker was a crazy idea. But for the first time ever, I think he might be on to something."

"'Course I am," said Junior. He pulled Toni close and planted a big smacker on her cheek.

"Car cooker?" said Sam. He cocked his head, wondering if he'd heard them correctly.

"And they're serious about wanting to make a deal?" pressed Suzanne.

"Well," said Junior, puffing out his chest, "it's about selling a patent, so I can't expect things to fall into place over night."

"You have a patent?" asked Suzanne.

"No, I need to get that settled," said Junior. "Plus they asked to see some kind of business plan. Something about consumer demand and purchasing behavior. So there's that hoop to jump through. And then I need proof of tech support."

"Good luck with that," said Suzanne, as a sudden clash of cymbals, a crashing drum roll, and a symphonic mix of trumpets, tubas, and French horns punctuated the night.

"The parade's starting!" said Toni.

"Led by our own Kindred High School marching band," said Suzanne as a line of flag twirlers in white parkas marched down the street.

They all rushed to the curb then, as the band, in their crisp red-and-black uniforms, streamed by unleashing a cacophony of sound.

"Nothing like a good old John Philip Sousa march," said Sam.

As the snare and bass drums passed by, the crowd clapped and cheered.

"Thrilling," said Suzanne, loving the moment, loving the fact that she was here with Sam, even feeling mildly charitable toward Junior, though that would surely pass.

After the band came the baton twirlers, trim and leggy in shiny red-sequined bodysuits. When one girl gave the signal, all six twirlers flung their batons high in the air, spun themselves around like tops, then caught their batons on the downward arc.

The crowd murmured a collective "Wow!"

Next up was the official Fire and Ice float. It was a red-foam structure that formed a slightly misshapen volcano with fluttering orange and red flames juxtaposed with a plastic arctic floe, complete with fuzzy polar bear.

"I've never seen that float before," said Toni.

"I think Mayor Mobley had it made special," said Junior.

"Spending hard-earned taxpayer dollars?" said Suzanne.

"Speaking of which," said Toni, "we haven't seen him in the parade yet."

A line of classic cars now snaked along, their horns beeping, their lights blinking. Junior was almost beside himself when he spotted a baby blue '56 Thunderbird, all smooth curves and classic design.

"You see that?" he sputtered. "Now there's a car!"

A group of earnest-looking women bearing torches marched along next. These were the proud members of the Library Guild.

Then came the dogsled teams. Nearly two dozen Alaskan huskies, handsome, proud, and beautifully groomed, pranced along as the mushers held their leashes.

Finally, two old, tough-looking World War II veterans came riding along, sitting on the back of an open convertible. Bundled in great coats and fur hats with ear flaps, they looked like they'd just returned from the Ardennes.

Junior raised a clenched fist and yelled at them as they passed by. "Go Army. Hey, you guys sure whipped them Nazis!"

Suzanne turned to Toni. "Does Junior realize World War II has been over for more than sixty years?" She was aware of a ragtag group of young skateboarders and bike riders who streamed along beside the floats.

"He knows," said Toni. "He just gets all whipped up over anything military. I think he still feels bad about getting turned down by Army recruiters years ago."

"Flat feet?" said Suzanne.

Toni tapped the side of her head. "More like low IQ."

After a gaggle of cute Girl Scouts and Boy Scouts trotted past, two shiny red fire engines from the town's volunteer fire department brought up the rear and finished off the parade. A great cheer went up, and then people turned and began to make their way down to Founders Park, where the crowning of the winter king and his princesses would be held.

"Having fun?" asked Sam as he squeezed Suzanne's hand.

"Nothing beats a small-town parade," said Suzanne. "And now we get to watch a coronation."

Sam's eyes crinkled. "Complete with real jewels?"

"Of course," said Suzanne, "direct from the five-and-dime."

A mass of people crowded the nearby park for the final event of the night—the big crowning of royalty. Of course, the king was always a prominent business leader, and the princesses were usually eighteen- and nineteen-year-old girls, looking a little nervous and expectant as they shivered in prom dresses recycled as princess gowns.

"Over here," said Sam. He pulled Suzanne through the park, past enormous blocks of ice that had been hauled in for the ice-carving contest, over to where a six-foot-high wooden stage had been whacked together by volunteers. Lit with bright tripod lights that had been brought in by the sheriff's department, it looked like an accident scene, except for the sparkling bunting and a string of colored lights.

Suzanne snuggled next to Sam, the two of them caught in a sea of townsfolk that seemed to ebb and flow as everyone awaited the arrival of the royal court.

But when someone prodded Suzanne in the back, she turned to look.

"Joey!" she exclaimed. There was Joey Ewald, her missing busboy, looking cocky and sassy with his battered purple skateboard tucked under one arm. Joey wore a black

Oakland Raiders jacket with his usual collection of crosses and skulls clanking around his neck.

Suzanne put her hand on his arm. "Joey, we need to talk."

Joey gave her a blank stare.

"I'm disappointed you gave your key to my café to Colby without asking me first," she said. "That was a complete breach of trust."

"Sorry about that, Mrs. D.," said Joey.

"You know you can call me Suzanne."

"Suzanne," said Joey, trying to pull away. "Hey, see ya later."

"We're not done here, Joey," said Suzanne, tightening her grip. "I need to know where your buddy Colby is."

Joey shrugged. "No idea. 'The Dude abides.'"

"I don't want a line from a movie," said Suzanne, "I want the honest truth."

"I don't know where he is," said Joey.

"Colby's not staying with you?"

Joey shook his head. "Nope."

"If I called your mom, I'd get the same answer?"

"That's right," said Joey.

"Okay," said Suzanne, "one more question. Is Colby dealing drugs?"

Joey did a double take, like he'd never before encountered the concept of teenagers and drugs. "Drugs!" he said, looking shocked as he rendered an Academy Award–worthy performance. "What kind of drugs?"

"You know darn well what I'm talking about. Grass, speed, meth, whatever."

"No way," said Joey. Then he amended it to "Not that I know of."

"If you knew Colby was dealing drugs, would you tell me?" asked Suzanne.

"Um . . . sure," said Joey. And this time he did make a clean getaway.

"Doggone kid," said Suzanne under her breath.

"Which one?" asked Sam.

"All of them," said Suzanne.

The crowd surged closer to the stage then, carrying Suzanne and Sam with them. Mayor Mobley, resplendent in a pinstripe suit that looked like he was starring in a remake of *Guys and Dolls,* trooped onto the stage, followed by the Fire and Ice royalty. The crowd cheered and Mobley grabbed a microphone.

"It is my great pleasure," said Mayor Mobley, with all the pomposity he could muster, "to present our newly crowned Fire and Ice king! Mr. George Draper!"

The crowd cheered and hooted again as Suzanne stared up at Draper. When she'd last seen him, he'd had poor Claudia hanging on his arm. Tonight, in his red velvet robe and faux-jeweled crown, George Draper looked absurdly pleased with himself, as if he'd slain a dragon or rescued a damsel in distress to actually *earn* the title of king.

Toni bumped up alongside Suzanne. "Look at that," she burbled. "King George. Do you think he realizes his robe looks like it was munched on by a pack of demented squirrels?"

Junior leaned in to add his two cents worth. "What you girls probably don't know," he said, "is that Draper is really the last-minute, pinch-hitter king."

"How so?" asked Suzanne.

"Ben Busacker was supposed to be Fire and Ice king," said Junior. He gave an elaborate eye roll. "But considering the circumstances, Mayor Mobley had to step in fast and appoint Draper."

"And how exactly do you happen to know this bit of town business?" asked Toni, perplexed.

"I have my ways," said Junior.

"Still," said Suzanne, "Draper is acting like he was elected in a landslide."

"But look at the court of royal princesses!" put in Toni proudly. "Kit Kaslik is one of the princesses!" Kit was a former exotic dancer at Hoobly's Roadhouse who Suzanne had convinced to quit her job and seek more suitable employment. "It's quite a step up, don't you think?" chortled Toni.

"From dancing under a blue light to a blue-blood princess," said Suzanne. "Isn't life grand?"

The band played a somewhat shaky version of Whitney Houston's "One Moment in Time," Mayor Mobley droned on, and the princesses continued to shiver in their strapless gowns. All in all, it was a wonderful small-town event.

"Can I get you guys some hot cocoa?" asked Sam. "There's a stand over there run by some of the ladies from Hope Church, I think."

"Sure," came the chorus from Suzanne, Toni, and Junior.

But when Sam stepped away, the crowd shifted, and Suzanne found herself standing next to Hamilton Wick. *Of all people*, she thought. Excellent! This was the perfect opportunity to speak to him.

"Hello," she said, forcing a sincere smile. "It's great to see you again."

"Quite a night out in Kindred, huh?" said Wick. He gave a perfunctory smile.

"Fabulous," said Suzanne. She edged closer to him. "And how are you doing? Any step closer to cinching the bank presidency?"

"I wish," said Wick. "Anything you could do . . ."

"I'll definitely put in a good word for you," said Suzanne.

Wick was so surprised he was practically speechless. "You would? Really?"

"Sure," said Suzanne, feeling like a liar. "Of course I will."

"You're a real friend, Suzanne," said Wick.

"I have to ask you something," she said. "And it's kind of a delicate matter . . ."

Wick's brows arched over watery blue eyes. "What's that?"

"Oh," she said, doing everything but stubbing her toe in

the snow, "it just seems to me that perhaps Ed Rapson and Ben Busacker might not have been on the best of terms."

"What do you mean?" he asked.

"I'm just wondering," said Suzanne, "if perhaps Rapson could have *wanted* Busacker out of the way."

"Out of the way," repeated Wick. "You know what you're saying?" He looked suddenly nervous.

Suzanne nodded. "Yes, I think I do."

"I don't know. It sounds a little far-fetched . . . though Rapson is a pretty tough character. Hard-nosed and demanding."

"You think Busacker and Rapson's relationship might have been adversarial?" Suzanne asked.

"I'm not sure," said Wick. He hesitated, as if he wanted to say more, then shook his head.

"What?" said Suzanne. "Tell me more about Busacker. Help me understand him. What was he really like?"

Hamilton Wick gazed into Suzanne's eyes. "Look, I didn't know him all that well. We were never particularly close."

"But you must have gleaned something from him," said Suzanne. "You two worked together. You were bank colleagues."

A hard look came across Wick's face, as if remembering some slight or insult. "He did have a few secrets."

"Like what?" Suzanne asked.

Wick lowered his voice. "For one thing, Ben and his wife, Claudia, weren't getting along all that well."

"Is that so?" Suzanne's heart started to pound a little faster. This was the kind of information she wanted. She leaned in just a little closer to Wick, hoping he'd tell her more.

"It's more of a rumor than anything," Wick said hastily.

"Uh-huh," said Suzanne. "But rumors are so often rooted in truth."

Wick continued to hem and haw as Suzanne kept cajoling him.

Finally, Wick spit it out. "The thing is . . . Claudia was having an . . . an assignation."

Suzanne tried hard not to register surprise, because she didn't want to spook him. But her first thought was *That sneaky Claudia!* That little lady put on a darned good show this morning and again this afternoon. "You mean she was having an affair?" said Suzanne. "Really." She pondered this for a few more seconds, then took the plunge. "Do you know who she was involved with? *Is* involved with?"

Wick's eyes drifted toward the stage, then back to Suzanne. "I don't really know."

"Does anyone else know about this?" asked Suzanne. *Like Sheriff Doogie?*

"I haven't said a word to anyone," said Wick "You're the first person I've mentioned this to. And I don't know why I did that, except that maybe I trust you. I'm not the kind of man who spreads rumors. I'm in the Rotary Club, for goodness sake."

"I understand completely," said Suzanne. *But tell me more.* "Is there anything else you can tell me?"

"With Ben gone . . ." said Wick. He stopped abruptly and licked his lips.

"With Ben gone," Suzanne repeated. She put a hand on Wick's arm and gave an encouraging squeeze.

"Well," said Wick, "there's the insurance policy."

"What insurance policy? Oh, you're talking about Busacker's policy?"

"That's right," said Wick. He pulled himself up straighter and said, "You realize, I'm the go-to guy at the bank for insurance. I'm the one who handles the various policies and annuities."

"I know you are," said Suzanne, letting a little admiration creep into her voice.

"So, the fact is," said Wick, "I happen to know that Claudia stands to inherit a rather tidy sum."

"How tidy would that sum be?" asked Suzanne.

"Let's just say seven figures," said Wick.

"A million or more?" said Suzanne.

"A million five," replied Wick, right on cue.

"Interesting," said Suzanne, striving to keep her reaction to a bare minimum. But inside she was thinking, *Hot dog! Is that the kind of money someone would kill for?* And as she watched Sam return with multiple cups of hot cocoa, her answer was, *Oh yes, it is. Most definitely it is.*

CHAPTER 17

SUZANNE moved her glass of beer in tight little circles as she listened to Sam. They were ensconced in a deep, dark booth in Schmitt's Bar. The aroma of grease and spilled beer hung heavy in the air, and there was the reassuring rattle of billiard balls being racked.

"Excuse me," said Suzanne, "what did you say?" Suzanne couldn't get that number, $1.5 million, out of her head. It kept bouncing around like the cue ball on the back pool table, worrying her to death. And even though her exchange with Hamilton Wick felt like some kind of strange dream hangover, she knew it had just happened. It had *really* happened.

"I said you haven't heard a thing I said," said Sam, taking a swig of his beer. "Here I am going on and on about poor Mrs. Hillstrom's hammertoe, and you don't care a lick."

Suzanne tried to focus. "I *do* care. Is that what you just said, really?"

"No, I was testing you. There is no Mrs. Hillstrom and there is no hammertoe," said Sam. He gazed at her affectionately. "But, sweetheart, you look like you're worried sick about something. Have been for the last ten minutes." Sam reached across the table and grasped her hand. "Now what gives? What *happened*?"

"I had a short conversation with Ham Wick," said Suzanne. "When you were off getting cocoa."

"Ham Wick," said Sam. "Sounds like one of your luncheon specials."

"Wick's the guy at the bank. The *other* guy. The one who's still alive."

"Oh, sure," said Sam, scrunching his face, "the little guy with the bow tie who sits at his desk staring at endless columns of numbers."

"Bingo," said Suzanne.

"What about him?"

"I was kind of buddying up to him," said Suzanne, "and pumping him for information about Busacker. And he let slip some fairly damning details."

"Damning to who?"

Suzanne leaned in closer. "To Claudia, Ben Busacker's widow."

Sam held up a hand. "Stop right now." He looked unsettled. "Do I really want to hear this?"

Suzanne fought a rising tide of panic. "I have to tell *someone!*"

Sam took a deep breath. "Okay. Lay it on me."

"Here's the thing," said Suzanne. "It seems that, in the wake—no pun intended—of Ben's death, Claudia is set to receive a one-point-five-million-dollar insurance settlement."

Sam let loose a low whistle.

"Exactly," said Suzanne. "So, you can see, that number's just been added to what's already a baffling equation."

"Sounds like a new suspect's been added, too," said Sam. He glanced sideways. Freddy, the aging hippy bartender who owned Schmitt's, was suddenly poised with his order pad and pencil.

"Help you?" said Freddy. He wore blue jeans, suspenders, and a T-shirt that read: I'm not Weird, I'm Gifted.

"Burger basket?" said Sam, looking at Suzanne. She nodded. "Two burger baskets," said Sam.

"Onion strings?" asked Freddy.

"Naturally," said Sam. He generally ate healthy, but made an exception for Freddy's grilled hamburgers. Done on an old-fashioned cast-iron grill cranked up to about a thousand degrees, they were like creosote on the outside, but pink and juicy on the inside.

"Cheddar or blue cheese?" asked Freddy.

"Yes," said Sam.

"Good man," said Freddy, writing it all down.

"So," said Sam, when Freddy had left, "are you going to tell Sheriff Doogie about this mega insurance policy?"

"I think I pretty much have to," said Suzanne.

"I think you do, too," said Sam. "Unless he knows about it already."

Suzanne sighed and leaned back against the cracked vinyl of the booth. She glanced at the crowd, saw lots of familiar faces in the knotty pine-paneled bar with its displays of softball trophies, tin signs tacked to the walls, and faded photos of Kindred bowling teams in their glory days. Freddy had added a new sign to his collection, too: Our Glasses Are Clean, But Our Martinis Are Dirty.

As the tinkling sounds of John Mellencamp's "Pink Houses" spilled out from the jukebox that hugged the far wall, Suzanne drained the last of her beer and smiled. She liked this congenial little bar with its crazy collectibles. But her smile faded the moment her eyes shifted and she caught sight of Charlie Steiner. He was hunched at the bar, wearing overalls and a worn Carhartt jacket and drinking all by himself. The downcast look on his face pretty much conveyed to everyone that he was disgusted with life in general. And as he took a swig of beer, he smacked his lips, then practically slammed his mug down on the counter.

"Hey," said Suzanne, prodding Sam with her toe. "Look who's at the bar."

Sam glanced over. "Steiner," he said. "Your prime suspect."

"Maybe not anymore," said Suzanne. She watched as Steiner muttered unhappily to himself. "Do you think Doogie's been nipping at his heels again, asking questions?"

"Probably," said Sam. Then he reconsidered. "I don't know, that's kind of your territory, isn't it?"

Suzanne's head snapped back and she stared at him. "What is?"

"Investigating. Though it pains me to say it, and scares the crap out of me to know you're running around questioning suspects."

"I'm really not," said Suzanne, trying to soft-pedal her own involvement. "They all just seem to find me."

"Except Claudia," said Sam.

"Oh no, she showed up today, too."

"Seriously? On the day of her husband's funeral?"

"I invited her to the tea," said Suzanne. "Told her it would do her good."

"Okay," said Sam.

"And when she did attend, I figured she was just looking for a little solace. But who knows? Maybe she was really just trying to win friends and influence people?"

Five minutes later, Freddy was back at their table with their piping-hot order. "Here you go," he said. He set two cheeseburger baskets in front of them. "Get 'cha anything else?"

"Maybe a couple more beers," said Sam. "Schell's if you got it."

"Sure thing," said Freddy as the front door swept open and about a dozen more people tumbled in.

"Business is good tonight," acknowledged Sam.

"Business is good every night," said Freddy. He looked pleased as he paused to scratch his ample belly. "Thing is, we're gonna punch through the wall next week and add another nine hundred square feet."

"Big time," said Sam.

Freddy grinned. "Gonna call our new addition the Boom Boom Room."

"Good grief," said Suzanne. "Please tell me you're not going to add strippers to your repertoire!"

"Why, Suzanne?" said Freddy, grinning. "Did you want to audition?"

*   *   *

BUNDLED up in their parkas again, Suzanne and Sam strolled back down Main Street. The lights still twinkled merrily, and displays in the front windows of Kuyper's Hardware and Sherri's Stationery looked cheery. But, for the most part, the center of town was pretty much deserted.

"Everybody's cleared out," said Sam.

"Everybody's in Schmitt's Bar," said Suzanne. She shivered. "Brrr. Where are you parked?"

"Another block down. By the bakery."

"Good," said Suzanne, "you can give me a ride to my—"

A muffled scream suddenly drifted toward them on the chill wind! Followed by sounds of a scuffle—maybe around the corner? And then a loud metallic *thunk*, like someone's car being clobbered with a shovel.

"What on earth?" said Suzanne.

There was the distinct sound of footsteps pounding down pavement; then they grew fainter.

"Come on!" said Sam, breaking into a sprint.

Rounding the corner, they spotted a dark shape, partly sprawled on the sidewalk, half slewed up against the front bumper of a pickup truck. Some poor person had been flung there like a discarded rag doll!

"Careful!" warned Suzanne. It was dark, and she couldn't really see what was going on. But Sam was down on his hands and knees by the time she caught up to him.

"It's a kid," said Sam.

Suzanne skidded to a stop and gazed down at the dark shape, which was making low moaning sounds. Then she saw the purple skateboard turned upside down. "It's Joey!" she cried. "Joey Ewald!"

"Your Joey?" said Sam.

Suzanne nodded, her teeth chattering. Poor Joey lay sprawled on the cold pavement, his black boots scraping the street as he made half-hearted motions. He was trying to get up but failing miserably.

"Joey," said Sam. "Can you hear me?"

Joey's eyes half opened as his hands went to his stomach, his face, and finally his head.

"I want you to lie still," said Sam, "and let me take a look at you."

"Oh man, he's bleeding," said a dismayed Suzanne as she knelt beside Sam. Dark rivulets of blood seeped from a cut on Joey's skull and smeared across his face, streaking his cheeks like a Navajo warrior. "It looks bad."

Sam ran a practiced hand across Joey's head, peered into his eyes, checked his pulse and respiration. "Head laceration," he said. "We should transport him to the hospital. He's going to need stitches and maybe a head CT." Sam pulled out his cell phone and called 911, relayed instructions to the dispatcher, requested an ambulance.

Suzanne pulled off her scarf and gently wiped blood from Joey's face. "I'm here," she crooned, trying to calm herself as well as the injured boy. "You'll be okay. We'll take care of you."

Joey moaned again, and his eyes fluttered. Sam took off his parka and draped it across Joey, trying to keep him as warm as possible.

A few minutes later, the ambulance arrived, its lights flashing and siren blatting. Which drew a small crowd out onto the street to watch Joey being placed on a backboard and then carefully loaded into the back of the ambulance. Sam climbed in to be with Joey; he'd get his car later, and Suzanne would meet them at the hospital.

As the ambulance pulled away into the dark night, Suzanne cast her eyes toward the gathering crowd. And wondered, *Did one of you do this? Did one of you hurt this child?*

ONCE Joey was safely lodged in a cot in a hospital exam room and had been cleaned up by the nursing team, Sam put on his doctor's coat and went to work. He injected Joey with a syringe of lidocaine, waited a few minutes for the anesthetic to take hold, then expertly made three small stitches in Joey's skull.

Shortly after that, Sam came out to the waiting room, where Suzanne sat jiggling her foot, nervously leafing through the pages of *Nursing Today.*

"How is he?" she asked, when she caught sight of him.

"Resting comfortably. Took a few stitches."

"Poor guy," said Suzanne. She was still shaken up because she knew this wasn't just a routine skateboarding accident. Whatever had happened to Joey had been a vicious, calculated *attack.* "Did somebody call Joey's mom?"

Sam nodded. "Mom's on her way." He paused. "Now you can't be mad at him anymore. For giving the key to the Cackleberry Club to Colby."

"I was never really mad at him."

"You were a little spicy."

Suzanne shook her head. "I still don't get it. I mean, who would *do* this to Joey? And why? Did he say anything to you?"

"Just says he got jumped from behind."

"Jeez," said Suzanne. "He's just a kid. A pain in the keister sometimes, but basically a good kid." Suzanne rubbed the back of her neck, where a throbbing pain seemed to have settled. "You don't suppose . . ."

"What?"

"That Colby had a hand in this. I mean, maybe they had a fight or something?"

"Could have happened," allowed Sam.

"You know how teenage boys are. They fight tooth and nail over some stupid DVD or Xbox game or imagined girl-friend."

Sam's eyes shifted. He gazed past Suzanne, and muttered, "Doogie."

"Huh?" She turned her head and saw Doogie lumbering toward them with his trademark flat-footed walk.

"Just heard about the Ewald kid," said Doogie.

"You should go talk to him," said Suzanne. "See if he remembers anything."

"Kid still awake?" asked Doogie, hitching up his belt.

"For now," said Sam. "But he's gonna get drowsy real fast."

Doogie nodded. "Got a question for you guys. Did either of you see Charlie Steiner tonight?"

"Sure," said Suzanne. "He was sitting in Schmitt's Bar."

"Hitting the sauce?" said Doogie.

"I guess so," said Suzanne. *He wasn't exactly sipping a pink lady.* "He was sitting at the bar all by his lonesome. Why are you asking? Do you think Charlie . . . um . . . attacked Joey?"

"I don't know," said Doogie. "I still don't know what's going on. But I'll tell you one thing: we found the same kind of wire that killed Ben Busacker out at Charlie Steiner's place. Strung around his hog pen."

Suzanne's eyes widened like Frisbees. "Was a piece cut from the wire? Just like from Ducovny's fence?"

Doogie wore his serious face. "Yup."

"So, now what?" asked Suzanne. "What does it mean?"

"I've got to send the wire up to the state BCA," said Doogie. "The Bureau of Criminal Apprehension. They've got specialized labs and can analyze it more carefully."

"You really need fancy forensics?" asked Suzanne. "Can't you just go around to the local hardware stores and see what kind of wire they've sold lately?"

"Already have," said Doogie.

SAM had told Suzanne to drive safely, and the notion worried her. He hadn't just tossed it off as an afterthought, a good-bye thought. In light of Joey's getting his skull bashed in, Sam had really meant it. And so she navigated the streets of Kindred with a watchful eye until she pulled safely into her garage. Then it was a matter of a skip and a dash until she was in her back door and the dogs were swirling around her, tails wagging and begging for treats.

"Treats for everyone," Suzanne told them. She pulled a handful of Liva Lova treats from a can while she put her teakettle on the stove. Five minutes later, the dogs were still licking their lips and Suzanne was sipping a nice steaming cup of jasmine tea, very conducive to relaxation and promoting sleep.

With her mug in her hand, she strolled through her living room, thought about catching a few minutes of *Letterman*, then decided against it. She walked out into the hallway, feeling slightly at odds and ends, and glanced into Walter's office.

Walter.

She strolled into his office slowly and looked around. It was exactly the same as when Walter had still been alive. Nice wooden desk, file cabinets, bookshelves filled with medical books, political thrillers, and books on trout fishing. She spotted a photo of the two of them in a gold frame that he'd always kept on his desk. Taken during a trip to New York City one December. Walter had his arm around her and her head was resting on his shoulder. They were standing in front of Rockefeller Center, the big Christmas tree glowing and glittering behind them. It was a sweet shot from early in their marriage.

Such a precious time.

Suzanne smiled for a moment. And took a sip of tea. Turned away from the desk and studied the room in general.

Maybe it's time to turn this room into a library, she thought. *This house could use a library. And . . . I think I've waited long enough to make this change.*

Toenails clicked against the hardwood floor.

Suzanne turned and saw Baxter looking up at her, his dark eyes both loving and inquisitive.

"What do you think, fella? Think that's the right thing to do?"

He let out a low "Grrrf."

"Glad you concur," she said.

Upstairs, Suzanne washed her face, brushed her teeth, changed into a big, comfy T-shirt, and slid into bed. As she settled there in the dark, covers bunched over her, she felt her heartbeat gradually slowing. Still, her thoughts turned to Joey.

Who could have launched an attack on him? One that was so sudden—and brutal.

Suzanne rolled onto her side and snuggled in, willing herself to put Joey out of her mind for the next eight hours. Nighttime was reserved for rest and renewal, not for replaying ugly scenes.

Ugly scenes. And ugly innuendos.

What if Hamilton Wick was wrong about Claudia? she wondered. What if she wasn't having an affair, after all? What if Wick was just imagining things? Could be. Maybe he was just jealous.

Just as Suzanne was about to drop off to sleep, an image drifted into her head. She saw George Draper, the funeral director, being so gentle, so caring, so solicitous to Claudia. Gazing at her with soft, shining eyes. Almost like a lover.

And then she remembered Hamilton Wick denying that he knew the identity of Claudia's lover, but glancing up at the stage. Looking directly at George Draper, who'd just been crowned king.

Suzanne drew a sharp intake of breath and was suddenly wide awake again, her eyes popped open wide. Because, in that instant, she was pretty sure that Claudia Busacker and George Draper were lovers.

The big question was: Had they conspired to murder Ben Busacker?

CHAPTER 18

SUZANNE'S eyes snapped open at 5:59 A.M. Exactly one minute before her trusty little CD player/alarm clock was set to explode with chatter from WLGN's exuberant morning DJ.

"Joey," she whispered in the chill darkness. "I gotta go see Joey."

Throwing her covers off, Suzanne sat up and rubbed the scratchies from her eyes. She hoped Joey was okay, that nothing had changed overnight: no fever, no swelling on the brain. She'd had foggy, frightening dreams about him, about finding him lying in a puddle of blood, the heels of his boots drumming feebly against the icy pavement.

Suzanne slipped into her pink terry cloth robe and fuzzy pink slippers, the ones Baxter sometimes pretended were bunnies and liked to stalk and pounce on when his wily little dog brain slipped into playful mode. Padding downstairs, she held the back door open and let the dogs meander outside to do their business.

"Make it snappy, guys, it's cold!" she warned them.

Standing at the door, Suzanne inhaled a small sip of frosty air. The night sky was just beginning to lighten in the east, streaks of gray morphing into eggshell blue with tints of rosy pink. Very pretty, but a little threatening, too. Like a hint of snow was lurking somewhere to the west, maybe already slicking roads and weighing down power lines in Colorado or Montana.

Once the dogs were back inside, she filled their bowls

with fresh water and gave them each a scoop of dog food. She stood, watching them plunge their muzzles into their bowls, spilling kibbles everywhere.

Oh well, they'll just gobble them up off the floor.

Then she glugged down a quick cup of strong, black coffee and hurried upstairs to take a shower.

As the hot, soothing water pelted down upon her back and neck, Suzanne stood there an extra few minutes, enjoying every drop. Still, her mind kept racing to thoughts of Joey. Why had he been attacked? Was this an indication of some new kind of crime wave in Kindred? Or was it somehow linked to Busacker's murder? All frightening questions with no clear-cut answers.

THIRTY minutes later, Suzanne was striding down the clean, bright, antiseptic halls of the hospital, headed for Joey's room on the second floor. People bustled all around her. Nurses checking on patients, orderlies stacking fresh linens, a cart full of breakfast trays rattling its way from room to room, smelling of scrambled eggs and cinnamon toast.

The door to Joey's room was partially opened. Suzanne gave a sharp knock and called out, "Joey?"

He was sitting up in bed, a breakfast tray on his lap. His hair stuck straight up in a few places, and a fresh gauze bandage covered the spot on his head where Sam had sutured him last night.

"Hey!" said Joey, glancing over and giving a shy smile.

"How are you feeling?" asked Suzanne, stepping into his room.

"Doing okay," said Joey. He reached for the TV remote and turned down the sound on *SpongeBob SquarePants.* "I got three stitches!"

"I heard," said Suzanne. She noted that Joey's cheeks were a healthy pink, and his eyes seemed bright and inquisitive. Good, she thought. Probably no residual ill effects.

Shrugging out of her parka, Suzanne hung it on a peg by the door. "Looks like you got breakfast in bed," she said, smiling. She walked over to him and settled into an uncomfortable plastic armchair parked next to his bed.

Joey chuckled. "The scrambled eggs are pretty decent. And look, I got pancakes, too." He pointed to a silver dollar-sized cake and a miniature bottle of syrup.

"Vermont maple syrup," said Suzanne. "Very impressive. Just like room service at the Four Seasons."

"They even brought me coffee," said Joey. "You want some? I never touch the stuff myself."

"Why not?" said Suzanne. She grabbed the little silver pot and filled a cup.

"It's kind of fun being waited on," said Joey. "Like when I was a little kid and I'd stay home from school with a cold or something." Then he crinkled his brow and offered a faux-serious expression. "Guess I can't come in to work today, huh?"

"You take all the time you need to recover," said Suzanne. "Don't worry about us."

"I'm sorry about last night," said Joey. "I shouldn't have been so . . . abrupt. I mean, when I saw you the *first* time. In the park."

Suzanne waved a hand. "It's okay, Joey." Then she edged forward in her chair and said, "But I would like to ask you about your getting hit last night."

"Getting clunked!" said Joey.

"Can you recall anything about that?" asked Suzanne. "Now that you've had a little time to kind of look back and reflect. Can you remember anything about the person who attacked you?"

Joey touched a hand to the white gauze bandage, and his face clouded up. "Not really," he said. "I was, like, coasting along on my skateboard, headed for home. And suddenly, it was like a ninja assassin or terrorist attack. *Ka-boom!*" He embellished his story with accompanying teenage-boy sound effects.

"That's it?" said Suzanne. She took another few sips of coffee.

Joey nodded. "Pretty much. It was like getting slugged with a baseball bat. Down I went. *Bam!*" More sound effects.

"Did you have any sense of someone leaping out from between parked cars or rushing up from behind?"

"Nope, they pretty much caught me by surprise."

"Do you think it was someone taller than you? Or maybe someone around your own age?" *Like Colby?*

"No idea." Joey gave a strangled grin. "Those are the same questions Sheriff Doogie asked me last night."

"Well, there you go," said Suzanne. "We're both interested in figuring out who your attacker was."

"Probably just some jerk from school," said Joey.

"Probably," said Suzanne. *Or maybe not.* She stood up, reached a hand out and touched his shoulder. *Nice boy. Please be safe.* "You take it easy, kiddo. Get plenty of rest."

"I will. I'm probably going home later today."

Suzanne turned to the coatrack and reached for her parka again. Her eyes fell upon the jacket hanging there next to hers. Black and gray with a shield motif and a pirate wearing a football helmet. She blinked, studied it for a moment, then said, very slowly and deliberately, "You traded coats with Colby." It was a statement not a question.

"Yeah," Joey replied. "Couple of days ago. What of it?"

"And you did that why?"

Joey shrugged. "'Cause he had a Raiders jacket. It's way cooler than my puffer jacket."

"Let me take a wild guess here," said Suzanne. "In exchange for Colby's Raiders' jacket, you gave him your puffer coat and the key to the Cackleberry Club?"

Joey looked chagrined, but he wasn't about to deny it. "Yeah." He sniffled, was about to dig a finger into a nostril, then thought better of it. "Are you real mad at me?"

"Joey," said Suzanne, "I think that jacket is the reason you were attacked last night."

Joey looked puzzled. "What are you talking about?"

"Somebody saw the Raiders' jacket you were wearing and thought you were Colby."

"Who would think that?" Joey stabbed his fork at the last bite of pancake.

Suzanne had nowhere to go but straight to the truth. "The killer."

"What?" Joey's fork clattered to his tray, and his voice rose a good three octaves. "You mean I was almost shot or stabbed or something?"

"I'm afraid so."

Now Joey twitched nervously beneath his blankets. "Wa-wait a minute. You said *killer?* Are you talking about the same person who killed that snowmobile guy?"

"That's a very distinct possibility, yes."

Suzanne could see the wheels spinning in Joey's head, making hasty connections.

"Is somebody gonna come after me?" he asked. "I mean, am I in some kind of danger?"

"No, honey, you're not," Suzanne assured him. "I'm going to call Sheriff Doogie, and he's going to take care of this."

"Promise?" Joey looked terrified, and Suzanne felt sick at heart.

"I promise," said Suzanne.

HOPPING into her car in the hospital parking lot, Suzanne started the engine and cranked up the heater full blast. Then she pulled out her cell phone and punched in Doogie's number. "Be there, Doogie," she hissed out loud. "Be at work *now.*"

He picked up on the first ring. "Yeah," he said. "Doogie here."

"I know why Joey Ewald was attacked last night," Suzanne said, in a breathless, over-caffeinated rush of words.

There was a pause and then Doogie said, "What are you talking about? Slow down, Suzanne. Explain yourself."

"Joey's attacker thought he was Colby!"

"Colby? The runaway?"

"Here's the thing," said Suzanne. She fought to keep her voice level. "I just came from visiting Joey, and he had Colby's Raiders jacket."

"The Oakland Raiders?" said Doogie.

"Yes," said Suzanne. "The key point being that the two boys *exchanged* jackets!"

"You're still not giving me a plausible explanation as to why Joey was attacked," said Doogie.

Suzanne fought to get her words straight. "Late yesterday, when I talked to Colby at the Cackleberry Club, I quizzed him about maybe seeing something the night Busacker was killed. Just because he'd been hanging around here, sleeping in the barn across the way. And Colby suddenly got all nervous and hinky, which led me to believe he *had* seen something. I mean, you should have seen his reaction! When I mentioned Busacker's snowmobile accident, it was like he'd been poked with a hot wire!"

"Yeah?"

"And then, a few hours later, Joey, wearing Colby's jacket, was brutally assaulted."

"And you think our killer did this," said Doogie. "That he thought Joey was Colby and came back to try to finish off a potential witness?" He didn't sound convinced.

"Yes, that's it exactly!"

"Huh."

"It really does make sense," said Suzanne. She felt like she'd just deciphered the Rosetta stone or something.

"You could be on to something," allowed Doogie. "But we've got to nail things down a little more. First off, we need to locate this Colby kid and really sweat him. Where'd you say he was now?"

"That's the problem," said Suzanne. "Nobody's got a clue."

"Not even Joey?"

"He says no."

"Okay, then," said Doogie. "I'll issue a bulletin. That way we'll have him by noon."

"You hope," said Suzanne.

"I'm the long arm of the law, Suzanne," said Doogie. "If we really want him, we'll catch him."

"There's something else I need to talk to you about," said Suzanne. She was dying to tell him about the very real possibility that George Draper and Claudia Busacker were having an affair. And about their $1.5-million-dollar motive to get Ben Busacker out of the way. But she wanted to deliver that juicy little nugget in person.

"What else are you fussing over?" said Doogie.

"Look," said Suzanne, "just stop by for lunch today, okay? Then we can talk in person."

"I might be busy," Doogie hedged.

"Too busy for chicken potpie?" asked Suzanne. She knew it was one of his all-time favorites.

"You're a wicked woman, Suzanne. Plus you drive a hard bargain."

"See you around noon," said Suzanne.

WHEN Suzanne walked into the Cackleberry Club, it smelled of fried onions, fresh cracked pepper, and malty Assam tea.

"Heaven," said Suzanne as she kicked off her boots.

Petra turned from her stove and smiled. "Got my breakfast casserole baking away."

"Smells like it," said Suzanne.

Then the swinging door banged open, and Toni came barging in. "So how's Joey?" she asked.

Suzanne was taken aback. "How'd you hear about Joey?"

Petra posed with a hand on an ample hip. "Are you for real? Some moron's been tweeting about it. The news is all over the dang county!"

"You can't turn around and let loose a good fart these

days without somebody tweeting or twittering or whatever about it," said Toni.

"Toni!" said Petra. "Gross!"

"It's the darned truth," Toni muttered.

"So how *is* Joey?" asked Petra. She grabbed a basket of cocoa brown eggs and proceeded to crack them into a large aluminum bowl. "I take it you stopped at the hospital?"

"Joey seems to be recovering fairly well," said Suzanne. "Eating pancakes and watching SpongeBob."

"Sounds just like Junior," said Toni.

"It's weird how that assault on him came out of no-where," said Petra, picking up a wire whisk and attacking her eggs. "Do they know . . . was it kids? Some kind of gang activity?"

"Nooo," said Suzanne. Then she decided she'd better come clean. "I have a theory about that. In fact, I already pitched it to Doogie."

Petra's whisking suddenly ceased. "What are you talking about?"

Suzanne quickly shared her discovery about Joey and Colby trading jackets. And then carefully explained to her friends how she thought the killer had targeted Joey, thinking he was Colby.

"Shut the front door!" whooped Toni. "Are you serious?"

"Afraid so," said Suzanne.

"I don't like the sound of that one bit," said Petra.

"That's for sure," said Toni. "It means the killer's still in town."

"It means the killer was at the Fire and Ice Parade last night," said Suzanne.

"That's a chilling thought," said Petra. "I mean, I wasn't there, but you two were."

"How much credence is there to the rumor that Charlie Steiner might be the killer?" asked Toni. "I mean, he could have been the one who conked Joey on the head last night."

"Could have been," said Suzanne, recalling how angry and morose Steiner had been at Schmitt's Bar.

"I hate to ask this," said Petra, "but was Ducovny around last night?"

Suzanne and Toni glanced at each other.

"I didn't see him," said Suzanne.

"Me neither," said Toni.

"He didn't do it," said Suzanne.

But Petra wasn't convinced. "A couple of days ago, I would have put my hand on a Bible and swore he didn't do it. But yesterday, when he turned up at our back door . . . man, he sure looked angry."

"He didn't do it," Suzanne repeated, her words sharp and clipped. But deep in her heart she thought: *Dear lord, what if he did?*

THEY turned their full attention to breakfast then, shaking off their worries, getting the tables set and ready. Toni brewed pots of Kona green-bean blend, a buttery, rich coffee with hints of cinnamon and clove. Suzanne pulled out three Chinese teapots and measured out servings of raspberry tea, Darjeeling, and Moroccan mint.

"With fresh tea leaves available, why would anyone use tea bags?" she mused.

"The same reason people eat frozen pizza versus making fresh," said Toni. "They don't know any better."

"Or they don't have a good pizza dough recipe," said Suzanne.

Toni nodded. "Yeah, that's probably it."

When their breakfast customers came tumbling in out of the cold, Suzanne and Toni revved up their activity level, pouring coffee, taking orders, then hustling them in to Petra.

"Whoa," said Suzanne, when she popped into the kitchen. Petra had an enormous mound of shredded cheese piled up on the butcher block counter. "It's like the Big

Rock Candy Mountain, only made out of cheese. Think you got enough cheese?"

"I'm not sure you can ever throw in enough cheese with quiche," said Petra, and she was dead serious.

"But it's in the egg batter *and* the topping," said Suzanne.

Petra nodded. "Sometimes I even pile an extra inch or two on top of my quiche before I bake it."

"It's a good thing this cheese is low cal and low cholesterol," said Suzanne.

"Oh, absolutely," grinned Petra.

By nine o'clock there was one open table, a two top near the window. Which was when Reverend Yoder came stumping in.

"You just got our last table," Suzanne, smiling, told Reverend Yoder as she seated him. "Otherwise you'd be doing takeout." Reverend Yoder was the minister, fund-raiser, caretaker, and all around go-to guy at the Journey's End Church next door. He was tall and rail-thin, with silvered gray hair and an austere bearing that many people found intimidating. But beneath the hard-shell exterior of a religious aesthete beat the heart of a pussycat. He was always kind, understanding, and cordial. And even after surviving a terrible fire at his church, as well as being felled by a heart attack, Reverend Yoder remained hard at work, ministering to his small but dedicated flock.

Reverend Yoder bobbed his head at her. "Nice to see you, Mrs. Dietz."

"Suzanne," she said. "Call me Suzanne."

"As you wish," said Reverend Yoder. He paused. "I've been doing a kind of traveling ministry these last few days, so I just yesterday returned to town." He eyed her with interest. "But I understand you had some terrible trouble here." His furry brows wrinkled like twin caterpillars. "Ben Busacker?"

"Afraid so," said Suzanne.

"Do they know . . . er, does the sheriff have any suspects?" he asked.

"Suspects, yes. Arrests, no," said Suzanne. She tapped a finger on the table. "So you be careful, okay? Keep your doors locked until this *whoever* is apprehended." Reverend Yoder had a small office in the back of the church and lived in the small sitting room, kitchen, and bedroom downstairs.

"Don't like to lock the doors," said Reverend Yoder. "It sends an unfriendly message."

"Then keep a sharp eye out," said Suzanne. She touched her pen to her order pad. "What can I get for you?"

"Just oatmeal," said Reverend Yoder, "with a little fruit. Blueberries, if you've got them." He shifted in his chair. "You know we're planning to hold our dedication in a few weeks. We're pretty excited about how fast we were able to rebuild after the fire and how lovely the church looks. We even purchased a new statue, hand painted in Italy." He paused. "I know you're not part of our congregation, Suzanne, but you'd be most welcome."

"I'd love to come," said Suzanne. "If you'd like, the Cackleberry Club can even handle the refreshments. Do coffee and cookies, maybe even bake a nice sheet cake."

"You'd really do that for us?" Reverend Yoder seemed pleased and a little surprised.

"Of course I would," said Suzanne. "That's what neighbors are for."

"Thank you," said Reverend Yoder. "That means a lot to me."

CHAPTER 19

"IT'S time," Toni said, nudging Suzanne at the counter. "For the clue."

"Right! The big number three," said Suzanne. She reached up and turned the radio on low while Toni grabbed paper and pen. Then Paula Patterson's friendly voice chirped out the third treasure-hunt clue:

Look left, look right, and straight on in.
It's closer now, so you can win.
Keep steady with the hand you're dealt.
Just make sure it doesn't melt!

"I have no earthly idea what she's babbling about," blurted Toni. "All these clues ever talk about is snow and ice, which we have way too much of in these parts." She turned pleading eyes on Suzanne. "You're still gonna help me figure this out, aren't you?"

"I thought Junior was going to help you. I thought he did help you last night."

Toni gave a delicate sniff. "Please. There's a reason Junior's an auto mechanic and not first officer on a nuclear sub."

"That bad?" said Suzanne. She knew Toni probably had a valid point. Junior's idea of hunting for the treasure probably involved driving around town and challenging people to drag races while he cooked a pot roast.

"Maybe we could study the clues and kind of poke around tonight?" Toni said hopefully. "After the play?"

"Oh my goodness," said Suzanne. "Tonight's the play. We've been so busy I almost forgot."

"*Titanic*," said Toni, who was really looking forward to it. "But do you think we could still look afterward?"

"I think we could probably do that," said Suzanne.

A few customers lingered in the café while Petra hummed along to the radio in the kitchen. This was the time of day Suzanne liked to savor. The forty or fifty minutes between the end of breakfast service and the start of lunch. Everything slowed to a nice, leisurely pace, and she could sip a cup of tea or pop into the Book Nook and stretch her creative muscles by making some kind of fun arrangement. They'd just gotten in some new books on finances, real estate, and the stock market, so maybe she could do something with her old crank adding machine and a few rolled up copies of the *Wall Street Journal.* Lord knows, money, or lack of it, seemed to be on everyone's brain these days.

"Petra?" Suzanne called out. The humming in the kitchen suddenly stopped. "What's our soup today?"

"Well, it started out as chicken noodle," Petra called back, "but I had leftover cheese, so I tossed it in . . . um, let's just call it chicken cheese soup?"

"Got it," said Suzanne. Cheesy chicken soup. If you could even find a few chunks of chicken in Petra's swirling magma of cheese.

Suzanne added chicken potpie, turkey and swiss cheese sandwich, Monte Cristo sandwich, and blond brownies to her menu. Just as she finished printing it all out on her blackboard in colored chalk, her eye caught a flash of chrome out the front window. Doogie's tan-colored cruiser had just rolled into their parking lot.

"How ready are those chicken potpies?" she called.

"Five more minutes," said Petra, peering out the pass-through. "Why?"

"I'm gonna need one," she said. "Pronto."

"Oh," said Petra. "For the sheriff?"

"That's right. We're going to have ourselves a little confab."

"Good luck," said Toni, as the door whooshed open and Sheriff Doogie stomped in. With typical noisy bluster, he pulled off his giant-size mitts, peeled off his parka, and whooped out *hellos* to everyone. His khaki shirt had bunched around his belly, looking untucked and unkempt, but Doogie didn't seemed to mind. Or care.

"Come on over here," Suzanne said, waggling her fingers at him. "Sit at the counter so we can talk while I work."

"Or you can work while I talk," guffawed Doogie.

"Whatever," said Suzanne. She reached into the pie saver and pulled out a sticky roll covered with thick caramel frosting and a scatter of pecans. "Lunch isn't quite ready, so how about a little appeteaser?" She slid the roll onto a plate and held it up like she was about to train a circus bear.

"Sure thing," said Doogie. "And coffee if you got it."

Suzanne set the roll in front of Doogie, then splashed coffee into a ceramic mug. "Have you thought about what we talked about?" she asked.

Doogie bit into his sticky roll and chewed thoughtfully. "You had a good insight," he said, "about Joey being mistaken for Colby. I'll admit that."

Suzanne's heart leapt. Now they were getting somewhere!

"Is there any word yet on Colby?" she asked.

Doogie continued to chew. "Nope. If he's still in the area, he sure as heck found himself a bolt hole to hide in. Because we've been actively looking. I even sent two deputies over to the Crossroads Mall in Jessup. They poked around, asked questions, even went into a couple of those crazy stores that the kids hang out in. Whadya call 'em—

head shops? But no Colby. And no kid that fit his description either."

"You're going to continue searching for him, aren't you?" asked Suzanne.

Doogie shifted uncomfortably. "How much can we really look? I mean, my department's got limited resources. You know that."

"But Colby could be the key to everything!" said Suzanne. "Plus, he's a runaway."

"I don't have a missing person's report on file," said Doogie. When Suzanne started to interrupt, he said, "You gotta look at it from my perspective. We got no last name, no background information, no worried parents making inquiries. So I'm flyin' blind here, Suzanne."

"I hear you."

"And don't forget, I still got Mayor Mobley badgering me like a duck on a beetle to solve Busacker's murder. And that wackadoodle banker guy Ed Rapson is backing him up. They say they can't bring in a new bank president until this murder is solved. They say nobody wants to take the place of a murder victim!"

"I suppose they've got a point," said Suzanne.

"So that just puts more pressure on my department," said Doogie.

Suzanne thought for a moment. "Have you heard anything more about Lester Drummond getting the bank presidency? *He* wouldn't mind sitting in the office of a dead guy."

"He's a cold-hearted son of a gun," Doogie agreed. "But Drummond surely doesn't seem like the proper candidate for the job." Doogie whisked a scatter of crumbs off the front of his shirt. "It'd be like he was transitioning from bail bonds to treasury bonds."

"Hey, Doogie," said Toni, as she swung by with a stack of dishes. "What do you know about the new warden out at the prison? I hear they call him Weasel Face."

"Who calls him that?" asked Suzanne. "The prisoners?"

Doogie chuckled. "Actually, pretty much everybody at city hall is calling him that."

"Isn't it wonderful," said Suzanne, "how Warden Fiedler has established such a high standard of trust and respect so early on. That there's so much collegiality."

"Got a chicken potpie here!" called Petra.

Suzanne stepped to the pass-through and grabbed it. She set it, all golden and steaming hot in front of Doogie. Then she placed a checkered napkin, knife and fork, and glass of ice water next to it.

Doogie's eyes lit up when he saw the potpie. "Doesn't that look good!" He grabbed his fork, ready to dig in.

"Poke it first," called Petra, "and let the steam out. Otherwise your tongue and brains will explode."

"Thanks for the warning," called Doogie, as he prodded it with great anticipation.

Suzanne edged closer to Doogie and lowered her voice. "I've got something else for you, but you have to keep it under your hat."

Doogie gave her a flat-eyed stare. "Okay." He took an enormous bite, juggled it around inside his mouth, then flapped a pudgy hand in front of his blistered lips. "Good," he said. What he really meant was "hot."

"I'm pretty sure Claudia Busacker is having an affair with George Draper," said Suzanne.

Doogie almost had his water glass up to his mouth. Upon hearing Suzanne's words, his hand wavered and he sloshed a few drops down the front of his shirt. He hastily set his glass down and hissed, "The heck you say! The crepe hanger?"

Suzanne nodded. Almost laughed. "The funeral director, yes."

"How do you know this?" asked Doogie. "From one of your stitchy bitchy groups or romance reader clubs?"

"Ham Wick heavily implied it," she told him, "when I ran into him at the coronation last night."

"But he didn't say it was the gospel truth, did he?" said Doogie.

"What Wick said was that Claudia and Ben had a very unhappy marriage, and that she was seeing someone else on the sly."

"So how did you come to the conclusion she was seeing George Draper?" asked Doogie.

"I kind of put two and two together," said Suzanne. "From watching the two of them . . . um, interact."

"Yeah?" Doogie, almost dazed, was staring at her.

"It's a guess," Suzanne admitted. *Or maybe even a psychic vision.* "But I'm ninety-nine percent sure that I'm right."

Doogie squinted at her. "That high?"

"Okay, maybe ninety percent," said Suzanne. "But you saw them together at Busacker's funeral. That wasn't just decorum, that was . . . love." *Or lust.*

"Could have fooled me," said Doogie, "but I'm listening. Granted, I'm still skeptical, since most of this seems to be based on female intuition, which is a funny kind of instinct that tells a woman she's right even when she's not."

"No," said Suzanne. "I'm pretty sure their relationship is fact."

Doogie dug into his potpie again. "At best it's a hunch." He chewed methodically. "And you can't run an investigation on hunches."

Suzanne put her elbows on the counter and leaned forward even more. "Then how about this, cowboy . . ."

Doogie stopped chewing.

"Claudia had a one-point-five-million-dollar insurance policy on her husband. Which she's now poised to collect—and spend in any frivolous and disgusting manner she sees fit."

Doogie sat in silence, digesting this new information along with his potpie.

"So . . . you still think it's a crazy hunch?" Suzanne asked.

"Maybe not," Doogie said slowly. "Maybe not."

* * *

PETRA was flipping Monte Cristo sandwiches on the grill and Toni was plopping radishes and carrot sticks on white luncheon plates when Suzanne swung into the kitchen.

"I got something to run by you guys," she said. Doogie had finished his lunch and left, and the café was starting to fill up. She knew she had to hurry.

"What's up?" said Toni. "You got some juicy gossip for us?"

"Yes," said Suzanne.

Petra turned around and frowned. "Suzanne." Her voice carried a warning.

"Hear me out," said Suzanne. She quickly told them about the Claudia Busacker–George Draper affair.

"That's what you were whispering about with Doogie?" said Toni. "That's crazy interesting!"

"No, it's not," said Petra. "It's shameful innuendo."

"Wait a minute," said Toni. She cocked her head, as if deep in thought. "Suzanne, are you telling us that Claudia might have had a motive for wanting her husband dead? That maybe she hired some kind of . . . hit man?"

"Really," said Suzanne, "I suppose anything's possible."

"Suzanne," said Petra, gesturing with a wooden spoon. "You're the one who's always harping about motive. People don't generally kill indiscriminately, unless they're crazies like Charles Manson . . ."

"Or Hannibal Lecter," put in Toni.

"Plus there's no hard evidence and certainly no possible motive," continued Petra. "So let's just let it go."

Suzanne gazed at Petra, ready to drop her bombshell. "What I'm about to tell you ladies cannot go beyond the boundaries of this humble kitchen," she said.

"What? What is it?" cried Toni, eager for more.

"Claudia stands to inherit one-point-five-million dollars from her husband's death," said Suzanne.

Petra gasped, clapped a hand to her chest, and said, "What?"

"Holy bazooka!" said Toni. "Where's that payout coming from?"

"A big, fat life insurance policy," said Suzanne.

"Whoa," said Toni. "One-point-five-million dollars is a humongous pile of greenbacks!"

"This is for real?" said Petra. "You wouldn't just make this up?"

"Serious *dinero!*" said Toni.

"It's for real," said Suzanne. "Which makes this information kind of a game changer."

"The plot thickens," said Toni.

"Or my waistline," said Petra, looking unhappy. "Whichever comes first."

SUZANNE was at odds and ends. She was worried about Colby, musing about Claudia, and letting everyone else— Ducovny, Steiner, Ed Rapson, George Draper, and Lester Drummond—enjoy a walk-on roll in her roiling, overtaxed brain. Nothing made sense, nothing seemed to connect. And yet, there'd been a murder and an aggravated assault. So where did this all lead? How did it connect? And was the Claudia–George Draper affair just too perfect? Or was the couple's motive perfectly obvious?

Even the dead Busacker lurched through her thoughts, as if prodding her to cough up an answer!

Finally, Suzanne escaped to a small space next to the cooler, where she'd been thinking about putting in her Shabby Chic Boutique. She wanted to stock vintage items or fun things that had been distressed to *appear* vintage, all with a soft, minimalist, feminine feel.

One crafty lady had already brought in a few items to sell on consignment. *Hmm.* Suzanne stood poised for a moment, like a ballet dancer ready to execute an arabesque, then hurried into her office and pulled out a box from beneath her desk.

There was a lamp that had been painted eggshell white and trimmed with a pink fabric shade. Cute. And a spoon bracelet and a pillow stenciled with a French crown. Also very saleable. And here was a picture of Marie Antoinette in a vintage blue curlicue frame.

Suzanne gazed at Marie, and thought, *Poor lady lost her head, too. Just like Busacker.* Which sent her mind reeling back to the events of this past week. And last night . . . with Joey. And how he'd switched jackets.

I wonder if . . .

Suzanne stopped right there and quickly dialed Joey's house. She made polite chitchat with his mom for a few minutes, then finally got Joey on the line.

"How are you feeling?" asked Suzanne.

"Pretty good," said Joey. "Mom just made my favorite lunch, sloppy joes."

"Joey," said Suzanne, "do me a favor. Look in the pockets of that jacket Colby gave you, okay? See if there's anything in there."

There was a moment of silence. Then Joey said, "Huh?"

"Just do it, honey, okay? I need to know if there's anything in there."

"Okay."

There was the *clunk* of the phone being set down, then Suzanne listened to dead air for thirty seconds. Finally, Joey came back on the line.

"I dug through all the pockets and pretty much came up empty," said Joey.

"There was nothing at all?"

"Just a piece of gum, kinda smells like spearmint or something, and a ticket stub for a concert."

"What's it say on it?"

"The gum?"

"No, the ticket stub."

"Uh . . . Fire Spokes," said Joey.

"That's a group, right?"

"Yeah. Slammin' sound. I got most of their stuff on my iPod."

"What's the venue?" asked Suzanne.

"The what?"

"The place where the concert was held."

"Um . . . wait a minute." More silence, then Joey came back again. "It says First Avenue. In Minneapolis."

"Anything else?"

"Not really."

Suzanne thought about this small shred of evidence. Colby had attended a concert at First Avenue in Minneapolis and had claimed that he'd once worked in a Minneapolis restaurant. So is that where he was from? Maybe. Possibly.

"Okay, Joey, take care," said Suzanne. "And thanks for your help."

"Bye," said Joey.

The minute the line disconnected, Suzanne punched in Doogie's number. She waited while her call was transferred; then he came on the line.

"Doogie," she said quickly into the phone, "get in touch with the Minneapolis police. See if they have a missing kid that matches Colby's description."

"What's this all about?" asked Doogie.

Suzanne hastily told him about the ticket stub in the pocket of the Raiders jacket.

"Minneapolis, huh?" said Doogie.

"Look, it's worth a shot," said Suzanne.

"Maybe," said Doogie, and promptly hung up.

Suzanne gazed at the wall across from her desk where photos, paintings, and some memorabilia were hung. Petra had stenciled a lovely photo of a dark green woods onto raw canvas and then had embroidered the words *The best way out is always through*. It was a quote from Robert Frost.

"I wonder," said Suzanne, "how we'll all make it through?"

CHAPTER 20

"THE thing for us to do now," said Toni, "is sit back, relax, and enjoy the show."

"The play's the thing, huh?" said Suzanne.

Suzanne and Toni were shoehorned into straight-backed wooden seats in the tenth row of the cavernous high school auditorium. All around them, people coughed, hiccupped, talked in excited whispers, and jiggled in their seats, anxious to see the stage presentation of *Titanic* put on by the Community Players, the local troupe dedicated to the performing arts. If you could call *Titanic* and last year's presentation of *The Producers* actual art, that is.

A red velvet curtain hung across the stage, creating an air of drama and mystery as more people filed in, rattling paper programs and glancing about.

"Nothing like live theater," said Toni, glancing around. "It's always thrilling. You never know when a hunk of scenery will topple over or somebody will miss their cue."

"To say nothing of forgetting their lines," said Suzanne, as she rifled through her bag for some cinnamon-flavored mints, then popped one in her mouth.

"Jeez Louise," said Toni, scanning her program. "Everybody and his brother has a bit part in this thing. Lookit." She tapped a finger against the cast list. "I never knew Lester Drummond was into acting. And not just any role, either. He's playing the ship's captain."

"It's tailor-made for him," said Suzanne. "Playing another loser."

"Huh," said Toni, still studying her program. "Carmen's in this, too. It's like old home week."

"What role is she playing?" asked Suzanne.

Toni studied her program. "I think she plays the witchy rich woman who's trying to marry off her daughter."

"Whoever did the casting," said Suzanne, "was really quite perceptive."

"Too bad Sam couldn't make it tonight," said Toni.

"He's working a shift at the hospital."

"Still," said Toni, folding her program, "it's nice to do girlfriend stuff."

A moment later, the house lights dimmed.

"This is so exciting!" whispered Toni.

The red velvet curtains flew open to reveal the large wooden prow of the ill-fated *Titanic*, as it sat docked and ready for its maiden voyage. Then the characters appeared and the story kicked into high gear.

For the next hour and a half, the entire audience was held rapt by impressive set changes, lots of action, dialogue that was sharp and crisp, and haunting music that seemed to foreshadow the end.

Suzanne kept thinking how wild it was to see Lester Drummond stride across the stage with his commanding, muscular presence and deliver his lines with authority. How long had he nursed these acting ambitions, she wondered, while he was serving as the head of a prison?

Carmen Copeland was also a natural onstage and seemed to bask in the limelight of her role. Her broad arm motions, haughty demeanor, and head tosses made her convincing as a sort of villainess.

Carmen was one lady who never suffered from stage fright, Suzanne decided. She had her acting down pat. In fact, her character seemed very much in keeping with Carmen's real-life persona!

Missy Langston was also cute and believable in her role, looking vulnerable and frightened as the iceberg loomed and shards of real ice were sent spilling and clattering across the stage.

And then, the heartbreaking ending rushed to a conclusion. Lifeboats—really two Lund fishing boats—were yanked across the stage. Women wept, survivors screamed, and an enormous cardboard cutout of the *Titanic* dipped its prow and seemed to disappear forever as stage lights slowly winked out.

When the final curtain fell and the house lights came up, the entire audience jumped to its feet, applauding and cheering enthusiastically.

Toni was ecstatic. "I loved every minute! I mean, they really pulled it off!"

"Really quite amazing," Suzanne agreed.

"And so authentic," said Toni, "especially when the people were scrabbling around in lifeboats and everything, biting each other's heads off." She gripped Suzanne's arm. "Why don't we go backstage and congratulate everyone just like they do at those big Broadway openings? Can we, huh? I've always wanted to do that!"

"And then we'll have drinks at Sardi's," said Suzanne. "Sure. Why not?"

THEY wove their way through throngs of people and eased into the warren of rooms behind the stage. Painted scenery was stacked everywhere—flats depicting elegant staterooms, steerage accommodations, a fancy dining room, and a ship's corridor. Overhead, a network of ropes and pulleys looked like an intricate spider's web as more sets hung in the darkness far above their heads.

The cast and crew were whooping it up in a large, mirrored dressing room. A crush of well-wishers swirled around them, some bearing small bouquets of red roses wrapped in crinkly paper.

"Fabulous job!" the director, a retired school teacher, was telling the cast.

"Yes, bravo to you all!" said the casting director, who was also Kindred's postmaster. "Your performance was a triumph!"

With several bottles of champagne already uncorked, people poured bubbly and passed drinks around, clinking glasses, toasting, and hugging each other as they recalled how smoothly the performance had gone and how receptive their audience had been.

"It wasn't flawless," Suzanne heard one actor say. "I flubbed a line in act two and had to ad lib to cover it up."

"We barely noticed!" exclaimed a gushing family member.

Just as Suzanne pushed into the room to look for Missy and Carmen, she overheard Lester Drummond's blustery voice from down the hall. His back was turned to her as he addressed several of his fellow cast members.

"From the seat of power at the prison to the executive office at our bank," Drummond said, in what seemed to be a rush of adrenaline-fueled words. "Imagine that."

"Just goes to show, Lester," responded one of his listeners, a man who'd played his second mate in the play. "You never know what's around the next turn."

"I always make my own luck," Drummond bragged. "I play my cards right and leave nothing to chance."

Startled, Suzanne turned away, hoping Drummond wouldn't catch sight of her. She sucked in a breath and tried not to be overly obvious that she'd been eavesdropping.

She was thinking: *The play ended five minutes ago, and Drummond is already back to beating his drum about that bank job.*

Did this mean Ed Rapson had finally made up his mind and given Drummond the good news? Or was this all conjecture on Drummond's part? All brash ego and over-the-top chutzpah?

"What a blowhard," Toni sneered. She'd caught an earful of Drummond's braggadocio, too.

"Maybe he really does have the job all sewn up," Suzanne said in a low voice.

"I hope not," said Toni. She gazed at Drummond with a look that was part fear and part fascination, the kind of look one might accord a poisonous reptile.

Suzanne tugged at Toni's sleeve. "Let's get out of here. Go find Missy or something."

They eased down a narrow corridor and into a room filled with racks of costumes.

"Hey, Missy!" Suzanne called, when she spotted her friend. Missy had just shrugged out of a long jumper and cape.

"You came!" Missy squealed, as she rushed over to hug Suzanne and Toni.

"You were great," Toni told her. "Brilliant. Far better than Carmen."

"You think?" said Missy, pleased. "But, of course, I had a much smaller role."

"Why is that?" asked Suzanne. "Because Toni's right, you were terrific up there."

"Probably because I'm working all the time," said Missy. "When we were first cast for the roles, I told Mr. Murray I didn't have a lot of spare time for rehearsals."

Every evening, when Suzanne drove past Alchemy, the lights were on. And she was pretty sure it wasn't Carmen who was logging those long hours. "Carmen's keeping you busy," she said.

Missy nodded, and for the first time her blue eyes looked tired and her narrow shoulders sagged. "You have no idea."

"Maybe working at Alchemy isn't the best job for you?" said Suzanne.

"No, it's not," said Missy, "but at the same time, I'm learning tons about fashion and styling. And, of course, how to run a retail operation."

"Maybe you'll have your own boutique some day," proposed Toni.

"Don't I wish," said Missy. "But until that magical moment . . ."

"Business as usual," said Suzanne. She knew it wasn't easy to step off the merry-go-round and work for yourself. You had to develop a unique concept, write a business plan, garner financing, and then make it all happen. No, it was darned near impossible. And even if you did pull it off, you had to have an unshakeable vision.

"Hey," said Missy, "I'm just glad you guys liked the play."

"Liked it?" said Toni. "We loved it!"

SUZANNE and Toni hung around for another ten minutes, congratulating the various players.

"You want to say hi to Ham Wick over there?" asked Toni. "Tell him what a great cabin steward he made?"

"Pass," said Suzanne. Instead, they enjoyed another glass of champagne and made chitchat with Laura Benchley, editor of the *Bugle,* and a couple other friends.

"This stuff is giving me the burps," said Toni, smacking a hand against her chest. "Too much carbonation."

"We should take off anyway," said Suzanne. The celebration was winding down. Without their makeup, the actors just looked tired from their workout onstage and seemed ready to head home.

"Okeydoke," said Toni, as they stepped out into the hall and looked around.

"Maybe we should go out the back door," Suzanne suggested. "Since we're parked out that way."

"Sure," said Toni, as they started down the corridor. "If we can get through. There's so many sets and props and things."

They inched around a dining table that was lying on its side, and hooked a left. It was darker back here and quieter, too.

"Spooky," said Toni.

"Just the back of the theatre," said Suzanne. "Nothing to worry about."

But as they eased past a tea cart, they heard a strange creaking sound.

"What's that?" asked Toni, looking nervous.

"Just the theater settling for the night," said Suzanne. "It's—"

Toni glanced up. "Ahhh!" she screamed. Grabbing Suzanne's arm, she pulled her back a step as she cried, "Watch out!"

There was an ear-splitting crack and a sudden rush of air from above.

"Holy bushwhackers!" cried Toni as a huge piece of scenery crashed down in front of them, shaking the floor and missing them by mere inches.

Frozen in place and clutching each other for dear life, Suzanne and Toni stared in wonderment at the hunk of fiberglass. It was crystal clear with jagged teeth all around—obviously one of the pieces that had served as an iceberg in the play!

"Where did that come from?" asked Suzanne, tilting her head back and staring up into the rigging.

"I don't know," said Toni, "but it almost clobbered us! We were almost killed by an iceberg! Two more victims of the *Titanic*!"

Suzanne continued to stare—and listen. "Anybody up there?" she called.

"Maybe a wire just worked loose," said Toni.

And maybe not, thought Suzanne. Maybe somebody who was in the play or had attended the play had engineered this little disaster? Maybe someone had followed them back here? Could have happened that way. After Busacker's murder and the attack on Joey, Suzanne was wildly suspicious about anything out of the ordinary.

Toni reached a hand out and touched the faux iceberg. "You don't think somebody did this on purpose, do you?"

"I'm not sure what to think," said Suzanne. "But from now on, let's be a whole lot more careful."

"Okay," said Toni, bobbing her head wildly. "For sure."

Carefully, quietly, they eased their way to the back door and headed for Suzanne's car.

As they buckled into their seatbelts, Suzanne promised Toni a quick and safe ride home. But as they cruised down Magnolia Lane, Toni's favorite country-western station playing "You're Gonna Miss This" by Trace Adkins and the heater spewing warm air, they started to relax.

And Toni was suddenly feeling mischievous. "Do you really believe Claudia Busacker and George Draper are having an affair?" she asked.

"I think so," said Suzanne, turning down the heater a bit. Between the raging heater and the snow melting off their woolen mittens, her car was beginning to smell like a wet dog.

"Do you think they're together right now?" asked Toni. "You know, having a little Friday-night delight?"

"No idea," said Suzanne. She was suddenly thinking that Petra had the right idea: don't spread gossip and innuendo.

But Toni wouldn't let it go. "Maybe we should drive by Claudia's house."

Suzanne's hand jerked hard on the steering wheel. "Right now?"

"Sure," said Toni. "What better way to set a rumor to rest?"

"It's awfully late," said Suzanne. But, truth be told, she was suddenly curious, too.

"It's not like we're gonna ring the doorbell and run away like a bunch of hobgoblins," said Toni. "We'll just do a little quiet reconnaissance. See what we can see."

"Well . . . I suppose," said Suzanne. She slowed at the intersection of Milton and Fremont, and turned left. Into the part of town where the larger, grander homes were situated.

Every town has a neighborhood like this, Suzanne thought to herself. A part where those-that-have happily reside, and the have-nots stay away in a kind of unwritten agreement. A neighborhood where bank presidents, company owners, and fat-cat politicos lived and hobnobbed among themselves.

They drove past a block of rather stately mansions, then turned into the cul-de-sac where Ben Busacker had lived. Where Claudia still lived.

"That's it," said Toni. "Right there."

Suzanne let the car coast to a stop as they stared at a large white clapboard home fronted with two sets of white columns. Even in winter it was showy and imperious-looking, with a four-car garage and a snow-covered hedge that stretched around to the back of the yard.

"Big place," said Toni. She was acutely aware that she worked her butt off every day and still lived in a one-bedroom apartment.

"Probably not paid for," said Suzanne. "Claudia probably has very little equity in that house. Most of it's owned by the bank."

"Yeah," said Toni, "her husband's bank." She stared out the frosted car window and said, "Well, we know somebody's home." Lights shone brightly from almost every window on the first floor.

"But no car parked in front."

"It wouldn't be," said Toni. "If Claudia and Draper are having an affair, he probably pulled his car into the garage."

"You think?" said Suzanne.

Toni nodded. "That's how they do it on the soap operas. That's how Deidre and Troy do it on *Days of Love.*"

"But this is *real* life," said Suzanne. *And real stupid, too, if we get caught.*

"Let's just take a peek in one of the first-floor windows," suggested Toni.

"What?" squawked Suzanne.

"Don't go freaking out on me," said Toni. "Think of it as

investigating. That's what you've been doing all this week, isn't it?" She cocked a knowing eye.

She's got me there, thought Suzanne. "But if we get caught . . ."

Toni flapped a hand. "Then we'll make up some humpus-bumpus story about selling magazines or Mary Jane makeup."

Suzanne sat there, wanting to take a look, feeling a little chicken.

"Don't worry," said Toni, easing open the car door, "we'll make it real quick."

CHAPTER 21

AGAINST her better judgment, Suzanne climbed out of her car and followed in Toni's footsteps. Ducking down and keeping to the shadows in the side yard, the two friends slowly crunched through the snow, angling their way toward the house. Suzanne knew if they got caught now, she'd really have to do some fancy tap dancing. *My dog ran away.* Or *I think I dropped an earring.* Yeah, right.

Ten steps from Claudia's house, they had a partial view through a bow window into what was either a den or family room.

"Careful," Suzanne whispered. "Not too close."

So, of course, Toni tiptoed closer. And Suzanne cautiously followed.

Now Suzanne could see the tops of bookcases and paintings on the wall. Den, she decided. Or library. Whatever. Claudia had nice things, fine things. Things that cost a good deal of money.

Just ahead, Toni slipped through a bush that was dotted with little red berries and touched a mittened hand to the windowsill. She rose up on tiptoes, cocked her head, and whispered, "Holy cow."

Curiosity burning like a red-hot poker, Suzanne slipped closer, too. She pressed up toward the window and peered in.

They were there, all right. Sprawled across Claudia's prim, white cabriole-style sofa. Claudia and George Draper, locked in a passionate embrace.

"Hot diggity dog!" Toni whispered. "Beneath that brittle exterior is a red hot tamale!"

Amid shocked but muffled giggles, they beat a hasty retreat back to the safety of their car. When they were a block away, Toni said, "We should tell Doogie!"

"Tell him what?" said Suzanne. She was still slightly out of breath and amazed at what she'd seen. "That the local funeral director is getting more action than he is? Besides, I already mentioned this possible scenario to him this morning."

"But now it's a real scenario. As in real hot."

"Granted that it's weird," said Suzanne, "but there's no law against it." *Infidelity doesn't count if the husband is dead, right?*

"The thing that makes this so creepy," said Toni, "is that Busacker was killed only a few days ago—and now Claudia's in the arms of another man. It makes me think Claudia *wanted* Ben dead!"

Suzanne was quiet for a moment. "Or maybe it's Draper we have to worry about. Maybe George Draper engineered the whole darn thing."

"So he could get Claudia as well as the money?" said Toni. "Wow. Wouldn't that be a barrel full of crazy!"

ONCE again, Suzanne pointed her car in the direction of Toni's apartment, but Toni had another burning issue on her mind.

"You said we were going to hunt for the treasure tonight," said Toni. She was slightly pleading, half pouting.

"It's after ten," said Suzanne. "Way past my bedtime."

"The shank of the evening," said Toni. "Besides, where's your sense of adventure? When we were younger, we didn't even go out until nine o'clock."

"And we listened to Madonna and Devo," said Suzanne. "And wore shoulder pads the size of pillows. Hey, things changed. We got a little older."

"I'll split it with you," said Toni.

Suzanne eased off on the gas. "The reward? I wouldn't expect you to do that." Then she added, "Finding the treasure medallion means that much to you?"

Toni nodded. "It does."

"Okay," said Suzanne. "Let's give it half an hour."

"Hot dang!" said Toni. She was suddenly rifling through her purse, digging out the clues.

"Let's look at the most recent one," said Suzanne, "and try to figure out the basic gist."

"Look left and right," Toni mumbled, "yadda yadda steady hand, make sure it doesn't melt." Toni took a breath. "Every clue so far has pointed to something frozen, which is barely any help at all."

"The clues could be referencing Fish Lake," said Suzanne, "where they're holding the ice-fishing tournament tomorrow."

"Maybe," said Toni, but she didn't seem convinced.

"Or just referring to the town's snowbanks and frozen streets?"

"Which narrows it down to nothing," said Toni.

Suzanne thought some more. "What about Catawba Creek?" Catawba Creek was the little stream that meandered through the west end of Kindred. In summer it was a lovely stream for trout fishing and bumping along on inner tubes. In winter, people who lived along the banks of the creek swept it clear of snow for the purpose of ice skating. Thus, intrepid skaters could coast along for several picturesque and uninterrupted miles.

"You think the treasure medallion could be hidden in the ice?" said Toni. "But where?"

"If I had to take a wild guess on where to look," said Suzanne, "I'd search for it close to Creekside Park. It's where the creek widens out and kids play hockey and such. Plus, there's a little parking lot and picnic tables."

"You think we should start there?" asked Toni.

"It's as good a place as any," said Suzanne.

They cut over to Ivy Lane and hit Catawba Parkway, the narrow street that wandered along the creek.

"Park's just ahead," said Toni. She was all whipped up, ready for adventure.

"Nobody here," said Suzanne as she angled into a parking spot. A single streetlight cast a yellow glow on the parking lot. But out on the ice it was pitch-black.

"This is good," said Toni. "The fact that nobody's here means nobody's figured this out yet." She cocked an index finger and tapped the side of her head. "Except us smarties."

They bundled up again, pulling on scarves and mittens, and hopped out of the car. Suzanne went around to her trunk and dug out two flashlights.

"You got flares, too?" said Toni.

Suzanne shut the lid. "It's a treasure hunt, not an accident zone."

Toni turned on her flashlight and let the beam dance across a grove of dark, gnarled oak trees. "This feels right," she muttered to herself. "It's close to town, but lonely. And everything's nice and frozen."

"If I was one of the treasure-hunt instigators," said Suzanne, "I'd hide the medallion in the middle of the stream, maybe even between those hockey nets."

Toni swept her flashlight toward the ice. "Dug into the ice?"

"Maybe embedded in the ice," said Suzanne. "Level with it."

"So it's still smooth, and you might even skate right over it," said Toni, liking the idea.

"It's a thought," said Suzanne. "A hunch."

"A good one," enthused Toni, as she crunched down the embankment and set foot on the ice.

"Slippery," said Suzanne, following her. "Be careful. We don't want any broken bones."

But Toni was already half shuffling, half running across the ice toward one of the hockey nets. When she was a few feet from it, she gave a good, hard kick and slid her way into it.

"Goal!" she cried, raising both hands in the air.

But Suzanne was focused on something else. She was halfway across the ice when she saw a small shadow ghost through the birch trees on the other side of the creek. *What was that?*

Then the shadow moved again, and Suzanne saw two bright eyes. *Coyote?*

It was a coyote. A small, shaggy animal with a wary, rugged appearance.

Suzanne's heart immediately went out to the poor creature. It looked cold and alone and probably hungry. Improbably, she felt she should somehow find it some food. Feed the scrawny little thing before it starved to death.

Where was its pack? she wondered. Or was it lost? Or, worse yet, expelled by a rival?

Toni had seen the coyote, too, and was watching it a little nervously.

Then the coyote lifted its head and tipped up its muzzle delicately, as if sipping some new scent that had drifted along on the wind. Suddenly, the coyote bunched its furry body and spun. There was a flash of tail, and then the animal was gone, melting back into the shadows.

"What do you think . . . ?" Toni began, just as the high-pitched whine of a motor sounded nearby.

Now what? Suzanne wondered. And before that thought had completely formed in her brain, a snowmobile suddenly came roaring straight at her from out of the darkness!

"Watch out!" cried Toni, ducking behind the hockey net.

But Suzanne was caught out in the middle of the frozen stream, and the rider was aiming directly at her, the snowmobile's yellow headlight bobbing and throbbing! The rider was garbed in black gear and a helmet with a smoked face mask. A demon driver who intended to harm her!

Thirty feet, twenty feet, ten feet—the machine was closing on her in mere seconds. No time to think, barely time to act!

Suzanne waited until she was positive the snowmobile wasn't going to change direction before she leapt sideways. A crazy, bounding leap of faith that sent her flying through the air until she landed hard on her right hip.

"Watch out!" Toni screamed, "he's coming back!"

Scrambling to her feet, trying to gain some traction, Suzanne fought to shuttle across the open ice and reach the safety of the hockey net.

But she wasn't going to make it in time. The snowmobile, with its menacing high-pitched drone, had cut a sharp turn and was roaring back at her!

Suzanne continued her mad, awkward shuffle toward the net.

"Come on, come on!" cried Toni. She was gesturing frantically. "You can do it!"

But Suzanne just couldn't! She turned to face her aggressor, balancing on the balls of her feet, knowing she'd have to launch herself out of his deadly path once again.

Just as the snowmobile was within twenty feet of her, it slowed slightly.

Trying to fix his aim? Suzanne wondered. Coming in for the kill?

The snowmobile whined and revved and moved in closer, again aiming its black, shiny, wasp-shaped nose directly at her. But this time Suzanne waited an extra beat. And just before she leapt out of its way, she hurled her flashlight directly at it.

Whipping end over end, splashing little bits of light, the flashlight crashed directly into the snowmobile's windshield. Fragments of hard plastic flew everywhere, and the rider, obviously surprised, swerved hard.

"Take that!" Suzanne screamed. Her blood was up, and she was angrier than she'd ever been. She gnashed her teeth like a wild woman and shrieked again, ready to chase after her aggressor and run him down. Then a steady hand on her arm tugged her back to reality.

"Easy, easy," said Toni. "He's gone. That crazy person is gone."

Suzanne stared at the retreating light, lips curled. "If he comes back!" she threatened, waving a fist. "If he comes back . . ."

"Down girl," said Toni as she tightened her grip on Suzanne and slowly led her back across the ice toward the parking lot.

"I'll kill him!" Suzanne vowed. "I will. I surely will."

"You know," said Toni, as they clambered up the frozen creek bank, "maybe I should drive."

Toni did drive, and Suzanne muttered angrily all the way to Toni's apartment. When she pulled up, Toni bounced her hands nervously against the steering wheel, and said, "I've never seen you lose it quite like that."

"Sorry," said Suzanne, puckering her brow. "I shouldn't have . . ."

"No, no," interrupted Toni, "you had every right to be angry. That guy tried to run you down!" She shook her head. "I'm just sorry you didn't knock his helmet completely off his fool head. That was good thinking, pitching your flashlight at him."

"Shattered his windshield," said Suzanne.

"With a cracked windshield like that, it might be easier to track him down."

"Maybe," said Suzanne. "But I don't want to think about that right now, okay?"

Toni scrunched over and gave Suzanne a big bear hug. "Okay." Then she wiggled back to the driver's side and opened the door. "You gonna be all right? You're gonna go right home?"

"Of course."

But Suzanne didn't go right home. She couldn't. She was still too revved up. On a whim, she drove to Ducovny's farm. The yard light was on, spilling its faint glow across the snow, outlining the barn and a couple of sheds. But no lights glowed from within the house.

They were in bed, Suzanne decided. Of course, there was another possibility: they weren't home yet.

Getting out of her car, she walked up to the barn door. Sliding the door open, Suzanne walked down a row of stalls. It was dark inside the barn, but a faint glow from the yard light shone through the low windows.

Good enough. Just enough.

Mocha Gent, her horse, was attuned to her scent or her footsteps or maybe he was just animal psychic. Because he let out a low whinny as she approached and pressed his chest up against the stall door.

"Hey, fella." Suzanne reached out and scratched Mocha behind his ears. Then she ran the flat of her hand down his fine Roman nose and under his bristly chin. As an extra goodwill gesture, she bent over and blew out a small puff of air. Horses liked that. It meant you were friendly, trustworthy.

In the stall next to Mocha, she could hear Grommet shuffling about. "Hey, nobody's leaving you out," she told him. She stepped sideways and gave him a pat as his big ears flicked forward. "Nice guy," she told him. "Love you, too, you big galoot." She didn't ride Grommet, but he made a dandy companion for Mocha.

Taking a step backward, Suzanne glanced around the barn. Her eyes had gradually become accustomed to the dark, and now she could make out different shapes. The tack hanging on the wall, an old wagon, bales of hay and straw stacked ten high.

Then her eyes moved to the narrow ladder that led to the hayloft.

Could Colby be up there? Hiding out in the hayloft? He said he'd spent a night there before. Maybe he'd come back. With the body heat from the animals and a warm blanket, he could easily be comfortable up there.

"Colby?" she called out. Then she called his name a little louder, a little more insistently. "Colby?"

She waited, but heard nothing.

Still, Suzanne had a funny feeling that Colby might be nearby. Doogie would scoff at her intuition, make man jokes about it, but she knew it was real. It was the same intuition most women possessed. That edgy feeling that a person or situation might be a little dangerous. A knowingness that it was always better, as a woman, to be safe than sorry.

Stepping out of the barn, Suzanne spotted Ducovny's snowmobile. She didn't recall seeing it when she first arrived. Huh? Had she missed it? She walked slowly toward it, wondering if it could be the one that had terrorized her tonight.

She crept closer and stared at the Plexiglas windshield. It was completely intact.

Wait a minute, didn't Ducovny have two snowmobiles? Where was the other one? Hidden somewhere away from prying eyes? Or just sitting in one of the sheds, needing a new carburetor?

Suzanne gazed at the farmhouse and wondered: Was Ducovny a danger? Could he be the killer after all?

She didn't think so. At least she hoped not.

TWENTY minutes later, Suzanne was safe and sound in her own home. *Finally.* She'd put on gray sweatpants, a pale pink sweater, and UGG slippers, and was sipping a glass of milk. She'd poked through her CD collection and picked out a Lady Antebellum album. Now, Lady Antebellum's "Need You Now" was playing, and she was humming along with the heartfelt lyrics.

"It's a quarter after one, I'm all alone, and I need you now . . ."

A knock sounded at the front door, startling Suzanne. She doused the living room light and padded to the entryway. Carefully, slowly, she peered through the tiny window in the front door.

Letting out a squeal, Suzanne pulled open the door and stepped into Sam's arms.

"Need a hug?" asked Sam.

"Need you now," said Suzanne.

CHAPTER 22

RED and green peppers sizzled in Petra's big cast-iron skillet along with chicken-and-apple sausages, the Cackleberry Club's lighter, healthier alternative to the pork fat and cracklings normally ingested by their customers.

It was Saturday morning, and they were only serving breakfast today. An abbreviated menu that included pepper frittatas, pancakes, English muffins, and the sausages. The plan was to close at eleven so Suzanne and Toni could head out to the big ice-fishing contest. Petra was going to stay behind and supervise the snow plowing of the parking lot, the erection of a large open-sided tent, and the installation of a cauldron, all necessities for their Winter Blaze party tomorrow night.

"What am I gonna tell folks if they ask for pork sausage?" said Toni. She stood in the kitchen, a pencil poked behind one ear, wrapping the ties of her apron around her narrow waist.

"Tell 'em we're fresh out," said Petra.

"Permanently?" said Toni. "Cause some of those farm boys do love to chow down on their real-deal sausage links."

"Tell them to please give our chicken-and-apple sausages a chance," said Petra.

"I'll tell 'em," Toni muttered in a singsong voice, "but they won't like it."

"Suzanne," Petra called, "have you found my unsalted butter yet?"

Suzanne backed out of the cooler with a stack of boxes. "Yup, got it right here."

"That's another thing they're not going to like," said Toni.

"Unsalted butter?" said Suzanne. "Why? It's what some of the finest chefs use. It's practically a staple in French cooking." She'd recently found a small local creamery, Sun Vista Creamery, that specialized in artisanal butter.

"*Foreign* cooking," said Toni.

"You sure have a case of the grumps," Petra said to Toni as she poured her egg mixture into a baking pan. "What's that all about?"

"Aw, I'm just . . ." Toni's eyes slid over to Suzanne. "Should we tell her?"

"Tell me what?" asked Petra.

Toni bit her lower lip. "About last night."

Petra stopped pouring batter. "This isn't about the play, is it?"

"I'm afraid it's après play," said Suzanne.

"Oh dear," said Petra. "What happened?"

And so they told her. About snooping around Claudia's house, deciding to hunt for the treasure medallion, then being terrorized by a crazed snowmobiler in the dark of night.

"Snowmobiler," said Petra, practically spitting out the word. "You think it could have been the same nutcase who strung that wire out back?"

Toni shrugged. "Probably not."

"If you say no, it probably was," said Petra. She let loose a deep and reluctant sigh. "You guys really go out of your way looking for trouble, don't you?"

"It all just kind of . . . happened," said Suzanne. She felt bad that Petra was so unsettled about it.

"Have you related any of this to Doogie yet?" asked Petra.

"Lot of good that will do," said Toni.

"Tell him anyway," said Petra, "and let the chips fall

where they may. He'll either blast you to kingdom come or use the information to figure things out."

"Maybe," said Suzanne.

"No maybe," said Petra. "Just do it." She gazed at Toni, who was edging toward the door, trying for a clean getaway. "You make sure Doogie hears about all this stuff, okay?"

"Yeah, okay," said Toni, finally making her exit.

"PETRA's really crabby, huh?" said Toni. She was stacking glazed donuts and strawberry muffins in the pie saver while Suzanne brewed a pot of English breakfast tea.

"She's just worried about us," said Suzanne.

"We can take care of ourselves."

Suzanne thought about last night, how frightened they'd been out on the ice. *Maybe, maybe not.* She waited a few moments, watching the tea leaves slowly unfurl. "Sam came over last night."

"Did you tell him what happened?" asked Toni.

"No. I wanted to, but . . . no."

"Good girl," said Toni. "I bet we figure this mess out yet. Maybe even before Doogie does."

"There are just so many strange pieces to this puzzle," said Suzanne. "The murder, the affair, the attacks on Joey, and . . ."

Toni held up a finger. "But we're not going to worry our fuzzy little heads about any of that today, are we? Because today—we ice fish!"

Suzanne couldn't help but laugh. Toni looked so serious and gung ho. "When did you turn into such a confirmed angler?"

"When I found out first prize was a hundred bucks," said Toni. "I tell you, we're all set. Junior gave me a couple of spincast rods and a bucket of minnows." She glanced out the window at her car. "That's if they haven't frozen solid. Aw heck, they'll thaw out. It's not like they're fancy filets or anything, they're just itty-bitty things."

"Very appealing," said Suzanne. The last time she'd tried to bait a hook was at Bible camp when she was ten years old. She'd ended up in tears with a worm stuck down the back of her blouse.

"And we'll take the Jungle Cruiser, so we can drive all over the lake." The Jungle Cruiser was Toni's nickname for her old Chevy. "We'll motorvate, as Junior calls it. He even put on a set of studded tires for super traction."

"Aren't those illegal?"

Toni held a finger to her mouth. "Shhhh."

"Suzanne, Toni!" called Petra. "What's going on out there?"

BREAKFAST slipped by fast. Toni did most of the order taking and serving, while Suzanne hunkered at the old brass cash register, making change and dashing out to clear tables and pour refills when the need arose.

They worked quickly and efficiently, with Toni only taking thirty seconds off to listen for her fourth treasure-hunt clue, chewing on her eraser once she'd finished writing it down.

By eleven fifteen, they were on their way, bundled into warm gear and humping along in Toni's Jungle Cruiser as it spewed black clouds of oil and telegraphed every rut and pothole.

"I've been thinking about last night," said Toni as she downshifted, grinding her gears.

"Okay," said Suzanne. She cracked open her side window, fearing Toni's car was dispensing a lethal dose of carbon monoxide.

"Do you think Claudia and George saw us?"

"Why would you think that?"

Toni slammed a cassette into an old-fashioned player from which red, yellow, and green wires stuck out, like a festive bowl of spaghetti. "I got to thinking, maybe George Draper was the mad snowmobiler last night," said Toni. "Maybe he's the one who came after us."

"He seemed rather . . . occupied, wouldn't you say?" suggested Suzanne.

Toni snickered. "Yeah, I guess."

"But still, somebody was trying to send us a warning. To scare us off, or stop us."

"Yes, they were," said Toni. As they approached a four-way stop, she pumped her clutch wildly and fought with her stick shift even as it continued to grind away, stuck somewhere in the nether region between second and third gear.

"The question still remains," said Suzanne, coughing slightly and rolling down her window even more, "who was it? Who came roaring after us last night? That's the burning question."

THEY rolled past a faded green boathouse, all boarded up for the winter, and down an ice-covered ramp. Ahead of them, covering some two thousand acres, was Fish Lake. It was a smaller lake, known for yielding rough fish, like eelpout and carp. But the Department of Natural Resources had stocked it with walleye fingerlings some four years ago, so there remained a glimmer of hope for today's ice-fishing contest.

"Holy lug nuts!" Toni exclaimed as they headed out onto the ice. "Will you look at this?"

"It's a veritable carnival," said Suzanne.

And it was. An entire village had sprung up practically overnight in the middle of the lake. There were popcorn wagons, a red-and-yellow-striped beer tent, a hot pretzel booth, and various church-sponsored booths selling chili con carne, tacos, fried cheese curds, buffalo wings, and pickles on a stick. And more than two hundred ice-fishing fans dressed warmly in snowmobile suits, pac boots, camo jackets, and ski jackets.

But the most amazing sight was the proliferation of fish houses. There must have been at least fifty of them, some as large as a Winnebago, others the dimension of a small outhouse.

Toni chuckled. "Like the good book says, give a man a fish, and he'll eat for a day. Teach him to fish, and he'll sit in one of those stupid little shacks guzzling beer all day."

"What book says that?" laughed Suzanne.

Toni touched a thumb to the front of her snowmobile suit. "My diary."

Toni parked the car, then jumped out to unpack their spin-cast rods and bucket of minnows. Suzanne pulled on a pair of pac boots she'd borrowed from Petra and pushed a woolen hat down on her head.

"They've augered plenty of fishing holes," said Toni, looking around, "so I guess we just pick one and toss in our lines."

"Works for me," said Suzanne. Settling in, she baited her hook with a minimum of trouble, then tossed the pathetic little minnow into their small bubble of water, where it promptly sank. "Now what?"

"Now we kind of hunker down," said Toni. "You see that red bobber?"

"Yup."

"If it goes under, grab your line and start hauling like crazy."

"Sure thing," said Suzanne. She had some expertise at fly fishing, and had even caught a few brook trout and rainbow trout. But this type of fishing, this kind of passive fishing, was new to her. As she stared at her immobile bobber and shifted from one foot to the other, she began to understand why fish houses were so well stocked with beer and rigged with satellite TVs. Anything to alleviate the mind-numbing boredom.

"Hey!" said Toni, "look who just showed up. It's the Doog-meister!"

Sheriff Doogie's tan-and-cream cruiser crept past them. Doogie was surveying the entire spectacle from behind aviator-style mirrored sunglasses. It was an affectation he'd picked up from a friend who served with the highway patrol.

They watched as Doogie parked his vehicle off to the side, climbed out, hitched up his pants, and wandered leisurely from group to group, nodding and shaking hands. He was also, Suzanne decided, turning a blind eye to all the drinking that was going on. Beer, sanctioned by the city and served by the local VFW, was okay. Hard liquor was not. When Doogie finally sauntered over to join them, Suzanne jumped on him right away, eager to pump him for information.

"Did you call the Minneapolis police?" Suzanne asked. "Did you get any sort of line on Colby?"

Doogie looked at her like she was daft. "Are you kidding? They got dozens of missing kids! They told me around sixty at last count."

"And no one who meets Colby's description?" asked Suzanne.

Doogie snorted. "They *all* do! They're all skinny and waifish and wear dark clothes."

"Colby is kind of Goth-looking," Toni piped up. "Did you mention that?"

"I did not," Doogie said, "because I have no idea what that means." He frowned at her. "Do *you* know what it means?"

He had her there. "Um," said Toni, "maybe like those kids in the *Twilight* movies?"

"I still don't know what that means," said Doogie.

"Sheriff," said Suzanne, "we had a somewhat strange encounter last night."

Doogie pulled out a hanky and blew his nose with a loud honk. "Huh?"

Suzanne quickly told him about the mad snowmobiler who had tried to run them down. Being of the discreet sort, she purposely left out the part about seeing Claudia and George Draper locked in a more-than-fond embrace.

"On Catawba Creek?" said Doogie. "You shouldn't have been there in the first place."

"We were looking for the treasure medallion," said Toni.

"Darn fool thing to run a treasure hunt when there's a manhunt going on!" said Doogie. He wiped at his nose again and edged away from them. "You gals gotta stay the heck out of the investigation."

"Really," said Suzanne, feeling frustrated, pretty much talking to his retreating back now, "I get that." But she knew she was already in it up to her ears.

"ARE you bored?" asked Toni. She was plopped on the ice, sitting Indian style on a blanket.

"Not too much," said Suzanne, even though she'd decided ice fishing was akin to watching paint dry. "But maybe we could get something to eat?"

Toni perked up. "A cup of chili?"

"With shredded cheese and sour cream, I hope," said Suzanne, eager for anything to break the monotony. "I'll go grab us some."

She dashed off through the crowd toward the food stands, happy to be moving and mingling with people she knew. As she dodged around ice holes, she saw lots of fish being pulled out, fairly good-size ones, too. And wondered if the minnows Junior had given them were total duds.

"Suzanne!" called a cheery voice.

Suzanne turned as Missy Langston rushed up to greet her. "If it isn't Theda Bara herself," said Suzanne. Then she decided that Missy, who was a few years younger than she was, might not catch the reference. So she said, "How's Kindred's very own celebrated actress?"

"Doing okay," said Missy. "Carmen actually closed the boutique today, so I have some time off."

"That's great," said Suzanne.

"Well, she wants me to enter the ice-carving contest tonight, so I'm back at it in a few hours."

"What are you going to carve?" Toni and Petra had talked about carving a giant cake, but Suzanne wasn't sure if they'd follow through.

"Oh," said Missy, "probably a woman's figure of some sort. But very high fashion, you know?"

"Like a fashion sketch or a dress form?" said Suzanne.

Missy nodded. "Something like that."

"Missy!" called a rough voice.

They both turned to see Lester Drummond hustling toward them.

"Oh no," said Missy, looking suddenly nervous. "Him again."

"Drummond's been bothering you?" said Suzanne.

"Endlessly," said Missy. "Says he wants to take me out on a date."

"Don't do it," Suzanne said under her breath as Drummond suddenly planted himself in front of them.

"You're looking fresh-faced and radiant today," said Drummond, casting a harsh smile at Missy. "All recovered from last night's play?"

Missy just nodded.

"Hello, Lester," said Suzanne.

"Yeah, hi," said Drummond, barely glancing at her.

"Can I buy you a bratwurst?" asked Drummond.

"Gosh, I just had one," said Missy brightly. "And I'm right in the middle of something with Suzanne. So . . . gotta run." She grabbed Suzanne's arm and together they moved off.

"Catch you later!" called Drummond. "For sure!"

"Eeyuh," said Missy, giving a little shiver. "He makes my skin crawl."

"Join the club," said Suzanne.

"He was forever trying to cozy up to me at rehearsals," said Missy. "And I don't want anything to do with him. He reminds me of some kind of Craigslist stalker."

"Just tell Carmen that Drummond's keeping you from doing your job," suggested Suzanne. "That'll get her to chase him off soon enough!"

"Good idea," said Missy.

"Whoa," said Suzanne, suddenly stopping in her tracks as a car put-putted toward them. "I think that's Junior!"

"Toni's husband? Er, ex-husband?" said Missy.

"Soon-to-be-ex, I think."

"Why is his car smoking like that?" asked Missy. They watched as great gluts of dark smoke poured from the front of Junior's car, then whirled skyward like a mini tornado. "It looks like his engine's caught fire."

"Come on," said Suzanne. "This you gotta see."

CHAPTER 23

SUZANNE and Missy moseyed up to Junior, who was dressed in a black ski jacket, jeans, and a pair of sparkly blue vintage moon boots.

"Whatcha cooking, Junior?" asked Suzanne.

Junior's face lit up when he saw her. "Oh hey, Suzanne! And Missy. Howdy do, ladies." He made a sweeping gesture as he clumped around to the front of his car. "You're just in time. I'm doin' hot dogs and beans in my car cooker."

"Car cooker?" said Missy, making a face.

"Tomorrow I'm gonna do barbecued ribs," Junior boasted.

"As you can clearly see," said Suzanne, "Junior has a new invention."

"A pretty strange invention, too," said Missy. "But what I want to know is, does it really work?"

"Does it work? This here's the *future*," proclaimed Junior. "I'm gonna personally put an end to fast food and greasy diners."

"Is that so," said Missy, clearly not impressed.

"Say," said Junior to Suzanne, "you and Toni got any minnows left? If I dredge 'em in enough batter, who's to know they're not fried smelt?"

Vrooom! Ratatatata!

Out of nowhere, a snowmobile suddenly careened directly toward Suzanne. Shocked, terrified it might be the same person who had tried to run her down last night, her first instinct was to duck and hide. But would someone really dare run her over in front of two hundred eyewitnesses?

Suzanne's question was quickly answered when the snowmobile roared to a stop not two feet from her. And the driver yanked off his helmet.

Suzanne blinked. "Sam?" Was it really *her* Sam sitting astride that throaty-sounding snowmobile? Yes, it certainly was.

"Surprise!" said Sam, a big grin on his face, his hair all askew.

"What are you *doing* with that thing?" she demanded.

Sam climbed off the snowmobile. "It's a special surprise! I rented it just for you!"

Suzanne took a step backward. "I can't ride a snowmobile," she blurted. Fresh in her mind was the nasty, threatening, droning machine from last night. *Sam, you have no idea what happened to me last night.*

"Sure you can." Sam reached out and patted the seat. "Hop on, we'll take a quick spin around the lake."

"Do it," coaxed Missy. "It'll be fun."

"Maybe later," said Suzanne, still hedging.

"Maybe now," said Sam, reaching out and catching her hand. "Come on, climb on back." He handed her a shiny red helmet. "I'll give you a lesson. Snowmobiling 101."

She climbed on reluctantly, put her arms around Sam's waist, and laced her gloved fingers together. She'd grit it out, she decided. Close her eyes and hang on for dear life. In a few minutes it would all be over. She'd tell Sam she'd had a wonderful ride, thank him profusely, and that would be the end of it. *Good-bye, snowmobile.*

Except it didn't quite work out that way.

Thirty seconds into the ride, Suzanne found she was beginning to crack a smile. Fish houses whipped by, tiny little pellets of snow stung her face, and she suddenly felt like she was flying. The ride was scary, exhilarating, and liberating, all at once. Then they were clear across the lake and zooming up a snowy embankment and into a frozen pine forest. She was full-out grinning now as they slalomed in and out of trees, carving big S-turns, and whooping as they went.

"Disclaimer!" Sam shouted. "Do not attempt at home!"

"Professional driver on closed course only," Suzanne shouted back.

Sam rocked the machine to a stop. He turned in his seat, gave her a kiss, and said, "Your turn."

"Really?" She wanted to drive it, but was still a little nervous.

"Sure, it's easy," he told her. "Throttle's on the right handlebar, the brake is on the left."

"So, it's kind of like a motorcycle," she said. She'd owned a scooter in college and had loved it.

"Something like that," said Sam. "Only easier."

They traded places, and Suzanne took off, tentative at first, until she started to get the hang of it. She found that stopping in deep snow was a cinch. You just took your hand off the throttle, and the snowmobile pretty much stopped. Ice was a little trickier. Stopping on a slick surface meant braking like a car. Pumping gently, then easing off.

By the time she'd circled the lake twice, Suzanne was having a blast. She headed for Toni's fishing hole, made a showy stop that blew up a ten-foot-high rooster tail of snow, then pulled off her helmet for a big reveal.

"That's you?" said Toni. "Holy buckets! I didn't think you knew how to drive a 'bile."

"I didn't," said Suzanne, climbing off, feeling a sense of pride, "until now. Sam rented it for me."

Toni glanced at Sam, who still sat straddling the machine and gave a thumbs-up. "Right on, dude," she said.

Suzanne glanced down at Toni's feet, where a skinny, greenish fish was flopping about wildly. "Hey, you got one!"

"Just pulled it out," said Toni. "Northern pike. Gotta go get it weighed."

"I'll come with you," said Suzanne, feeling guilty about not bringing the chili back. "Okay?" she said to Sam.

"See you guys later," he said, revving up the snowmobile again. "Go have fun."

TONI'S northern pike weighed in at eight pounds, one ounce.

"That puts you in third place," the head of the judging committee told her. His name was Burt Finch, and he ran the local sporting-goods store.

"What's that pay?" asked Toni.

"Twenty-five dollars," said Finch. He was a big, burly guy in brown thermal overalls with a tufted fur hat that looked like the kind Khrushchev used to wear.

Toni shook her head. "Have to do better than that."

"You got time," said Finch. "There's still three hours left." He looked past them, and said, "What have you got there, Charlie?"

Suzanne and Toni turned to find Charlie Steiner holding up a good-sized walleye. His wife Elise stood behind him.

"Got the prize winner right here," said Steiner, bulling his way in.

Finch hooked the fish onto his handheld scale and read the numbers. "Twelve pounds, two ounces. That puts you in third place, Charlie." He gazed at Toni. "Knocks you down to fourth."

"Big whoop," said Toni. "Now I'm out of the money."

"Hah!" Steiner cackled. "My luck is starting to turn!"

Suzanne had the feeling Steiner might not be referring solely to his fish.

"How's that, Charlie?" she asked. She was aware of Elise throwing her a hopeful look.

Steiner gave a nasty, snaggletoothed grin. "First they stuck that bank fellow Busacker in the ground, so I got a kind of reprieve on my property, and now my fish is in the money. Nothing wrong with that!" As he talked, his breath plumed out, carrying the distinct odor of cheap whiskey.

"You fool!" shouted Ed Rapson, startling them as he

suddenly rushed up out of nowhere and insinuated himself in the mix. "You got maybe a one-month reprieve! Once I put a new bank president in place, your property is toast!" He stared at Steiner with hate in his slitty, piggy eyes. "Just like that stupid fish of yours, you're still on the hook!"

Steiner suddenly lost it. He grabbed his fish from Finch and slapped it hard against Rapson's chest! Snow, fish scales, and bits of fish goop stained the man's coat.

"Charlie, don't!" wailed Elise.

"What are you accusing me of?" growled Steiner. "You think I had something to do with that snowmobile accident that killed Busacker? Go ahead and *prove* it! I dare you!" He shook with anger as Elise pulled him away from the melee.

"I'll not only prove it," shouted Rapson, "I'll help slap the handcuffs on and personally escort you to jail!"

"Hey!" shouted Finch, looking disgusted. "Enough of this nonsense! This is a *family* event! Charlie, take your danged fish and get out of here." Then he shook a warning finger at Rapson, who was muttering and brushing fish scales off the front of his black wool coat. "And *you*, back down. Don't run around accusing people of things you can't prove. Don't think you can take the law into your own hands!"

"We'll see about that!" shrilled Rapson, as he stalked off angrily.

Toni stared at Finch. "Does this mean I'm back in third place?"

OVER cocoa and kettle corn, Suzanne and Toni replayed the nasty event.

"Charlie Steiner just got elevated to suspect *numero uno* in my book," said Toni. "He's one scary, unstable buckaroo."

"No kidding," said Suzanne. She'd also been shocked and dismayed by the nasty scene that had just played out. So had everyone around them.

"Steiner could have easily been the jackhole on that

snowmobile last night," said Toni. "Because he's not just a hothead, he's a mean hothead. Arguing and snapping at Rapson like that proves it."

"If you ask me," said Suzanne, "either one of those guys is crazy enough to be the killer."

They shuffled over to the chili booth and got in line.

"Watch it," said Suzanne, bobbing her head. "Here comes George Draper."

"What? No Claudia?" said Toni, under her breath.

"I think this lake scene might be a little too folksy for her big-city sensibilities," Suzanne murmured back.

"Plus, she'd probably freeze her sweet little tush off," said Toni.

Suzanne waved as Toni sang out, "Hey, George. You doing some fishing today? Must not be any business back at the funeral home, huh?"

George pulled his stocking cap down over pink ears, and said, "Not right now, not today, but January is actually one of my busiest months."

"You have seasonal activity?" asked Suzanne. It sounded a little creepy, even as she said it.

"Oh yeah," said Draper, looking enthusiastic. "Older people, they always manage to hang on by their fingernails through the holidays. Guess it's all the gifts and family cheer that punches up their spirits. But then, when January rolls around, they sort of give up the ghost. Maybe it's the cold and ice that gets to them. I don't know. Or they figure they can't hold out until spring."

"Jeez, George," said Toni. "That's totally weird."

George glared at Toni, looking like he needed to defend his words. "Not when you think of it as smart business analysis."

"Some business," said Toni.

"Somebody has to do it," said George.

Suzanne decided it was time to change the subject. "Are you going to throw in a line today, George? Did you enter the fishing contest?"

"No," said Draper, "but I'm in the ice-sculpture contest tonight. One of my assistants and I are carving an Egyptian sarcophagus."

"A sarcophagus," said Toni, frowning. "That's like a . . ."

"Tomb," said Draper, smiling.

"Good luck to you," said Suzanne, grabbing Toni by the elbow and steering her away.

"What a creep," muttered Toni. "I wonder how Claudia feels, knowing he was, like, sucking blood out of dead bodies right before he, um . . ." Her voice trailed off.

"You don't have to say any more," said Suzanne. "I get the picture."

"So back to the old fishin' hole," said Toni. "Hope I can hook myself a lunker."

"What is a lunker?" asked Suzanne.

"Anything bigger than a bread box," said Toni. She gazed across the ice. "Hey, what's the problem with Doogie's cruiser?"

Suzanne put a hand up to diffuse the sun's glare as she stared at Doogie's car. It seemed to be listing heavily to one side. "Looks like it started to go through the ice."

"I'm not surprised," said Toni. "There are so many holes augered around here it's like a bunch of prairie dogs set up camp."

But when they got to Doogie's cruiser, it wasn't ice holes that were the problem. Somebody had poured salt near his left rear wheel, and that part of his car had partially sunk into the ice.

"Salt?" said Toni. "Who would do that?"

"That's what I'd like to know!" said Doogie. He was hopping mad, kicking at the mushy ice, sending spatters of slush everywhere. He'd put in a call to Deputy Driscoll to come tow him out. Now the deputy had fixed a towline under Doogie's front bumper and was cranking methodically.

"You think that's going to work?" Suzanne wondered.

"It better!" said Doogie. He checked to make sure the

line was taut, then said, "Okay, take it ahead, Eddie. Go easy, though." With an ungainly leap, he hopped into the driver's seat, revved his engine, and spun his wheels as Driscoll inched forward in the tow car.

"That's really weird," said Toni. They both looked around at the horde of people. "Somebody here did this?"

"Had to be," said Suzanne. "Maybe his investigation is right on track and getting a little too close for comfort."

"Lots of suspects," Toni agreed, chipping a frozen minnow out of her bucket.

"Unfortunately, not a lot of answers," murmured Suzanne.

CHAPTER 24

SUZANNE squirted a tiny spray of perfume on her wrists and rubbed them briskly together. Euphoria Blossom by Calvin Klein. A soft scent of citrus, peony, and white musk that lingered in the air and made her smile. *Mmm. Nice*, she thought.

Looking in the mirror and tilting her head, she grabbed a rat-tail comb and puffed up her ash blond hair a little bit more in back. She'd done the blowout thing, juggling hair dryer and fat boar-bristle brush, spritzing on a little mousse until she'd coaxed her hair into a loose bob.

Satisfied with her do, Suzanne looped on a gold chain necklace and smoothed her clothes. She'd decided on a black cashmere sweater, scoop necked and flattering in all the right places, paired with a black wool skirt and shiny black leather boots. She'd seen the look in a fashion magazine, a trifle austere with a hint of sexy. So she'd shopped her closet and come up with her own version.

"Perfect," she said to herself in the mirror. Grinned, and added, "At least I hope so."

Sam was picking her up for what was supposed to be a leisurely yet romantic dinner tonight. Honestly, she thought, the man was so full of surprises. What with the rented snowmobile today and showing up on her doorstep the night before. Still, he didn't come on strong, and he didn't push. But he'd ignited a huge spark of excitement in her life. And what woman didn't love that?

* * *

KOPELL's Restaurant and B&B in nearby Cornucopia offered a romantic, cozy dining room. In fact, the first thing Suzanne and Sam saw when they hustled in out of the cold was a robust fire crackling in a stone fireplace that practically dominated an entire back wall.

"So cozy," said Suzanne. They were seated so close to the fire that they could hear the pop and hiss of green logs and feel the comforting warmth of the flames. "Now all we need are a pair of deer hounds stretched out beside us."

"This place does look like a Black Forest *schloss*, doesn't it?" said Sam.

Deer antlers, moody paintings of castles in dark forests, and a shelf of antique beer steins added to the Germanic atmosphere. Upstairs, the bed and breakfast featured sleigh beds, billowing featherbed mattresses, textured wallpaper with intriguing patterns of ribbon and gold, and plenty of old-world charm.

As they relaxed at their table, a waiter brought ice water, a basket of fresh-baked molasses bread, and menus in ornate leather holders. But before they had a chance to peruse their menus, Bernie Affolter, the owner and head chef, strolled over to greet them. A large, stout man with a commanding presence, he had a full head of dark curly hair and a waxed moustache to match.

"Good evening, folks," Bernie said, smiling broadly.

"My good man," said Sam. They'd dined here before and had gotten to know Bernie fairly well. It also didn't hurt that they usually ordered a fine Bordeaux from Bernie's cellar.

"I've got a nice Pomerol stashed away," said Bernie, in a conspiratorial tone. "Want me to decant it for you?"

"Sounds good," said Sam. He nodded toward one of the mounted deer antlers. "Is that your doing?"

Bernie eyed the antlers. "Those are from my younger

days," he said, with a chuckle. "Before the notion of char-cuterie, glazed oysters, and wine *terroirs* ever crossed my mind. These days, instead of hunting deer, I'm much more interested in marinating it in organic red wine, smoking it on the grill, and serving it up with pecan chutney."

"Sounds fantastic," said Suzanne.

"You two are familiar with our menu," said Bernie, "but we have a couple of specials tonight." He reached into the pocket of his XXL white chef's jacket and pulled out a hastily scrawled list. "Muscovy duck with coriander, honey, and cooked carrots; Copper River salmon with celery root puree; and juniper-crusted bison."

"What's best?" asked Sam.

"Depends on what you're in the mood for," said Bernie.

"I'll have the Muscovy duck," said Suzanne.

"Bison for me," said Sam.

"Excellent," said Bernie. "And I'll send along a side dish of grilled winter vegetables."

When Bernie had moved to another table, Sam asked in a low voice, "What are winter vegetables? I mean, nothing grows in winter, does it?"

"How about snow peas, chili peppers, and iceberg let-tuce?" Suzanne joked.

Once the wine was poured, swirled, tasted, and exclaimed over, Suzanne and Sam gazed across the table at each other.

"This is nice," said Sam.

Nice? thought Suzanne. *It's fantastic!*

"Mmm," she said. "Very relaxing after such a tough week."

Sam looked at her. "I'm sorry that murder had to land at your doorstep like that."

"So am I," said Suzanne. "Because it kicked off an ava-lanche of problems."

"Did you ever locate that kid you told me about? What was his name?"

"Colby?" said Suzanne. "He's probably hightailed it into the next county by now."

"Or maybe he just went home," said Sam.

"I hope so," said Suzanne. But for some reason, she didn't think he had. She had a funny feeling that Colby might still be lurking somewhere close by. Then, not wanting their lovely evening to focus on the murder or anything remotely relating to it, she said, "You really surprised the heck out of me with that snowmobile."

"I thought you'd get a kick out of it." Sam was pleased that she was pleased.

"Once I got the hang of driving it," said Suzanne, "it was quite an adrenaline rush."

"See, you're a sledhead already," Sam laughed. "I knew it!"

Their food arrived, and it was fabulous. After they'd carefully exchanged bites and poured refills on wine, they tucked into it with gusto.

"I had no idea I was this hungry," said Suzanne.

"You were outside all day probably burning up a zillion calories."

"Doubtful," said Suzanne.

"Plus the wine is helpful in replacing electrolytes," said Sam, topping off her glass again.

"Wine does that?"

He winked at her. "It does for me."

With the accompanying clink of crystal, Mozart on the sound system, and the golden haze cast by the fire, Suzanne felt that she'd tumbled down a magical rabbit hole. A year ago she had been a widow weighed down with worry over the future. Now, here she was, keeping company with a great guy and reveling in his comforting and very real presence.

They lingered over dessert and coffee, sharing a rich chocolate mousse with two spoons.

"Chocolate," said Sam, practically scraping the bottom of the glass bowl, "is my ultimate downfall. Dangle a Belgian truffle or bonbon in front of me and I'm yours for life."

"Really?" said Suzanne. She might have to take him up on that.

"I'm a terrible chocoholic," admitted Sam.

"In that case," said Suzanne, "I'll have to whip up my famous German chocolate layer cake."

He stared at her. "You really know how to make that?"

"With ease."

"What else do you have in your bag of tricks?"

"How about dirty fried chicken," said Suzanne.

Sam's gaze was long and lingering. "Wow."

SOME twenty minutes later, they were back in downtown Kindred. Main Street was brightly lit and thronged with crowds of people.

"The sleigh rides," said Sam, nosing into a parking space.

"And the ice-sculpture contest just kicked off," said Suzanne.

"So, what's first?"

They got out of Sam's car just as an enormous brown Belgian draft horse clopped by, bells jingling. The animal was pulling an old-fashioned sleigh with red velvet seats.

"Definitely a sleigh ride," said Suzanne.

"You really have a thing for horses, don't you?" said Sam.

"They're the best," said Suzanne, smiling as the big horse negotiated a tight turn at the end of the block, arched his neck with pride, and came back toward them.

They waited in line for just a few minutes, and when it was their turn, they clambered in and the driver tossed a striped Hudson's Bay blanket over their legs.

"And away we go," said Sam.

They flew down Main Street, the rushing wind chilling their faces as the enormous Belgian horse pulled their sleigh with effortless vigor. Lampposts strung with twinkle lights flew past, friends waved, a couple of kids chased after them.

When they were dropped at the park, Suzanne was

stunned at what a beehive of activity it was! It seemed like everyone and his brother-in-law had a pick axe, hammer, or shovel, and was chipping and chopping at enormous blocks of ice, trying to coax them into some semblance of an ice sculpture.

George Draper, with no sign of Claudia nearby, was chopping away with help from his assistant. Their horizontal piece of ice had already taken on the dimensions of a grand sarcophagus, complete with handles on the side and two small lions crouched on top. Certainly a tomb befitting an emperor!

"Get a load of this one," said Sam, pointing to the block of ice Ham Wick was working on. They walked up to it.

"What is it?" Suzanne asked Wick.

"It's a bit of a secret right now," said Wick, sounding a little mysterious. "But it has to do with money."

"Is it a cash register?" asked Suzanne.

"Can't say," answered Wick.

"Stack of dollar bills?" proposed Sam.

Wick shook his head. "Still can't say."

"Okay, then," said Suzanne. "Good luck."

Sam and Suzanne strolled on. Some of the nurses from Westvale Clinic were trying to create a giant stethoscope.

"Come on over and give us a hand, Doc," called one of the nurses.

"Tonight's my night off," Sam called back, grinning.

Brett and Gregg from Root 66 were bearing down on what looked like a giant pair of scissors. And Darrel Kronsky, a local wood-carver, was using his chainsaw to craft an elaborate polar bear out of a tremendous block of ice.

Just as they were about to leave, they discovered Toni and Petra, who'd entered the contest—sure enough—at the very last minute. They were doing a six-tiered wedding cake, complete with fancy decorations. Only, right now, it seemed to be listing to one side.

"Howdy, ladies!" said Suzanne. "I see you're whipping up an irresistible dessert."

"Trying to," said Toni. "Only problem is, this dad-burned cake isn't straight."

Sam cocked his head to one side. "Looks fine to me."

Toni snatched up a mitful of snow, formed it into a fast snowball, and tossed it at him in mock anger. "It's whacked!" she cried. "We need to straighten this crazy thing out, and fast. Petra, what the heck are we gonna do?"

Petra was tromping around, squinting at their sculpture. "Make an adjustment?" she said.

"Well, I know *that*," said Toni. "The question is how?"

Sam moved a little closer. "Maybe if you add a little more snow to the left side . . ."

But Suzanne had suddenly tuned them out. Instead, she was hyper-focused on a dark figure, a slight figure, who'd just darted behind a half-formed Pegasus sculpture.

He looks familiar . . . Could it be . . . ?

But when she'd crunched over a few steps toward the Pegasus, the person was gone.

Gone where?

She strained her neck, hoping to catch another glimpse of him. For, surely, it had to be Colby. But where had the little dickens run off to?

She spun around, taking in the bright lights, glinting sculptures, and ice carvers moving about in their colorful jackets and hats. But just outside this magic circle was darkness, where shadows danced and blue-black evergreens swayed in the night wind.

Orienting herself, looking back at Sam, Toni, and Petra, Suzanne took a few steps toward the trees, riveting her gaze on that copse of darkness. But when she got to the tree line, no one was there.

She stood rock still, a little unnerved. Were her eyes playing tricks on her?

No, there it was again. A sylph-like shadow slipping behind a snowman made of ice.

Suzanne dashed over, ready to confront Colby. But he wasn't there.

Then where?

She strode around the park now with purpose in her stride, peeking behind hunks of ice, keeping a keen eye out for the kid.

When she'd looked behind and around every single ice sculpture, even those half finished or barely begun, she still didn't see him.

Oh . . . crud.

Standing on the edge of the park, gazing at the sculptures and all the folks who'd come out to try their hand, Suzanne suddenly felt helpless. Colby wasn't here. And if he had been, he'd certainly outfoxed her.

But there was a lot of that going around this week.

Doogie and his investigators had been outfoxed so far, too. And even as the fine residents of Kindred jostled in the park, enjoying the task at hand, not minding the cold one bit, she knew it wasn't even close to being small-town perfect.

After all, a killer was still on the loose.

CHAPTER 25

FIFTY pounds of bratwurst special-ordered from Sheboygan, Wisconsin, rested in the cooler. Three enormous kettles of beans sat soaking in water on Petra's industrial-size stove. Suzanne had arrived at the Cackleberry Club at one o'clock this Sunday afternoon, anxious to make sure everything was primed and ready for their big Winter Blaze party tonight. And even though her morning with Sam had been leisurely—she'd made cheddar cheese egg strata, and they'd perused the *New York Times*—tonight's party had been niggling away in the back of her mind.

But, really, all Petra had to do was add molasses, sugar, and onions to her beans and set them to baking. After all, they were only handling the brats and beans part, everything else was . . .

Boots stomped loudly on the back steps leading to the kitchen door.

"Being delivered," said Suzanne out loud. She pulled open the wooden door and peered through the screen door. Yup, there was Bill Probst from the Kindred Bakery, struggling under a tower of cardboard boxes.

"Got some bratwurst buns for you," said Probst.

"Bring your buns right in here," said Suzanne.

Probst eased past her. "Couldn't resist, could you?" he said, the corners of his mouth turning up just slightly. "People love to say that."

"Sorry," said Suzanne. "I guess I should have tried for something a little more original."

"That's okay," said Probst, stacking the boxes on the butcher-block counter. He looked around. "Where's Petra? I figured she'd be here worrying and fussing over everything."

"She'll probably show up any minute. And then she'll start worrying and fussing."

"Okay," said Probst, giving a tip of his red felt cap. "Cheers. See you at the party tonight."

Suzanne was just about to shut the door when she heard laughter and high-pitched voices. She looked out, saw an animated Toni and Petra chatting with Mr. Probst. Then, a few seconds later, her cohorts came rushing in with a burst of cold air. Toni looked like a ski bunny in her pink ski jacket and fuzzy white hat. Petra wore a puffy blue down coat.

"You'll never guess what happened!" said Toni, pulling off her cap and tossing it in the air.

"Doogie apprehended the killer," said Suzanne. *Please let me be right.*

"Nooo," said Toni.

"Then what?" said Suzanne.

Toni was dancing in place, giggling like a goofy teenager. "You tell her, Petra."

"It's kind of unofficial," said Petra, a broad grin on her kindly, open face, "but the simple fact is, we won."

"What!" cried Suzanne. "Are you talking about the ice-carving contest?"

"According to Missy, who kind of tipped us off because she's going out with one of the judges, our six-tiered wedding cake took third place!" said Toni. "Can you believe it?"

"Yes, I can believe it," said Suzanne. "You guys were chipping away like fiends last night."

"Petra's the one who really clinched it for us," said Toni, "because she's decorated so many real cakes."

"The most difficult part was getting the layers just right," said Petra.

"When we got to the top layer," said Toni, "everything looked a little crooked and off center."

"I remember," said Suzanne.

"So we just packed on handfuls of snow and molded it," said Toni. "With a little help from Sam, of course."

"Kind of like Play-Doh," said Petra.

"And then our brilliant Petra here took a spray bottle and spritzed everything with water," said Toni.

"So it pretty much froze instantly and turned to ice," said Petra, peeling off her voluminous coat. "And took on a nice glaze."

"We're going to get a ribbon and everything," said Toni. "Mayor Mobley's going to announce all the winners tonight at the party."

"Who won first place?" asked Suzanne. She'd seen so many fanciful sculptures last night, they'd all seemed prizeworthy.

"We don't know that yet," said Petra. "For the ice carving or the ice-fishing contest."

"I don't much care about ice fishing anymore," said Toni, "since I've probably dropped to tenth place by now."

"You gave it a good shot," said Suzanne.

"I guess," said Toni. She reached down, picked up her hat, and said, "So what needs to get done around here?"

"I'm going to focus on my baked beans," said Petra. "So maybe the two of you could haul the buns out to the café and line up all the paper plates and cups and plastic forks and stuff. Have it ready so we can shuttle everything outside in a couple of hours and be ready for the thundering horde."

"How many people do you think will show up?" asked Toni.

"I'm guessing two hundred," said Suzanne. "At least, that's what we've planned for."

"What if we get more?" said Toni. "What if we run out of food?"

Suzanne gave a lopsided grin. "In that case, we'll have to depend on Junior and his car cooker. Hope for the best."

"Dear lord, no," said Petra, grabbing a bottle of molasses.

"THIS isn't working," said Toni. She stood in the middle of about ten strings of mini lights. "I'm trying to get them into one long string, but all I have is a ginormous tangle."

"These lights are tricky," said Suzanne, crunching across the snowy parking lot toward her. "Here, you take one end—"

"I can't *find* one end," Toni huffed.

"Then let's unplug all the strings and start over."

They picked and plucked and finally got ten strings of mini white lights untangled and laid out straight.

"Now we'll just loop them around the top of the tent," said Suzanne. She knew the twinkle lights would lend a fun, festive air once it got dark.

"All of the lights?" said Toni. "How about I hang a couple of strings in the pine trees?"

"If you can climb up there without falling and breaking a hip, sure," said Suzanne. She looped her lights around the tent, then muscled three shallow metal cauldrons into the middle of the parking lot. In another two hours, they'd build fires inside them and the cauldrons would become cozy beacons of cheer for their party guests.

Dan Mullin, owner of Mullin's Dairy, had trucked in a load of hay bales, and Suzanne and Toni dragged those around, setting them in concentric circles around the cauldrons to serve as seating.

"Good thing I grew up on a farm," said Toni, flexing her arms in a muscle-man pose. "I can still heft a hay bale."

"You're remarkably strong for your weight," said Suzanne.

"Yeah," said Toni. "Junior says I'm all sinew and gristle."

"That Junior's a sweet-talkin' man," said Suzanne.

"If we want to catch some of the sled dog races," said Toni, "we better head over there now."

Suzanne and Toni skirted around the Cackleberry Club, pushed their way through the woods, and came out on the edge of what had been a green undulating alfalfa field just a few months earlier.

"Whoa, Nelly!" said Toni. "This looks like a real racetrack!"

Plows and snowmobiles had plowed and flattened a one mile oval in the snow. Now it was packed hard and fast, ideal for sled dog racing.

"They did a great job," said Suzanne, "creating banked turns and everything."

"Even the dogs approve," said Toni.

Across the way, swirling packs of Siberian huskies and Alaskan malamutes yipped and yapped with unbridled enthusiasm as their harried owners struggled to strap them into their tandem harnesses. At least fifty or sixty people were positioned around the track and ready to cheer on their favorite canine teams.

"This is so exciting," said Toni, as the wooden sleds were hooked on and six teams lined up at the starting line. "How many times are they going to go around?"

"No idea," said Suzanne. This was her first dogsled race, and she had no clue if there was a set number of laps or if the dogs just ran until they got pooped.

An air horn released a noisy belch, and just like that, the teams were off!

"Look at those pooches run!" cried Toni. The teams were running full-out, already rounding the first turn.

"This would have been wonderful inspiration for Baxter," said Suzanne. "To see actual dogs in an all-out sprint."

"Right," Toni said in a dry tone. They both knew Baxter was a confirmed couch potato and didn't really relish the cold. Plus, he was getting up there in years, as much as Suzanne tried to overlook that fact.

The teams had already made a complete lap, with two teams pulling out in front. One team had slowed down considerably.

"Did you see that they're all wearing paw covers?" said Toni.

"Thank goodness for that," said Suzanne. She hated the idea of the dogs' paws getting cold and scratched from the ice and snow.

"And here they come again," Toni whooped, as the dogs flew by them for the second time. "Oh, oh, somebody's waving a flag over there."

"Must be signaling the final lap," said Suzanne.

"The bell lap, kind of like in NASCAR racing," said Toni.

Now three dog teams were neck and neck as they flew around their final lap. People were really starting to scream and shout now.

"Gonna be close," said Toni.

"But one team is pulling ahead," said Suzanne. "Oh, wow, they're really pouring it on."

The dogs flew past them a third and final time, ears back, muzzles thrust forward, headed for the finish line as the crowd urged them on.

"Fantastic!" said Toni, as the lead team crossed the finish line and the dogs, as if realizing they'd won, braked immediately. Barking, yipping, and wagging their plumy tales, they seemed to be celebrating and congratulating each other with nips and slobbery kisses.

"We'd better head back," said Suzanne, when the excitement had died down a bit. She glanced at her watch. "It's three-thirty already. Our guests should start arriving around five."

"There's a couple more races," said Toni. "I think maybe an eight-dog hitch."

"Still . . ."

"Okay," said Toni.

"Did you listen and write down this morning's treasure-hunt clue?"

Toni walked along with her head down. "Aw, I've pretty much given up on the treasure hunt. It's just not in the cards for me."

THE Bogus Creek Bluegrass Boys had just arrived, so Suzanne met with them and showed them where to set up, close to one of the blazing cauldrons so they'd hopefully stay nice and toasty.

"You guys play a little country, too?" she asked. They were four men in quilted jean jackets, trapper hats, and pac boots who each played a different instrument—mandolin, fiddle, banjo, and guitar.

Their leader, Teddy Grinnel, nodded solemnly. "We play bluegrass, country, some Methodist, and a touch of revival for good measure."

"You need an extension cord?" she asked. "To mike your instruments?"

"Mike?" said Teddy. "No, that's Buddy over there."

By quarter to five, the bonfires were lit, the musicians had already run through a peppy rendition of "Walking the Dog," and Petra and a small group of volunteers had arranged three Weber grills under the tent. A group of men, honchoed by Whitey Milburn, who worked for the power company, had set up six stanchions of glowing lights. By the time Suzanne turned on her mini lights, the whole place sparkled and shimmered like a scene inside a snow globe.

With a burp of oil and a sizzle of grease, Junior's car cooker rattled into the parking lot and stopped right next to Suzanne's rented snowmobile. Right on his tail was Sam's BMW.

While Junior got out and fussed under his hood, Sam

made a beeline for Suzanne. They kissed each other in greeting.

"Need any help?" he asked her. Before she could answer, he looked around and said, "Gee, everything looks terrific."

"I think we actually have it under control," said Suzanne. She'd changed into jeans, a black faux-fur jacket, and her shiny black boots.

"Excellent," said Sam. "I'm not exactly a light-your-briquettes kind of guy."

You sure enough warm my briquettes, thought Suzanne.

"Hey," said Sam. "Got something for you." He reached into the pocket of his shearling jacket and handed her a dark blue leather box etched in gold.

A jewelry box, thought Suzanne. *Oh my. Oh dear.*

"Go ahead, open it."

Suzanne took a deep breath and opened the little box. There, nested on a pillow of blue velvet, was a tiny Fabergé egg pendant. It was very wintry looking, all gold and perfect and studded with hundreds of tiny white crystals.

"Oh my goodness!" said a shocked Suzanne. "It's beautiful! But . . . what is this for? What did I do to deserve this?" She was fumbling her words, a little bit embarrassed, but secretly pleased, too.

Sam leaned over and kissed her on the forehead. "It's our three-month anniversary."

"We're counting months?"

"I am."

Suzanne smiled to herself. Any man who counted weeks or months in a relationship was a good man. A keeper. She held up the pendant again, thrilled at how the light caught the crystals and made them sparkle like fire. "And it's real Fabergé?"

"Well, it wasn't exactly handcrafted by Carl Fabergé in between making priceless treasures for Czar Nicholas. But it's from the Fabergé family, yes." Sam grinned. "Probably the brother-in-law." He chuckled. "Fritz Fabergé."

Suzanne removed the pendant from its velvet box and hung it around her neck. It gleamed and sparkled as it settled into the little notch below her throat. "I love it." And she truly did. It made her feel warm and safe, as if she were back in college and had been solemnly asked to wear someone's fraternity pin.

"I had to order it from a jewelry store in Chicago," said Sam. He had the pride that all men have when they've put themselves out there and gotten the gift thing right.

"But I don't have anything for you," said Suzanne, suddenly worried.

Sam pulled her close. "Oh yes, you do."

The spell was suddenly broken by Toni stomping across the lot. She stopped, stared at Sam's boots, and said, "It takes a real man to wear UGGs." Then she turned toward Junior, and screamed, "Junior! Don't you dare park that ugly clunker there!"

Junior turned to her, palms up, in a gesture of appeasement. "I'm just making final *adjustments*," he told her. "Besides, I gotta log a few more miles. My ribs aren't quite cooked yet. I want them falling-off-the-bone tender."

Suzanne and Sam strolled over to Junior's car, where Sam watched Junior peel back his hood and baste his rack of ribs.

"I'm fascinated by this," Sam said to Junior. "You came up with this invention all on your own?"

Junior tapped a grubby index finger against the side of his head. "My brain's always whirling away. I'm always on the lookout for the next triumph in engineering."

"And you're doing barbecue," said Sam, staring at the ribs in Junior's makeshift cooker.

"Baby back ribs," boasted Junior. "Basted with my own secret sauce."

"What's so secret about it?" asked Toni. "You probably threw together a squirt of ketchup, a little mustard, and maybe a toot of horseradish."

"You can't expect me to reveal the *precise* ingredients,"

said Junior, indignantly. "Some big food conglomerate might get wind of it and try to steal my recipe out from under me."

Suzanne thought, *Fat chance*, but instead said, "That's smart thinking, Junior."

But Sam was still fascinated by Junior's invention. "So you use a meat thermometer and everything?"

Junior shrugged. "Naw, I just poke 'em with the dipstick."

CHAPTER 26

THE mercury was hovering at barely twenty degrees, but the people who thronged outside the Cackleberry Club didn't seem to mind. Brats sizzled and popped over hot coals, hot cider steamed, and the fire cauldrons blazed as the Bogus Creek Bluegrass Boys cranked out "Wreck of the Old 97."

"This is fantastic," said Petra. "We really pulled it off." She stood next to Suzanne with one of her hand-knitted angora shawls pulled tightly around her shoulders, watching the two hundred guests mill and mingle.

"And the volunteers," said Suzanne. "I can't believe how many people pitched in to help."

"Pitched in and chipped in," said Petra. "That's what small towns are all about. Everyone working together."

Suzanne didn't want to bring up the fact that there was a killer stalking this particular small town, so she didn't. But the notion burned inside her. For all she knew, the killer could be here tonight, on this very property once again, smiling and joking, drinking cider or cocoa, and doing the two-step. As much as one could maneuver the two-step wearing clunky winter boots.

And still people poured in. Ed Rapson showed up, though Suzanne sincerely wondered why, with Ham Wick trailing him like a hopeful puppy dog.

Sheriff Doogie and his deputy Eddie Driscoll had staked out a place on the sidelines, sipping cocoa and watching the festivities with their cool law-enforcement eyes.

Suzanne wondered if they knew something she didn't. Then decided she had to stop obsessing, if just for one night. Yes, that was it. She'd give herself a break. Tonight she'd simply enjoy herself, and tomorrow she'd go back to worrying about the murder and everything else. Her hand crept inside her jacket, and the tips of her fingers touched the egg pendant Sam had given her. What a delightful surprise from a man she was fast falling in love with.

"Dear lord," Petra murmured, "will you look at that."

Carmen Copeland had just arrived in her white Mercedes-Benz SLK, and edged the nose of her car past Junior's car cooker.

"Come to slum," said Suzanne. She watched as Carmen got out of her car, gave Junior's wreck a disdainful look, and minced toward a group of people. Not only was Carmen wearing a mink hat to match her full-length mink coat, but when her coat fell open, it revealed a red and gold spangled wool sweater.

"What on earth is she wearing?" said Petra. "I know it's probably expensive as all get-out, but it looks more like the Ice Capades."

Toni strolled up to them. "Mayor Mobley says he wants to give out the awards in a few minutes."

"Fine with me," said Suzanne. "Maybe after this song? Then he's clear to take center stage."

"More like take over," said Toni. "But, yeah, I'll tell him."

"Tell Junior to move that crappy car of his, too," said Petra.

"Already did," said Toni, giving a helpless shrug. "About a zillion times."

"Suzanne," said a low voice behind her.

Suzanne turned to find Reed Ducovny standing there and gazing at her.

"Could we have a word?" Ducovny asked.

"Of course," said Suzanne, slipping away from Petra. She guided Ducovny over to one of the sparkling pine trees and said, "What's up?"

"I know it's January and all," said Ducovny, "but I sure am getting the cold shoulder from a lot of people."

"Oh no," said Suzanne, feeling awful.

"Seems like people still think I'm a suspect," said Ducovny. He paused. "Am I?"

"I'm the wrong person to ask," said Suzanne as diplomatically as she could. "You should be having this conversation with Sheriff Doogie."

"Which I've tried to do," said Ducovny. "Countless times. But he ends up doing all the talking. Asking me about my business with the bank, what I was up to last Monday, stuff like that."

"I'm sure Doogie's just trying to be thorough," said Suzanne. "I know he's under tremendous pressure."

"So am I," said Ducovny, kicking snow with his toe. "I don't think I've had a decent night's sleep since that awful snowmobile accident out back of your place."

Not accident, Suzanne thought for about the twentieth time. *Murder.*

"I'm sorry," said Suzanne, and she was. Sorry that Ducovny was a suspect, sorry that nothing had been resolved yet, sorry that she'd let herself get dragged into this awful mess.

"If you can put in a good word for me," said Ducovny, "I'd sure appreciate it."

"I'll certainly try," said Suzanne, knowing she really couldn't do that and hating herself for not being more helpful to him. She watched as Ducovny wandered off, then focused her attention back on the party. It was in full swing now, with food being dished out and people really enjoying themselves. She saw Lester Drummond approach Missy Langston, presumably to ask her to dance. Missy shook her head and pulled away even as Drummond followed her.

Persistent son of a gun, aren't you? Suzanne thought to herself as a loud, high-pitched squeal suddenly burst forth from the PA system. She glanced at the band and saw that

Mayor Mobley had commandeered a microphone and was posturing grandly.

Ah, she thought. *Award time.*

"May I have your attention, please?" Mayor Mobley's voice blared out above the noise of the crowd. When the crowd finally settled down and turned their attention his way, he said, "First of all, I want to welcome all of you to our Winter Blaze party!" A loud cheer went up, and Mobley grinned and nodded, as if he'd carried off the entire evening all on his own. "What a fitting conclusion to our town's wonderful Fire and Ice celebration!" There were more cheers and a couple of boos.

That'll get his dander up, thought Suzanne. Mobley wasn't a fan of negative opinions.

"My cohorts tell me," said Mayor Mobley, "that although many of you have come very *close* to finding the treasure medallion, no one has actually plucked it from its hiding place yet. So you've still got a few hours left in which to win the three thousand dollars in prize money, which our own lovely Carmen Copeland has graciously donated." There was more applause, a riff of music from the band, and then Mobley continued. "Now I know you're anxious to find out who won our ice-fishing contest and our ice-carving contest. So I don't intend to keep you waiting any longer." He grinned and glanced around, milking the moment and making people wait even though he said he wouldn't. Finally Mobley announced, his voice sounding almost jubilant, "With a prize-winning walleye that weighed in at an amazing twelve pounds and four ounces, our first-place winner is Mr. Charlie Steiner!"

There was a spatter of reserved applause as Charlie Steiner stumped up to Mayor Mobley to receive his hundred-dollar check.

I didn't even know Steiner was here tonight, Suzanne thought to herself. Very interesting. She slipped through the crowd, searching for Sam, as Mobley plowed ahead, announcing the second- and third-place winners.

This time there was lots more applause, but still no Sam in sight.

Where are you? Suzanne wondered as Toni suddenly grabbed her sleeve.

"This is it," Toni murmured.

"And now for the ice-carving contest," said Mayor Mobley, his voice booming out. "We had a record two-dozen entries this year! And some of the sculptures were real doozies!" He glanced out at George Draper, and said, "I never saw an ice sarcophagus before today!" The crowd roared its approval, and Draper bobbed his head. "But after much deliberation by our judges, the first-place blue ribbon goes to Darrel Kronsky for his polar bear sculpture!"

"Can't say I'm surprised," said Toni, as she clapped politely and watched Kronsky accept his ribbon. "After all, Kronsky's a professional wood-carver who really knows his stuff."

"Second place," Mayor Mobley said now, "goes to Chalmer's Meats for their ice castle." He handed a fluttering red ribbon to Bud Chalmer and his employees. "And third place, fittingly enough, goes to our delightful hosts here at the Cackleberry Club!"

There were cheers and whoops as Toni and Petra raced up to collect their ribbon.

"For their six-layer wedding cake!" Mayor Mobley added.

Toni grabbed the white ribbon and waved it above her head as Junior honked his horn and shouted, "Whoop, whoop!"

"Congratulations," said a voice at Suzanne's elbow.

She turned to find Reverend Yoder. He was dressed in a long dark coat that was practically threadbare at the elbows. And even though it made him look like the grim reaper, his eyes were kind and crinkled with mirth.

"Thank you," said Suzanne, "but I didn't lift so much as a pinky finger. Toni and Petra did all the carving, so they deserve all the credit."

"Good for them," said Reverend Yoder. "But my thanks to you for hosting this lovely event."

"I hope you're going to stay and have a cup of hot cider with us," said Suzanne. "And enjoy some grilled brats and baked beans."

"You're always so kind," said Reverend Yoder, "but I'm afraid I have some pressing business."

"Well, it is Sunday," said Suzanne. "Your busy day." She wasn't a member of his congregation, but she had friends who were.

Reverend Yoder smiled. "No, I just have to get back to my young guest."

Suzanne wasn't sure she'd heard him correctly at first—and was instantly on alert, all her pistons firing at once. She clutched Reverend Yoder's arm, and said, "Young guest? You have somebody staying with you at the church?"

Reverend Yoder nodded. "Yes, but only temporarily. Until I can contact the boy's parents."

"Oh my gosh!" said Suzanne. "Colby!"

"That's right," said Reverend Yoder, breaking into a slow grin. "How on earth did you know his name?"

Suzanne gripped his arm again, her fingers pressing so hard that Reverend Yoder practically winced. "Is he there now?" she asked. Her words were terse and filled with urgency.

"Yes, of course," said Reverend Yoder.

Suzanne looked around frantically for Sheriff Doogie, but didn't see him. Never mind, she told herself. I'll go over and get Colby myself. Maybe it's better that way; then he won't feel like he's under arrest or something. I'll just sort of invite him to the party and let things play out.

"This is important," Suzanne said to Reverend Yoder, fighting to control her emotions. "I need to talk to Colby right now!"

BUT it was easier said than done. Because Colby certainly wasn't happy to see Suzanne, and he sure didn't want any part of leaving the church.

"Why?" Colby whined at Suzanne, staring directly into her eyes. She looked him over, saw that physically, anyway, he seemed fine. Then the boy's eyes slid over to Reverend Yoder. "You told me I could stay here. Now you went and sold me out!" Colby was bitter, accusing, lying on his cot with some manga comics spread out around him.

"I did no such thing," said Reverend Yoder. "But it appears you haven't exactly been honest with me, young man. I had no idea people were looking for you, let alone law enforcement."

"But I didn't *do* anything!" Colby protested.

"We know that," said Suzanne calmly, hoping to settle the boy. "But I need to talk to you and so does Sheriff Doogie."

"So bring him over," said Colby.

"I'd rather you come next door and join the party," said Suzanne.

Colby was still reluctant. "What if I don't want to?"

"Trust me," said Suzanne kindly but firmly. "You want to."

EVEN though he mumbled and grumbled the entire time, Colby slipped into his puffer jacket and walked across the frozen ground with Suzanne and Reverend Yoder.

"This is what you wanted me to see?" Colby asked, when he saw the Winter Blaze party. "Big friggin' deal. A small-town hoedown."

They stood on the outer fringe of the event, Suzanne hopeful, Colby mistrustful. Reverend Yoder was still a little befuddled by the whole thing.

"I want you to do something for me," said Suzanne.

"What?" said Colby.

"Listen to me very carefully," said Suzanne. "I know you witnessed something that night. The night the man on the snowmobile was killed."

"No way," said Colby. His voice was firm, but his eyes skittered away from her.

"So I want you to help us."

Colby stood there, practically dancing on the balls of his feet, throwing off wave after wave of nervous energy.

"I know you saw *someone* that night," said Suzanne, "so all I want you to do is look around right now and see if you recognize anyone."

Colby turned pleading eyes on Reverend Yoder. "Do I have to?"

Reverend Yoder nodded. "Help us out," he said in a quiet voice. "You can do that; I *know* you can do that. I have great faith in you, Colby."

Colby let loose a deep sigh, and said, "You mean, do I recognize the guy who strung the wire that night?"

Suzanne's heart lurched wildly. "Do you?"

Colby gazed around, his brow furrowed, his eyes moving from one person to another. "I dunno," he said.

"Take your time," said Suzanne. "Just kind of think about it."

"I am," said Colby. He continued to search the crowd, studying face after face. "No, I don't think so." He was seemingly ready to give up and call it quits when something flickered in his eyes. A tiny spark of recognition.

"Do you see someone you recognize?" Suzanne asked, her voice barely a whisper.

Colby nodded slowly.

"Who is it?" asked Suzanne.

Colby stood still for a long thirty seconds. Then, slowly but surely, he lifted a hand and pointed. To none other than Hamilton Wick.

CHAPTER 27

AT that exact moment, Ham Wick was perched on a hay bale, taking a sip of hot cider. He was sitting next to Gene Gandle, who was jotting something down in his ever-present reporter's notebook. When Wick realized he'd been spotted, when he saw Colby pointing at him and figured he was quite probably a marked man, he dumped his drink on the ground and sprang from his hay bale. Sprinting through the throng of guests, he headed for the nearest car. Carmen's Mercedes. Only it was locked tight.

"We can't let Wick get away!" Suzanne cried, launching herself into the crowd. "We have to get Doogie!" She elbowed her way through the press of guests, searching frantically for Doogie, trying to keep one eye on Wick!

"Whoa!" said Toni, reaching out to grab her arm. "What's wrong, girlfriend?"

"Wick!" Suzanne sputtered. "Colby says he strung the wire! He's the killer!"

Toni whirled around, caught a flash of movement on the edge of the crowd, and, with dismay coloring her voice, cried out, "Oh no!"

"What?" cried Suzanne.

They watched as Ham Wick pulled open the driver's side door of Junior's idling car and hurled himself inside. There was a sickening grind of gears, a spew of oily smoke, and then Wick was rolling, picking up speed.

"He's using Junior's car cooker as his getaway car!" Toni cried.

"We gotta follow him!" Suzanne yelped. "Come on, we'll take my snowmobile!"

They made a mad dash for her rented snowmobile, jumped on, jammed helmets onto their heads. As Suzanne revved the machine and lurched forward, Toni clinging on back for dear life, Sheriff Doogie ran out to wave them down.

"What's wrong? What's wrong?" he cried. "What's going on?"

"We gotta go after Ham Wick!" Suzanne screamed. "Colby just fingered him for the murder!"

"For sure?" said Doogie.

"He's the one!" Suzanne cried. "Wick killed Busacker!"

Doogie rushed to his cruiser, had his hand on the door, before he realized it was sandwiched between two other cars. Hopelessly blocked.

Suzanne glanced over her shoulder at him. "Take one of the other snowmobiles!" she cried, waving toward a cluster of them. "And follow us!" She cranked the throttle and took off.

Doogie leapt onto one of the snowmobiles and instantly punched it to life. His modified Smoky Bear hat sailed neatly off his head as he lurched forward and joined the chase!

Two minutes later, zooming down the middle of Highway 65, cutting through the darkness, Doogie caught up to Suzanne and Toni.

Waving an arm at them, he motioned for them to pull over, to drop out of the chase. "Go back!" he yelled at them, fighting to be heard above the wind that buffeted both machines. "Let me take handle this!"

"No way!" cried Suzanne as she leaned forward and poured on even more speed. She could see Wick's taillights up ahead. Maybe a half mile in front of them. Could they catch him? They had to try!

The two snowmobiles, yellow headlights piercing the darkness, raced full throttle down the highway. In some spots the pavement had been scraped bare, so Suzanne and Doogie had to dodge and weave onto the shoulder to find navigable snow and ice.

Toni bent forward and screamed in Suzanne's ear, "I bet he's heading into town!"

Suzanne nodded as tears streamed from her eyes. Traveling at almost forty miles an hour meant the wind-chill temperature they were sustaining was something like minus five degrees. Plus she wasn't dressed for a wild chase at all. Her jacket and boots were more fashion items than survival gear. Still, Suzanne wasn't about to give up!

Where Highway 65 intersected with Bigsby Road, Suzanne finally throttled back. Somehow, they'd lost sight of him. Had Wick turned east or west? If he'd turned east, he was heading into downtown Kindred. If he'd turned west, he could be bumping across frozen farm fields and cruising down gulleys and deep ravines where they'd never find him.

"Which way, which way?" Doogie shouted, as he pulled up alongside them. His thin gray hair was blown back, as if he'd been spun through a wind tunnel. He was shivering, but determined.

"Not sure," said Suzanne, over the loud *tatatata* of the engines. She ground her teeth together and grimaced. Should she venture a guess? But what if she guessed wrong?

Doogie was gazing west, about to head out into the countryside and carry on his search, when Suzanne goosed her machine and coasted a few feet in the direction of town. It *felt* right to her, but she could be . . .

"Holy hiccups!" cried Toni, pointing a finger. "Is that blood?"

Suzanne glanced down, saw a splotch of red in the snow. Had there been an accident? Had Wick hit someone with his stolen car? Oh, dear lord, a hit-and-run. Could this get any worse?

Hopping off her snowmobile, Suzanne bent down on one knee. For some reason it didn't look like blood. On the other hand, it was bright red and . . .

She leaned closer and gave a suspicious sniff. "It's bar-becue sauce!"

Which caused Toni to tilt her head back, inhale deeply, and suddenly thrust out an arm. "He went thataway! I smell the lingering aroma of baby back ribs!"

Now they were a tag team of snowmobiles racing down Kindred's residential streets. Wick was ahead of them, all right, leading them on a crazy, high-speed chase from neighborhood to neighborhood. Sometimes he'd be a block or two ahead of them. Other times they'd catch sight of Junior's car sputtering along on a parallel street, so they'd have to roar down an alley, praying nobody would back their car out of the garage at that exact moment!

"Where's he going?" Toni wondered out loud into Suzanne's right ear.

"To the bank to grab some money?" said Suzanne. "Or to his house to pick up his car?" She took her hands off the handlebars for a second, making a helpless gesture. Somehow, Wick had made a tricky turn and eluded them.

"We lost him," said Doogie, pulling alongside. They were coasting quietly now, running past the old train station and feed mill.

"Maybe he's following the train tracks out of town," Suzanne called to Doogie.

"Maybe," said Doogie.

"Nope," said Toni. "I can still smell those ribs."

"So which way?" said Suzanne.

Toni gestured off to her left. "Maybe . . . that way?"

Suzanne kicked her sled into gear again and cut across a playground. They drifted past deserted swing sets and teeter-totters, then skimmed across a snow-covered base-ball diamond.

"This is hopeless," said Doogie, running alongside them. "We're never going to find him."

"Yes, we are," said Suzanne. She turned the nose of her

sled into a small copse of trees, bumped through what she knew was Mrs. Cooperfield's vegetable garden, and came out on Meadow Lane. And there, gliding by, not five hundred yards ahead of them, was Junior's car!

"There he is!" yelled Toni. "Doogie, Doogie, over there!"

Then they were after Wick again, nipping at his heels and chasing him over another couple of blocks, plowing through backyards when they had to, clattering down alleys and up onto a frozen sidewalk.

"He's gonna run out of town pretty soon," yelled Doogie.

"Then we have to get him now," Suzanne yelled back. If Wick made a break for open country, they'd never catch him. Simply because they'd never find him.

"He's headed for Main Street!" Toni whooped.

"Gonna run him down!" cried Suzanne.

They flew after Wick, crossing Turnbull Street, swerving around a gas station, and coming up on Main Street.

"There he is!" Toni yelled.

They were all flying down Main Street now, heading for the downtown business section of Kindred. They whipped past Kuyper's Hardware, Rexall Drugs, Schmitt's Bar, Marcus Brothers State Farm Insurance, and Root 66.

"You can do it!" Toni cried, egging Suzanne on. "You can catch him!" She bent forward, burying her face in the back of Suzanne's jacket as Suzanne redlined the snowmobile, taking it up to dangerous speeds.

Wick, seeing the bobbing headlights behind him, slalomed left, then right, hitting a parked car, nicking a light pole. All the while, Junior's rattletrap of a car was shaking and roaring like it was about to explode!

"He's pushing the engine too hard!" Toni yelled. "That clunker won't take it!"

Suddenly, Wick swerved the car off the street and drove directly into the park!

"He's heading for the ice sculptures!" Suzanne cried. She glanced back to see if Doogie was keeping up, saw that he was grim-faced and barely ten feet behind her. Then she swerved up and over a snowbank, catching some air and landing hard as she fought to stay on Wick's tail.

Wick was directly ahead of her now, weaving back and forth between the ice sculptures. He seemed to be trying to dip and dodge his way through the icy obstacles, but he was clipping them left and right as he flew past. Suzanne saw a head tumble from a Greek statue, an arm fly off a winged figure, and a giant fish wobble, then topple. It was as if Wick was shaving ice for a fancy drink!

George Draper's ice sarcophagus loomed into view, but when Wick tried to maneuver around the solid, seven-foot-long piece, he clipped his right front bumper. That was all it took. Junior's car spun out wildly, making a hair-raising three-hundred-and-sixty-degree turn, then crashed headfirst into the winning polar bear sculpture! The polar bear, hit low in its stomach, groaned loudly in protest. Then it toppled a few feet to the left and seemed to balance there precariously, like the Leaning Tower of Pisa.

Suzanne, fearing she wouldn't be able to stop in time, braked hard, hard, hard. She swerved left, skidding like mad, trying to avoid a huge collision. Then, when she knew it wasn't going to happen, when she knew she was going to hit *something,* she rammed the nose of her snowmobile directly into the front of Junior's car.

The hood crumpled like a cheap accordion, the car engine screamed and grunted like a dying dinosaur, and barbecue sauce flew up into the air in a nasty spray of red, spattering everything within a ten-foot radius!

Doogie was right on their trail. He slewed his snowmobile into a kind of hockey stop, managing to nick only the left wing of the Pegasus ice sculpture. Then he jumped off his sled with his gun drawn, and raced to Junior's car.

Shaken, feeling glad to still be alive, Suzanne cried, "Did Wick make it? Did he survive?"

Doogie was peering into the stolen car, bug-eyed and shouting. "Barely! Looks like he's bleeding to death!"

Suzanne limped over to find Ham Wick slumped in the front seat of Junior's car cooker, covered with copious amounts of viscous red liquid.

Toni loped up behind them, took one look, and said, "Naw, he ain't bleeding. He just got doused with Junior's special hot sauce."

CHAPTER 28

DOOGIE got on his personal radio then, putting out a special alert, requesting backup as well as an ambulance.

But much to Suzanne's amazement, the first car that rocked to a stop next to them was Sam and Junior in Sam's BMW! And they'd brought Colby along with them!

Colby hopped out, scared and almost hysterical. "Did you get him? Did you get him?" he called out over and over.

"Whoa, son," said Doogie, stretching out a big hand. "Take it down a notch. Our suspect's already been handcuffed and read his rights."

Doogie's deputy, Eddie Driscoll, pulled up one minute later in a cruiser, lights whirling and siren blasting like mad.

As Doogie jerked Ham Wick, handcuffed and extremely shaken up, to his feet, Wick pretty much broke down and confessed everything. Tears streamed down his face as he wailed out his tale of woe, saying over and over, "I didn't mean it! I only wanted to scare him!"

Suzanne didn't give a fig about Wick's remorse. "Did you read him his rights?" Suzanne asked Doogie, as Sam stood nearby. "Are you sure you did that?" She didn't want to see a stone-cold killer go free just because of some stupid technicality.

"Yup, yup," said Doogie. "Wick's been signed, sealed, and delivered on that count," he added, as Deputy Driscoll grabbed Wick and shoved him into the backseat of his cruiser.

"You jackhole!" Suzanne shouted at Wick. "You slimeball! You attacked Joey and then you tried to run me down with a snowmobile! What's the matter with you?"

"Easy, easy," said Sam, trying to get a hand on Suzanne. "It's over. It's finished."

"You jerk!" Suzanne called again.

Sam wrapped both arms around her now. "Easy girl, it's over. Time to stand down," he murmured in a soothing voice.

"I'll try, I will," said Suzanne, knowing she was yelling and chattering like a crazy woman as her adrenaline still pumped like crazy. She drew a few shaky breaths, looked up at Sam, and said, "There. Okay. Better now. I'm better now."

But Colby was the one whose nerves were still frazzled. He stalked back and forth, punching his fist at the ice sculptures.

Suzanne pulled away from Sam and went over to Colby. "You have to calm down, too," she told him. "Or you're going to hurt yourself. Really, everything's okay now. It's over. Wick's under arrest and charged with murder."

Doogie cocked a wary eye at Colby. "You better be sure Wick's the one, kid. This is no time to pull a funny act."

Colby bobbed his head vigorously. "Absolutely, he's the one," he chattered. He pointed at Ham Wick who was hunched miserably in the back seat of Driscoll's cruiser. "That's the guy who strung the wire."

"You'd testify to that in a court of law?" asked Doogie.

Colby, still angry and shivering, said, "Yes, yes. That guy was after me, too. I saw him in town a couple of times and I got the feeling he wanted to kill me!"

"Which he almost did," said Suzanne, "except he clobbered poor Joey instead."

Colby put his hands up to his face and shook his head. "Oh no. I didn't know that. Oh man!"

Suzanne gazed at Colby. "That's why you were hiding, wasn't it? Because you thought the killer was after you. Because he *was* after you."

Colby nodded. "Yeah, I guess he was. Sure, he was."

"But now you're going to go home," said Suzanne, in a kinder, gentler tone of voice. "You're going to let me call your mom, right? You're going to give me her number?"

"Maybe," said Colby.

"Yes, you are," said Suzanne. She nudged closer to him.

"If you call her," said Colby, "can you sort of smooth things over?"

Suzanne put an arm around Colby's shoulders and hugged him. "Of course I will. And I bet Reverend Yoder will help, too."

"Mom's gonna be awful mad."

"I'll just have to tell her what a hero you were," said Suzanne.

Colby gazed at her with gratitude. "You will, really?" he asked. Then, more shyly, "I'm a hero?"

Suzanne pulled him closer. "You are to me, kiddo."

"Looks like Charlie Steiner, Ducovny, and Drummond are all off the hook," said Toni, sidling up to Suzanne as they surveyed the crash site.

"And Claudia and George Draper, as well as Ed Rapson," said Suzanne "Though all of them have their own problems to work out."

"But look at poor Junior," said Toni. He was pacing back and forth, running his fingers through his shaggy hair, looking completely devastated as he surveyed his wrecked car. "He's a total basket case."

"My car cooker!" Junior moaned. "My *baby*. Not only was this fine piece of machinery carjacked, but it's been driven to wreck and ruin!"

Suzanne reached out and patted Junior's arm. "Look at it this way, Junior. Your car cooker served a higher purpose. A dangerous criminal was apprehended. You should be very proud."

Junior looked up hopefully, tossing his forelock to one side. "You think?" His voice was a sad warble.

"Absolutely," said Suzanne. "You might even get a citation from the mayor. Or at least your car will."

"Come on, Junior," Toni urged. "You can build a new car cooker. A *better* car cooker. You've always dreamed about jazzing up that old Ford Fairlane you got stashed behind Shelby's Body Shop."

"Have to rebuild the engine," Junior moped. "The transmission's completely shot."

"You can fix that," said Toni. "Plus you could spiff it up with that tuck-and-roll red vinyl upholstery you've always wanted. And think of the new attachments you could add. Like . . . uh . . ." Toni turned to Suzanne for help.

"A drive-by salad shooter?" said Suzanne.

"Yeah!" said Toni.

Doogie wandered over to Junior's car. "Say, those ribs are smelling pretty dang good!"

"I'll say," said Sam. "Do you think they're cooked?"

Doogie grabbed the hood latch and gave a good tug. As a hunk of crumpled metal slid off, the smell of burning oil and transmission fluid mingled with the piquant aroma of spicy barbecue sauce. "Heck you say!" Doogie exclaimed. "These ribs look like they're pretty much cooked to perfection."

Junior bent over his devastated car. "You better believe they are." He was all business now as he flipped up a metal plate that was wired near the battery. "Got some garlic toast here, too, if anybody's interested."

"Dear lord," said Toni. She ambled around Junior's car, just as the polar bear started to topple and shards of ice rained down upon her head and shoulders. "Eeey!" she cried. Then she stopped midscreech, her mouth open in amazement as she reached up with a mittened hand. "I don't believe it!" she shrieked. She poked tentatively at the polar bear's massive ice paw and, lo and behold, there was a sparkle of gold! "The . . . the treasure!" she whooped.

"You found it?" said Suzanne. "The treasure medallion?" She was shocked beyond belief but thrilled for Toni.

"Embedded in his paw!" said Toni, grabbing the shiny gold medallion and then holding it up for all to see. "What do you know about that!" She blinked, chortled again, and said in a jubilant voice, "I did it! I won!"

"You surely did," enthused Sam, putting an arm around Suzanne's shoulders.

"You deserve it," said Suzanne.

"Hoo yaw!" yelped Junior. "This means we can finance a new car cooker!" He pulled Toni close and planted a big smooch on her cheek.

"Love at first bite," joked Doogie, gnawing away on a rib.

Sam pulled Suzanne even closer and nuzzled her gently. "Well, I knew *that*."

Lemon Cornbread

1¼ cup brown sugar
½ cup oil
¾ cup sour cream
2 large eggs
2 cups all-purpose flour
½ tsp baking powder
½ tsp baking soda
¾ tsp salt
1 cup cornmeal
⅓ cup lemon juice
1 tbsp lemon zest

Cream together brown sugar, oil, sour cream, and eggs in a small mixing bowl. In a large mixing bowl, sift in flour, then add baking powder, baking soda, and salt. Stir together and add in cornmeal. Now pour creamed mixture into large bowl and stir until just combined. Then add lemon juice and lemon zest and stir again. Pour mixture into a greased 9 x 11–inch baking dish and bake at 400 degrees for 25 minutes.

Carrot Quiche

3 medium carrots, pared and sliced fairly thin
2 tbsp butter
½ cup onion, finely diced
4 slices of bacon, cooked and crumbled
9" pie shell, unbaked
1½ cups Swiss cheese, shredded
4 eggs
1 cup cream
Salt and pepper to taste

Place carrots in skillet with a little water and simmer, covered, for 20 minutes. Drain carrots and reserve for later. In skillet, melt butter, then sauté the onions for about 5 minutes. Add carrot slices and mix well. Place crumbled bacon in bottom of pie shell and sprinkle with the Swiss cheese, then add carrot and onion mixture. In a medium bowl, beat eggs with cream until frothy, then add salt and pepper. Now pour egg mixture into pie shell. Bake at 375 degrees on lower rack of oven for 40 minutes.

Cheggnog

3 cups eggnog, prepared
1 tsp vanilla extract
1 cup prepared liquid chai concentrate
Nutmeg

Combine eggnog, vanilla, and chai concentrate in blender until well mixed. Pour into glasses and garnish with a sprinkle of nutmeg.

Serves 2 to 3.

Red Velvet Chocolate Chip Pancakes

2 cups all-purpose flour
2 tsp baking powder
1 tsp baking soda
6 tbsp sugar
4 tbsp unsweetened cocoa powder
½ tsp salt
2 eggs
1½ cups buttermilk
½ cup sour cream
2 tsp red food coloring
4 tsp vanilla extract
¾ cup chocolate chips

Combine flour, baking powder, baking soda, sugar, cocoa powder, and salt in large bowl. In separate bowl, whisk together eggs, buttermilk, sour cream, food coloring, and vanilla. Add wet ingredients to dry ingredients and mix until combined. Fold chocolate chips into batter. Pour ¼ to ⅓ cup of batter onto lightly greased griddle to form pancakes. Cook until lightly brown and bubbles form, then flip pancake over and cook for two to three minutes. Serve with butter and maple syrup.

Egg Sammys

1 tbsp butter
2 eggs
2 slices cheese, Swiss or cheddar
2 English muffins
4 slices of bacon, already cooked and drained

Melt butter in saucepan, then crack eggs into it. When eggs are half fried, add a piece of cheese to each egg and continue to fry. Toast English muffins. Place a fried egg on the bottom half of each muffin. Top with bacon slices and press on the top half of each muffin. Makes 2 sammys. Hot sauce, ketchup, or mayo can be added for extra zest!

Cheddar Ricotta Quiche

6 eggs
2 tbsp flour
1 cup cheddar cheese, shredded
2 cups ricotta cheese
¼ cup melted butter
4 oz can green chilies, minced

Beat eggs in a bowl, add flour, and beat again. Mix in cheddar cheese, ricotta cheese, melted butter, and chilies. Divide mixture among 6 well-greased ramekins. Bake at 375 degrees for 45 minutes. To serve, top with sour cream and salsa.

Make Ahead Breakfast Casserole

1 lb ground sausage
6 tbsp butter
6 slices bread, no crusts
1½ cups cheddar cheese, shredded
5 eggs
2 cups half-and-half
1 tsp salt

Sautee sausage until no longer pink, then drain. Melt butter and pour into 9 x 12–inch baking dish. Tear bread into small pieces and sprinkle evenly over butter. Sprinkle sausage over torn bread. Now sprinkle cheese over the sausage. Beat eggs with half-and-half and salt until frothy, then pour over entire mixture. Cover and chill for 8 hours or overnight. Bake at 350 degrees for about 50 minutes or until set.

Dirty Fried Chicken

¾ cup flour
1 tsp salt
1 tsp paprika
¼ tsp cardamom
¼ tsp cloves, crushed or ground
1 cup buttermilk
3 tbsp hot sauce
1 chicken, cut up
Oil for frying

Mix flour, salt, paprika, cardamom, and cloves together in a shallow bowl. Mix buttermilk and hot sauce together in a second shallow bowl. Drip chicken pieces in buttermilk and then in flour-spice mixture. Fry chicken in hot oil on medium-high heat. When chicken is browned, reduce heat to medium and cook for an additional 30 to 35 minutes, turning occasionally.

Junior's Secret Barbecue Sauce

1 cup Jack Daniel's whiskey
1 cup ketchup
½ cup brown sugar
¼ cup vinegar

½ tsp dry mustard
1 tbsp lemon juice
1 tsp Worcestershire sauce
Salt and pepper to taste

Put all ingredients into a saucepan and simmer together for about 20 to 25 minutes. Pour into a container and let cool in refrigerator overnight. Now you're ready to use this zesty concoction on ribs, pork, or even chicken!

Turn the page for a preview of
Laura Childs's next Tea Shop Mystery . . .

Sweet Tea Revenge

Coming March 2013 in hardcover
from Berkley Prime Crime!

Rain slashed against stained glass windows and thunder shook the rafters as Theodosia Browning hurried up the back staircase of Ravencrest Inn. Her long, peach-colored bridesmaid's dress swished about her ankles as she balanced a giant box of flowers that had just been delivered to the inn's back door. It was the second Saturday in June, the morning of her friend Delaine Dish's wedding. Normally, Charleston, South Carolina, was awash in sun and steamy heat this time of year. But today, this day of all days, a nasty squall had blown in from the Atlantic, parked itself over the city, and turned everything into a soggy morass. Including, unfortunately, the bride's temper.

Theodosia reached the top step, stumbled, almost catching her heel in the hem on her dress, then quickly righted herself.

"Delaine!" she called. "Your flowers have arrived."

Delaine Dish rushed out into the dark hallway and threw up her arms in a gesture of sheer panic. "Finally! And, can you believe it, the power's gone out twice already!"

"I know," said Theodosia, trying to minimize the problem. "They lit candles downstairs for the guests. So all the parlors look quite dreamy and atmospheric." She hustled past Delaine, carrying the cumbersome box into the suite of rooms that Delaine was using as her dressing room. The groom, Dougan Granville, was cloistered in his own suite of rooms down the long, dark corridor.

"How does my bouquet look?" asked a jittery Delaine, as Theodosia carefully opened the box.

"Hang on a minute." Theodosia was practically as nervous as Delaine. All the bouquets had been ordered from Floradora, a florist she often counted on to create distinctive centerpieces for her Indigo Tea Shop over on Church Street.

"So many delays," worried Delaine as another flash of lightning strobed, giving the room the flickering, jittering look of an old-time black-and-white film. "My guests must be getting restless."

"Not to worry," said Theodosia. "Last I looked, Drayton and Haley were serving peach-and-ginger tea accompanied by miniature cream scones. Your guests were happy as clams." She pulled the bridal bouquet, a lovely arrangement of orchids, tea roses, and Queen Anne's lace, from its tissue paper wrapping and handed it to Delaine. "There you go. And it's perfect."

"It is, isn't it?" said Delaine, smiling as she accepted the bouquet. She stepped over to a full-length mirror and peered into its murky depths. "How do I look?" she asked.

"Beautiful," said Theodosia. And she meant it. She and Delaine had had their differences over the years, but today Delaine looked positively radiant. Her ivory strapless ball gown–style wedding dress, with its delicate ruche bodice, highlighted her dark hair and extraordinary coloring and set off her thin figure perfectly.

Delaine stretched a hand out to Theodosia. "Come over here, you."

Theodosia joined Delaine at the mirror and stared at her own reflection in the pitted glass. With masses of curly auburn hair to contend with, Theodosia sometimes projected the aura of a Renaissance woman captured in a portrait by Raphael or even Botticelli. She had a smooth, peaches-and-cream complexion, intense blue eyes, and often wore the slightly bemused look of a self-sufficient woman. A woman who in her mid-thirties, had found herself to be a successful entrepreneur, possessed a fair amount of life experience, and had hooked up with a nice boyfriend to boot. So life was good.

Delaine patted her dark upswept hair, and her eyes glittered. She was successful, too, with her Cotton Duck boutique. But she was of a predatory nature, always on the prowl for the next new experience or thrill. Theodosia, on the other hand, had found contentment. Her tea shop was cozy, charming, and filled to the rafters with good friends and guests. And Drayton and Haley, her two dear friends, worked there with her.

Delaine turned from the mirror and shrugged. Her nerves were fizzing and she could barely stand still. She whirled one way, then the other and asked, "Have you seen my sister? Where on earth is Nadine?"

"I know," said Theodosia. "She's late." Then again, Nadine was perpetually late.

"That woman would be late to her own funeral," Delaine spat out.

There was a *clump clump* from out in the hallway and then an overly chirpy cry of "Here I am!" Nadine charged into the room, looking damp, self-absorbed, and not one bit apologetic. "Sorry to be late," she chortled. "But did you know Bay Street actually flooded? My cab driver had to detour for *miles*!"

Delaine's mouth fell open as she stared in horror at her sister, who was practically the spitting image of her, even if a couple of pounds heavier. Nadine brushed rain from her Khaki trench coat as she struggled with the handle of a pink paisley umbrella.

"Close that umbrella!" Delaine cried.

Nadine stopped fussing, frowned distractedly, then stared down at the damp, half-open umbrella that was clutched in her hands. "What's wrong now?" she asked.

"Don't you know it's bad luck?" cried Delaine. "You *never* open an umbrella in the house." Delaine was a big believer in signs, portents, and superstitions.

"Sorry," Nadine mumbled. Then added, in a more acerbic tone, "But in case you hadn't noticed, it's raining buckets out there!"

"I noticed," said Delaine, gritting her teeth. "Really, do you think I *planned* for bad weather? Do you think I called the National Weather Service and asked for the *precise* day on which we were going to have a deluge of Biblical proportions?"

Nadine stiffened. "You don't have to get snippy!"

"Whatever," said Delaine.

Not wanting to get dragged into a sister-versus-sister fight, Theodosia continued to unpack the five smaller bouquets made up of tea roses and chamomile. These, too, were perfectly composed. Dainty and fragrant and frothy with blooms.

"Maybe you could take these bouquets into the next room," Theodosia suggested to Nadine. "And hand them out to the other bridesmaids."

"I suppose," said Nadine, whose nose was still out of joint.

When she was finally alone with Delaine, Theodosia said, "Okay, what else do you need?" She was finding maid-of-honor duties to be more trouble than she'd ever imagined. Good thing it would all be over in a matter of hours.

Delaine did a little pirouette, letting her enormous ruffled skirt billow out around her. Then she peered in the mirror again. "I really look okay?"

"Gorgeous," said Theodosia, trying to stifle a yawn. She'd been up late helping decorate and arrange seating in the downstairs Fireplace Room.

"I do feel we could have used a touch more planning," said Delaine.

"It is what it is," said Theodosia. "You had such a short engagement." *Like about four weeks.*

"Which is why I had to settle for this place," said Delaine, her mouth suddenly downcast.

"It's lovely," said Theodosia. Truth be told, Ravencrest

Inn, with its old-world cypress paneling, narrow hallways, and looming presence in the Historic District, was dark and a trifle shabby. The rooms were claustrophobic and furnished with mismatched pieces, and the plumbing clanked noisily. But Delaine had pushed everything ahead at warp speed so she could hastily tie the knot with one of Charleston's top attorneys. It was your basic Southern shotgun wedding without a baby.

"Did you see that this place even has a widow's walk?" said Delaine.

"Which makes it quaint," said Theodosia.

"It's a dump," replied Delaine.

"But this is a pretty room," said Theodosia, trying to find some spark of joy. Delaine was like a hummingbird; flitting, sipping, constantly in motion.

"You think?" said Delaine. She pointed to a shelf of antique dolls that stared blankly at them. "Look at that. Another silly collection."

"I find it interesting," said Theodosia, "that every room has been themed with a different collection. Teapots, dolls, angels, leather-bound books, you name it."

"But you know how I feel about dolls," said Delaine, tapping her foot.

"I really *don't* know," said Theodosia. *But I have a feeling you're going to tell me.*

"They're horribly creepy," said Delaine. "With their little glass eyes and puckered rubber faces. And look." She pointed a pink-enameled finger at the offending shelf. "There's even a bride doll swaddled in ghastly lace. Makes me think of *Bride of Chucky* or something nasty like that."

"This is not what you should be fretting about on your wedding day," said Theodosia, determined to stay upbeat. "Come on over here and let's pin your veil on."

Delaine ghosted across the room. "You know, I had a fight with Dougan this morning."

Theodosia gathered up a long veil of French lace and

held it a few inches above Delaine's swirl of dark hair. "That's probably normal. Frayed nerves and all that."

"Don't you want to know what it was about?" asked Delaine.

Theodosia knew when she was being goaded. "Not really." She centered the veil, then set it carefully on Delaine's head. Gently spread the sides of the veil over her bare shoulders.

"He wants to cut the honeymoon short," said Delaine. "Because of work. We screamed and hollered. I'm quite sure everyone here heard us."

Theodosia picked up Delaine's bouquet and shoved it into her friend's twitching hands. "Time to get you married." *Could I be any chirpier?* she wondered. *Could I be in any more of a hurry to jumpstart this wedding?* "Let's get you and your lovely bridesmaids all lined up at the top of the staircase so we can make any and all final adjustments. Then you, my dear, shall make the world's grandest entrance in front of all your guests."

The lights flickered once again and thunder crackled loudly as five bridesmaids, one maid of honor, and a nervous bride gathered at the top of the stairs.

"Remember," Theodosia told the bridesmaid at the front of the pack, a distant cousin of Delaine's who was supposed to lead the procession. "As soon as you hear that first note of music . . ."

Swish, swish, chuff. Someone was hurrying up the back staircase. They all turned en masse, silk and lace rustling, to look.

It was Drayton Conneley, Theodosia's tea expert and dear friend. Dressed in a slim, European-cut tuxedo with a plaid cummerbund, Drayton's patrician face was drawn and slightly flushed beneath his mane of gray hair. Despite his normally quiet reserve, his eyes were crinkled with worry.

Theodosia hastened over to meet him. "What's wrong?" she whispered.

Drayton put a hand to his chest to still his beating heart.

He was edging into his high sixties and not used to dashing up two flights of stairs like a gazelle. "We have a problem."

"No lights?" asked Theodosia.

"No groom," said Drayton.

"Typical." Delaine's voice floated out behind them. "He's probably holed up in his room texting away. Dealing with some important client or political bigwig." She sighed deeply. "That's my Dougan. Always puts his work first."

Before Delaine could get any snappier, Theodosia said, "I'll take care of this. I'll go get him."

"Please," said Delaine, in an arch tone.

"Thank you," said Drayton, turning on his heels and disappearing back downstairs.

Theodosia flew down the narrow hallway to Dougan Granville's room. Interestingly enough, Granville was her next-door neighbor. Her home, her quaint Hansel and Gretel–style cottage, had once been part of his larger, more grand estate.

She rapped on the door of Granville's suite. "Dougan, it's time," she called out. Theodosia knew he was a hard-driving attorney who was probably working right up until the last millisecond.

Nothing. No movement, no answer.

Theodosia leaned forward and put an ear to the door. Maybe he was . . . slightly indisposed? Maybe he really was a nervous bridegroom?

"Dougan? Mr. Granville? It's Theodosia. We're all waiting for you."

Still nothing.

Wondering what protocol she should observe for something like this, Theodosia hesitated for a few moments. Then decided it didn't much matter. Guests were waiting; it was time to get moving. She gripped the doorknob and turned it, pushed the door open a good six inches.

"Dougan," she called again, trying to put a little humor in her voice. "We have an impatient bride who's waiting for her handsome groom."

There was no sound, save the monotonous drumming of rain on the roof and the gurgling of water as it rushed through the downspouts.

Theodosia pushed the door all the way open and stepped across the threshold.

"Dougan?"

The room was completely dark and ominously quiet. Straight ahead, she could just make out a faint outline of heavy velvet draperies pulled across a bay window.

Did Granville fall asleep? He must have. Wow, this is one relaxed guy on his wedding day.

Shadows capered on the walls as she stepped past a looming wardrobe and another piece of furniture. The room had a strange electrical smell, as if an outside transformer had exploded. Theodosia tiptoed across the carpet, her silk mules whispering softly. When she reached the foot of the bed, she stared. A tiny bedside lamp shone a small circle of warmth on a battered bedside table, but there was no one lying on the bed. Nothing had creased the dusty pink coverlet.

What on earth?

Flustered, nervous now that they might have a runaway groom on their hands, Theodosia fumbled with the curtains and ripped them open. Lightning flashed outside, a sharp blade cutting through a wall of purple-black clouds.

Still, this is better. A little more light.

Just as Theodosia turned, something caught her eye. A fleeting image that she couldn't quite process but that unnerved her anyway. She slowly retraced her footsteps. Back to the sitting-room area that had been in total darkness, as thunder boomed like kettledrums in some unholy symphony.

That's when she saw him.

Dougan Granville was sprawled on a brocade fainting couch. His eyes were squeezed shut, his head had fallen forward until his chin rested heavily on his chest. On the small glass table in front of him was an empty glassine envelope and a scatter of white powder.

Theodosia tiptoed closer, her heart hammering in her chest, her brain shouting screams of protest. An unwanted shot of adrenaline sparked by surprise and fear had sent her blood pressure zooming. Still, she was mesmerized, hypnotized, by what she was seeing.

Was Granville just stoned? Or . . . something worse?

Theodosia moved closer and stretched out a tentative hand. The very tips of her fingers brushed the pulse point of his neck. Granville felt ice-cold and lifeless. There was no pulse, no respiration.

Revulsion and fear rose up inside her like sulfurous magma from a roiling volcano. Theodosia understood, logically and viscerally, that Granville hadn't just fainted on this fainting couch like genteel ladies of old.

This man was seriously, catastrophically, dead.